THE SKORZENY PROJECT

Recent Titles by Clive Egleton from Severn House

THE ALSOS MISSION
A CONFLICT OF INTERESTS
A FALCON FOR THE HAWK
OPERATION SOVEREIGN
THE ROMMEL PLOT

THE
SKORZENY PROJECT

Clive Egleton

This title first published in Great Britain 1998 by
SEVERN HOUSE PUBLISHERS LTD of
9–15 High Street, Sutton, Surrey SM1 1DF.
Originally published in 1982 in Great Britain under the title
Double Griffin and pseudonym of *Patrick Blake*.
First published in the USA 1998 by
SEVERN HOUSE PUBLISHERS INC., of
595 Madison Avenue, New York, NY 10022.

British Library Cataloguing in Publication Data

Egleton, Clive, 1927-
  The Skorzeny project
  1. World War, 1939-1945 – Naval operations - Submarine - Fiction
  2. World War, 1939-1945 - Naval operations, German - Fiction
  3. War stories
  1. Title II. Blake, Patrick. Double Griffin
  823.9'14 [F]

  ISBN 0-7278-5384-8

Printed and bound in Great Britain by
MPG Books Ltd, Bodmin, Cornwall.

This book is for the Campbells – all of them!

I would like to express my appreciation to Martin Arnold, Lesley Berger and Marion Donnelly of the *New York Times* whose help in researching the background material was invaluable. I should also like to say a special thank you to Lieutenant Commander (Retd) David Webb, RN, whose expert advice on anti-submarine warfare was so freely given.

PART I

GREY NOVEMBER

CHAPTER 1

Oranienburg near Berlin

Friday, 3 November 1944

Kapitän zur See Christian Wirth shook hands with Otto Skorzeny and smiled wryly, recalling the cautionary words of advice he had received in Kiel from Admiral Hans Georg von Friedeburg before leaving for Oranienburg. A small man with sharp pointed features and receding fair hair, Wirth found himself dwarfed by the powerfully built Skorzeny, found too that the prominent, rather bulging eyes and the dueling scar which ran vertically down his left cheek had a hypnotic effect on him. It was all very well for the Commander-in-Chief of the U-boat fleet to say that he should not allow himself to be intimidated by a mere Sturmbannführer, but the Admiral had never met Otto Skorzeny face to face.

'How was the flight to Berl?'
'Somewhat bumpy.' A large hand waved him to a chair and Wirth sat down, placing his briefcase on the polished oak table between them. 'The weather forecast for the next six hours doesn't look any too promising either. Unless there is an improvement, I may have to return by rail.'
'If it's humanly possible to do so, you'll fly. I'll see to that.'
The glib assurance would have been absurd had it been given by any other Sturmbannführer. Skorenzy, however, commanded exceptional power for a comparatively junior officer. For a man who in February 1940 had been rejected by the Luftwaffe on the grounds that at the age of thirty-one he was too old to be a pilot, he had certainly come a long way. Enlisting in the Leibstandarte as an engineer-cadet, he had served on the Russian front until invalided

9

home with gall-stones early in 1942. There were some who maintained that Skorzeny had been posted to Berlin as a driving instructor because he had failed the company commander's examination, but Wirth believed this to be purely malicious gossip. What was beyond dispute was the fact that his subsequent fame was in part due to Kaltenbrunner, a fellow Austrian, who had used his influence as head of the Reich Security main office to have him transferred to the Special Purposes Regiment at Oranienburg. Chosen personally by the Führer from commando officers of greater experience, he had succeeded in rescuing Mussolini from house arrest in the Campo Imperatore Hotel on top of the Gran Sasso, the highest point in the Apennines and accessible only by a funicular railway. After the reverses on the Russian front and the capitulation of Italy in 1943, the German people had been badly in need of a folk hero and Goebbels had made the most of his exploit.

The glider-borne assault had captured the imagination of the public, and while there was no denying that it had been an audacious feat, the German Propaganda Ministry had carefully avoided mentioning that the pilot of the Feisler Storch had had great difficulty in taking off from the rock plateau below the hotel with both the Duce and Otto Skorzeny on board. Although this slightly farcical note had been officially suppressed, Skorzeny's enemies in the SS had been quick to put it about that the return flight to Rome had been the only really hazardous part of the operation. The story could have tarnished his image, but ten months later on the twentieth of July, he had been able to enhance his reputation by playing a minor though important part in defeating the Bendlerstrasse conspirators. Although most of the credit for nipping the attempted putsch in the bud rightly belonged to Major Otto Remer of the Berlin Guard Battalion, it was Skorzeny who had quelled the air of panic that had gripped the SD and had organized the defence of the Gestapo headquarters in Prinz Albrechtstrasse. And it was he who had first persuaded the tank school formations which were converging on the Wilhelmstrasse area to remain loyal to the Führer. That he had been thrust into the limelight again was due to the intervention of Schellenberg, the number-two man in the SD. Unaware that an attempt had been made on Hitler's life at Rastenburg, Skorzeny had actually left Berlin on the six o'clock night express to Vienna, and on Schellenberg's instructions had been hauled off the train when it stopped in the suburb of Lichterfelde.

His star firmly in the ascendency, the Sturmbannführer had pulled off yet another coup less than three weeks ago. Learning that Admiral Horthy, the Regent of Hungary, was about to surrender unconditionally to the Russians, he had kidnapped his only surviving son from the Villa Petoefer in a last-minute bid to make him think again. A fool's errand, so it seemed at first, because by the time Ambassador Rahn secured an audience with Horthy to deliver the necessary ultimatum, the Regent had already broadcast the news of the surrender over Radio Budapest. Nevertheless, the Admiral had intimated that he was willing to abdicate in favour of Major Ferenc Szalasi, an offer that had been gratefully accepted because the gallant Major and his 'Arrow Cross' party were in favour of continuing the war. The fact that the whole affair had been something of a comic opera was of no consequence. So far as the Führer was concerned, Skorzeny could do no wrong, and in view of this, Wirth could well understand why he wielded so much power.

'What do you think of my idea?'

Wirth was suddenly aware that Skorzeny was gazing at him expectantly. 'It's certainly very audacious,' he said, choosing his words carefully.

'The best plans always are. Of course, in the end, success depends on having a resolute and skilled officer in command.'

'Quite.'

'So who do you have in mind?'

'Korvettenkapitän Erich Hartmann.' Wirth extracted a thin folder from his briefcase and passed it across the table. 'As you will see, he has a fine war record.'

'Another Kretschmer?'

Wirth shook his head. Before he'd been taken prisoner in March 1941, Kretschmer had sunk forty-four ships totalling more than two hundred and sixty thousand tons, and at this stage of the war no one would break that record.

'But you feel Hartmann is the right man for the job?'

'Yes. So does Admiral von Friedeburg.'

Skorzeny appeared unconvinced, but as he leafed through the service dossier, Wirth noticed that his sceptical expression gradually disappeared, as well it might. Although Hartmann wasn't numbered among the top aces, he had notched up an impressive enough score and was vastly more experienced than any of his surviving contemporaries. When he had commissioned U 195, Hartmann had assured his crew that they could rely on him to bring them back safe and sound. It had been no idle promise; just three days ago they had returned to Bergen having completed their twelfth operational patrol. Apart from the watch officers, Hartmann still had virtually the same crew he'd started out with three and a half long years ago and for sheer efficiency and high morale they were in a class of their own.

'I agree with your choice.' Skorzeny closed the folder and put it to one side. 'What about the rest of the personnel?'

It was really none of his business but such was his dominating personality that Wirth felt obliged to answer.

'Even if we wanted to, Hartmann would go through the roof if we changed any of his crew. As it is, he won't take kindly to the fact that some of his men will have to be left behind in order to accommodate the army detachment.'

'Is that necessary? I thought the new electro boats carried a much larger complement than the type VIIc?'

'They do, but Hartmann won't be getting one.'

'Why not?'

The first of the type XXIs had been launched on the seventeenth of July but the acceptance trials had not been completed yet and a number of teething problems remained. Production was also being hampered because seventy percent of the skilled workers in the shipyards had been drafted into the armed forces and much of the work was being done by old men, women and children who lacked the craftsman's touch. Neither of these facts would cut much ice with Skorenzy and Wirth suspected that the Sturmbannführer would go over their heads and take the issue to the Führer, which was the last thing he wanted. However, there were certain practical considerations which might persuade him to stay his hand.

'Suppose we do give him a type XXI. It would still have to be modified for this particular operation, and even working round the clock, the job can't be done in much under a fortnight. Once the refit is completed, the crew will then need at least another month in which to familiarize themselves with the new boat, and that's being optimistic. Time is at a premium, and if Hartmann is to meet your deadline, he must depart on the twenty-fifth of November at the latest.'

'I presume this refit will be done at Kiel?'

While not actually saying so, it was evident from the question that Skorzeny had accepted the force of his argument.

'No, we intend to airlift the labour force to Bergen. All being well, they will leave tomorrow.' Wirth smiled fleetingly. 'You need have no worries about security, Herr Sturmbannführer. The workmen will be confined to the naval base until their task is completed.'

'And the crew?'

'They're not due back from leave until the end of next week. They will have to cool their heels in Kiel for several days, but that's not unusual. Hartmann and I will fly to Bergen on Saturday, the eleventh of November, to make all the necessary administrative arrangements.'

Administrative arrangements was an all-embracing expression, but luckily Skorzeny did not press him for details. There are twenty-nine operational boats in the flotilla at Bergen and while half of these would be away on

13

patrol at any one time, isolating the crew of U 195 from the rest of the base was going to be quite a problem. Separate messing and recreational facilities would be required and this was only scratching the surface. The ban on shore leave would have to remain in force long after U 195 had sailed and that was bound to cause discontent.

'How much does Hartmann know about this venture?'

'Nothing. To have briefed him before he went on leave would have been very imprudent, to say the least. What about your man?'

'My man?'

'The officer in charge of the army detachment,' Wirth said, stifling his impatience. 'I assume somebody has been earmarked?'

'Major Reinhard Galen and he's in the artillery not the SS. Mind you, with his technical background he may well put two and two together when he learns that he is going to Bergen, but rest assured, he knows when to keep his mouth shut. Galen is serving with the 271st Missile Regiment and that's the most sensitive outfit in the whole damned Wehrmacht.'

'With the possible exception of the Special Purposes Regiment.'

Skorzeny glanced toward the window and then looked away again, his eyes suddenly narrowing. 'You would be well advised to forget what you have seen here, Herr Kapitän.'

Wirth felt stung by the rebuke and it was only with the greatest difficulty that he managed to control his temper. 'I already have,' he said in an icy voice.

"Good.' Skorenzy nodded emphatically. 'Now as to the vexed question of command and control ...'

It was a fundamental point, one that Wirth had discussed with the Admiral before leaving for the conference at Oranienburg. So far as the navy was concerned, the issue wasn't in doubt. The North Atlantic was their theatre of operations and therefore the executive orders to Hartmann would come from U-boat headquarters at Kiel. It quickly transpired that the army and the SS didn't agree. In their view, U 195 was simply a weapons platform, and that being the case, command should be exercised by the Gernal Staff through Major Reinhard Galen. Reaching an impasse, the two men arrived at a compromise and decided to establish a change of operational control line at seventy degrees west where Hartmann would defer to Galen's instructions except in matters of seamanship.

'I don't think my C-in-C is going to be very happy with this arrangement. He may take it up with Grossadmiral Dönitz.'

'That's his prerogative.' Skorzeny left the table, and opening the cupboard which stood in the corner of his office, returned with a bottle of Schnapps and two spirit glasses. 'But do you think that will change anything?'

Dönotz would be obliged to refer the problem to the OKW, the High Command of the armed forces, which in effect meant the Führer, who would undoubtedly back Skorzeny. There was a time when Hitler would have listened to the Grossadmiral and taken his advice, but the crushing reverses the navy had suffered in April and May of 1943 and the failure of the U-boats to stop the D-day landings had undermined his influence.

'No.' Wirth sighed. 'No, I'm sure it won't.'

'Then let's drink to the success of the mission, coupled with Operation Griffin.'

Wirth had never heard of Operation Griffin, but he had a shrewd idea that it might have something to do with the soldiers dressed in American uniforms he'd observed on entering the camp.

'The Amis have two nasty surprises coming their way and they won't know what hit them' Skorzeny smiled at him over the rim of his glass. 'You mark my words. Less than two months from now the whole course of this war will have changed dramatically.'

'In our favour, I presume?'

'But of course.'

Wirth had meant it as a joke but it seemed that Otto Skorzeny still believed in miracles.

CHAPTER 2

Bergen, Norway

Saturday, 18 November 1944

With its pressurized cabin, the Mark XVI photo reconnaissance version of the de Havilland Mosquito was able to operate at forty thousand feet and was fast enough to outstrip the high altitude Focke Wulf 190. On this occasion, however, Flight Lieutenant Thomas had been ordered to go in at very low level, and he just hoped the end result would be worth all the aggravation. There was a good chance that their low-level approach over the North Sea would confuse the long-range early warning radar, but even so, they could still expect to receive a warm reception from the flak defences. Until recently, Thomas would have regarded a photo recce of the U-boat base at Bergen as something of a milk run, but that cosy situation was unlikely to apply now. On Tuesday, the fourteenth of November, Lancasters from 617 Squadron had attacked and sunk the *Tirpitz* in Tromsoe Fjord and he reckoned the Germans were probably more than a mite angry about that.

'That's Sotra Island ahead.'

Thomas acknowledged the cool voice of his navigator, Sergeant James, and with one eye on the air speed indicator, opened both throttles to push the two-stage Rolls Royce Merlin engines to their limit.

The Mosquito was doing close to four hundred and ten miles an hour when they swept over Kors-fjord and ran into a barrage of flak from the 20mm guns guarding the Leroy Narrows. Two minutes and twelve miles farther on, the barrage became a wall of fire as the Eighty-eights from Forts Kvarven and Hellen joined in.

Slowly, all too slowly, the U-boat pens came in sight,

and then the massive concrete structure topped by a flat roof some forty feet thick was behind them, and they were flashing over the barracks area, the forward-facing cameras in the two underwing fuel tanks and the nose filming every detail on the ground. Banking sharply at the end of the run, Thomas then took violent evasive action and headed out to sea.

'Did you spot it?' Sergeant Janes asked him presently.

'What?'

'The wooden security fence inside the barracks, the one our Intelligence people were on about.'

'No,' said Thomas. 'I was too busy praying.'

'I didn't see it either,' said Janes. 'Maybe the Norwegians have got it wrong and the bloody thing doesn't exist.'

Kapitänleutnant August Peiper felt old, looked old and, at the age of forty-five, was regarded as being very old by ninety-nine percent of the crew of the U 195. To the first and second watch officers, Oberleutnant zur See Werner Best and Leutnant zur See Karl-Hans Dietrich, he was affectionately known as Grossvater, but to the diesel and electro mechanics he was next in line to God. Born in Hamburg before the turn of the century, it was only natural that the sea should have been in his blood. Still under training when the High Seas Fleet had mutinied, Peiper had joined the Hamburg-Amerika Line as a stoker shortly after his discharge from the navy in January 1919. Had it not been for the slump of '23 he would probably have remained a merchant seaman for the rest of his working life, but when the mark dropped through the floor and one American dollar was worth four billion, Peiper had found himself on the beach.

A succession of jobs had followed in the next five years but none had lasted more than a few weeks, and looking for security, he'd decided to rejoin the navy. Promotion had been slow and for a long time it had seemed he would be lucky to make petty officer. The scrapping of the Versailles Treaty and the Anglo-Germany Naval

Agreement of 1935 had changed all that, and with an eye to the main chance, Peiper had transferred to the newly reformed U-boat arm. Even so, he was still only a chief engine room artificer when the war started and he'd had to wait a further two years before the Kriegsmarine saw fit to commission him.

To reach the rank of Kapitänleutnant had been the height of his ambition and having achieved that distinction in '43, Peiper had had every reason to be content. What if the job was hazardous? He had a good wife, a beautiful seventeen-year-old daughter that any father would be proud of, money in the bank and a nice little house outside Wilhelmshaven that was almost paid for. That had been his philosophy then, but in the intervening eighteen months he had learned better. His old bounce and confidence gone, Peiper was filled with dread each time he had to go back to sea. Far too many of his contemporaries were now resting in steel coffins at the bottom of the Atlantic for him to have any peace of mind.

For the first time in his life Peiper had wanted to believe the scuttlebutt that had been going the rounds in the barracks at Kiel after the crew had returned from leave, had wanted to believe that they were going to be reassigned to one of the new electro boats. Most rumours were too fantastic to have any credibility but that one had sounded plausible. The navy hadn't been in a hurry to send them back to Norway and Korvettenkapitän Erich Hartmann had disappeared, reputedly to Bremen where several type XXIs were nearing completion. As it turned out, it had all been wishful thinking on the part of the crew; one week later the Movements staff had sent them on their way to Bergen.

Peiper finished the rest of the brandy and returned the hip flask to the pocket of his bridgecoat. Twenty-four hours on the ferry from Kiel to Oslo hadn't exactly improved his morale. The boat had been overcrowded, the food lousy and the Skagerrak so damned rough that most of the army and Luftwaffe personnel on board had been seasick. As the senior officer among those destined for

18

Bergen, the railway transportation officer at Oslo had appointed him OC for the train, something at least which had met with Peiper's approval, since it meant that he had a compartment all to himself. It wasn't that he didn't get on with the two watch officers; Werner Best and Karl-hans Dietrich were likeable enough young men, but he hadn't been in the mood for 'their company and still wasn't.

Werner Best was an ambitious officer whose conversation tended to be somewhat limited, especially when Dietrich was around, and endless talk about U-boats was the last thing Peiper wanted. U 195 had been his second love for the past three and a half years but, like a mistress who'd lost her appeal, he was now sick of the sight of her. He had come to loathe the sour smell of unwashed bodies within her womb, the garbage that had to be stored in her intestines until it was safe to excrete it and the way she broke out in a muck sweat. But most of all, Peiper was afraid of her, afraid because their next patrol together would be the thirteenth and he had a premonition that it would also be their last.

Peiper leaned his head against the window and closed his eyes. Of course, there was always Hartmann. Erich had brought them safely home on twelve previous occasions and there was no logical reason why he shouldn't do so again. Hartmann had a good head on his shoulders and was one of the most efficient captains in the U-boat fleet, which was hardly surprising considering the grounding he'd had from men like Prien and Schepke. He'd been the second watch officer on U 47 when Gunther Prien had penetrated the defences of Scapa Flow to sink the battleship *Royal Oak* while she lay at anchor; and Schepke, one of the leading aces of his day, had taught him a trick or two before he was selected for command.

Any apprentice worth his salt could have learned his trade backward from those two, but Hartmann had something far more important going for him. He seemed to be endowed with a sixth sense which was a damn sight more reliable than the Metox radar U 195 was equipped

19

with. He had proved that on their fourth patrol when they were cruising on the surface, shadowing a convoy two days out from St. John's. A heavy rainsquall had reduced visibility to just over a mile when suddenly, despite the fact that the lookouts hadn't seen anything and their hydrophones were silent, Hartmann had decided to take the boat down to periscope depth and prepare for action. Everybody on board had thought him mad, but exactly seven minutes later a Town Class destroyer doing close on twenty knots had appeared on a parallel course and they had put two fish into her broadside on.

Luck was another of Hartmann's star qualities, for had he remained with either Prien or Schepke, he would now be a dead man. Experience, skill, a sixth sense and luck: What more could a crew want from their captain? Peiper smiled to himself, catching at the straw that as long as Hartmann was in command they would come to no harm. It was a comforting thought to hang on to as the train approached Bergen.

Hartmann took one last look of U 195 and then left the subterranean pen where she was berthed to make his way to the flotilla headquarters above ground.

The type VIIc boats were the backbone of the fleet and such was their versatility that the basic design had been subjected to various modifications in the construction stage, particularly with regard to the number of torpedo tubes. The normal complement was five but some boats were not fitted with a stern tube. U 195 was different again in that, along with five others of her class, she only had a total of three tubes, two of which were in the bows. Certain external structural alterations had followed in October 1943, when they had returned to Brest for a refit after completing their ninth patrol. The 88mm quick-firing gun had been removed and the existing antiaircraft platform behind the conning tower enlarged to accommodate a quadruple 20mm. At the same time, a Metox radar and a rigid snorkel had been installed so that the diesel engines could be used to recharge the batteries

20

while cruising at periscope depth, a measure that was intended to combat the growing menace from the air. Although these modifications had not been a hundred percent effective, at least they had improved the U-boat's appearance, making her seem even more sleek than before, which Hartmann thought was more than could be said for this latest refit carried out at Bergen.

U 195 had been violated; there was no other way to describe what had been done to her. The foredeck casing had been strengthened and an upward-sweeping ramp now extended from the conning tower to the sharklike configuration of the Atlantic-type bows. The ramp resembled a backward-facing ski jump and consisted of two parallel rails supported by a lattice of metal struts, the vertical members gradually increasing in size to reach a maximum height of one metre at the bows. As he strolled toward the headquarters block where Kapitän zur See Wirth had installed himself, Hartmann wondered what the crew would make of the new look that U 195 had acquired in their absence, wondered too what they would make of the high wooden fence that had been erected around their barrack and mess hall accommodation.

Wirth's office was on the ground floor. Expecting to find him alone, he was annoyed to discover that Major Reinhard Galen was present. Although he had managed to conceal it so far, Hartmann had taken an instant dislike to the artillery officer, finding him arrogant and overbearing. His attitude and certain remarks he'd made regarding the Führer's method of conducting the war had convinced him that he was a fanatical Nazi. In appearance, Galen was the archetypal Aryan, the kind of man commercial artists liked to depict in the propaganda posters plasted on hoardings all over Germany. Tall, athletic and very blond, his handsome features were marred only by a thin Roman nose that was a shade too long.

'You've arrived in the nick of time, Erich." Wirth greeted him with a brief smile. 'Major Galen and I have been discussing what additional security measures should be taken, and we'd like your opinion. That reconnaissance flight by the RAF this morning was a nasty surprise.'

'Yes, it was. However, I doubt if they saw anything apart from the wooden fence around the barracks area. Of course, they'll have some oblique photographs of the pens, but not of the boats. They were too far back for the cameras to pick them up.'

'I must say I'm amazed at your complacency,' Galen said coldly. 'The RAF aren't in the habit of making casual visits.'

'I'm well aware of that.' Hartmann made a supreme effort to keep his temper. 'Obviously there was some careless talk and the Norwegian Underground passed the information on to London. I know everyone is confined to base, but fresh vegetables still have to be purchased from the market in Bergen.'

'And the civilian contractor was allowed to collect the swill from the mess halls as usual.' Wirth picked up a ruler and flexed it, bending it in a bow. 'The SD are questioning him now, along with the cooks and the ration storeman. I imagine it won't be long before we know who was responsible for the leak.'

'But that won't stop the RAF from paying us another visit. That fence is bound to increase their curiosity.' Hartmann rubbed his jaw reflectively. 'Not that it will make any difference to our plans. After all, we've already decided the acceptance trials will be carried out at night.'

'What about the preliminary briefing of your crew? Shouldn't we reconsider what you are going to say to them?' Galen turned in Wirth's direction, as if seeking his support.

'I don't see why,' said Hartmann. 'My men aren't fools; they know the Baltic is the only safe training area we have. In any case, there are a number of farms on Sotra Island, so I shall remind them that most Norwegians are not deaf, dumb and blind. You needn't worry, they won't question our decision.'

'Nevertheless, we can't afford to take any chances, Erich. We've given the matter some thought and Both

Major Galen and I think it inadvisable to screen the documentary film produced by Peenemünde. It's bound to cause a lot of speculation and one cannot be sure that our quarantine arrangements will prove a hundred percent effective. For instance, if one of your crew were taken seriously ill, we'd have no alternative but to send him to the military hospital in Bergen.'

'You have a point, sir, but, with all due respect, cancelling the film show won't put an end to the speculation. Their U-boat has been given a drastic face-lift and they will want to know what that ramp is for. In my view, seeing the film will make them appreciate why it's vital they keep their mouths shut.'

Wirth pursed his lips and looked thoughtful. As the silence lengthened, it became obvious to Hartmann that the Kapitän zur See was waiting for Galen to give his opinion before he made up his mind.

'On reflection, perhaps we ought to show the film tonight.' Galen cleared his throat noisily. 'The documentary will go a long way toward satisfying their curiosity and it will certainly help to give the men a sense of purpose.'

His crew had never been lacking in that, but Hartmann let it pass. Although the slight had probably been intentional, he decided it would be diplomatic to pretend otherwise; as it was, Galen would be a hard man to get along with in the confined space of the U-boat without him adding fuel to the fire before they set sail.

'I'm glad we were able to resolve that problem satisfactorily.' Wirth glanced at his wristwatch. 'Well now,' he said briskly, 'I see the troop train is due to arrive in ten minutes.'

It was another way of saying, 'Don't let me detain you any longer, gentlemen,' but Hartmann ignored the hint.

'I understand the naval architect is returning to Kiel tomorrow, Herr Kapitän?'

'Yes, he is. Naturally the other civilian workers will be staying on until the acceptance trials have been completed.'

23

'I'd like the naval architect to remain as well.'

'Oh?' Wirth raised his eyebrows. 'May I ask why?'

'I'm not very happy about one of the structural alterations that have been made to my boat. The forward hatch has been enlarged and there may be some weakness there.'

'Nonsense, Erich. Herr Jost is confident that U 195 is completely seaworthy.'

'Then he won't mind accompanying us tomorrow, will he?'

'That is out of the question. Herr Jost is heavily involved with the type XXI programme.'

'One day should be sufficient,' Hartmann said calmly. 'I can easily vary our programme and take her straight down to our maximum diving depth. It's rather like putting the horse before the cart, but I appreciate that Herr Jost is a very busy man. And besides, there is another point we should consider ...'

'Yes?'

'We don't want the crew to get the wrong idea, do we, sir? I mean, it would be most unfortunate if they thought Herr Jost had no confidence in his design.'

There was a long pause, and then Wirth gave in, just as Hartmann had known he would.

Although the mess hall was centrally heated, August Peiper couldn't stop shivering. The army detachment had caused a buzz of excitement among the crew when they'd trooped into the building, but their arrival had chilled him to the bone. His morale, having once again sunk to a low ebb, had dropped even further after Hartmann had begun his address by stressing that what they were about to see and hear was Top Secret. So far as Peiper was concerned, there could not have been a more ominous introduction which, coupled with the security fence around their living quarters, confirmed all his worst fears about the next patrol.

As he sat there listening to Hartmann, Peiper told himself that it was stupid to be superstitious about a

24

number. Thirteen might be unlucky for some, but offhand he couldn't recall a single instance where it had applied to him. And what if their next patrol did prove hazardous? They had been in tight spots before and Erich had always pulled them through. Hartmann was no fledgling out of the nest with the down still on his cheeks; he was twenty-eight years old and easily the most likable and efficient captain that Peiper had ever served under. One look at those broad shoulders and that strong face with its wide, generous mouth which always seemed ready to smile and you knew he was indestructible. That he was also a very brave man was beyond dispute; the Knight's Cross with oak leaves around his neck was a visible reminder of that.

Hartmann concluded his opening remarks and sat down in the front row next to Oberleutnant zur See Best, his senior watch officer. A few moments later the lights in the mess hall went out and the triumphant strains of 'We March Against England' blared through the portable speakers on either side of the canvas screen. The music faded away and was replaced by a deafening roar as the camera zoomed in on a Flakzielgerat 76. Peiper had seen newsreel shots of the V1 before, but not in colour, and the bright orange flame escaping from the pulse jet engine mounted on the torpedo-shaped bomb filled him with awe. As if shot from a catapult, the flying bomb sped up the inclined ramp and lifted off, the note of its engine changing to a deep-throated snarl, a noise that reminded Peiper of a heavy diesel truck with a loose baffle plate in the silencer. Turning onto a preset course, the V1 climbed rapidly to a height of four thousand feet and levelled out, the film then becoming noticeably jerky as the missile was tracked by an airborne cameraman. Presently the flying bomb tilted into a nose-down attitude and in that same instant the engine cut out. Like a gannet swooping down on its prey, the V1 plummeted toward the ground in a nearly vertical dive. Two minutes later the deathly silence was broken by a dull roar, and a column of debris rose into the air.

One sequence would have been sufficient but the film

director had chosen to lay it on with a shovel. Different bombs shown from different angles still amounted to the same thing and Peiper rapidly decided that once you'd seen one V1 you had seen them all. It was an opinion shared by the vast majority of the audience, who became increasingly restive and increasingly bored with the commentator whose lyrical description of the missile would have done credit to a high-powered car salesman. Suddenly, just as the documentary seemed to be drawing to a close, the whole tempo changed, becoming languid with an extended take of the sun slowly climbing above the horizon. As the light improved, one of the old type II U-boats belonging to the Baltic Training Division came sharply into focus and there was an audible gasp from the audience.

The U-boat was an eyesore, its clean lines disfigured by a ramp which extended from the conning tower to the bows. In a long list of harebrained schemes that had been mooted during the war, the idea of launching a V1 from a U-boat struck Peiper as being the most lunatic of all. Numb with disbelief, he watched the flying bomb leave the ramp and then the screen went blank and the martial strains of 'We March Against England' boomed through the speakers once more.

It was a stirring but singularly inappropriate way to end the film. Hartmann had disclosed nothing about the impending mission, but common sense told Peiper that this particular surprise package would not be directed against the British Isles.

CHAPTER 3

Bergen, Norway

Sunday, 19 November 1944

WINDS NORTHEAST. FORCE THREE TO FOUR.
VISIBILITY POOR. SLEET OR SNOW SHOWERS
AT TIMES.

Hartmann turned up the collar of his fur-lined leather jacket against the cold night air and sat down on the jump seat by the ventilating shaft situated on the port side of the bridge. The weather forecast for the next six hours looked fairly reasonable, but the meteorologists had been proved wrong before. The North Sea was very capricious at this time of the year and its mood could change dramatically within a matter of an hour or so, usually for the worse. There was no telling how U 195 would behave in a heavy swell with the added weight of the ramp on her bows, but there was an even chance she would wallow like a pig. However, at the present moment it was more pressing to know whether the enlarged forward hatch would prove watertight at their maximum diving depth, something which had to be established before Herr Jost, the naval architect, returned to Kiel.

'I can't say I'm looking forward to the next few hours, sir.' Werner Best cupped his hands together and blew on them. 'I think it's going to be damned cold out there in the Leroy Narrows. Still, the sea ought to be moderately calm. I imagine that will please Major Galen.'

'Anything's possible,' Hartmann said drily.

Galen was the sole military representative on board. There had been no need for him to come along but, to Hartmann's annoyance, the artillery officer had insisted on the grounds that it would give him an opportunity to familiarize himself with the routine at sea. After promising not to make a nuisance of himself, Galen had then promptly asked if he might have the use of Hartmann's cabin so that he could study the side elevation and deck plans of U 195. It seemed that, while the conducted tour of the boat by Leutnant zur See Dietrich that morning had been most helpful, the drawings would enable Galen to refresh his memory.

'Permission to carry on, sir?'

Hartmann looked up and nodded. Werner Best was a competent executive officer but he liked to do everything exactly by the book and lacked the imagination to make a successful U-boat commander. It wasn't entirely his fault. Werner had been a second watch officer under Kapitänleutnant Terboven, a man who, having spent most of his service on the battleship *Gneisnau*, should never have been transferred to the U-boat arm. Terboven was a stickler for spit and polish and had a reputation for running what he called a taut ship. Not surprisingly, many of his fads had rubbed off on the junior officer. Observing Best now as he called for reports from the engine room and Obersteuermann Frick, the chief helmsman, Hartmann couldn't help feeling that his senior watch officer would be more at home on the deck of a surface vessel.

It was, however, part of a captain's job to train his subordinates for command and the fact that so far he'd been unable to remold Werner or to convince him that competence had little to do with spit and polish, was an admission of failure on his part. Best was motivated by ambition but he was willing and anxious to learn.

"We'll have to vary the routine for leaving harbour. Werner.' Hartmann stood up and, leaning over the conning tower, glanced at the ramp below. Then he looked pointedly toward Kapitän zur See Wirth, who was watching them from the jetty. 'I expect that has already occurred to you?'

'Sir?'

The blank look and the hesitant tone of voice said it all.

28

Despite the broad hint, Best hadn't the faintest idea what he was getting at.

'We've got the best part of a junkyard on our superstructure,' Hartmann explained patiently. 'Added to which, it also happens to be pitch black out there. I don't want anyone falling overboard.'

'You want the men sent below as soon as we've cast off?'

'Exactly. This is one occasion when Kapitän Wirth will forgive us for dispensing with the usual pomp and circumstance.'

'I should have thought of that.'

The admission was typical of the first watch officer. It was this willingness to cheerfully acknowledge when he was in the wrong that made Hartmann respect him.

His confidence in no way diminished, Best gave instructions to cast off and then ordered all hands below before ringing for slow ahead on the telegraph. Moments later, U 195 began to inch her way out of the pen propelled by two diesel engines, each of which were capable of developing three thousand two hundred horsepower.

Galen placed the drawing face down on the table and, finding a sheet of paper, began to sketch the layout of the U 195 from memory. With an eye for detail, he first drew the outline of the boat and then, using his fountain pen, described the inner pressurized walls. Having done that, he subdivided the pressurized interior into a number of squares, each one representing a compartment which he proceeded to identify, beginning with the captain's cabin immediately forward of the control room and opposite the radio office. Working toward the bows, he next marked in the forward accommodation, the single toilet that served the entire crew of fifty-six officers and men, and the bow torepedo room. The forward battery room was belowdecks, sandwiched between one of the oil tanks and a torpedo storage compartment and extending from the captain's cabin as far as the toilet.

Satisfied that he had not forgotten anything, Galen :urned his attention to the control room in the conning tower, indicating the surface attack periscope which retracted into a well let into the number-three diving tank in the keel. Moving on from there, he drew an upturned cooking pot above the control room to represent the pressurized cabin in the conning tower used by the captain during a submerged attack, and then pencilled in the adjoining sky navigation periscope together with the rigid snorkel. On the bridge itself, various symbols were used to show the Hohentwiel radar, the Metox receiver and the radio direction finder. In the control room itself, a mass of wheels and dials depicted the trimming panel and the hydroplane controls, which operated a type of rudder that enabled the U-boat to go up or down.

The stern section was less complicated. Progressing from the engineers' quarters next to the control room, there was a small galley beyond which lay the diesel engine room and the rear torpedo compartment, which also housed the two electric motors. Impatient to complete his self-imposed task, Galen arrowed the trim tanks, propeller shaft, stern oil tanks and the aft battery room beneath the engineers' quarters. As a final touch, two downward sloping lines, stretching from the conning tower to the bows and stern, represented the jumping wires whose purpose was to prevent the U-boat becoming entangled in an antisubmarine net.

Comparing his rough sketch with the detailed drawing, Galen had reason to be satisfied. Apart from omitting the drinking and used water tanks next to the stern battery room and the fore and aft diving tanks which were outside the pressurized interior, his memory had served him well. His request for the side elevation and deck plans of U 195 had caused a few raised eyebrows among the officers, but their ill-concealed amusement hadn't bothered him. The hallmark of a good staff officer was the ability to think and plan ahead and it was entirely conceivable that the time might come when the knowledge he'd acquired would stand him in good stead. Despite the glowing report from the Kriegsmarine and Hartmann's admittedly impressive war record, Galen was in possession of certain information from the SD which led him to believe that the Korvettenkapitän was not to be trusted.

The family had first come to the notice of the Gestapo through the activities of Hartmann's uncle, a prominent lawyer who had been on very friendly terms with Karl Goerdler, the former Burgomeister of Leipzig and the driving force behind every conspiracy to overthrow the Führer. That in itself was not particularly damning, but in the hysterical aftermath of the July bomb plot, subsequent inquiries had brought to light the interesting fact that, for a brief period in 1941, Hartmann's sister, Lisette, had worked for Ludwig Pohl, the editor and publisher of the *Lübeck Zeitung*, who was later tried and executed for printing seditious leaflets. Whether Lisette Hartmann had been aware of Pohl's subversive activities during the time she was in his employ was far from clear, but she certainly had a talent for mixing with the wrong people. Shortly after leaving the *Lübeck Zeitung* she had announced her engagement to Hauptmann Friedrich von Oberg, a junior staff officer for whom a brilliant future had been predicted. Captured at Stalingrad along with the rest of Sixth Army, Oberg had joined the Free Germany Committee organized by the Russians and was thought to have written some of the speeches that had been broadcast from Moscow by Field Marshal Paulus.

None of this had anything to do with Hartmann directly, but Galen thought he was a man who would bear watching. The Korvettenkapitän was far too independent and outspoken, even for a U-boat captain, and there were grounds for thinking he was the kind of officer who might well disregard the orders of his superiors if he disagreed with them. If that should happen during the voyage, it would be necessary to replace him before the rest of the crew became disaffected. Oberleutnant zur See Best would be the logical choice to replace Hartmann in command, but as yet there was no telling which way he would jump if his loyalty were put to the test.

Galen glanced at his wristwatch and was surprised to see that more than two hours had passed since U 195 had slipped her moorings. Provided Hartmann had stuck to his original plan and maintained an average cruising speed of ten knots, they should be well south of Sotra Island by now and close to the area where the diving trial was scheduled to take place. As if to confirm Galen's supposition, there was an earsplitting blast from the Klaxon. Moving out into the passageway outside the cabin, he saw Leutnant zur See Dietrich close the circular pressurized hatch to the control room.

August Peiper didn't need to issue orders. With three and a half years of operational experience behind them, his men knew exactly what they had to do when the Klaxon sounded. Leaving the engine room, he walked through the galley and engineers' quarters to take his place at the trimming panel in the control room. By the time he reached the conning tower and was closing the watertight hatch behind him, all three diving tanks had been vented and the diesel engines shut down, their deep pulsating throb replaced by the quiet low-pitched hum of the electric motors.

The slick response of the diesel and electro mechanics was no more than Peiper expected. Although this was only an exercise, every man was aware that the next time they were called upon to make a crash dive, there could well be a long-range Liberator or a Catalina on the horizon. If you were caught on the surface by one of these bastards, there were just two things you could do. Either you stayed up and fought it out or else you went down into the cellar, and if it was the latter decision, you had to be damn quick about it. The battle of seconds started the moment the aircraft began its final run in for the kill. When that happened, the U-boat had to be ten metres below the surface within half a minute if it was to remain in one piece. The margin between life and death was narrow and only a well-trained crew could achieve that sort of time when the gun positions were fully manned, but under Hartmann's command they had succeeded in clipping a full two seconds off the existing record.

Peiper felt himself overbalancing and grabbed hold of a stanchion. The angle of descent was much steeper than he'd expected considering it was supposed to be a practice dive and he wondered what the hydroplane operators were playing at. If it was Hartmann's intention to put the forward hatch in the bows under maximum stress he was certainly going the right way about it. On the other hand, he was not the sort of captain who took unnecessary risks, so there had to be some other explanation for the way the boat was behaving.

It could be that the hydroplane controls were jammed, but in that case Hartmann would have immediately ordered the relief men to use the manual controls in the stern and below the torpedo room in the bows, which were there for just such an emergency. Peiper frowned. No, the ramp was the root cause of the trouble. He had known all along that they would have problems with that damn contraption. It had altered the whole trim of the boat and was taking them down like an express train. Still, there was no need to get alarmed yet. Hartmann was as cool as a cucumber and the hull was good for at least two hundred and fifty metres. That would give the hydroplane operators plenty of time to get used to the new feel of her.

The depth gauge went past fifty metres, moved on to sixty and then began to slow up. At sixty-five the hydroplane operators finally brought the boat under control and there was an audible sigh of relief from Werner Best. Sowly but surely they went down into the cellar. Hartmann using the tannoy periodically to check with Leutnant zur See Dietrich that the enlarged forward hatch in the bows was holding up. Ten minutes later they reached their maximum safe depth and Peiper trimmed the number-one diving tank in the stern to bring the boat onto an even keel.

'Well, at least we've learned one thing,' Hartmann glanced at Best, a wry smile on his face. 'If we're forced to make a crash dive in earnest, we know she'll sink like a stone. What do you say, Chief?'

'I only hope she bobs up again like the proverbial cork,'

Peiper said gloomily.

'You never used to be such a pessimist, August.' Hartmann edged past him and unclipped the forward hatch. 'You can take her up, Werner, while I have a few words with Herr Jost.'

'And Major Galen?'

'Not if I can help it,' said Hartmann.

The naval architect was a very articulate and enthusiastic little man. If Jost resented the fact that he had been obliged to stay on in Bergen instead of returning to Kiel, he certainly didn't show it. A few congratulatory words about the modified hatch were enough to spark off a long-winded and highly technical explanation of the stress factors involved, and Hartmann was soon groping for excuses to get away. When finally he did, it was only to find that Galen was waiting for him in the passageway outside the bow torpedo room.

'I trust everything is satisfactory, Erich?'

The sudden use of his Christian name surprised Hartmann. 'The hatch is watertight, if that's what you mean,' he said curtly.

'Good.' Taking Hartmann by the elbow, Galen steered him into the commander's cabin. 'Then we can presume that the acceptance trials will be completed on time.'

'Well, let's say we've cleared the first hurdle.'

'We can't afford to delay our departure beyond the twenty-sixth of this month, Erich.'

'I'm aware of that, but it will be a race against time to lick everyone into shape. We can't have any passengers on this trip.'

'Precisely what do you mean by that?'

'I've got to leave ten of my crew behind to accommodate your detachment. But we can discuss that problem later.'

'Why not now?' Galen sat down on the bunk and leaned his elbow on the table. 'Surely Oberleutnant Best can be left in command for a few minutes?'

Galen was right. The problem had to be faced sometime and now was as good a moment as any. 'The loss of those trained seamen is going to leave me very shorthanded. Of

34

course, we can slot some of your men into the various watches. They can take their turn up top with the other lookouts whenever it's safe enough to run on the surface, but that doesn't really solve the problem, Herr Major.'

'Reinhard.' Galen smiled. 'Please call me Reinhard. It's so much more friendly, don't you think?'

'Yes ... Reinhard.' The name struck in his gullet like a piece of undigested meat.

'You were saying, Erich?'

"Well, I was wondering if you could meet me halfway and reduce the size of your detachment. That second-in-command of yours, for instance?'

'Kleist?'

Hartmann nodded. Hauptmann Martin Kleist, a very studious-looking artillery officer with poor eyesight and a nervous habit of biting his nails.

'Yes, do you need him?'

'He's a scientist, Erich, a back-room boy. I'd like to help you, really I would, but every man in my detachment is a specialist. Reduce my numbers and the success of Operation Double Griffin will be severely prejudiced."

'Double Griffin?' Hartmann murmured. "Is that what they've decided to call this junket?"

'You know, Erich, I get the impression that you don't think much of this operation.' Galen creased his face in a smile that had all the warmth of an iceberg. 'Am I right?'

Hartmann leaned against the bulkhead, arms folded across his chest. The question was not as guileless as it appeared on the surface, and he had a feeling that Galen was trying to gauge his loyalty. 'Do you want an honest opinion?'

'Of course I do, I've no time for people who are afraid to speak their minds.'

'All right, if you're really interested, I just don't see what we hope to achieve by launching a ton of high explosive against some unspecified target on the eastern seaboard of the United States. Maybe I would feel differently about it if the V1 were an accurate weapon but, from what I've heard, a large percentage of the flying bombs aimed at London fell in the open countryside.'

There was a lot more Hartmann could have said, but he wanted to cut their conversation short and get up on the bridge where he belonged. The boat was running on the surface now; he could feel the cold night air venting through the interior and hear the pulsating throb of the diesel engines.

'They weren't radio-controlled from the ground,' Galen said calmly.

'From the ground?' Hartmann stared at the artillery officer, his eyes narrowing thoughtfully. 'Are you implying that we've got to put one of your men ashore before we can launch the missile?'

'No, that won't be necessary, Erich. You see, it just so happens that we've already got an agent inside the target area.'

'This spy, Reinhard – was he recruited by Admiral Canaris?'

'A long time ago. However, the Abwehr is no longer in business. Military Intelligence was absorbed into the SD in February of this year.'

'And he's a good agent?'

'One of the best, Erich. He's still at large.'

Hartmann digested the information in silence. Considering he was an artillery officer, Galen seemed to know an awful lot about the Reich Security Services.

CHAPTER 4

New York

Monday, 20 November 1944

Paul Webber poured a glass of orange juice from the carton in the refrigerator, popped two slices of bread in to the electric toaster and then lit the gas under the coffee percolator. Unlike most men who lived alone, Webber was thoroughly organized, a facet of his character which had little to do with the fact that he was forty-three years old and used to looking after himself.

He hadn't always lived alone however, and there was a time when his name had been spelled with one 'b'. He had been born Paul Weber, the only son of a captain in the Kaiser's Regiment of Foot Guards. The gallant captain had been killed during the first battle of Ypres in November 1914, cut down at point blank range, along with the rest of his regiment, by the 1st King's Regiment of the British Army who were holding Polygon Wood. Partly out of the sense of duty and patriotism instilled in him by his father, but mostly because he wanted to fly, Weber falsified his age and joined the Army Air Service. To his intense disappointment, the war ended shortly after he had been awarded his wings, and within a matter of weeks he was demobilized to join another army, the army of the unemployed. In October 1919, his mother having died of influenza in January of that year, he left Germany for good and emigrated to America to live with his maternal aunt in Milwaukee. Three years later, when legally eligible to do so, he applied for American citizenship and changed his name to Webber.

Flying was in his blood, but civil aviation was in its infancy and there were few openings for a fledgling pilot. As a result, for a long time it looked as if he were destined to remain a bank clerk for the rest of his life. The arrival in town of a group of barnstormers changed all that. They stayed a week, and every day Webber went out to the grass field where they had pitched camp, to see them perform. The night before the barnstormers were due to leave Milwaukee he approached the organizer and begged him for a job. He'd do anything — help with the cooking, pitch tents, drive one of the trucks, guard the planes at night — and they only had to give him bed and board. It was an offer no man could refuse and it maked a turning point in Webber's life.

The barnstormers toured the Middle West, moved to California and then worked their way north to Oregon and back again. In the two and a half years he was with

37

the outfit before it folded, Webber climbed the ladder from menial to stunt pilot. When this harum-scarum way of life ended in 1925, he was lucky enough to land a job with Spruce Airways, a small airline based in San Francisco. He was lucky in the sense that eleven months after joining them, Spruce Airways won the franchise to carry U.S. mail to Seattle and he was in on the ground floor. By 1931 he'd graduated to the Ford Tri Motor and was flying passengers instead of freight.

In between times, he had met, courted and married a Miss Avis Lawrence, a striking redhead who had a secretarial post with a firm of insurance brokers. Avis gave up her job to keep house for him, but less than three years later she decided she'd had enough. As the airline expanded, Webber was frequently away for days on end, and in her boredom and loneliness, Avis had formed an attachment with a high school teacher. After talking it over, they both agreed that their marriage had broken down and Avis took off for Reno to establish the obligatory residential qualification before filing suit for divorce. In 1936, acting on advice, Webber moved to New York and joined National Eastern Airlines, with whom he stayed.

Although as a senior captain with National Eastern Airlines Webber could have afforded something much better, he had no intention of moving from the apartment house on East 93rd Street. The apartment had everything he wanted and was in a good area, just a few strides from Fifth Avenue and Central Park. He also got on well with his neighbours, even the gushing Mrs. Langdon across the hall who kept inviting him to dinner in the faint hope that he would eventually take an interest in her thirty-two-year-old and very homely daughter, Cynthia. Apart from those considerations, the large bedroom, living-dining room, bathroom and kitchen were about as much as he could cope with.

Never one to eat standing up, Webber laid a place at the kitchen table and then switched on the radio to catch the eight o'clock newscast on WNYC which he had breakfast. It seemed that the war in Europe was bogged down. Even though six Allied armies were alleged to be advancing on a broad front, there were precious few gains to report either in the Aachen area or farther south where the Seventh Army was still extending its arc around Metz. It was much the same in the Pacific, where the battle for Leyte had become a hard and bitter slugging match. The home front was one long yawn, most of the local news concerning the sixth war-bond loan drive that had started rolling when Roosevelt had lit the torch of the Statue of Liberty reproduction in Times Square.

Bored with the news, Webber switched off the radio and rinsed the breakfast dishes in the sink. That done, he collected his overnight bag from the bedroom, put on a trench coat and left the apartment.

Mrs. Langdon intercepted him in the hall, but there was nothing unusual about that. No matter how much he varied his routine in an effort to avoid her, Mrs. Langdon always defeated him, as if she possessed some sort of built-in radar that told her exactly when he was about to leave.

'Good morning, Mr. Webber,' she said brightly. 'And where are you off to today?'

'Cleveland, Detroit and then Chicago — weather permitting.' Webber made a vague gesture with his thumb toward the ceiling and then started to edge away. 'The temperature's low and those dark clouds up there mean sleet or snow.'

'Will you be back tonight?'

'No, we have a stopover in Chicago.' Webber inched nearer the staircase.

'My, you do get around. When are young going to Washington again?'

Mrs. Langdon was up to her old tricks, fishing for information and hoping that in an unguarded moment he'd tell her something about a girl friend in Georgetown whom she firmly believed was wholly fictitious. Well, he didn't care what she thought; Christel did exist. She worked in the Swiss Embassy on Cathedral Avenue Northwest and they had a very special kind of relationship, one that he was determined neither Mrs.

Langdon nor anyone else should ever discover.

'Who can tell?' Webber shrugged his shoulders. 'I never know from one day to the next what my schedule will be. All the younger men are in the Army Air Force and we're kind of shorthanded.' He grinned ruefully. 'I only wish they'd let me put on a proper uniform.'

'You do your bit, Mr. Webber." She smiled, and scarcely pausing for breath, rushed in with, 'My husband and I were wondering if you'd like to have dinner with us on Thanksgiving Day?'

Desperately, Webber racked his brain for a convincing excuse to decline the invitation, but his mind remained obstinately blank. 'That's very kind of you, Mrs. Langdon,' he said with false enthusiasm. 'I'd like to very much.'

'Oh, that's just marvellous; Cynthia will be pleased. She doesn't get to meet many people of her own age, you know.'

There was no answer to that. Glancing at his wristwatch, he said he'd have to be getting along, otherwise he would be late, and started down the staircase. As he left the house, Mrs. Langdon leaned over the bannisters and told him to have a nice day.

Webber thought the day could hardly have started on a less auspicious note, but at least nobody had tried to tamper with the security lock on the gas tank of his car during the night. Climbing into the Studebaker two-door sedan, he was even more pleasantly surprised when the engine started at the touch of a button. But the feeling that it wasn't going to be such a bad day after all vanished shortly after crossing the Queensborough Bridge, when it began to sleet. By the time Webber reached La Guardia Airport, the sleet had changed to rain, becoming a torrential downpour in the process.

John Anderson had long since forgotten the name and the face of the skipper of the British merchantman who'd visited the operations room of Eastern Sea Frontier one bitterly cold day in February '43, but he could remember his words as if it were only yesterday. The skipper had taken one quick look at the U-boat plot and then had turned to him with a broad smile on his face. There must have been many times, he had remarked, when Anderson had reckoned his posting to New York the best thing to have happened to him since joining the Royal Navy. Although it had been said without malice, the casual observation had rankled. The posting had brought him promotion to Lieutenant Commander at the age of twenty-six and had removed him from the war zone, but in those early days there had been no reason to have guilty feelings about it. He was one of the few regulars to have specialized in anti-submarine warfare in peacetime, and with more than three years of active service in the North Atlantic, he'd had a lot to offer in the way of practical advice.

Now, almost two years later, it was a totally different story. The Americans didn't need his expertise and the war at sea had changed dramatically. The air gap in mid-Atlantic had been closed by long-range Liberators based in Iceland and the introduction of escort carriers. The Hudson River and the great anchorage of New York's Upper Bay were no longer jammed with ships awaiting convoy, because there were more frigates and destroyers available, and during the period June to October '44, the Germans had actually lost more U-boats than they had sunk merchantmen.

On the face of it, the only reason why the Admiralty hadn't moved him elsewhere was because he had taken on additional duties, thus releasing other men for active duty. Although he still used the same office in 17 Battery Place, he now combined the appointment of staff officer for Operations and Intelligence with that of Assistant British Naval Liaison Officer with special responsibility for overseeing the repair of HM ships in the Brooklyn Navy Yard. He was also the link man between the joint British-Canadian escort base on Staten Island and the U.S. Navy District, but that was a job in name only these days.

For well over a year now, Anderson had been fighting a

long running battle with their lordships at the Admiralty. Regularly each month he submitted an application for a sea-going appointment; regularly each month it was rejected on the grounds that only someone of his experience could fill the staff appointment at Eastern Sea Frontier. But the validity of that argument had been demolished for good just over a fortnight ago by Tom Sullivan.

Tom Sullivan had been his opposite number in the U.S. Navy, and Sullivan's greatest ambition had also been to return to sea duty. It had taken him fourteen long months to do it, but in the end his persistence had paid off and the navy had finally relented. Sullivan's unconcealed joy at being appointed to command a destroyer in the Pacific had been hard enough to bear, but it had been the American's replacement who'd really made Anderson feel sore. Even though two weeks had gone by since Sullivan had introduced him to his successor, he still felt vaguely uneasy every time he walked into Tom's old office and found Lieutenant (j.g.) Virginia Canford sitting behind the desk.

Virginia Canford was a disturbing young woman in more ways than one. There were any number of attractive blondes in New York, but she was undoubtedly the most intelligent and sophisticated one he'd met so far. She had all the poise and confidence in the world, which was hardly surprising given her background. After leaving the Shipley School in 1939, she had been introduced into society, following which she had graduated from Bryn Mawr and the Columbia University Law School. Prior to joining the Waves, she had worked for a brief time in the family law firm of Brooks, Canford and Ward. According to Sullivan, her mother was related to the Dupont family, her father was reputed to be worth four million dollars and, if that weren't enough, one of her uncles was currently a member of the Senate Committee for Foreign Relations. To put it in a nutshell, Virginia Canford had been born with a diamond-encrusted silver spoon in her mouth. That alone was enough to make him feel at a disadvantage, without the added impression that she didn't hold him in very high regard.

Anderson picked up the loose-leaf folder containing the Admiralty signals received in the past twenty-four hours and walked over to the window. He looked out across the rain-swept Battery Park and instead of seeing the East River, visualized the Thames Estuary moments before a mine had blown HMS *Valhalla* in two, killing sixty-one members of the destroyer's crew. Then, looking at the Upper Bay, he saw himself and six other survivors clinging to a life raft two hundred and fifty miles southwest of Reykjavik. They had spent eight hours in the water, close to death in the sub-zero temperature, and anyone who had been through that kind of experience could never hope to be the same man again. Certainly Anderson knew he'd changed in mind and body. His face looked harder, there were flecks of grey in his dark hair and he'd been told there was a steeliness in his eyes that hadn't been there before. His family and friends also said that he'd become introspective which, in a way, was only to be expected. The corvette had been his first command and most of the ship's company had gone down with her when she was torpedoed. With the best will in the world, that was not the sort of memory one could shrug off overnight. Someone like Virginia Canford could never understand what the war at sea was really all about and certainly he had no intention of opening her eyes to the facts of life and death in the North Atlantic. That would be too much like pleading for tea and sympathy.

Crossing the room in a few strides, he rapped on the communicating door and then entered her office.

'Good morning, Virginia.' He had never used her first name before and she looked up with a faint smile of amusement. His face expressionless, he placed the loose-leaf file on her desk. 'These are the Admiralty signals for the past twenty-four hours.'

'Do they affect the U-boat plot we already have on the board, sir?'

Anderson frowned. He wished to God she would stop

addressing him in that way. 'No, but you can alter your scorecard for the month. A U-boat was sunk off Falmouth yesterday morning, so the running total is now five.'

'Five U-boats against three merchantmen.' Virginia Canford shook her head. 'I'd say the Kriegsmarine has just about had it.'

'I wouldn't underestimate them; they could still give us a nastry surprise.' It sounded pompous, even to his ears, but somehow this attractive American girl invariably brought out the worst in him. 'For instance, there's an item here that could be interesting.' Anderson moved round the desk and was immediately aware of a fragrant smell of perfume as he stood beside her and sorted through the signals in the file. 'The Norwegian Underground reported that the 11th U-boat flotilla had been confined to base until further notice. In view of this, the RAF sent a Mosquito over to Bergen on Saturday to see what the Germans were up to. They didn't find much, except that one section of the barracks had been fenced off.'

'That's kind of odd, isn't it, sir?' Virginia looked up at him with a puzzled expression. 'I mean, why the additional security measures?'

'Search me. Your guess is as good as mine.'

'I'm a lawyer and we don't go in for guessing games.'

A slim hand closed the file and placed it in the pending tray, a gesture that closed the subject and effectively terminated their conversation. Anderson was prepared to concede that the signal was probably unimportant, but Virginia didn't make his job of liaising with the U.S. Navy exactly easy. He'd never had any touble communicating with Tom Sullivan, but it was a whole new ball game with her. Halfway to the door, it suddenly occurred to him that it wasn't altogether her fault; after all, he hadn't made any real effort to get to know her better.

'I was just wondering ...' he said. 'How would you like to have dinner with me at the Astor tomorrow night?'

The Astor would swallow most of his pay for a whole month, but he reckoned it was the sort of place she was used to.

'I'm on duty in the Ops Room.'

The regretful smile suggested that she would have accepted had she been free. Mulling it over, Anderson decided that Thursday was probably out, it being Thanksgiving Day.

"How about Wednesday?"

'I'm afraid I already have a dinner date.'

It was the polite brush-off and he got the message. 'Some other time then,' he said coolly.

'We could meet for cocktails if you like.'

Her manner was hesitant and he noticed she was biting her lip, as if realizing she'd committed a social faux pas. Girls who'd been to Bryn Mawr didn't do that sort of thing, did they?

'Fine. I know quite a nice little bar on west 45th Street.'

'Good. I'll look forward to Wednesday, sir.'

'John,' he said firmly.

'John,' she repeated and smiled. 'I was beginning to think you'd never thaw.'

Slattery's Bar on York Street in Brooklyn was no distance from the subway, which was one reason why Larry Novak had arranged to meet George Eltsberg there to discuss a possible business deal. Some five years back, a bad fracture of the right fibula had left Novak with one limb shorter than the other, and the game leg gave him hell whenever he was on his feet for any length of time. Of course, there were other reasons for choosing Slattery's; the bar was off the beaten track, dimly lit and frequented by the kind of people who knew when to turn a blind eye and keep their mouths shut. The same went for the neighbourhood cops on the beat.

The place was usually three parts empty around midafternoon and today was no exception. A brassy-looking blonde was perched on a stool at the far end of the bar, her raincoat unbuttoned to reveal a tight-fitting pastel-coloured dress with a large bow on one hip. She had raised the hem high enough for anybody who was at all interested to have a good idea what was being offered, but as yet there were no takers. Although the leg show was obviously intended for the two sailors at the opposite end of the bar, their pale faces suggested they had just been discharged from the navy hospital on Flushing Avenue, and it was possible they weren't exactly keen to be readmitted with a dose of clap.

Eltsberg was waiting for Novak in a corner booth, his back toward the entrance. There were two other men with him, both of whom were strangers to Novak. One looked to be in his late thirties, had dark curly hair, broad shoulders and the misshapen nose and scar tissue above the eyes that were the trademarks of an ex-boxer. The younger man had light brown hair, a thin face and eyes that reminded Novak of a weasel. As he approached the booth, Eltsberg turned about, his moon-shaped face breaking into an eager smile.

'Hi, Larry,' he said, 'we were just talking about you.'

'Yeah?' Novak sat down beside Eltsberg and stared at the two men facing him. 'I don't think I know your friends, George.'

'This is Heine Kalmbach.' Eltsberg pointed to the broad-shouldered man. 'You may have heard of him. He went ten rounds with Braddock at the Garden a few years back.'

'When was that?'

'Before the war,' said Kalmbach. 'Before Braddock went on to become the lightheavyweight champ.'

'And this is Steve Mirnick. He's got a job as a welder in the Brooklyn Navy Yard.'

'Is that a fact?' Novak wiped a dewdrop from his nose. 'So why aren't you there now, Steve?'

'I'm sick, ain't I?' Mirnick gave a hollow cough. 'It's my chest, I always get bronchitis this time of year.'

'That's tough. What do you do when you're not working, Steve?'

'Aw, a bit of this and that – you know how it is, Larry.'

'Sure. Times are hard. It's getting so's a man can't make a fast buck anymore.' Novak twisted round and signalled the bartender to bring him a beer. 'Look at them gasoline operators the cops busted in Brooklyn, Manhattan and Queens last Wednesday. According to the Office of Price Administration, they had cornered the market in stolen and counterfeit ration coupons.'

'We read the papers too,' said Kalmbach.

'So?'

'So we didn't come here to listen to you making small talk. If you've got a proposition to put to us, let's hear it. Otherwise, don't waste our time.'

'You're free to leave anytime you want,' Novak said coldly. 'I only do business with people I know. Like George here.'

'Now don't be like that, Larry,' Eltsberg said hastily. 'These guys are friends of mine. They want in.'

'Do they now?'

Novak saw the bartender approaching their table and leaned back to give him elbowroom. While they had been talking, one of the sailors had made the acquaintance of the blond hooker at the end of the bar and was furtively stroking her knee while he held a whispered conversation with her. There was no sign of his companion, who was evidently less adventurous. Presently, the blond slipped off the high stool and, linking arms with her prospective client, led him out of the bar.

'What's the going price these days?' asked Novak.

The bartender followed his gaze. 'That one charges a sawbuck.'

Eltsberg shook his head. 'Some guys must have money to burn.'

'From what I seen of him,' said the bartender, 'that gob has more than money to burn.'

The wisecrack wasn't particularly funny, but it seemed to amuse Mirnick who threw back his head and neighed like a horse. Fishing a dollar bill out of his pocket, Novak told the barman to keep the change and buy himself a drink, which was another way of saying they wanted a bit of privacy.

'This proposition of yours,' Kalmbach said in a low voice. 'What's it going to cost us?'

47

'Two C's up front for the information and five percent of the take.'

"Two C's is kind of steep, ain't it?' Kalmbach produced a pack of Camels from his jacket and offered them around. 'I mean, what are you giving us for that?'

'A loan shark,' Novak said calmly. 'You can hit him anytime you like. There's never less than ten grand in the safe.'

'Then how come you aren't pulling the job?' Mirnick put his empty beer glass on one side and leaned forward. 'Is it because you're afraid you won't be able to run fast enough with that game leg of yours?'

'You tell him, George.' Novak struck a match and lit his cigarette.

'It's like this,' said Eltsberg. 'Larry here has two previous convictions for armed robbery.'

'You get the picture?' Novak glared at Mirnick. 'One more time and I get life. Now, do we have a deal or don't we?'

'I don't know,' said Kalmbach.

'What's the matter? Is it too big for you? Maybe you should try hijacking a truckload of turkeys. Thanksgiving is only three days off and I hear there ain't enough to go around.'

'Tell me about your gammy leg.' Kalmbach reached under the table with his left hand and dug his fingers into the tendons behind Novak's right knee, making him wince with pain. 'How did you get it, Larry?'

Novak gritted his teeth. There was a lighted cigarette in his hand and he wished he had the balls to use it on the big man, but Eltsberg had said that Kalmbach had gone ten rounds with Braddock and he didn't fancy his chances.

'It was a misunderstanding. Some of the guys on Tenth Avenue thought I was trying to muscle in on their territory, so they decided to straighten me out with a sledgehammer.'

'I heard different.'

'Then you heard wrong, I ain't no stoolie. You ask George.'

48

'Leave him alone, Heine,' Eltsberg said quietly. 'Larry's okay. If you're not interested in what he has to sell, just say the word and I'll find somebody else to go in with me.'

Kalmbach released his grip. 'Aw, shit,' he snarled, 'if that's the way you feel, give him the fucking two hundred.'

Eltsberg took an envelope from the inside pocket of his jacket and placed it on the bench seat between them. 'It's all there, Larry – fives and tens, just like you said.'

'I'll take your word for it.'

'So give,' said Mirnick. 'Tell us how we're going to get rich.'

'The loan shark is a guy called Passaretti, Vince Passaretti. He runs his business from Ziggermann's, a small outfitters on West 48th Street off Eleventh Avenue. The outfitters is a front run by an old man by the name of Jacob Levy with the help of an assistant. Levy and the assistant won't give you no trouble, but Passaretti has two strongarm men working for him and they're always around. The loan office is in back of the shop, with an exit into the alleyway behind the block.' Novak reached for his beer, gulped it down in one go and then wiped his mouth on the back of his hand. 'That's about it,' he said, 'the rest is up to you.'

'How come you know so much about Passaretti?' Kalmbach asked him softly.

'How is my business, but I got eyes and ears and I can use them.'

'And nobody seen you snooping around?'

Detective Benjamin Delgado from the 18th Precinct had, but Novak wasn't going to admit to that. It had been a chance meeting; Delgado had wandered into the lunch counter across the street from Ziggermann's and had spotted him sitting in a booth by the window. That Delgado had made a point of exchanging a few words with him was only natural. The wop had arrested him two days after he'd pulled his first armed robbery at the age of eighteen and they had known each other from way back.

'What do you take me for – a schmoe?' Novak stuffed the envelope into his pocket and stood up. 'If you screw it

49

up, don't point the finger at me. I did my job but good. Nobody seen me casing the joint.'

With a curt nod to Eltsberg, Novak left the bar and walked out into York Street. Before he reached the subway, the rain which had eased off around three o'clock started bucketing down again.

CHAPTER 5

New York

Tuesday, 21 November 1944

Kalmbach turned away from Mirnick and stared through the window at Ziggermann's outfitters across the rain-swept street. Watching Mirnick eat one hot dog after another, his mouth wide open, his uneven teeth discoloured with a mixture of ketchup and French mustard, was enough to turn anyone's stomach.

'No sign of it letting up,' he said moodily.

'What?' Eltsberg lowered his copy of the *New York Daily News* and followed Kalmbach's gaze just as a Nash Ambassador ploughed through a pool of water and raised a bow wave that swept across the sidewalk. 'Oh yeah, the rain. Could be India, the amount we're getting.'

'Why India?' Mirnick grunted with his mouth full.

'They have monsoons there.' Eltsberg rustled the newspaper. 'Didn't stop people going to the Garden last night, though, did it? Says here that twenty thousand people turned out to see and listen to the stars. "Let Yourself Go" with Ray Block's orchestra, George Burns and Gracie Allen doing something called "Doctor I.Q.," as well as Edgar Bergen and Charlie McCarthy. Raised a hundred million in war bonds, they did.'

'Aw, for Chrissakes, George,' Kalmbach muttered wearily, 'you're worse than Novak.'

'Something eating you, Heine?'

'We got better things to talk about – like you know what.'

50

'Oh, I thought we'd already been over that.' Eltsberg nudged the brown-paper parcel lying between them on the bench seat. 'Cost me twenty-five bucks to see the inside of that dump. Another ten, maybe fifteen, and I could have gotten myself a real snazzy suit from Gimbels.'

'What are you complaining about? You'll get your money back.' Kalmbach kept his voice low and spoke out of the corner of his mouth. It was a mannerism which he shared with the other two men, both of whom had also done time. 'It's only a question of seeing the manager. Tomorrow might be a good day to do that.'

'Tomorrow?' Eltsberg folded his newspaper in half and put it on one side. 'That's kind of sudden, isn't it?'

'Thursday is out. They could be closed for Thanksgiving, and we can't afford to hang around until Friday. I don't trust Novak. I mean, what's to stop that little runt peddling his information to somebody else?'

'Larry wouldn't do a thing like that.'

'Yeah?' Kalmbach lit a cigarette and drew the smoke down into his lungs. 'Well, we'd look pretty stupid if we found ourselves at the end of the line.'

'All right, have it your way — we'll go call on the man tomorrow. You realize we'll need an extra pair of hands?'

Kalmbach didn't like it but he knew Eltsberg was right. Somebody would have to mind the shop while he and Mirnick cleaned out the office. George couldn't do it because Jacob Levy and his assistant had already seen him and they'd smell a rat if he showed up again the following day. In any case, George ought to be waiting for them at the top of the alley behind the wheel of a car.

'I know somebody who might be interested.' Mirnick took a toothpick from the jar on the table and began to probe the gap between his front teeth.

'Yeah? Who? Kalmbach asked.

'Earl Shaffer.'

'Never heard of him.'

'Earl's okay. We was in Riker's together. He drew one to five for assault with a deadly weapon but he's out on parole now, working nights at some plant making ball bearings.'

'Looks the same as you, does he?'

'Naw, Earl's a regular choirboy, got a face like an angel. All the women go for him.'

'What do you think, George?'

'We need someone who'll make a good impression. That old kike who runs the shop is one suspicious bastard.' Eltsberg shrugged his shoulders. 'You could give this Shaffer the once-over.'

'Earl lives downtown,' Mirnick said helpfully. 'Has a couple of rooms on Coenties Slip.'

'Okay, we'll go see him just as soon as this rain eases up.' Kalmbach stubbed out his cigarette. 'What you got planned for this afternoon, George?'

'There's no point in me going back to Brooklyn. I figured I'd kill some time at the movies before looking out a car.'

In Eltsberg's vernacular, 'looking out' was another way of saying that he intended to steal an automobile. As soon as it was dark, he planned to take the subway on Queens and see what he could find. He had decided on Queens because there was always a risk of getting snarled up in the traffic in Manhattan, the Bronx was too far from home and Brooklyn was out because he didn't believe in fouling his own doorstep.

'We don't want anything fancy, George. In fact, I think you should go for a family sedan.'

Advice from Kalmbach was one thing Eltsberg didn't need. He already had a set of plates and the registration papers had been forged by a real artist. All he required now was the right make, year and model to go with them.

'I had a Ford in mind – a four-door sedan.'

'You picked out the colour yet?' Mirnick asked him facetiously.

'Grey,' said Eltsberg.

Grey paint was easy to come by, especially when you had a friend working in the Brooklyn Navy Yard. A quick spray job, the odd dent in the fender and body to make it look right, and even the original owner wouldn't be able to recognize his own automobile.

52

The convoy sailing conference which assembled at 17 Battery Place at eleven-thirty that morning was attended by forty-three men and one woman. If Virginia Canford found the odds daunting and felt at a disadvantage, it was not apparent to John Anderson. Observing her closely, he thought she seemed poised and confident and not in the least bit worried that, before the meeting was over, she would have to brief and take questions from thirty-five ships' masters who had been sailing back and forth across the Atlantic while she was still in her sophomore year at Bryn Mawr.

The conference was both a starting and culminating point, depending on which side of the fence you happened to be. For the merchant navy men it was the first intimation that they would be sailing in Convoy HX 320 the next day, whereas for the staff officers of Eastern Sea Frontier it marked the time when the end results of their work would be translated into action. The size of the convoy had been determined by the number of escorts available, and from this base line the Port Director had then decided on the actual composition. The letters HX denoted a fast eastbound convoy, while the figures indicated that it was the three hundred and twentieth of that particular category.

The main factor governing the Port Director's selection had been speed, and any ship waiting in New York which could not maintain an average of ten knots had automatically been relegated to SC 189. This was a slow eastbound convoy which would sail on Saturday, the twenty-fifth of November, although as yet this information had not been communicated to the various captains involved.

The planning of every convoy was a complex and complicated business because there was no overall supreme commander. A change of operational control at longitude 35 degrees west effectively divided the ocean in two. The Americans controlled the western Atlantic while the British looked after the eastern half. Although the Convoy and Routing Section of the Navy Department in Washington was responsible for the detailed planning of all eastbound traffic, the choice of route from New York to the Western Ocean Meeting Point off Newfoundland was decided by Eastern Sea Frontier. The Admiralty in London was also involved, as they selected the route from the halfway point in mid-Atlantic to the final destination. As a result of this loose arrangement, it was part of Anderson's job to ensure that the recommendations made by the Royal Navy were incorporated in the final plan.

Once underway, the sailing conference followed a long-established and well-tried format. The Port Director opened the proceedings by informing the ships' captains what position they would take in the convoy, and he was followed by the New York harbour master who covered the route down-water as far as the swept channel. The Commodore, a reserve officer selected for the voyage by the British Naval Liaison Officer, spoke next and went over the daily routine to be observed during the passage across the Atlantic. He, in turn, gave way to the Escort Commander, and then Virginia Canford took her place at the rostrum to an appreciative buzz from the audience.

'I can see the look of apprehension on your faces,' she began, 'and I'd like to put the record straight. You're not alone – I'm worried too.'

Her timing was perfect; the slight pause had the audience waiting for the punch line and there was a ripple of laughter when she delivered it.

'I don't have to tell you that the situation has changed dramatically in the last twelve months,' she continued. 'You all know that better than I do. According to the latest information we have from the submarine tracking rooms in Washington and London, there are two or possibly three U-boats operating in the area latitude 58 degrees north, longitude 20 degrees west, approximately three hundred miles due west of South Uist in the Outer Hebrides. In other words, gentlemen, there are no wolf packs waiting for you. However, please don't run away with the idea that we're complacent. Just to be on the safe side, Task Force 223 will be operating off to one flank and their presence should discourage any U-boat from getting too close to the convoy. For obvious reasons, I can't give you the composition of Task Force 223, but I can tell you that it has already sailed from Norfolk, Virginia.'

There was no need for any elaboration. The reputation of Task Force 223 had been established in June of that year and their exploits off the Ivory Coast had received a great deal of publicity on both sides of the Atlantic. A hunter-killer group made up of the aircraft carrier *Guadalcanal* and the destroyers *Pilsbury*, *Pope*, *Flaherty*, *Jenks* and *Chatelain*, the task force had surprised U 505 on the surface when she was recharging her batteries. The U-boat had immediately crash-dived, but two Avengers from the carrier had marked her position with machine-gun fire and the *Chatelain* had dropped a pattern of depth charges, damaging the boat and forcing it to surface again. Despite the fact that U 505 was out of control and making seven knots, the task force had managed to get a prize crew on board and tow the U-boat across the Atlantic to Bermuda.

Virginia came to the end of her notes and scanned the faces of her audience. 'Are there any questions you'd like to ask?' she enquired politely.

'Only one, miss.' A broad-shouldered merchant navy captain with a soft Hampshire accent stood up. 'What exactly is a Wave?'

'The initials stand for Women Appointed for Voluntary Emergency Service.'

'I see.' A faint smile appeared on the captain's face. 'Well, miss, if ever I'm faced with an emergency,' he said gravely, 'I hope you're around to volunteer your services.'

Somebody said, 'Amen to that' and there was another ripple of laughter. Still very cool and poised but with an amused smile on her lips, Virginia Canford left the rostrum and returned to her seat.

The Port Director turned to the next item on the agenda and then, having reminded everyone present to sign for their sailing orders before leaving the room, brought the meeting to a close.

Like so many others that had gone before it, the

conference had been routine. It would be succeeded by another in three days' time, when those who were sailing in the slower moving convoy, SC 189, would assemble in the same room. The only connecting link between the two would be Task Force 223 which, acting independently of the close escorts, was scheduled to cover both convoys. The relevant orders had been drafted by Tenth Fleet, but neither the staff in Washington nor anyone at Eastern Sea Frontier in New York could have foreseen that these instructions to Task Force 223 would bring the hunter-killer group into juxtaposition with U 195 six days after Hartmann sailed from Bergen.

Coenties Slip was mostly warehouses and office blocks with the odd seedy rooming house sandwiched in between. Earl Shaffer had a couple of rooms on the fourth floor of a tenement building on Water Street, which backed onto the 'S' curve of the Second Avenue elevated. At first, it looked as if he wasn't at home, but then Kalmbach gave the door another pounding and a disgruntled voice yelled, 'For Chrissakes, I'm coming as fast as I can, dammit.' Presently the door opened a fraction and half a face appeared in the gap.

'Hi,' said Mirnick. 'It's me – Steve. Mind if we come in for a minute?'

'Who's we?' Shaffer grunted.

'This here is Heine.' Mirnick jerked a thumb at Kalmbach. 'We've got a proposition that might interest you.'

'Like what?'

'Like one that's big enough to take you out of this dump,' said Kalmbach.

The chain came off the latch and Shaffer stepped back, clutching a blanket around his middle.

'I see you been catching up on your sleep, Earl,' Mirnick said, grinning.

'I work nights. You know that.'

Kalmbach followed both men into the living room and

56

glanced about him, his nose wrinkling in disgust at what he saw. A threadbare carpet covered part of the floor, both armchairs looked as if they had been rescued from a rubbish heap and grimy net curtains hung in a window that hadn't been washed in months. There was a stack of dishes in the sink, the gas stove in the corner was covered in black grease and there were stale bread crumbs on the table. Shaffer might have the face of a choirboy, but it seemed he was more at home in a pigsty.

'Nice place you got here,' said Kalmbach in a voice loaded with sarcasm.

'What's it to you how I live?' Shaffer pushed a hand through his tousled blond hair. 'I thought you guys wanted to talk business?'

'That we do,' said Mirnick.

'So make your pitch; I'm listening.'

'You want to get dressed first?' Kalmbach suggested.

'What for? I'm not cold. As soon as you leave, I'm going back to bed.'

'Somebody keeping it warm for you?'

'What do you think?'

'I think I'd better take a look.' Kalmbach crossed the room and opened the door to the bedroom. 'You don't mind, do you?'

'Be my guest,' said Shaffer.

The room was shadowy, the thin curtains drawn to shut out the elevated railroad that was on a level with the window. However, it was light enough for Kalmbach to see the dress and raincoat draped over the back of a chair and the black underwear on the seat. The dark-haired girl who stared back at him from the bed wasn't bad looking from what he could see of her, but he thought she could have done with a layer or two less makeup on her face.

'You want something?' she asked in a cold voice.

'Not a damn thing.' Kalmbach backed out of the room and closed the door behind him. 'Who's the hooker?' he asked Shaffer.

'Louise Dudzinski. She hangs out on Tenth and 44th, but

she ain't no hooker.'

'Go tell that to the Marines.'

'Okay, have it your way.' Shaffer grinned at him from the armchair. 'Can I help it if she can't resist me?'

'Just tell her to get her ass out of here before it starts raining again.'

The smile vanished, the blue eyes narrowed and the round face became less angelic. 'Go fuck yourself,' said Shaffer.

'Two, maybe three grand hangs on it,' Kalmbach said calmly.

'That's different.'

In a much more reasonable frame of mind, Shaffer got up out of the chair and walked into the bedroom.

Paul Webber parked outside the apartment house on East 93rd Street and switched everything off, the car radio, the headlights and the ignition. Grabbing his overnight bag, he got out of the Studebaker and locked the door. It had been a lousy two days. The bad weather on Monday had delayed their flight departure time from La Guardia and magneto trouble had subsequently held them up in Chicago, so that it was past six-thirty when they finally touched down in New York again. The drive home from the airport hadn't exactly filled him with joy either; a mile from the Queensborough Bridge he'd had to pull over and change a flat.

All Webber wanted now was a good stiff drink and a long hot bath. Letting himself into the house, he crept up the stairs, determined that this was one time Mrs. Langdon wouldn't intercept him. But both the bath and the drink would have to wait. As he unlocked the door to his apartment, the telephone began to ring, and leaving his trench coat and the overnight bag in the hall, he hurried into the living room to answer it.

A familiar voice said, 'Is that you, Paul?'

'Christel?' Webber took a deep breath and steeled himself to remain calm. 'This is a pleasant surprise. How have you been?'

58

'I'm fine. And you, Paul?'

'I've had a lousy two days, but you've made it better.'

'That's nice. When am I going to see you again?'

'I wish I knew.' Webber clenched his left hand, digging the nails into the palm. Christel was out of line. Theirs was strictly a one-way channel and she had better have a good reason for breaking the rules to call him. 'National Eastern have been switching me around lately and I'm not sure when I'll be in Washington again.'

'Never mind. Perhaps we can get together when I'm in New York on Thursday?'

'Thursday?' Webber repeated blankly.

'Yes. The Embassy has given me the day off and the Butchers have invited me to spend Thanksgiving with them. You remember Amy Butcher, don't you, Paul?'

Webber remembered Amy Butcher all right. Amy Butcher was the key phrase that spelled out an emergency. 'Sure I do,' he said slowly. 'Unfortunately, Thursday is a bad day for me. I'll be in Chicago again. I could sound out the other guys to see if any of them will agree to switch schedules with me, but I don't hold out much hope of that. How about tomorrow night? Can you catch at train after work?'

'Well, I suppose I could ask the Butchers to put me up for the night.'

Webber had to admire her. Christel had struck exactly the right note to give the impression that while she would like to see him again, there were certain practical difficulties. It was a well-acted charade, but a necessary precaution in case the long distance operator was listening in to their conversation.

'I'm sure they'd be only too delighted,' he said. 'But if you don't feel like imposing on them, I can always book you into a hotel.'

'Could you?'

'Certainly. It'll be a pleasure. Listen, I'll meet you at Penn Station around seven and then we'll have dinner together. Okay?'

'I'll look forward to that, Paul.'

'So will I, honey,' he said with false enthusiasm. 'Till tomorrow then.'

Webber put the phone down and decided he needed that drink more than ever now. For ten years he had been living a double life, both as the upright, patriotic American citizen and as the Abwehr intelligence agent. It had all started back in 1934 when he was still living in San Francisco and after Hitler had repudiated the Versailles Treaty. That announcement had rekindled the old love of Fatherland that his father had instilled in him as a child, and had made him see where his duty lay. He had gone to the German Consulate and offered his services, because it was obvious to him that the Luftwaffe would need all the trained pilots they could get.

The consular official had listened to him courteously and then sent him on his way, saying that he would get in touch with him in due course, after he had heard from Berlin. Two months later, Webber received a telephone call from another man suggesting they meet for dinner at a restaurant on Fisherman's Wharf. In agreeing to meet the stranger, Webber made a decision that was to change his whole way of life.

It transpired that there was no shortage of pilots for the Luftwaffe, but the Third Reich was anxious to create an intelligence network in the United States and he had all the necessary attributes for the making of a good agent. Webber was led to understand that he was not to be a spy in the conventional sense; on the contrary, Berlin was far more concerned to know what the American people thought of the Third Reich. In short, he was to look upon himself as a sort of opinion pollster, a man who didn't ask questions but who kept his eyes and ears open.

Webber had known it wouldn't stop there, but it was something he wanted to do and the risks involved had been an added stimulus. Not that he'd run into any danger before the war. Despite his newfound political convictions, he'd avoided having anything to do with the German American Bund and he'd never committed anything to paper. The information had always been passed by word of mouth at a time and place of his choosing and never to anybody remoted connected with the German Consulate. Then, shortly after the Wehrmacht had marched into the Rhineland, it had been suggested to him that it would be a good idea if he moved to New York and lay low for a while.

In 1940 he had been reactivated and put in touch with Christel Zolf, a secretary in the Swiss Embassy. His briefing officer had said that the same ground rules would apply, but there had been one proviso. Christel had to have a number where she would reach him in a dire emergency. What had seemed an unlikely contingency at the time, had now become a reality and Webber felt distinctly uneasy.

He thought it unlikely that Christel Zolf shared his misgivings. In the four years he'd known her, Webber could not recall a single occasion when she hadn't been cool and emotionally detached, but of course he didn't know her that well. Christel was a very secretive person and it was difficult to get anything out of her. What little he had managed to discover about her background could be summarized in a few sentences.

The only child of a prominent physician and a wealthy socialite, Christel had been born in Zurich on the twenty-eighth of October, 1912. Educated at a private school until the age of eighteen, she had then progressed to Geidelberg where for the next three years she'd read modern languages. During that time it seemed that two entirely unconnected events had shaped the rest of her life. Shortly before graduating, Christel had been very shocked to learn that her parents intended to separate, and then, a few weeks later, she had attended the Nuremberg Rally of 1933 together with a crowd of her student friends. If you could believe Christel, listening to the Führer's speech had given her a sense of purpose, and from that moment on she'd been an ardent National Socialist, although, of necessity, she'd had to conceal her political beliefs.

Just when she had offered her services to the Third Reich was anybody's guess, but Webber fancied it must have been long before she joined the Swiss Diplomatic Corps in the autumn of 1936. That was the sum total of his knowledge and it didn't add up to much. Christel was a very attractive woman but she kept to herself, and, looking at it dispassionately, Webber supposed that was one of the reasons why the Abwehr had chosen her to run the intelligence network on the eastern seaboard.

Still feeling in need of a drink, Webber fixed himself a large scotch on the rocks and downed it in one go.

CHAPTER 6

New York

Wednesday, 22 November 1944. Morning.

Shaffer got off the bus at the stop before West 48th Street and started walking north on Tenth Avenue. Steve and Heine had said they would be waiting near the intersection, and as he turned the corner and headed toward Ziggermann's, he spotted Mirnick gazing into the window of a druggist's across the street from him. Thirty yards farther on, he strolled past Heine who was examining a collection of pot-bellied stoves on the sidewalk outside a hardware store.

Kalmbach thought everything was looking good. The 'choirboy' had showed up on time in a presentable suit and a dark grey overcoat that was only a fraction too long for him. There were no squad cars in the vicinity and the only patrolman he'd seen that morning had been walking east toward Ninth Avenue. Unless he'd gotten himself snarled up in the traffic somewhere along the way, Eltsberg should now be approaching the intersection at Eleventh Avenue and 42nd Street. Waiting until Mirnick was almost abreast of him on the other side of the street, he started after Shaffer.

Mirnick quickened his stride, overtook Kalmbach and steadily closed the gap between himself and Shaffer. The zipper bag he carried in his left hand was filled out with old newspapers packed around a Smith and Wesson .38 calibre revolver. The thought that in a few minutes the old newsprint would be exchanged for a different and more negotiable kind of paper was enough to set his pulse racing. Drawing ahead of Shaffer, he went on past the lunch counter to the traffic lights at the intersection, where he stopped and glanced to his left.

A slow smile spread across his face when Mirnick saw that Eltsberg was already in position and waiting for them in a grey four-door sedan. The car was parked by the curb just short of the alley behind Ziggermann's and facing up Eleventh Avenue exactly as they had planned. As soon as the lights changed, Mirnick crossed the street and paused by the delicatessen on the corner.

Shaffer waited for Mirnick to give him the okay and then walked into the outfitters. From the description he'd been given he immediately recognized the layout. Jacob Levy and the assistant were standing behind a counter that took up the length of one wall and was at right angles to the entrance. Directly opposite the counter on the other side of the room were two small cubicles. The rest of the available space was taken up by several hanging racks, two of which had been wheeled into a position where they partly screened the door at the back of the shop.

'Can I help you, sir?'

Shaffer turned to face the assistant and smiled. 'I was thinking of buying a suit,' he said. 'Nothing too fancy. Something in dark blue or maybe charcoal, but without a pinstripe.'

'I'm sure we have what you're looking for.' The assistant, a thin, weedy man whose thick glasses made his eyes seem enormous, moved round the counter and came toward him, a tape measure draped over both shoulders like a vestment. 'If I could just take your measurements, sir?'

Shaffer removed his overcoat and hung it over a rack. Levy remained where he was, seemingly disinterested, his heavy eyelids drooping as if he was about to fall asleep on his feet. It was a deceptive post. One false move on his part and Shaffer knew the old man would press the alarm button under the counter.

The assistant took his chest and waist measurements, wrote them down on a piece of paper and then proceeded with midshoulder to elbow and crooked elbow to wrist. That done, he knelt down on one knee and was about to take the outside leg when Mirnick entered the shop, walked up to the counter and placed his zipper bag on the glass top.

'I'd like one of them striped shirts you got in the window,' said Mirnick. 'I fancy green and white. Do you have one in my size?'

Levy looked him up and down. 'What size is that?' he asked.

'Fifteen. I'm kind of scraggy round the neck.'

Levy nodded and stooped below the counter. As he did so, Mirnick unzipped the bag and curled his fingers around the butt of the Smith and Wesson. Using the revolver like a hammer, he leaned over the counter and smashed the barrel into Levy's skull. Taking his cue from Mirnick, Shaffer stepped back one pace and kicked the assistant in the face and stomach. Seconds later, Kalmbach entered the outfitters and, closing the street door behind him, sped through the shop, a .45 Remington automatic in his right hand. Like two line-backers running interception for him, Mirnick and Shaffer wheeled the clothes racks out of his way so that he could hit the far door with his shoulder and burst into the office.

Kalmbach had the advantage of speed and surprise. Passaretti had waxed fat and prosperous on loan sharking and as a result had become a shade too overconfident. The Police Department never bothered him because the neighbourhood patrolmen were on his payroll. The people who borrowed money from him at exorbitant rates of interest never complained or tried to renege on a debt, because they knew what would happen to them if they did. There were never less than two enforcers on the premises, and while the alarm system had never been put to the test, Passaretti had no reason to suppose it wasn't foolproof. After four trouble-free years, the idea that anybody would have the audacity to rob him in broad daylight in his own office had become such a remote possibility as to be

64

laughable. His complacency had obviously rubbed off on his associates, and in the circumstances it was hardly surprising that all three men were caught off guard.

Kalmbach looked at their startled faces and grinned. Passaretti, fat, dark-complexioned and with a Clark Gable moustache on his upper lip, gaped at him openmouthed from behind the desk, his eyes almost popping out of their sockets. The two henchmen, one seated by the exit into the alley, the other in the near corner on Passaretti's left, were still clutching the comic pages they had been reading when he'd burst into the office.

'Surprise, surprise.' Kalmbach waved the Remington at the two enforcers. 'Now get up on your feet and face the wall — over here near the desk where I can keep an eye on you.'

'You men have got to be crazy,' Passaretti said in a hoarse whisper. 'Don't you know who I am?'

'Sure we do, that's why we looked you up.' Mirnick closed the office door and then tossed the zipper bag at Passaretti. 'We're after a loan.'

'A loan?'

'That's right. All you've got to do is tip the newspapers into the wastebasket and then fill the bag with greenbacks.'

Passaretti hesitated fractionally, apparently of two minds, but then, with a slight shrug of his shoulders, he emptied the bag and took it over to the safe. Pulling a bunch of keys from his pocket, he unlocked the door and swung it open.

'How do you want it?' he asked casually. 'In fives, tens, twenties or what?'

'We're not particular, Vince,' said Mirnick. 'We'll take anything and everything you've got.'

'That figures.' Holding the bag in one hand in such a way that neither man could see what he was doing, Passaretti reached inside the safe and grabbed the .32 lying on the middle shelf. 'I guess this just isn't my lucky day, is it?' He half turned toward them, his face assuming a rueful expression that was still there when he squeezed the trigger.

The bullet hit Mirnick between the eyes and went straight through his skull, removing several fragments of bone and splattering the wall behind with brain tissue.

That Passaretti should choose to shoot it out rather than hand over the money was the last thing Kalmbach had expected. Although taken by surprise, an animal-like instinct for self-preservation asserted itself, and whirling round, he shot the loan shark in the chest. In that same instant, a sudden movement caught his eye and swinging back in the reverse direction, he emptied the rest of the magazine into the two enforcers, killing one outright and fatally wounding the other.

Kalmbach looked around the office, his mind numb and uncomprehending. The money in the safe was still there for the taking, but suddenly it didn't seem to matter anymore, and giving way to panic, he unlocked the back door and ran out into the alley.

The gunfire in the office had sounded like an artillery barrage and Shaffer reckoned just about everyone in the entire neighbourhood must have heard it. Until a few moments ago, everything had been going beautifully, but now it was a different story and his first thought was to get the hell out of there before some passer-by raised the alarm. Snatching his overcoat from the rack, he slipped it on and hastily fastened the buttons. The street was only a few strides away, but Shaffer reasoned that if he was right about the noise being heard, he could find himself in all kinds of trouble. Mirnick had often remarked that life had dealt him one lousy break after another, and it would be just his luck to bump into some guy who was aching to be a hero.

The alley then? If he could make it to the car he would be all right, but that meant going through the office. Shaffer stared at the door, his mouth suddenly dry, his palms oozing sweat. Surely if Passaretti were still alive, he'd have sent one of his associated to check out the shop by now? Knowing the mustn't hesitate any longer, he took a deep breath and pushed open the door.

Mirnick was lying flat on his back just inside the entrance and there were three other bodies sprawled in ungainly attitudes by the wall. The safe was ajar and he saw that the money inside had been left untouched. He also noticed that the rear exit was wide open, but several seconds elapsed before it dawned on Shaffer that Heine had run out on him. When the penny did finally drop, he ran towards the door, mouthing a string of obscenities.

Throughout a lifetime of lousy breaks, Shaffer now collected one more to prove the worst of all. As he jumped out into the alley, one of the men whom Kalmbach had left for dead found the strength to shoot him in the back with a .32 calibre automatic. The low velocity bullet went in just below the left shoulder blade and failed to exit. Although its impact was not unlike a hard punch, his body immediately felt numb from the waist up. But, somehow or other, despite the pain and the shock, he managed to keep going, telling himself that everything would be all right if only the others were prepared to wait for him.

But that was something Eltsberg and Kalmbach were not inclined to do, and he still had some distance to go when the grey four-door sedan pulled out from the curb and headed uptown. By the time Shaffer reached Eleventh Avenue, there was no sign of the car, and a blind, helpless rage boiled up inside him to spill over in a repetitive outburst of four-letter words. The stream of invective didn't make him feel any better and within a matter of seconds his anger evaporated and was replaced by despair.

The tenement building in Water Street seemed to be a million light years away, and in his present condition he would pass out long before he reached Coenties Slip. The shirt on his back must already be soaked with blood and it was only a question of time before it seeped through his overcoat. His legs felt as if they no longer belonged to him and there was a fuzzy haze in front of his eyes. Louise Dudzinski? Shaffer pinched his eyes in a desperate attempt to clear his vision. Her place wasn't too far away and there was just a chance she might be prepared to help him. If nothing else, the Polish hooker would know a quack who could dress his wound.

Gritting his teeth and making a determined effort to ignore the pain, Shaffer set off to walk four blocks south to West 44th Street. An interminable half hour later, he staggered into the brownstone house on Tenth Avenue where Louise Dudzinski was living and banged on the door of her apartment.

Benjamin Delgado considered himself a very fortunate man. He was married to a lovely Italian girl called Gina and he had two very bright and loving children, a son of eight and a teenage daughter, both of whom had inherited their mother's good looks. He lived in a nice apartment on East 92nd, which was a far cry from Mulberry Street in Little Italy where he'd spent the first twenty years of his life. By way of an added bonus, he also happened to like his job. In fact, he could only recall one occasion when he'd been disenchanted with it, and that had been shortly after Pearl Harbour when he'd tried to enlist in the Army Air Corps. Just about everybody had put a stop to that, from the Police Commissioner right on down to Captain Burns of the 18th Precinct and Lieutenant Caskey who commanded the squad. In their collective view, the criminal fraternity would still be in business, war or no war, and good detectives were hard to come by. It was an argument that had carried a lot of weight with the local draft board, and although at first their decision to place him in a reserved category had rankled, Delgado had eventually come to accept it.

In a sense, he too was fighting a war, but sometimes the people who were supposed to be on his side were not exactly the most helpful of allies. The bank clerk whose wallet had been stolen was a case in point. Just why Mr. Ambrose had waited twenty-four hours to report the theft was something to do with the contents of his wallet. The billfold had contained twenty-five dollars, his social security card and some 'A' and 'B' type gasoline coupons which, contrary to regulations, Mr. Ambrose had forgotten to endorse with the license number of his car. He couldn't remember exactly when the theft had occurred, but he was pretty sure the wallet had been on his person when he left the bank and it most certainly hadn't been there when he came to pay the bill for lunch. He recalled that while crossing Broadway a

68

man had apologized for accidentally bumping into him, but of course he hadn't paid much attention to his face.

In Delgado's experience, pickpockets usually worked in pairs, but he hadn't bothered to mention that. If the victim couldn't describe the man who'd given him the heave with any accuracy, it was extremely unlikely that Mr. Ambrose would have noticed the accomplice to whom the poke had been passed. Instead, Delgado merely took down his complaint and then asked him to look through what mug shots they had of convicted pickpockets. A faint hope that he might recognize a face, however, was doomed to disappointment.

'No luck then?' Delgado retrieved the book of mug shots with a sympathetic smile. 'Well, don't worry about it, Mr. Ambrose, we'll get him sooner or later.'

'I wish I could believe that.'

'You can take a rain check on it,' Delgado said firmly. 'Tomorrow is Thanksgiving Day and every pickpocket in town is going to be out on the street. We know that, and we'll be looking for them. By this time Friday, we should have quite a lineup.'

'And you think there's a chance I might get my wallet back?'

'Well, to be absolutely honest, I very much doubt if you will.'

Mr. Ambrose buttoned up his overcoat and moved toward the corridor. 'I was afraid of that,' he said morosely. 'What do you advise I do about the gas coupons?'

Delgado thought it obvious that he would have to get by without them, but that was hardly the kind of advice Mr. Ambrose was looking for. It would also be bad for public relations and scarcely in keeping with the favourable image of the precinct which Captain Burns wished to project. So, although Mr. Ambrose was unlikely to get any change out of the officials concerned, Delgado advised him to see his local Office of Price Administration and then sent him on his way with a friendly smile.

Returning to the squadroom, he found Lieutenant Caskey waiting for him, and within the space of a minute flat, learned that he had another case on his hands and a new partner to go with it. The new partner was Detective Jack Ganley, who just happened to be the only other available officer, and the case was a multiple homicide on West 48th Street. Caskey's instructions were short and simple: They were to hold the fort until he arrived with reinforcements. He made it sound like Custer's last stand at Little Big Horn.

Ziggermann's outfitters had rapidly become the focal point of interest for the immediate neighbourhood. By the time Delgado and Ganley arrived on the scene, the press were already there in force and a sizeable crowd had gathered outside the lunch counter across the street. Apart from a couple of ambulances and several squad cars, there was really nothing for them to see. Yet, in spite of this, nobody seemed willing to move on, and the officers who were trying to steer people away from the area were becoming increasingly harassed and bad-tempered.

The outfitters was chaotic and offended Delgado's sense of order. The place was crowded with too many people trying to do too many things at once, with the result that they kept getting in each other's way. The medical examiner, a photographer and three officers from the police laboratory were jammed into the office, and the shop reminded him of the out-patients' department of Roosevelt Hospital. The only familiar face, apart from Jacob Levy, was a young patrolman from the 18th Precinct on West 54th Street whom Delgado immediately buttonholed.

'Well, Joe,' he said cheerfully, 'how are things shaping up?'

'They aren't, Ben.' The patrolman jerked a thumb at the ambulance men who were clustered round Levy. 'Nobody's paying any attention to me, they're all too busy doing what they're doing. I tell you, nothing I learned at the Police Academy prepared me for this clambake.'

'Okay, let's take it from the beginning, Joe. Who raised the alarm?'

'I did. I happened to be passing when the old man over

70

there staggered out into the street with blood all over his face. I helped him back inside and that's when I saw the assistant lying inside one of the changing rooms. As a matter of fact, Ben, he was in such a bad way the medics insisted on rushing him to the hospital before you arrived. They want to have Levy X-rayed as soon as possible too.'

'Have you got any kind of statement from him?'

'For what it's worth.' The patrolman opened his notebook and leafed through several pages. 'Levy is still pretty concussed but it seems at least two men were involved. One was medium height, medium build and very young looking. Levy says he had a real innocent kind of face – like a choirboy. The other man was thin, had light brown hair and was not very prepossessing. He's the one who's lying flat on his back in the office with a bullet between the eyes.'

'Are there any other witnesses?'

'None that I could find, Ben.'

Delgado nodded. Nothing was ever easy. At least two men had entered the shop and somebody somewhere must have seen them. Finding that somebody could take days, maybe even weeks.

'The lieutenant will be here any minute,' Ganley said quietly.

In his tactful way, Ganley was suggesting they establish some kind of order before Caskey arrived. The chances were that Caskey wouldn't be the only man they had to contend with either. Passaretti's death was bound to attract the Chief of Detectives and the Chief of the Organized Crime bureau.

You've got a point, Jack.' Delgado scratched his chin. 'This place is kind of crowded. What if we let them take Levy off to the hospital?'

'I don't see why not,' said Ganley. 'We can always question him later.'

'That's what I figured. There's not much we can do about those reporters outside. They won't move on until they've seen the lieutenant.'

'I could compare notes with Joe here and rough out a

71

statement if you like, Ben.'

'Right,' said Delgado. 'You do that while I see how the guys in the office are making out.'

The office was a slaughterhouse, the walls splattered with blood and skin tissue. Passaretti was no stranger to Delgado. Some five years back, before Caskey was in charge of the squad, he had tried to build a case against the loan shark but the Assistant District Attorney had decided the evidence wouldn't stand up in court. Seeing him now, curled up in a fetus position by the open safe in the corner, Delgado couldn't help wondering if Passaretti wouldn't have been better off if he hadn't intimidated the witness who at one time had been prepared to testify against him.

It wasn't difficult to piece together what had happened. At some stage in the proceedings, Passaretti had decided to be brave, and, as a result, he and three other men had died. Judging by the size of the bullet holes in the wall, the guy who had done most of the shooting must have been using a cannon. At a guess, Delgado thought he was probably armed with a .45 automatic, but ballistics would be able to confirm that in due course, just as Organized Crime would be able to identify the dead man inside the entrance from his fingerprints. It didn't look as if anything had been taken from the safe, which suggested the robbers had panicked and run out into the alley. Knowing the geography of the place, he also figured that a getaway car had been waiting for them on Eleventh Avenue.

'What do you reckon, Ben?'

Delgado jumped at the sound of the voice behind him and swung round. For a big man, Caskey was suprisingly light on his feet and this wasn't the first time the lieutenant had caught him unawares.

'I think four men were involved, Lieutenant.'

'Four?' Caskey frowned. 'Ganley tells me only two men entered the shop.'

'Well, that's according to Levy. As I see it, the robbers would have left one man to watch the street in case somebody else happened to drop by. The fourth would have been waiting in the getaway car on Eleventh Avenue.'

72

'You'd better start knocking on a few doors then. You might run down a witness who saw the car.'

'There's also another lead which might be worth following.' Delgado produced a packet of cigarettes and offered one to Caskey. 'It's a bit of a long shot, but I'd like to have a talk with Larry Novak.'

'Novak?' Caskey lit his cigarette and inhaled. 'I don't think I know him.'

'Novak has two convictions for armed robbery. I met him a couple days ago in the lunch counter across the street. I'm not saying he took part in the robbery, but he could have helped to set it up. That's more his style these days.'

'Do you have an address?'

'We've known each other a long time, Lieutenant. I know where to find him.'

'All right,' said Caskey, 'you and Ganley had better get on it. I'll have somebody else question the people on Eleventh Avenue.'

Larry Novak lived on the lower east side, in what passed for an apartment house on Madison Street. It took Delgado and Ganley just five minutes to establish that he wasn't at home, and twice that long to rouse the janitor, who was more than a little drunk. When finally the did gain admittance, it was clear from the state of his room that either Novak had left town in a hurry or else he was lying very low someplace else in the city. The fact that he had disappeared was enough to convince Delgado that they should put out an APB for him.

CHAPTER 7

New York

Wednesday, 22 November 1944. Early Evening.

The Theatre Bar and Restaurant at 273 West 45th Street was a popular haunt with the acting fraternity. It was also one of the few night spots in New York where Anderson could afford to take Virginia Canford. In this instance, take was not strictly correct because they had arrived separately, albeit within a few minutes of one another. It wasn't Anderson's style, but Virginia had insisted that it would be ridiculous for him to go miles out of his way merely to pick her up. Anderson was quartered with the joint British-Canadian Escort Group on Staten Island, while Virginia, as one of the few Waves attached to Eastern Sea Frontier, was allowed to live out. She shared an apartment with three other girls somewhere in Greenwich Village, the precise location of which appeared to be a closely guarded naval secret.

Right from the moment he'd first seen her, Anderson had thought Virginia was one of the few women who could put on a uniform and still look feminine. Yet, attractive as she was in naval rig, she looked even better out of it. Even though the three-quarter-length Bergdorf Goodman sable and the simple black dress she wore under it weren't entirely for his benefit, and they were just going to have a drink together before she went on elsewhere, Anderson had felt a proprietary glow as Virginia came toward him.

He had looked on their date as a means of getting to know her better, but like so many of the best-laid plans, it didn't work out quite the way he'd intended. Virginia posed all the questions, leaving him to provide the answers, much as if they were in a courtroom and he on the witness stand. She had started by asking where his parents lived, and within a very short time he'd told her just about everything there was to know about his family.

Home for Anderson was a farmhouse on the outskirts of Hook, a small village near Goole in the East Riding of Yorkshire. His people farmed two hundred acres which his father had inherited from his father, and which in time would almost certainly be handed on to his younger brother, David. At least, Anderson presumed it would, because he'd decided long ago that he wasn't cut out to be a farmer. David was different; he had a feeling for the land and farming was in his blood. Anderson didn't know how his sister, Judith, really felt about that. He supposed that having been brought up on a farm, she was capable of running the place as well as any man, but somehow he couldn't see Judith taking it on should anything happen to David. Judith was married to a bomber pilot in the RAF who had ambitions of becoming a barrister when he returned to civilian life.

'Two hundred acres may not sound a lot to you,' said Anderson, 'but I sometimes wonder how the old man manages it with David away.'

'You didn't tell me that David had left home,' said Virginia.

'Oh, didn't I? Well, he joined the RAF four months ago.'

Anderson reckoned his brother-in-law had had a lot to do with that. He was stationed at Great Driffield, only fifteen miles from Hook, which meant that Judith could live at home and he was able to see her whenever he wasn't flying. With his Distinguished Flying Cross and bar, he had undoubtedly made a profound impression on David, who was only just eighteen.

'Isn't farming a reserved occupation in England?'

'It is, but apparently David wanted to leave school and join up and I suppose my father felt he could hardly stop him. After all, he had done the very same thing in the First World War.'

'Is he going to be a pilot too?'

'Air gunner,' said Anderson.

Air gunner was not what he would have wished for his

brother, but David had failed the PNB selection board. It took a year to train a pilot and only slightly less time to turn out a navigator or a bombardier. On the other hand, if the RAF took you on as an air gunner, you could find yourself on operations within four months of putting on a uniform. Six weeks basic training followed by a six-week gunnery course with a sergeant's stripes at the end of it. It was the quickest way to get into the war and the quickest way of getting yourself killed.

'What made you want to join the navy?' Virginia toyed with the dry martini, circling the rim of her glass with a moist finger. 'I mean, it isn't as if you lived by the sea or there was a strong tradition in the family, is it?'

'Well, Goole happens to be a small port on the Humber and my father was keen on sailing. We used to spend a week on the Norfolk Broads every year.' Anderson smiled. 'That mightn't sound a very convincing reason to you but it's the only one I can think of. Anyway, I was sufficiently motivated at thirteen to sit the entrance examination for Dartmouth Naval College.'

'I'd say that was kind of young to take such a momentous decision.'

'My mother thought it was, but on the whole, I can't say I've ever regretted it.'

'Are you telling me that there hasn't been one single occasion during the last fifteen years when you haven't had second thoughts about it?'

'I can see you've been doing your homework,' Anderson said drily.

'What do you mean?'

'How did you know I've been in the navy that long?'

'Somebody must have told me.'

'I wonder who that could have been?'

'I think it was Tom Sullivan, my predecessor.' Virginia opened her handbag and began searching through the contents, which he suspected was simply a ploy to hide her obvious embarrassment. 'Anyway, you haven't answered my question.'

'Every job has its lousy moments.' Anderson swallowed

the rest of his scotch on the rocks. 'I lost some very good friends on the *Valhalla*.'

'If I remember my Norse mythology, isn't that the great hall where Odin feasts the souls of heroes slain in battle?' Virginia pursed her lips and looked thoughtful, 'I think I'd be rather superstitious about sailing in a ship with that name.'

'Perhaps you're right, though *Valhalla* was an Admiralty "V" Class destroyer launched in 1917. It was twenty-two years later, and one month after the outbreak of war, that she hit a magnetic mine in the Thames Estuary and broke in two.'

'Were you serving on her at the time?'

'What a lot of questions,' said Anderson. 'I think it's time we had another drink and talked about you for a change.'

'Oh, my life hasn't been nearly as interesting as yours. Besides, I really ought to be leaving.'

'Have one for the road then.'

Virginia hesitated, glanced at her wristwatch and then smiled. 'I shouldn't, but you've talked me into it."

Paul Webber glanced up at the clock inside the entrance to Pennsylvania Station and hurried down the steps into the main concourse. The train from Washington had arrived some ten minutes ago and he thought it unlikely that Christel Zolf would still be waiting for him at Gate 14. Half the population of New York plus a sizeable proportion of the armed forces seemed to be milling around in the concourse, so that getting from one end to the other was like weaving in and out of a maze.

The main waiting room was equally crowded. Gazing around this triumphant piece of pseudo-Roman architecture whose marble columns soared up to a fifteen-storey-high roof, Webber eventually spotted Christel near the information booth. She was wearing a navy blue coat cut on military lines, with square shoulders and a narrow waist. Her light brown hair had been combed back and was for the most part hidden by a navy-coloured peaked cap similar in style and shape to a Wac's, except that it was worn at a more rakish angle. There was, however, nothing martial about the high-heeled shoes which emphasized her shapely legs.

'Christel.' Webber touched her lightly on the elbow. 'I'm sorry I'm late. Have you been waiting very long?'

'About ten minutes.' Christel turned to face him, her eyes narrowing, a sign that she was annoyed with him. 'What kept you, Paul?'

'The damn car broke down on me on the way back from the airport.' Webber leaned closer, pecked Christel on the cheek and then picked up her suitcase. 'I had to leave it in a garage.'

'Poor old you.' Christel fell in step beside him as they moved toward the exit. 'How will you get to La Guardia tomorrow?'

'My copilot's offered me a lift. I'm to meet him on Fifth and Central Park South at nine-fifteen. That should give me enough time to go back and change.'

'Go back where?' she asked with a puzzled frown.

'To my apartment,' said Webber. 'I thought it would be best if we both stayed at the Paramount.'

'In separate rooms, Paul?'

'Adjoining.' Webber smiled fleetingly. 'After all, we don't want to draw attention to ourselves, do we?'

Although Webber had no way of knowing it, they were about to do just that. A ten-minute wait for a cab combined with a heavy build-up of traffic on Eighth Avenue were destined to put them in the wrong place at the wrong time. The hazards of a partial dim-out and a bad decision taken in the heat of the moment would do the rest.

Shaffer thought he could hear someone calling his name, but the voice was a long way off and distorted by a curious noise that sounded like running water. After a while, the voice became sharper and more insistent and then a hand shook him none too gently and he opened his eyes. The blurred face peering down from above gradually swam into focus and he saw that it was Louise Dudzinski.

'Can you hear me, Earl?'

'Sure I can,' he groaned.

'How are you feeling?'

'Rough.' He licked his lips. Rough was an understatement; there was an excruciating pain in his back and his whole body seemed to be on fire.

'It's time we were leaving.'

Leaving? Shaffer wondered what the hell Louise was talking about. He wasn't in a state to go anywhere.

'You have to get dressed now.' She snapped her fingers in his face, urging him to get off the bed. 'The doctor wants to operate on your shoulder and we can't keep him waiting.'

Shaffer threw the blankets aside, turned over onto his right hip and gingerly placed both feet on the floor. The rest wasn't so easy, but somehow he managed to push himself up into a sitting position. From the waist up, his body felt constricted, as if encased in a suit of armour. Looking down, he saw there was a wide adhesive bandage across his chest.

It didn't make sense. Why would Louise say that the doctor was waiting for him when the wound had already been dressed? Thinking about it, he was almost sure he remembered a little man with birdlike eyes who'd taken his pulse with a stethoscope. The details were hazy, but he recalled a black bag and a long, thin scalpel that had given him a lot of pain before he passed out.

Shaffer raised his head and stared at Louise. Her face was heavily made up, the eyebrows pencilled in black, the lashes spiky with mascara. Bright red lipstick had transformed the shape of her mouth into a cupid's bow and the musky perfume she used was overpowering. She was wearing a tight-fitting sweater and a skirt that outlined the rounded contours of her thighs.

'You're trying to get rid of me,' he mumbled.

'How's that?'

'A John's coming to see you. That's why you want me out of here.'

'You've got it all wrong, Earl.' She tossed her head angrily. 'If you had heard me talking on the phone a few minutes ago, you'd know it was the Doc ringing to say

79

everything is ready.'

'He did, huh?' Shaffer pointed to his chest. 'Then how come I'm all bandaged up? Don't tell me you did that.'

'Of course I didn't. You know I can't stand the sight of blood.' Louise turned away from him and picked up a brand new shirt lying on top of the bureau. Using both hands, she ripped off the cellophane wrapper and then unpinned the shirt from the carboard backing. 'The doctor was here earlier. He stopped the bleeding and patched you up as best he could, but the bullet is still in there and it has to come out.'

'So what stopped him?'

'What kind of place do you think I've got here? A hospital?' Louise got his arms into the sleeves and then pulled the shirt on over his head. 'Listen, the bullet's in deep and that means a general anaesthetic. It could be you'll need a blood transfusion too.'

Scarcely pausing for breath and chattering at machine-gun speed, she explained why they had been able to do so little before nightfall. It had been too dangerous to move him in daylight. The robbery had made all the headlines and station WMCA had reported it in every one of their news bulletins. Besides, he had been too weak to leave the house earlier, but he was much stronger now, wasn't he?

Nothing Louise said rang true, but he was too feeble and exhausted to care. He just sat there like a tailor's dummy while she dressed him, tucking the shirt into his pants and buttoning it up to the neck. Obediently he raised one leg at a time so that she could put his shoes on and lace them up. Stand up, sit down, arms raised, arms lowered; first for the jacket and then the overcoat. Head up, eyes shut while she combed and brushed his hair. The docile robot waiting patiently until Louise had put on her hat and coat and was ready to lead him out of the house.

The night air was cold and blustery, but Shaffer didn't feel it. His skin was on fire, burning to the touch, and beads of perspiration oozed from every pore. The sidewalk rocked and swayed beneath his feet, but Louise held him close, one arm about his waist. There were few people about and

80

those who were didn't spare them a second glance. They were simply two young lovers out for an evening stroll, pausing now and then to kiss one another, or so it seemed. Slowly, at little more than a snail's pace, they made their way toward Ninth Avenue.

Virginia Canford glanced again at her wristwatch and smiled ruefully. 'It really is time I was leaving,' she said.

'Yes, of course you must.' Anderson raised a hand and signalled the waited to bring him the check. 'You're going to be late as it is.'

'Yes.'

'Will he mind?'

'No, I don't think so. He's grown accustomed to it.'

In other words, Virginia and this unknown admirer had known each other for a long time. Taking a realistic view, Anderson thought they had probably been friends from childhood, and with that kind of relationship, it so often developed into something far more permanent. He supposed it was only natural and, as his father was fond of remarking, it was inevitable that like should marry like.

'What is it you British say – a penny for your thoughts?'

Anderson laughed. 'I'm not sure they're worth it.' He broke off long enough to glance at the check and leave a five dollar bill on the tray. 'I was just thinking I wouldn't be quite so patient were I in his shoes.'

'Young men rarely are.' Virginia stood up, and Anderson, reaching for the fur coat, helped her into it. 'Thank you, John.' She smiled and laid a hand on his arm. 'I can't remember when I've enjoyed an evening so much.'

'We must do it again sometime,' he said.

'I'd like that.'

'Good. We'll fix a date while I walk you to a cab.'

'Oh, there's no need for you to do that.'

'I insist,' he said firmly. 'Eighth Avenue is no distance from here and the fresh air will do me good.'

Ignoring her protests, he took Virginia by the arm and led her out into the street. There were something like fifteen thousand licensed cabs operating in New York, but at that

81

precise moment in time, it seemed that not one was available for hire. Rather than hang about in the chill night air, they started walking south toward 44th Street.

Webber lit two cigarettes and passed one to Christel. The cab journey from Penn Station was taking longer than he'd expected and they had run out of small talk long ago. Not that they ever had much to say to one another that was of a trivial nature; theirs was strictly a professional relationship, and that was a very restricting factor when it came to making conversation for the sake of it.

'Forty-second Street,' he muttered. 'Not much longer now.'

'I hope not,' said Christel.

The lights changed and they started moving again, the traffic suddenly flowing more freely than it had before. The cab driver made the most of it, jockeying into the outside lane in time to beat the stoplight at the next intersection.

Shaffer breathed through his mouth, making a hollow rasping noise that sounded like a death rattle. He had no idea where he was or where he was going and what little strength he still possessed was rapidly draining away.

'It's not much farther now, Earl. That's Eighth Avenue straight ahead.'

He wanted to ask Louise what she meant by that, but although his lips moved, the words wouldn't come.

'You can make it from here.' She stopped and turned to face him, one arm still encircling his waist. 'The address you want is 131A West 44th. Have you got that?'

He nodded dumbly, not really comprehending why he had to remember the address.

'The doctor said you were to come alone. Do you understand what I'm saying, Earl? I can't go with you.'

Her mouth curved in a bright smile, the kind she flashed on the street whenever a John seemed interested, and then her arm was no longer around his waist and she was walking away from him, back the way they had come.

Shaffer stared after her. Slow to grasp that Louise wasn't

coming back, he eventually turned about and moved on. His vision was blurred, and unable to see that the lights were against him, he stepped off the curb into the path of the oncoming traffic.

Webber saw the man step off the curb a split second before the cab driver did, but even so his warning shout made not an iota of difference. In the dim-out, with neither time nor room for manoeuvre, an accident was inevitable. Although the driver stamped on the brakes and swerved to the right, the car was still moving forward at close to thirty miles an hour when the left fender caught the pedestrian a glancing blow and knocked him high into the air. Skidding wildly into the next lane, the cab rammed into a Mercury station wagon and then slewed round tail-first to end up opposite the Squire Theatre and facing in the wrong direction. Some forty yards back down the street, a small crowd had already gathered around the crumpled figure lying on the sidewalk.

'Sweet Jesus.' The cab driver stared through the windshield. 'Sweet Jesus, did you see that guy?'

'It wasn't your fault,' Webber said swiftly. 'The man was obviously drunk.'

'You reckon?'

'Damn right he was. Look at the way he was swaying when he stepped off the curb. I'll bear witness to that.' Webber leaned across Christel and opened the door on her side. 'Lose yourself in the crowd,' he whispered furiously. 'I'll meet you in the lobby of the Paramount Hotel just as soon as I can.'

'What's going on, mister?' The cab driver swivelled around to face them. 'Where does your lady friend think she's going?'

'You only need me as a witness.' Webber dipped into his pocket and tossed a crumpled ten dollar bill onto the bench seat in front. 'The lady is married to someone else and I don't want her involved.'

'I get the picture,' said the cab driver. 'If there was a lady with you, I didn't see her. Right?'

'Right,' said Webber and got out of the cab.

There were a number of other eyewitnesses to the accident, among whom were John Anderson and Virginia Canford, who were only a few yards from West 44th Street when it occurred. They were, however, on the opposite side of the street, and by the time they arrived on the scene, somebody had already draped a coat over the victim's face. One of the onlookers asked if anyone had thought to send for an ambulance, and since nobody appeared to know, Anderson decided he'd better do something about it. Looking round for the nearest telephone, Virginia suggested he try the Squire Theatre up the street.

As he neared the theatre, a girl in a military-style coat and hat got out of the damaged cab and hurried past him, her face averted from his gaze.

CHAPTER 8

New York

Wednesday, 22 November 1944. Night.

Benjamin Delgado opened a can of beer and settled back in his armchair to listen to the radio. Matthew, his eight-year-old son, was already in bed, and Francesca, a carbon copy of her mother, would be on her way too in just over an hour from now. Ten o'clock was maybe a little late for a thirteen-year-old girl to still be up, but Francesca had wanted to hear the Eddie Cantor show at nine-thirty on station WEAF, and his daughter had always been able to twist him around her little finger. Eddie Cantor was a laugh a minute, but Delgado knew it was his guest star who was the real attraction for Francesca. You walked into her bedroom and there was Alan Ladd, an enigmatic smile on his lips, looking down on you from a dozen different places. It was all part of the business of growing up, and he supposed that in another year some spotty-faced neighbourhood kid would be competing with Alan Ladd to become her latest heart throb.

Francesca was growing up fast, just like her mother had. Delgado glanced at Gina, who was sitting on the couch opposite him, and wondered how it was that his wife could possibly feel comfortable with one leg tucked under her rump. Raising the beer can to his mouth, he surreptitiously admired Gina's trim figure, his eyes roving from the curve of her slim hips to the swell of her pert breasts under the dress. At thirty-two, his wife could lop eight years off her age and no one would be any the wiser. Her mother had run to fat, but Gina never would. She watched her diet, avoided anything that was fattening and took plenty of exercise.

'How many beers have you had today, Ben?'

'This is my first tonight, honey.'

'That's what I call an evasive answer.' Gina smiled at him and then went back to her book. 'Just be sure it's your last. I don't want to see you develop a pot belly.'

'You get the message, Pop?' Francesca, who was lying on the floor, raised her head and made a face at him. 'Watch that waistline or Mom will give you the old heave-ho.'

'I should be so lucky,' said Delgado.

'What did you say?'

Gina still had her nose buried in the book and he couldn't see the expression on her face, but her voice was cold, like an icy wind blowing from the Arctic.

'Nothing,' he said hastily, 'it was just a joke.'

It had been full of innuendo, too, but with his daughter present it was a mite difficult to explain that the sight of Gina curled up on the sofa made him feel amorous.

'If that's your idea of a wisecrack, Ben, it wasn't very funny. I don't care for remarks that imply you'd like to be rid of me.'

'Now you know I didn't mean anything of the kind.'

Of course he didn't. Gina was a wonderful woman and he couldn't imagine what life would be like without her. So all right, they quarrelled once in a while, but what married couple didn't. They'd never had a serious fight except maybe over the choice of name for their son. He had wanted to call him Mario, but Gina had insisted on Matthew and no one, not even the Holy Father himself, had been able to

85

persuade her to change her mind. 'What does she want?' his mother had asked him. 'That your son should grow up thinking he's only half-Italian?' Well, a man didn't have to be a psychiatrist to know that the choice of name was symbolic of Gina's determination that their son should have a better start in life than they'd had. New York wasn't only a cosmopolitan city, it was a pyramid with the Negroes at the bottom and the white Anglo-Saxon Protestants at the peak. Precisely which strata the Italians occupied was far from clear, but they sure as hell were a long way from the top.

It was easier for some people to fulfil the American dream that it was for others. Delgado had climbed partway up the ladder, but the Police Department was dominated by the Irish, and no matter how good he was, Delgado was convinced his name would never appear among those promoted to lieutenant. Gina clung obstinately to the belief that if you had drive, determination and ability, nothing was impossible. She was fond of citing Mayor La Guardia as an example of what she meant, but of course he was a politician, not a cop. If they enjoyed a standard of living that was far beyond the reach of his parents, it was only because Gina had a well-paid job. Without her money, they could never have afforded this apartment on East 92nd.

'Will somebody please answer the telephone?'

Gina's voice interrupted his reverie and he looked up, startled. As he reached out to turn down the volume on the radio, Francesca scrambled to her feet and reached to take the call. Delgado couldn't remember a time when his daughter had shown such alacrity. Usually when her mother asked her to do something, Francesca was apt to respond with all the energy and enthusiasm of a tired old woman. Was it possible that the spotty-faced neighbourhood kid had materialized a year earlier than he'd anticipated?

'It's for you, Pop.'

The disappointed tone and the crestfallen expression said it all. For Francesca, like most other teenager girls, growing up was a painful experience.

Delgado took the phone and listened attentively. Two minutes and several grunts later, he hung up, sourly reflecting that he could say good-bye to the Eddie Cantor show and the rest of the evening.

'Who was that, Ben?'

'Jack Ganley.'

'Who?' Gina laid her book aside.

'My new partner. You haven't met him.' Delgado smiled ruefully. 'He joined the squad a month back and I think he's trying to make a name for himself. Anyway, something's come up and apparently it can't wait until morning.'

'You're going out?'

'I don't have any option.'

'I see.'

Her frosty attitude suggested otherwise. The wealth of meaning Gina was able to convey in a few words never ceased to amaze him.

'Look, I don't like it any more than you do,' Delgado said patiently. 'But this has to do with the Passaretti shooting and I just can't walk away from it.'

'How long will you be?' Her voice was much warmer now and concerned too, a sign that a rapid thaw had set in, as it always did.

'I don't know, but I'll be as quick as I can. Visiting a morgue at this time of night isn't my idea of fun.'

Gina uncurled herself from the couch and came toward him. Entwining both arms around his neck, she pressed her body against his and kissed him fiercely. The sky didn't actually fall in, but their daughter whistled loud and long.

The morgue on West 50th was pretty much like any other. It was spotlessly clean, wholly functional, very stark and cold, so cold that Delgado couldn't stop shivering. The body was lying on a slab in the centre of the room, its torso covered by a sheet. According to the label on the big toe of the right foot, the corpse had been a man called Earl Shaffer.

'Who identified the body?' asked Delgado.

87

'I guess I did.' Ganley reached inside his overcoat and produced a crime sheet. 'One and the same man, wouldn't you say, Ben?'

Delgado compared the mug shots with the body on the slab and then returned the crime sheet to Ganley. 'It's Shaffer, all right,' he said quietly. 'How did you make the connection?'

'Remember the guy who was lying flat on his back inside the office with a bullet between the eyes? Well, Organized Crime identified him as Steve Mirnick and they also gave me a list of his known associates. Anyway, I was still checking through the list when the desk sergeant rang through about a fatal traffic accident at the intersection of Eighth Avenue and West 44th. Although the victim had been pronounced dead on arrival at the hospital, one of the interns who carried out the examination reported that the deceased had a bullet wound in the back. That set me thinking and I went back to Mirnick. Most of his associates were either still in jail or had moved on elsewhere. The exception was this Earl Shaffer, who had just been released on parole. Since he and Mirnick had shared a cell on Riker's Island, I pulled his record sheet and came around her on the off chance.'

Ganley had done a good job and Delgado said so. There were, however, a number of loose ends that had to be tied up before they could definitely link Shaffer with the armed robbery at Ziggermann's.

'Have they done an autopsy?'

'Only a preliminary one,' said Ganley.

"Why are we talking in whispers?' Delgado hunched his shoulders and wished he could stop shivering. 'Anybody would think this place was a church.' His voice echoed and sounded unnaturally loud.

'I guess it's because that's where most people go from here.'

'Not Shaffer,' said Delgado. 'At least not until that bullet has been removed from his back.'

'Right. That's why I've arranged to have the body transferred for a postmortem examination by our people.'

88

Ganley was certainly on the ball, remarkably so, considering his lack of experience. It was rapidly becoming apparent that his new partner was a flier, a man who was destined to go a long way, maybe even as far as Commissioner.

'I think Shaffer was probably involved,' said Delgado. 'But we can't be sure of that until Ballistics compares the bullet with the handguns we found at Ziggermann's.'

'Well, we already know that Passaretti didn't shoot him. Only one bullet was fired from his .32 and he put that into Mirnick.'

'Have we had a report to that effect?'

Ganley nodded. 'It was delivered about an hour ago.'

Delgado wondered what else his new partner was keeping to himself. 'Was there anyone with Shaffer when the accident happened?' he asked.

'Not according to the eyewitnesses.' Ganley produced a notebook from his pocket. 'Leon Janowski, the cab driver, is definite that Shaffer was alone and his evidence is supported by a Mr. Paul Webber who was seated behind him on the side nearest the curb. Webber is a senior captain with National Eastern Airlines.'

'And you think that makes him infallible?'

'No, but I'd say it made him a pretty reliable witness, Ben. And there are two others in that category – a Lieutenant Virginia Canford of the Waves and an officer in the Royal Navy, a Lieutenant Commander John Anderson.'

Four reliable witnesses could be mistaken, but Delgado thought it unlikely. The attempted robbery had occurred shortly before midday, and if Shaffer had taken part in the abortive holdup, somebody must have been hiding him in the meantime.

'Was Shaffer badly wounded?'

'He might have survived with proper medical care. Somebody had tried to patch him up, but they didn't do a very good job of it. The intern reckoned he must have lost a lot of blood. I was talking to him shortly before you arrived.' Ganley consulted his notebook again, leafing through several pages until he found the entry he was looking for. 'The guys who were making inquiries on Eleventh Avenue came up with one witness who remembered seeing a grey sedan parked near the alley behind Ziggermann's. He didn't see it pull out and he could only give Lieutenant Caskey a vague description of the man who was sitting behind the wheel.'

'You can bet the car was stolen, and not from this borough either.'

'That's what I figured, Ben.'

Ganley was beginning to depress him. He was so damned sharp that an outsider would be hard pressed to tell who was the rookie.

'But it doesn't get us very far, does it?'

Delgado closed his eyes and wondered what further brilliant observations Ganley was about to make.

'Auto Theft puts out a list of stolen vehicles to every precinct and all we can do is wait for some sharp-eyed patrolman to come across one that fits the vague description we've been given.'

It had been a lament, not a profound observation, and Delgado recovered some of his lost ego. 'I'd be a lot happier if your hypothetical patrolman found Larry Novak for us. I'm pretty sure four men were involved in that robbery and I've got a hunch he can name the other two.'

'Maybe he can, Ben, but where do we go from here?'

'Home,' said Delgado. 'That's where I'm going, and if you take my advice, you'll do the same.'

Webber got up from his chair and opened a window to clear the stale atmosphere. He'd lost count of the number of cigarettes he'd smoked since bidding good night to Christel Zolf, but the contents of the ashtray and the blue-grey haze in the hotel bedroom suggested it was probably close to twenty. In the past, a cigarette had always helped him to unwind whenever he was feeling tense, but not on this occasion. Webber supposed that was hardly surprising, considering what an eventful night it had been.

Eventful was putting it mildly. He had been living on his

90

nerves ever since the traffic accident. Trying to look at it dispassionately, he came to the conclusion that bribing the cab driver had been a bad mistake. Although Janowski hadn't said anything to the police about Christel, the cab driver now knew his name and address and was therefore in a position to blackmail him if he had a mind to. That alone was enough to worry him sick, without Berlin making things even worse. Right from the time Christel had telephoned him on Tuesday night, he had been filled with a sense of deep foreboding, but never in his wildest dreams had Webber imagined that he would find himself involved in a suicide mission.

No matter what Christel said, there was no other way to describe operation Double Griffin. Even the code name stank: A Griffin was a mythological creature, part lion, part eagle, an animal that could only exist in fantasy. It was, however, a singularly appropriate name for an operation that was one long fantasy from beginning to end. Maybe the bomb could hit the target with pinpoint accuracy as she claimed, but he just couldn't see how one two-thousand pounder was going to change the course of the war. The fact that he had been given two possible objectives, with no firm date for either one, was an indication of the muddled thinking and lack of decision by the planners.

Absorbed in his thoughts, it was some moments before Webber realized that Christel had been calling to him from the adjoining room.

'I saw your light was still burning.' Christel smiled at him from the doorway. 'May I come in?'

Webber stared at her dressing gown and wondered if she had deliberately left it undone so that he could see the champagne-coloured satin nightdress underneath. 'It seems to me you already have,' he grunted.

'I can't sleep either.' She looked round for somewhere to sit, hesitated between the ladder-back chair at the writing desk and the single bed and then finally perched on the edge of the low coffee table. 'I suppose it's because I'm excited.'

She was too; he could see it in her dark eyes, the way they shone. He thought the same zealous expression had probably been there the night she'd attended the Nuremberg Rally back in '33.

'Well, there's the difference,' said Webber. 'I'm just plain worried.'

'About the operation?' Christel leaned closer, her knees brushing against his. 'You needn't be. Those who planned Double Griffin know exactly what they are doing.'

Her voice was soothing, and she spoke to him as if he were a frightened child whose nameless fears she was determined to allay. No one had ever talked down to him like that, and he found it difficult to conceal his irritation. He wanted to take Christel by the shoulders and shake her until the teeth rattled in her head, but instead he got to his feet and closed the window. For some moments, Webber stood there looking down at the deserted street, until at last his anger evaporated and he returned to his chair.

'Whoever authorized the operation belongs in a lunatic asylum,' he said wearily. 'We've no hope of winning this war; we lost it at Stalingrad. Unconditional surrender may seem harsh, but it's preferable to total destruction, and that's what will happen to Germany unless the generals do something about it.'

'The war may be lost, Paul, but the peace can still be won.'

That the vanquished could suddenly become the victors was a new one on him, but as she expounded on her theme, Webber began to see the force of her new argument. Although the Americans were riding high and believed the end was in sight, a major setback might persuade them to consider the advantage a negotiated peace could bring. As surely as night followed day, the Soviet Union would emerge from the war as a world power strong enough to challenge the United States. Roosevelt had been elected to a fourth term on the slogan, 'Victory and a Lasting Peace', but there would be little chance of that if Europe were under Russian domination. America needed Germany as a buffer between East and West, but only an operation on the scale of Double Griffin could bring that lesson home to the politicians.

'One bomb is not enough.'

'Who said it was, Paul?' Christel took his hand and squeezed it gently. 'I didn't. We've only been told as much as we need to know.'

Her meaning was clear enough. There would be no more questions. He had been given a job to do, and Berlin expected him to get on with it.

'You know,' he said, 'I can't help feeling that somewhere some anonymous intelligence officer has decided that you and I are both expendable.'

'If we are, then we're in good company.'

Webber supposed that Christel was referring to the fifty-six officers and men of the U-boat, but somehow he found it difficult to relate to them.

CHAPTER 9

Bergen, Norway

Friday, 24 November 1944

Acceptance Report U 195

RE: MODIFICATIONS 11/7917. 11/7819

1. The evaluation trials in connection with the above modifications were completed on Thursday, 23 November 1944.
2. *Forward hatch* (Modification 11/7917). This proved watertight at maximum diving depth and no structural weaknesses were observed.
3. *Launch ramp* (Modification 11/7918). Due to the added weight on the foredeck casing, the hydroplane operators experienced some difficulty in keeping the boat on an even keel at the correct depth when snorkeling. The ramp also exerts a noticeable drag, with the result that the maximum submerged speed is reduced from seven point six knots to five point nine. Surface speed is not adversely affected, but U 195 now has a marked

93

tendency to roll in a heavy swell.

4. Notwithstanding the observations in Pargraph 3, I consider U 195 is seaworthy in all respects.

(E. Hartmann)
Korvettenkapitän

Satisfied that there were no typing errors, Hartmann signed all three copies of the report in the space provided and then returned the folder to Kapitän zur See Wirth.

'Perhaps it's just as well you were able to complete the acceptance trials one day ahead of schedule.' Wirth placed the report in the out-tray and leaned back in his chair. 'The RAF have been a damned sight too inquisitive for my liking. We were lucky they never caught you on the surface.'

Hartmann nodded. With the benefit of hindsight, it was obvious that segregating the crew of U 195 from the rest of the base had been a mistake. The high security fence around their quarters had aroused the curiosity of the RAF photographic interpreters to such an extent that Bergen had rapidly become a number-one priority target for the PR Mosquitoes. Although the fence had been removed last Wednesday, its sudden disappearance had failed to achieve the desired effect. The RAF had made their customary visit the following day and had flown yet another sortie earlier that morning.

'That extra twenty-four hours you saved could prove invaluable, Erich.' Wirth pointed to the acceptance report in the out-tray. 'I expected the ramp to affect the submerged speed but not to the extent you have indicated.'

'It's certainly going to hold us up until we're south of the Great Circle route, sir.' Hartmann smiled briefly. 'As you may have already guessed, I spent most of last night studying the charts that were issued with the sailing instructions.'

'And there are a number of questions you'd like to raise before Major Galen arrives?'

'Well, they don't affect the army and I thought it might save a certain amount of time if we aired them now. For instance, I calculate that we shall cover approximately

94

three thousand nine hundred nautical miles on the outward leg, and that's not taking into account any diversions which may be forced upon us. I haven't been given the route back yet, but I trust it will be more direct, because our radius of action at cruising speed is exactly eight and a half thousand miles.'

'You will be refueled at sea, Erich. Your sealed orders will tell you where and when to rendezvous with the "milk cow".'

'Milk cow' was the nickname for the type XIV class which were designed to resupply the fighting boats so that they could stay at sea longer and operate farther afield. Displacing some seventeen hundred tons, the type XIVs were slow to leave the surface, which made them an easy prey for radar-equipped aircraft. Hartmann had always been under the impression that all ten 'milk cows' had been sunk in quick succession.

'I didn't know we had any left?'

'Strictly speaking, we haven't.' Wirth picked up a ruler and flexed it into a bow, a habit that Hartmann had become familiar with during the past two weeks. 'It's merely a convenient way of describing the type XB minelayer we're using for that purpose.'

The large minelayers were completely unsuitable for convoy battles in the North Atlantic. Apart from the fact that they were only equipped with two stern torpedo tubes, they suffered from the same defects as the type XIVs in that they were clumsy to handle and took far too long to submerge. However, as resupply boats they still had their uses.

'Do you have any other questions, Erich?'

'A couple,' said Hartmann. 'What do my sealed orders have to say about standard operating procedures?'

'You will receive the usual daily intelligence report.'

'Which I am expected to acknowledge?'

'Of course. How else can we keep track of you?'

'I want to maintain complete wireless silence until we're clear of the Great Circle route.'

'I'm afraid that's out of the question.'

95

'Times have changed,' Hartmann said quietly. 'We're no longer the hunters but the hunted. Even if I were to send only four coded digits, the British could still pinpoint my position with their high-frequency direction finders.'

'The answer is still no. The Führer has a personal interest in the progress of Operation Double Griffin and he wishes to be kept fully informed.'

Hartmann could recognize a brick wall when he saw one. The Führer had spoken and that was that as far as the Kapitän zur See was concerned. Since Wirth obviously lacked the moral courage to do anything about it, the order would have to be circumvented. Technical faults were not unknown and U 195 had had her share in the past. Before they reached the Shetland Islands, their wireless would go on the blink and it would stay that way for the next twelve hundred miles. Galen would probably scream blue murder, but that was a problem he would face with the time came.

'And the second question?' Wirth said impatiently. 'What does that concern?'

'The Arctic weather station at Spitzbergen. Is it still functioning?'

'No, I'm afraid we had to withdraw our people while you were on leave, Erich. Things were becoming a little too hot for them.'

Cape Mitra had been their last secret weather station in the Arctic. There had been others on Bear Island and on the coast of Greenland, but the British had tracked them down one by one. Now that Spitzbergen had gone, it would be impossible to forecast the weather for the mid-Atlantic with any accuracy.

'Naturally, steps have been taken to put this right. One of the U-boats from the 14th Flotilla up at Narvik has positioned two automatic buoys off Bear Island.'

The wheel had turned almost full circle. The buoys had been introduced in 1942 to replace the weather ships that had been sunk. The same shape as a torpedo, the equipment consisted of a battery-powered radio transmitter and instruments to measure the temperature, specific gravity and wind speeds. Discharged from a

96

torpedo tube, the buoy floated vertically to the surface. Once the nose was above water, a weight in the tail was automatically released to unwind a thousand metres of steel wire which anchored it in position. At the same time, an aerial containing the instruments was projected two metres into the air. Controlled by a clock which switched the apparatus on twice a day, the buoy would then transmit accurate readings until the batteries were exhausted approximately six months later.

'I assume these weather buoys are not entirely for our benefit?'

'Is that a question or an observation, Erich?'

'A bit of both.'

'I think you're manufacturing difficulties.' Wirth studied him thoughtfully. 'It's my impression you are not wholeheartedly enthusiastic about this operation.'

'I'm not qualified to pass judgment until I receive my sealed orders.'

'You're hedging, Erich, and that's not like you.'

The supercilious smile and the tone of voice were not lost on Hartmann. In a none-too-subtle way, Wirth had implied that he was afraid to voice his opinion. No one had ever accused him of that before and he didn't try to disguise his contempt.

'I'm not a cheerleader, Herr Kapitän. I leave that sort of thing to Major Galen.'

Faced with that kind of impertinent remark, nine captains out of ten would have hauled him over the coals, but it seemed Wirth was one of the exceptions. Instead of the expected outburst there was only a weak smile.

'Yes, I know what you mean, Erich. Major Galen can be rather trying at times.' Wirth glanced at his wristwatch and frowned. 'In fact, very trying. He should have been here ten minutes ago. I wonder what the devil's happened to him?'

'Hauptmann Kleist was experiencing some difficulty loading the missile through the forward hatch. When I saw him last, Major Galen was telling Kleist how it should be done.'

'He would,' said Wirth with some feeling.

Obersteuermann Wilhelm Frick dismissed the working party and made his way forward to the control room from the galley. A squat, barrel-chested man with red hair, he was the senior enlisted man of U 195 and as chief helmsman was responsible to the captain for the maintenance of discipline. Apart from his other duties, Frick was also in charge of provisions, a sideline that had earned him the affectionate nickname of 'Grocer Willie' among the crew. It was his job to check the supplies on board and see that they were neatly stowed away which, in view of the lack of space, called for a good deal of ingenuity. The galley was little more than a cubbyhole and, as usual, it had been necessary to store the fresh vegetables in the engine room accommodation. It was bad luck for the diesel and electro mechanics; with sacks of potatoes and cabbages stored under their bunks, there was no room for their personal gear, but like the rest of the crew, they had grown accustomed to the fact that life on board a U-boat was no pleasure cruise.

The control room was deserted, but through the open hatchway Frick could see enlisted men using the hoist to load the port bow tube with one of the T5 acoustic torpedoes that had been stowed on board earlier that morning. Barely sparing them a second glance, he climbed the ladder up to the bridge where a poker-faced Oberleutnant zur See Best was watching the antics of the army detachment below.

Had it been left to the Kriegsmarine, the missiles would have been stashed away long before now, but Frick had been present when Major Galen had made it very clear to the executive officer that he welcomed neither advice nor help from any outsider. With clockwork precision, his artillerymen had removed both wings from the V1 and shackled the missile to the hoist, at which point their efficiency had temporarily deserted them. Although they had watched the crew prepare the torpedoes for striking down, hoisting the V1 on board and positioning it at the right angle above the forward hatch was not the simple task they had imagined. As of that moment, the bomb was suspended in midair, swinging gently to and fro like a vast pendulum while Major Galen harangued the assembled detachment for their incompetence.

'That's not the same V1 I saw an hour ago, is it, sir?' Frick asked in a low voice.

'I'm afraid it is,' Best turned about and grinned at him. 'I don't know when I've seen such a clumsy lot.'

'Neither do I.' Frick clucked his tongue in disgust. 'They will need to be a lot more lively when we put to sea.'

'At the rate they're going, I can see us being stuck her for the next week.'

'Well, sir, we're all ready to go. The rations have been checked and stowed away and both water tanks have been filled. Incidentally, I took the precaution of removing the tap from the drinking tank. I've put it in my foot locker.'

'Why did you do that?'

'Because of the army detachment,' said Frick.

Best could see what the chief helmsman was getting at. There was only a limited supply of drinking water and the atmosphere inside the pressure hull was apt to become very humid when the boat was submerged for any length of time. In the circumstances, one of the artillerymen might well be tempted to help himself to a drink, but knowing Major Gallen, he thought it highly unlikely that anybody would have the nerve to do so.

'I think we ought to put it back. Some of us may be wearing a different uniform but we're one crew, and the last thing we want is bad feeling between the army and the navy.' Best saw the dour expression on Frick's face and gave him what he thought was an encouraging smile. 'I suggest you take their Oberfeldwebel aside and have a few quiet words with him.'

Frick tried to conceal his irritation. He could talk to Warrant Officer Meyer until he was blue in the face but it wouldn't do any good. The Oberfeldwebel took his orders from Major Galen and the executive officer was living in never-never land if he thought Meyer would pay any attention to him.

'Will you also be seeing Hauptmann Kleist, sir?' he

99

asked diplomatically.

'What about?'

'Well, I understand that the Herr Major expects his men to be spick-and-span at all times.'

Best nodded. Among other things, spick-and-span meant that Galen wanted his men to be clean-shaven and that simply wasn't possible. The tank of washing water was barely sufficient to meet the needs of the officers and senior enlisted men. The ordinary seamen were provided with a block of saltwater soap and had to get by as best they could. 'Tar your clothes – the white is showing' was an old saying among U-boat men, but putting that message across was not going to be easy. Best turned about, and noticing that Galen had departed while he had been talking to the chief helmsman, decided to make the most of the opportunity.

'All right,' he said crisply, 'leave it to me, I'm sure we can straighten things out. In the meantime, you'd better see to the freshwater tank.'

Frick snapped to attention and left the bridge. Descending into the control room, he made his way forward to the bow accommodation room, collected the tap from his foot locker and returned to the galley. He still thought the executive officer was making a big mistake, but orders were orders and he knew better than to argue. The tap replaced, he opened the galley hatch aft of the conning tower and went up on deck again.

Kapitänleutnant August Peiper, the chief engineer, was standing on the jetty, both hands stuffed deep in the pockets of his brown overalls. His eyes were downcast, fixed on the hose lines that were feeding one hundred and fourteen tons of diesel oil into the storage tanks. There was the usual puckered frown on his forehead, an outward sign of his conviction that he had the cares of the world on his shoulders. A sudden cheer from the army detachment made him look up, and catching sight of Frick, he pulled a face.

'They'll have to be better than that,' Peiper said morosely.

Lately, the chief engineer had been prone to look on the

black side of everything, and although by nature he was not a pessimist, in this instance Frick shared his misgivings. It had taken Galen's men the best part of two hours to strike one missile down into the bow torpedo room and God help them all if they took that long to launch the damn thing. To spend two hours on the surface off the enemy coast was tantamount to committing suicide.

Hartmann placed the letter to his parents in an envelope and sealed it, a privilege that was not accorded to the enlisted men, whose letters were read by the censor before they were sent on. Censorship was necessary in wartime but it was a distasteful job, and Hartmann was thankful that he no longer had to do it. Writing a letter home was the last thing every man in the crew did before they put to sea, and Hartmann remembered how embarrassed he'd been when as a junior officer it had fallen to his lot to go through the ship's mail. Every seaman hated having his mail read, but their reactions varied. Some had no hesitation in expressing their opinion of the censor, while others were so self-conscious that their letters were reduced to the 'I am well – how are you?' kind. Of course there had been exceptions, men who were not inhibited by the thought of a stranger looking over their shoulders and not too shy to tell the women in their lives how much they loved and missed them.

Hartmann wished it were possible to send such a letter to Jeanne Verlhac, but the postal service to Brest had been terminated somewhat abruptly by the Americans. Jeanne Verlhac and Erich Hartmann – a French schoolteacher and the U-boat commander – a mismatch that had been doomed from the start. Jeanne had known that, but he had refused to see it.

They had met by chance in the town centre of Brest one bitterly cold Saturday afternoon in January 1943, when the pavements had been treacherous and she had slipped and fallen on a patch of ice. Jeanne had virtually landed at his feet and when he'd stooped down to pick her up, Hartmann had discovered that she had sprained her ankle very badly. At the same time, he'd also discovered that she was a very attractive young woman. Despite Jeanne's protests, he had insisted on taking her to the nearest doctor and then to her home on the outskirts of town.

From the very outset, her parents had shown their disapproval of him with an icy politeness that had initially rubbed off on Jeanne, but in the end, through sheer persistence, he had finally won her over. It hadn't been easy, but the long refit which had followed their ninth patrol had enabled him to lay a protracted siege and eventually she had capitulated. He had wanted to marry her, and still did, but there had been too many obstacles in their way. Her parents had objected strongly and the Kriegsmarine had made it very clear that they did not approve. Faced with that kind of opposition and ostracized by her friends, Jeanne had begged him to wait until the war was over.

He knew now that he should never have listened to Jeanne, but anything was preferable to losing her altogether and he had reluctantly agreed. He had seen her for the very last time the day before he had been ordered to leave Brest and join the flotilla at Bergen, although of course neither of them had known then that it might be the end of the war before they saw each other again. Jeanne had told him that she thought she was pregnant, and he had said it was the best news he'd heard in months because now they would have to get married.

The best news in months? Well, that just showed how wrong he'd been, because now Jeanne was alone and without a single friend in the world. She was also at the mercy of the French Resistance and that was something that didn't bear thinking about.

Hartmann got up from the desk and walked across the room. His kit was already packed, but Jeanne's photograph in the silver frame was still on the bedside table and he never went anywhere without it. Placing it face down on top of his spare uniform in the valise, he drew the zipper fastener and then put on his bridge coat. Although the crew were not due to muster until 1800 hours, he saw little point in killing time just for the sake of it, and leaving the officers' mess, he made his way over to the headquarters block.

There was no sign of Kapitän zur See Wirth, which was something of a relief because they hadn't parted exactly the best of friends after the final briefing. The petty officer in charge of the regulating office accepted the letter to his parents without comment, and pausing only to collect an up-to-date forecast from the Met Section, Hartmann went on down to the U-boat pens.

Ten minutes later, his kit unpacked, the photograph of Jeanne Verlhac on the shelf above his bunk, he settled back to await the arrival of his crew.

U 195 slipped her moorings at 1830 hours Central European time and put to sea. Escorted by an E-boat, she left Bergen by way of North Byfjord. None of the top brass were there to see them off, but after guiding them through the protective minefield, the E-boat flashed a farewell message to U 195. It read: 'Good luck and God speed.' Hartmann just hoped the Almighty would take note.

CHAPTER 10

New York

Saturday, 25 November 1944. Morning.

Anderson had spent the previous night watch-keeping in the Operations Room, a duty that came around once every ten days. Rather than go back to his quarters on Staten Island, he shaved in the washroom at 17 Battery Place, changed into a clean shirt and, giving breakfast a miss, went straight to his office. The slow eastbound convoy SC 189 had sailed at 0700 hours that morning, and, if precedent was anything to go by, Anderson thought it possible that he could be landed with one or two problems to sort out. The number of merchant seamen who jumped ship was remarkably small, but rarely did every ship sail with a full complement. HX 320, the fast convoy that had departed on Wednesday, had been an exception in that no one had fallen sick at the last moment or gone AWOL or had been so hung over that they couldn't make it back to the ship on time.

A copy of the daily intelligence summary from the Admiralty for the period ending 1800 hours GMT, the twenty fourth of November, had already been placed in his in-tray by the Yeoman of Signals. Glancing through it, he saw that the RAF had been over Bergen again, taking yet more photographs of the submarine pens and the naval barracks with the same apparently negative results. There was also a press handout from the U.S. Navy District with a message from the Senior British Liaison Officer. The press handout concerned an invitation to members of the public to view the *Bonhomme Richard*, the newest aircraft carrier of the Essex Class, while the message suggested it would further Anglo-American relations if he put in an appearance. Just how his presence tomorrow would achieve that was beyond Anderson, but he marked it in his diary.

A circle around the date on the calendar reminded him the time had come to submit yet another application to their lordships at the Admiralty requesting that he be considered for a seagoing appointment. Opening the bottom drawer in the desk. Anderson took out his personal file and flagged it at the appropriate page. Once that was completed, he wrote a brief note to one of the secretaries referring her to the correct page and asking her to type an updated letter for his signature.

Following that spate of activity, he found there was nothing else to do until the day staff came in, and settling back in the chair, he propped his feet up on the open drawer. The room was decidedly warm, his lids felt heavy and presently his head dropped forward.

He was awakened by a light knock on the door and a feminine voice saying, 'Oh, I'm sorry, I'll come back later.'

Anderson opened one eye, saw it was Virginia Canford and straightened up. 'God, you're an early bird,' he said, yawning. 'What time is it?'

'I make it ten after nine.'

'Really? As late as that? I must have dropped off.' Completely unruffled, Anderson picked up the intelligence summary and handed it to her. 'This came in during the night,' he said. 'Take a look at the third paragraph.'

Virginia read the signal, her eyebrows gradually meeting in a puzzled frown. 'I don't understand,' she said eventually. 'The RAF has been over Bergen before. What's so special about this latest sortie?'

'The security fence is no longer there. Right?'

She nodded. 'As I recall, they discovered that interesting fact last Wednesday.'

'But the flak was the heaviest yet and the Mosquito pilot reported that four FW 190s tried to intercept him.'

'After seven missions in a row, I'd say that was only to be expected.'

'The Norwegians reported that the 11th U-boat Flotilla had been confined to base until further notice,' Anderson reminded her. 'The RAF then found that part of the barracks had been screened off. Finding the security fence had aroused the curiosity of our people; the Germans removed it, hoping we would lose interest, and when we didn't, they brought in more antiaircraft guns. To me that means they've got something to hide.'

'Like what, for instance?'

'According to one of the earlier reports, there were four huts inside that security compound. Men have got to eat, sleep, shower and go to the lavatory. Take away a dining hall, the ablutions and the latrines and you are left with one barrack block large enough to accommodate a crew of a U-boat. Now you don't think they would go to all that trouble unless they had a very special mission planned for that U-boat, do you?'

'It's a very interesting theory.' Virginia returned the signal to the in-tray on his desk. 'And you could be right ...'

'However ...' he prompted.

'Well, I hate to sound like a lawyer, but where's your hard evidence?'

'You've got me there ...' Anderson broke off to answer

the telephone.

The Canadian voice at the end of the line was very brisk and businesslike and he barely had time to grab a memo pad before the called launched into the message. Using a form of shorthand that only he could decipher, Anderson made a note of the salient points, checked that he had the facts straight and then hung up.

'Sounds like someone has jumped ship,' Virginia said quietly.

'Someone has,' said Anderon. 'Gunner Harold Yates of the Royal Artillery.'

'An army man?'

'From the Maritime Artillery Regiment. Yates is – or was – a member of the antiaircraft detachment on board the SS *Queenstown Bay*. I daresay he found New York infinitely preferable to the North Atlantic, but he won't enjoy it for long. Either the shore patrol will pick him up or else the police will.'

At least, he presumed they would. The Canadian executive officer of the escort base on Staten Island had assured him that everybody had been informed and had then asked if he'd mind collecting Yates's documents sometime, as it would save them a trip. The ship's master had left his regimental and battery conduct sheets with the coast guard detachment at the French Line Ocean Terminal near the Weehauken ferry, which meant that Anderson would have to take a cab uptown.

Although there was no hurry, Anderson thought he might just as well collect the documents now while his in-tray was still empty. He briefed Virginia Canford as to where he was going and was halfway to the door when he thought to ask what she had wanted to see him about.

'A party tonight.' She lowered her eyes and her manner became slightly flustered, which wasn't like her at all. 'My roommates decided it was time we held one. They've invited a few nurses from the navy hospital on Flatbush Avenue and a host of officers from the Brooklyn Navy Yard and Staten Island. We're having our neighbours in too.'

'Sounds like quite a gathering,' he said noncommittally.

'Yes – well – I know it's kind of short notice, but I just wondered if you would like to come along as well?' She smiled hesitantly. 'That's if you've nothing better to do.'

'I'd like to very much. Where do you live?'

'In Greenwich Village.'

'I already know that,' Anderson said, smiling. 'I was after the address.'

'Oh. It's 5A Washington Mews – right opposite the square. The party starts at seven, okay?'

Her complexion had turned a delicate shade of pink and he wondered what had happened to the cool, confident and very poised Virginia Canford and why she was behaving like a shy and embarrassed schoolgirl all of a sudden.

'I'll be there on the dot,' he told her, and walked out of the office.

The room he'd moved into on 175th Street in the Bronx had rapidly become a prison for Larry Novak. It had seemed a good idea to drop out of sight before George Eltsberg and his friends hit Vince Passaretti, because Delgado had seen him in the lunch counter across the way from Ziggermann's and the wop detective was pretty good at putting two and two together. The only trouble was that he hadn't run far enough. With two C's in his pocket he could have gone to Miami and soaked up the sun, but five percent of the take had seemed one very good reason for staying in New York.

The robbery should have been a pushover but Eltsberg had picked two deadbeats to go in with him and had then allowed Mirnick to recruit a fourth man, some jerk by the name of Shaffer. Novak thought George should never have done that, but there were no prizes for guessing that he'd listened to Kalmbach and had gone along with what the big man had said. Kalmbach had started to call the shots when they'd met in Slattery's Bar last Monday, and Eltsberg had taken a back seat because the ex-prizefighter had a reputation. He had gone ten rounds with Braddock and that made him a hero, the kind of man you could depend on when you were in a jam. Maybe this Shaffer had felt the same way about him, which was his big mistake, because when the chips were down, Kalmbach had shown he was full of chicken shit.

Novak got up from the bed and walked over to the window. He felt trapped, caged like an animal at the zoo. What angered him most of all was the knowledge that he wouldn't be in this fix if he'd caught the twelve-thirty news flash of the robbery on station WNEW on Wednesday. He could have slipped out of town then before anyone thought to cover the bus depots and the railroad stations, but of course he hadn't been able to stay home and listen to the radio. The janitor was a goddamned nosy bastard and he'd had to spend the entire day killing time in various bars and at the movies to fool the shithead into thinking he had a job to go to. By the time he saw the headlines in the *Post* that evening, it was too late to do anything except go underground like some fucking mole.

For more than two days now he'd been cooped up in this poky little room, a portable radio his only link with the outside world. He hadn't had a bite to eat, he was out of cigarettes and he was slowly going nuts thinking about Kalmbach and Eltsberg. If it wasn't for the fact that Lieutenant Caskey had suddenly become the most quoted man in town, he wouldn't have known what the hell was going on. Even so, the news bulletins on the radio raised more questions than they answered. Caskey had said the police were pretty sure four men had been involved in the robbery, and that since Mirnick and Shaffer had shared the same cell on Riker's Island, it was more than likely one of them had been acquainted with the other two men. By acquainted, the lieutenant meant they had known each other for some considerable time, an assumption which made Novak sweat because it certainly applied to Kalmbach and Mirnick. Sooner or later the cops would get to Kalmbach, and when they did, the big man would talk and talk.

Novak returned to the crumpled, unmade bed, sat down and switched on the radio, tuning in to station WMCA to catch the twelve o'clock newscast. Reports of bitter street fighting in Budapest, the stalemate in the West, the clash

108

between British troops and Communist guerrillas in Athens and the slugging match on Leyte were of no interest to him. When the reporter finally did get around to it, the local news was a complete anticlimax.

There was no mention of the holdup on West 48th. Instead, he found himself listening to a long spiel about the Regional War Labour Board which had ordered a five-dollar-a-week rise for meat truckdrivers whose one-day strike in October had paralyzed the city's supply, and then, before he knew it, the newscaster was into the sports roundup for the day. Suddenly and quite inexplicably, it seemed that Lieutenant Caskey's popularity rating had dropped to zero and the crime was no longer considered newsworthy.

No wiser now than before the bulletin, Novak figured he could do one of two things. Either he continued to sit tight or else he took a chance and called Eltsberg from a phone booth on Jerome Avenue. Unable to make up his mind which choice to take, he flipped a quarter, deciding that if it came down heads he would stay put. For a full minute, Novak stared at the eagle on the reverse side of the coin and then, slipping on a raincoat, he left the room, went on downstairs and let himself out of the house.

A fine drizzle was falling from an overcast sky and there weren't too many people about. Jerome Avenue was busier, but not like it usually was on a Saturday morning. Five minutes after leaving the house on 175th Street, he found a pay booth and called Eltsberg at his home in Brooklyn. Their conversation was somewhat stilted, and while Novak got the impression that George wasn't any too pleased with him, it was a relief to know that he was still in circulation. Eltsberg didn't volunteer any information about Kalmbach and he didn't bother to ask, figuring that if the cops had the big man in custody, George wouldn't have been around to answer the phone.

Leaving the phone booth, he made straight for a lunch counter and ordered a cup of coffee and two hot dogs which he ate ravenously while thinking about his next move. The heat wasn't off yet, but give it another day or two and he figured it would be safe enough to leave town. Boston seemed a good place to go because he had friends there. Perhaps that was stretching it a bit, but he knew at least one guy who would take him in. It wasn't much of a plan, but for the first time since Wednesday night, Novak thought he could see a glimmer of light at the end of the tunnel. Nothing could have been farther from the truth. Less than five minutes later while on his way back to 175th Street, the sky fell in on him.

The two patrolmen appeared from nowhere. The taller one asked if he was Larry Novak and before he could answer, the other said, 'Of course it's him, I'd know that ugly face anywhere.' And then they frisked him, cuffed his wrists together behind his back and shoved him into the squad car. The short drive to the 46th Precinct station at 2120 Ryer Avenue was the longest mile Novak had ever known.

CHAPTER 11

New York

Saturday, 25 November 1944. Evening.

Larry Novak's greatest asset was his reputation for being a good Joe. As far as his friends were concerned, this meant he was a man who could be trusted to keep his mouth shut. Delgado knew this, but unlike some detective who would have used their fists to break him, he preferred more subtle methods. Novak might seem a tough nut to crack, but with two previous convictions for armed robbery on his sheet, Delgado reckoned he was vulnerable. Capitalizing on this, he arranged to have Norvak placed in a fake lineup where he was immediatley identified by Ganley and a police officer from the 46th Precinct posing as civilian eyewitnesses. To apply further psychological pressure, Delgado then left Novak to stew on his predicament for a good two hours before attempting to question him. When he finally did walk into the interview room, Novak gave every sign of being ready to crumble.

'Hello, Larry.' Delgado pulled out a chair and sat down at the table facing Novak. 'I thought your lawyer would have been here by now,' he said casually.

'My lawyer?' Novak stared at him, his eyes bulging. 'For Chrissakes, what chance have I had to call him? I've been given the bum's rush ever since I was brung here.'

'Well, that's too bad.' Delgado clucked his tongue and half rose from the chair. 'Tell you what – I'll get an extension plugged in and you can phone him now.'

'What for?'

'What for?' Delgado sank back into the chair, the expression on his face a picture of total incredulity. 'Because I'm going to read you your rights and then charge you with armed robbery – that's what for.'

'Bullshit. You can't pin anything on me and you know it. Listen, I was drinking in a bar on the Grand Boulevard right here in the Bronx when those guys hit Ziggermann's.'

'And that's your alibi, is it?' Delgado shook his head. 'Hell, Larry, you'll have to do a lot better than that.'

'I've got witnesses.'

'So have I – two of them. They picked you out in the lineup, remember? One witness is pretty sure you were the guy he saw in a grey four-door sedan parked near the alleyway behind Ziggermann's on Wednesday morning. The other saw you walking away from the Ford after leaving it under the Eighth Avenue El opposite Clements's cigar store on 111th Street.'

'That's a load of crap. You're trying to frame me with a couple of fake witnesses.'

It was a nice try, but it didn't throw Delgado because he knew that Novak had never met either Ganley or the other police officer, which was why they'd been chosen.

'The car,' he continued relentlessly, 'was stolen on Tuesday night. It belonged to a Mr. Enrico Conti who lives on Lorrimer Street. That's in the Williamsburg section of Queens. It was found by a patrolman from the 24th Precinct yesterday morning.'

This time he wasn't bluffing. The details of the auto theft were completely authentic and the implications weren't lost on Novak.

'You're trying real hard, Delgado, but it just won't stand up. You know why?' Novak hunched his shoulders and leaned forward, his elbows resting on the table. 'Because my prints aren't on that sedan.'

'We don't need your prints, Larry. We've got two independent witnesses, and I saw you in the lunch counter across the street from Ziggermann's two days before the attempted holdup took place.' Delgado produced a packet of Chesterfields and lit a cigarette. 'I figure it happened this way. Mirnick and Shaffer were supposed to break into the office and persuade Vince Passaretti to open his safe, but they fouled it up and there was a shoot-out. Mirnick was killed instantly and Shaffer got himself badly wounded. You heard the shooting, lost your head, and drove off before Shaffer could reach the car.'

'Four men took part in that robbery.' Novak whispered hoarsely. 'Lieutenant Caskey said so. I heard it on the radio.'

'Yeah, I know.' Delgado pursed his lips and blew a smoke ring towards the ceiling. 'As a matter of fact, that was my theory, and I've changed my mind. I believe only three men were involved – Shaffer, Mirnick and you.'

'There were four.'

'I'm prepared to settle for three, and you know something, Larry? That's quite a coincidence, because you'll be a three-time loser.'

'You think I don't know that?' Novak licked his lips. His face had turned white and there was a nervous tic below his left eye. 'Look, if I give you some names, do we have a deal?'

It was the opening Delgado had been working toward, but there was a little matter of ethics. It would be difficult to deliver the assurance Novak was looking for, and he thought it only right to lay his cards on the table.

'Maybe you weren't directly involved, Larry, but we both know you set it up. Now I don't know if the DA will agree to waive a charge of conspiracy, but I'll certainly make a strong recommendation to that effect. Of course, you'd have to be very cooperative, which means giving evidence in court.'

Delgado hoped it wouldn't come to that. A good lawyer would crucify Novak in cross-examination. The defence might also try to infer that the police had deliberately used him as an agent provocateur.

'You don't give a man much choice, do you, Ben?'

'I'm not pushing you, Larry,' Delgado said quietly.

'No, I guess you aren't.' Novak drummed his fingers on the table, beating a nervous tattoo. 'George Eltsberg and Heine Kalmbach,' he said presently. 'They're the guys you want. George lives in Brooklyn, but I don't know where Kalmbach hangs out. He used to be a prizefighter.'

Delgado produced a notebook and pencil and placed them in front of Novak. 'You want to write down his address, Larry?'

There was a momentary hesitation and then Novak picked up the pencil and printed Eltsberg's address in a shaky hand. 'What happens now, Ben?' he asked anxiously.

'Well, I'll phone Lieutenant Caskey and he'll arrange to have you transferred to our jurisdiction. Provided there are no hitches, we'll then take you back to the 18th Precinct with us and get your statement in writing.'

'Yeah, that's what I figured.' Novak eyed the packed of Chesterfields on the table. 'Can I bum a smoke from you, Ben?'

'Sure.' Delgado flicked the packet at him. 'In fact, you can have what's left.'

Delgado reckoned he could afford to be generous. Thanks to Novak they had cracked the case in record time. It was a natural assumption, but in truth, Delgado had seen only the tip of the iceberg. Although he didn't know it yet, the Ziggermann affair was far from being a closed book.

The apartment in Washington Mews, which Virginia Canford shared with two other girls, dwarfed any flat Anderson had seen in England. The living room alone ran to some thirty by twenty-five feet, but even so it was proving inadequate on this occasion. By eight-thirty the party had spilled over into the hall and was rapidly encroaching on the kitchen. Half the servicemen stationed in New York appeared to have been invited, and there was a strong contingent of nurses from a navy hospital in Brooklyn. There were also a few civilians and their wives, neighbours from above and below whose presence ensured there would be no complaints about the noise.

One of the first to arrive, Anderson had been gradually eased farther and farther back into the room until finally he'd wound up in a corner. Penned in on all sides, he had then been buttonholed by a Mr. Ralph Inglis, who turned out to be one of Virginia's neighbours. An earnest little man in his early thirties, Inglis had been determined to explain why he wasn't in uniform. The reasons were complicated, but toward the end of a long-winded discourse, Anderson had gathered that, apart from his wife and three children to support, Inglis also had a slight heart murmur. He had seemed so guilty about it that Anderson had felt compelled to say that no doubt he was engaged in essential war work, which proved to be a big mistake, because Inglis had then proceeded to tell him all about his job with the Office of Price Administration.

Once started, there was no stopping him. The recital went on and on until there was very little he didn't know about the man, his wife or his whole family. The ice cubes in Anderson's scotch melted away to nothing and he began to regret having accepted Virginia's invitation. A silent prayer that somebody would rescue him was answered by a freckled-faced girl with an upturned nose.

'Hi,' she said. 'My name's Judy Usmar. You must be Lieutenant Commander John Anderson. Right?'

'Yes. How did you know?'

'That's easy – you're the only Royal Navy man here.' One eye closed in a broad wink. 'Besides, I'm one of Virginia's roommates and she's told me a lot about you.'

There wasn't much he could say to that without seeming either coy or downright vain. Judy Usmar was a good head shorter, and across the crowded room he could see Virginia dancing with a tall, broad-shouldered marine.

'Aren't you curious to know what she said?' Judy smiled up at him, her head tilted slightly on one side.

'Not really,' he said.

'Uh huh. Well, keep it up, you're doing fine so far.'

'What?'

'With your technique,' said Judy. 'The fact that you don't appear to be too interested in her is the thing that interests Ginny. You follow me?'

'Ginny?' he murmured, ducking the question. 'Is that what you call her?'

'It's a nickname she got at Bryn Mawr. Anyway, as I said, Ginny is used to having men chase after her, but you're different and that's why she's intrigued.'

'I think you're having me on.' Anderson smiled. 'In fact, I know you are.'

'You want to bet?' Judy seized his free hand and turned to Inglis. 'You will excuse us, won't you, Ralph?' she said brightly. 'There's someone who's dying to meet John.'

Anderson thought the lie so blatant and transparent that he almost felt sorry for Ralph, who nodded and smiled indulgently. Keeping a tight grip on his hand, Judy threaded her way across the room until finding a space near the hall, she stopped and turned to face him.

'You have an empty glass, John,' she said, and made it sound like an accusation. 'What are you drinking?'

'Scotch on the rocks.'

'Okay, you stay right there and I'll fix you another.'

'I thought someone was dying to meet me,' Anderson said with a mocking grin.

'Someone is.'

'Like who?'

'Turn round and see for yourself,' said Judy.

Even before Anderson did so, he knew that Virginia was standing behind him. The crush of people in the room had raised the temperature to the point where he felt like a boiled lobster, but she looked very cool and very elegant in a sleeveless blue dress cut on simple lines.

'Enjoying the party?' she asked softly.

'I am now,' he said.

Paul Webber was hard pressed to recall an evening when the time had passed so slowly, nor could he remember dating anyone who was quite so insipid as Cynthia Langdon. She was heavy going, for she lacked charm and was utterly humourless, but taking her out was one way of repaying the Langdons for their hospitality on Thanksgiving Day. But there had also been an ulterior motive, one that had to do with Times Square and the scaled-down replica of the Statue of Liberty.

Always a cautious man, Webber's natural anxiety to preserve his cover had become almost paranoic following his meeting with Christel Zolf on Wednesday night. It was this newfound mania for secrecy that had convinced him it would be taking an unjustifiable risk to reconnoitre the target area on his own. He needed a companion in case some eager patrolman suspected he was loitering with intent and decided to question him. Cynthia Langdon would turn no one's head and she filled the bill perfectly.

After cocktails at the Algonquin, he'd taken her to the Music Box and then on to Sardi's for a late night dinner.

'It was absolutely marvellous, Paul.'

After such a long period of silence, Webber wasn't quite sure whether Cynthia was referring to the show or the dinner. Noticing that her plate was empty, he made a stab at it and guessed wrong.

'No, I meant the play, silly. Weren't Oscar Homolka and Mady Christians absolutely wonderful in their parts? I should think *I Remember Mama* will be a huge success.'

'I guess it's likely to enjoy a long run.' Webber groped for something else to say and then added, 'of course, I'm no judge. I don't go to the theatre very often these days. Somehow, I never seem to have the time.'

'Because of your job?' she suggested.

'Yes. Most of the younger men went off to the war, so we're short of pilots. Other airlines have the same problem.'

'How long have you been with National Eastern, Paul?'

'Eight years,' he said. 'I'm almost the most senior captain they have – a regular greybeard.'

'You look much too young to fit that description,' Cynthia said coyly.

Flattery will get you nowhere, he thought, especially when there's hardly a grain of truth in it. He was forty-three years old and looked it. His light brown hair was decidedly thin on top and there were crow's feet at the corners of his eyes. A couple of inches under six feet, he weighed a hundred and seventy-five pounds, and although he watched his diet and exercised whenever possible, the spare flesh around his waist refused to go away.

'Yours is a minority view,' he said and smiled.

'That doesn't alter my opinion.'

First she had bored him to tears, now she was doing her best to embarrass him.

'Would you like some coffee?' he asked quickly.

'No, I don't think so, Paul. Coffee always keeps me awake at night.' Cynthia glanced at the tiny gold watch that encircled her thin wrist. 'My word,' she breathed, 'just look at the time.'

It was the moment Webber had been longing for all evening and he swivelled round to his right, hoping to catch the waiter's eye. As he did so, his leg brushed against hers and much to his surprise, Cynthia did not react in the way he would have expected. Instead of withdrawing, she pressed her thigh against his and stared straight ahead, her chest rising as she breathed a little faster. The invitation was obvious and would lead to complications unless he did something about it. Cynthia Langdon had served a purpose, but from now on he would keep her at arm's length. The fact that she was unattractive had nothing to do with it. His decision was based on the need for secrecy, hardened by the knowledge that sometime during the next three weeks Christel Zolf would tell him how and when he was to establish contact with U 195. In view of the risks involved in that, Webber simply couldn't afford to have a close relationship with anybody.

CHAPTER 12

Latitude 62 degrees 35 minutes north
Longitude 2 degrees 12 minutes west
Approximate position at 1830 Central European time,
30 nautical miles due west of Shetland Island.
Winds northeast, Gale 9.

Sunday, 26 November 1944

'The weather is very bad and, as was predicted, U 195 has shown a marked tendency to pitch and roll. The Shetlands are maintaining their usual reputation. The water in this area is exceptionally rough and the army personnel have suffered accordingly. With the exception of Major Galen, the entire detachment has been prostrate with seasickness for the second day running. The atmosphere in the bow accommodation room is absolutely foul, the smell of vomit almost overpowering.

'Today's run has been disappointing, although not altogether surprising, given the circumstances. Oberleutnant Werner Best has calculated that we have made barely eighty-four nautical miles, whereas we achieved just over twice that distance in the previous twenty-four hours. The adverse weather conditions are partly to blame for our slow progress, but the main reason is that within eight hours of leaving Bergen, it was no longer safe to cruise on the surface, even at night.

'Intense enemy air and naval activity has forced us to remain submerged, which is no more than I expected, and it is my intention to proceed with the utmost caution until we are clear of the Great Circle route. I doubt if this will meet with the approval of Major Galen, but as long as we maintain wireless silence there is very little he can do about it other than make himself thoroughly unpleasant ...'

'I'm not disturbing you, am I, Erich?'

Hartmann looked up, one arm surreptitiously hiding the diary from Galen's view as the artillery officer pushed the curtain aside and stepped into his cabin. 'Not in the least, Reinhard,' he said in a voice heavy with ivory. 'I'm always available.'

'Good. Then perhaps I may claim a few minutes of your valuable time?' Without waiting to be asked, Galen sat down beside him and came straight to the point. 'I'm rather concerned that we haven't made better progress. I know the trials were completed a day ahead of schedule, but at our present slow speed it won't be long before this gain is wiped out.'

Although Galen couldn't have seen the log, he sounded very sure of his facts, and there was only one conclusion Hartmann could draw from that. The man had obviously been talking to one of his officers, probably Leutnant zur See Dietrich. Karl-Hans was somewhat young and gullible and certainly naïve enough not to realize when he was being pumped for information.

'I wouldn't worry about it if I were you, Reinhard,' Hartmann said coolly. 'We'll make up whatever time is lost once we're clear of the shipping lanes.'

'I'm glad to hear it. Perhaps you can also set my mind at rest on another point?' Galen stared at the photograph on the shelf above Hartmann's bunk, his eyes narrowing thoughtfully. 'I refer of course to our radio. I'm told we can receive but not transmit.'

'There's nothing wrong with the set,' Hartmann said quietly.

'I see. You just took it upon yourself to disobey orders, is that it?'

'This is our thirteenth patrol and I'm not about to commit suicide because some desk-bound idiot in Berlin wants to move a pin on a map. If you can convince me that you have a vital message for OKH, I'll order the radio operator to break wireless silence. If not, no one is going to hear a peep from us until we're in safer waters. When we are, you can send a nightly greeting to our beloved Führer, for all I care.'

Hartmann broke off, frowning. To say the least, he had been indiscreet, but undoubtedly that had been Galen's aim. He had deliberately set out to needle him, hoping he would shoot his mouth off.

'I don't want you to get the wrong impression, Reinhard,' Hartmann continued. 'I may not be the Sieg Heil type but I know my duty. I'll get you to within striking distance of the target and bring everybody back safe and sound. You have my word on that.'

'And your impressive war record, Erich.' Galen clapped him on the shoulder, presuming a friendship that didn't and never would exist between them. 'Believe me, I have every confidence in your seamanship. And so, I imagine, have a lot of other people.'

'No captain could ask for a better crew.'

'Oh, I wasn't thinking of them.' Galen's mouth twisted in the semblance of a smile, but his eyes were fixed on the girl in the photograph. 'I had in mind their wives and families.'

'Her name is Jeanne Verlhac,' Hartmann snapped.

'What?'

'The girl in the photograph. Isn't that what you wanted to know? You've been staring at her for the last five minutes.'

'I'm sorry, but I couldn't help admiring her. After all, she is a very attractive young woman.'

'She also happens to be French.' Hartmann stood up and began to edge past Galen. 'Now, if you'll excuse me, I have work to do. Among other things, the batteries have got to be recharged.'

Contrary to popular belief, a U-boat was not capable of remaining submerged indefinitely. Although the type VIIc was the workhorse of the Kriegsmarine, like any other class it had been designed to operate on the surface for most of the time. Indeed, during the early years of the war, the number of occasions when Hartmann had been forced to submerge by the enemy had been so few and far between that he'd found it necessary to hold regular checks to ensure U 195 was still capable of diving. Of course, those had been the 'happy days' when the U-boats had had things pretty

120

much their own way. Nowadays it was a vastly different situation. The war at sea had changed so dramatically in the last eighteen months that they now spent most of their time in the 'cellar'.

Hartmann ducked through the watertight door and entered the control room. As he did so, he noticed that August Peiper had already joined the officer of the watch who, along with two hydroplane operators and a helmsman, manned the control room during silent hours. There was really no need for the chief engineer to be present. He had two engine room artificers, both of whom were quite capable of keeping the boat at periscope depth, but Peiper rarely allowed them to operate the trimming panel. This failure to delegate also applied to Werner Best, although to a lesser extent. By rights, Leutnant zur See Dietrich should have been on watch, but Hartmann assumed the executive officer has sent him off duty when he'd fixed their position at 1830 hours.

'All present and correct, sir,' Best said in a low voice.

'Very good, Werner.' Hartmann positioned himself at the sky-navigation periscope. 'Let's take her up nice and slow.'

Trimmed for neutral buoyancy, U 195 was lying at a depth of twenty-five metres. Blowing the water from the diving tanks with compressed air was one way of bringing her to the surface, but this was only resorted to in an emergency. Although it was a far slower method, using the hydroplanes to do most of the work had one distinct advantage in that it conserved their supply of electricity.

Hartmann watched the illuminated depth gauge and waited until the needle was on the three-metre mark before raising the navigation periscope to sweep the horizon. Visibility was extremely poor and at first he experienced some difficulty in distinguishing sea from sky, but gradually his eyes became accustomed to the prevailing light. The weather up top was even worse than their rolling motion had suggested when they were fully submerged. Lashed by gale-force winds, the sea resembled a boiling cauldron and some of the waves looked higher than an average-sized house.

'You're going to have your work cut out, August,' Hartmann said grimly. 'This is one of the worst storms we've experienced in a long time.'

'It'd take more that a little storm to upset U 195, sir.' Peiper winked at Best. 'I could trim this boat for snorkeling for the middle of a typhoon.'

'I must remember to put that in my book, Best murmured. 'It's the best line I've heard since joining the navy.'

Even under favourable conditions, trimming the boat at periscope depth was a fine art. The balance was so delicate that one seaman walking from bow to stern could upset the equilibrium. Reliable though they were, Peiper was convinced that neither of his two engine room artificers possessed a fine enough judgment to tackle the job properly when the weather was bad. However, although forewarned by Hartmann, Peiper found the task more difficult than he'd expected, and it was a good twenty minutes before he was able to report that the boat was on an even keel. With the rigid snorkel approximate six metres above the surface, the diesel engines then took over from the twin seven hundred and fifty horsepower electric motors.

The rigid snorkel was intended to combat the H2S anti-surface-vessel radar of the long-range Liberators and other aircraft of RAF Coastal Command. It enabled a U-boat to recharge its batteries while submerged, and to that extent it could be counted a success. Its disadvantage was that the air mast was liable to snap off if the speed exceeded six knots, and in consequence the snorkel in no way improved their offensive capability. At six knots they could barely keep pace with a slow convoy, while a fast one left them floundering in its wake. Furthermore, it was extremely difficult to find a convoy in the first place, since the lookouts were restricted by the narrow field of vision afforded by the two periscopes.

In one respect the device was positively dangerous. The snorkel was essentially a breather tube, but the designers had foreseen that in a rough sea it could ship water into the pressurized hull. To prevent this happening, the air mast was capped by a head valve incorporating a large ball cock. A wave surging above the snorkel pushed the ball cock up an inclined plane to effectively seal off the air intake. Once the wave had spent its force, the ball cock was then free to roll down the inclined plane and allow air into the breather tube again. However, as a safety device, the head valve had one serious defect. It gave no prior warning, which meant the diesel engines frequently sucked most of the air out of the boat, creating a near vacuum before they could be shut down.

The diesels had only been running for a few minutes when a large wave swept over the head valve and cut off the air supply. To Hartmann, it seemed as if his chest was being crushed under a giant press. As he reeled away from the navigation periscope, he saw that the other men were similarly affected. Werner Best was staring at him, his eyes bulging from their sockets, while Peiper's face was contorted in agony. Obersteuermann Frick, the chief helmsman, was gasping for breath and both hydroplane operators looked as if they were having an epileptic fit.

The near vacuum was relieved by a gush of cold air as the ball cock rolled down the inclined plane. Hartmann felt his ears pop and the pain gradually subsided in his chest. Still slightly deaf, it was some time before he heard the high-pitched scream.

Best saw the questioning look in his eyes, and said, 'Sounds as if it is coming from somewhere aft.'

Hartmann switched on the intercom and, in a crisp voice, ordered the second watch officer to check the stern accommodation and report his findings to the control room.

'It's probably one of the soldiers,' said Best. 'Either Major Galen, Hauptmann Kleist or Oberfeldwebel Meyer. They're bunking in with the petty officers aft.'

'Well, whoever it is, let's hope the poor devil hasn't suffered any permanent damage.'

'About the diesel engines, sir?' Peiper cleared his throat. 'Shall I give orders to start them up again?'

'And have the same thing happen again?' Hartmann shook his head. 'I think not, August.'

'The batteries are almost exhausted.'

Hartmann didn't need his chief engineer to tell him that. Nor was it necessary for Peiper to point out that they couldn't survive without them, which would be the situation if they were going to spend the following day in the cellar. It would take three hours to recharge the batteries and that was a hell of a long time to be on the surface when they were no great distance from the Shetlands. The Metox receiver was unable to detect an aircraft with H2S, and he had very little faith in the Hohentweil radar although it was better than nothing. Yet, when all was said and done, he was left with no alternative but to surface.

'Get me a sou'wester and oilskins,' he said abruptly.

'We're going to surface?' Best asked in a doubtful voice.

'That's right, Werner. And then I'm going up top to see what it's like outside.'

'I'll come with you.'

'And leave Dietrich in command? If both you and I should be swept overboard, he will be the only executive officer left. Hadn't that possibility occurred to you, Werner?'

'No, sir.'

'No, I thought not ...' Hartmann broke off, suddenly aware that Dietrich had joined them in the control room and had probably overhead every word he'd said. 'My apologies, Karl,' he said quickly. 'My remarks were not intended to be a reflection on your ability. It's just that I think you lack the necessary experience to take command.'

'Yes, sir.' The observation had rankled, but Dietrich was in no position to refute it. He would have to bide his time, wait for the right opportunity and then prove to Hartmann how wrong he was.

'Do you have anything to report?' Hartmann asked.

Dietrich nodded. 'Yes, sir. Hauptmann Kleist is in considerable plain. I'm no doctor but it looks to me as if his eardrumgs have burst.'

'You'd better get hold of the medical chest and do the

best you can for him. Try olive oil. If that doesn't work, give him a shot of morphine.'

Kleist was the V1 expert: If he hadn't fully recovered by the time they reached the target area, the successful outcome of Operation Double Griffin would become even more problematical. Hartmann put the thought out of his mind. Right now he had more important things to attend to.

'Blow one and two main tanks,' he snapped.

Peiper repeated the order and opened two of the direct flow valves. Compressed air screamed through narrow steel pipes to the diving tanks at the bow and stern, forcing out and replace the water so that U 195 surfaced like a whale.

'Start main engines. Half speed ahead both.'

Peiper relayed the instruction to the engine room over the voice pipe and the diesels thundered into life again.

A few minutes later, Best returned with the oilskins and sou'wester. Leaving Hartmann to put them on, he unclipped and opened the hatch to the pressurized cabin above the control room and then stepped back out of the way.

'I wish you'd let me go instead,' he muttered.

'And let you grab all the glory?' Hartmann said with a broad smile. 'Not on your life, Werner. If there are any medals going, I want them. Just close the hatch behind me — all right?'

'Yes, sir.'

'Well, don't look so damned miserable. I'm not dead yet.'

Hartmann made it to the pressurized cabin above the control room, waited until Best had closed the hatch behind him and then opened the upper one to the bridge. Taking a firm foot and handhold on the iron rungs, he went on up.

The spray and wind deflectors on the conning tower might not have been there for all the good they were doing. As he emerged from the hatchway, a wave broke over the bridge and deluged him from head to foot. As he struggled to his feet, the gale-force wind sent him lurching sideways.

Buffeted by the angry sea, U 195 plunged into a trough, tilted over to starboard and slowly righted herself to meet

125

the next wave head on. Wrapping one arm around the navigation periscope to steady himself, Hartmann leaned over the conning tower to see how the ramp was faring. Incredibly, despite the pounding they were taking, the guide rails looked as robust and ugly as ever.

The weather was vile, the worst he could remember, but it would take more than a Force 9 gale to ground the RAF. With its H2S radar, a long-range Liberator could track them down with the same degree of certainty as that shown by a guide dog leading a blind man.

Their own radar was unlikely to give them adequate forewarning of a hostile aircraft. The RAF were wise to that and had perfected a technique to outfox the Hohentweil impulse receiver. As soon as the RAF radar operator had a firm contact, it was usual for him to swtich off the anti-surface-vessel radar and inform the pilot of the approximate position of the U-boat. The pilot then moved into a favourable attacking position while losing height for the run-in over the target. On a dark night such as this, the ASV would probably be switched on and off several times in order to check that the plane was on the correct course, but even so, Hartmann reckoned that they would get precious little warning. Like as not, they would still be on the surface when the Liberator's powerful Leigh Light suddenly cleaved through the darkness and lit them up. If that should happen, they could only stay up top and fight it out.

Hartmann edged his way toward the voice pipe. With the boat rolling from side to side like a bobbing cork, a man could easily be swept overboard, but running blind on the surface was courting certain disaster. Removing the cover, he whistled up the control room and spoke to Werner Best.

'I want two lookouts on the bridge and the 20mm guns on the upper platform manned.'

The executive officer said, 'Yes, sir,' in a voice that was completely emotionless.

'It's pretty rough up here, Werner.' Hartmann turned his back to the wind and wiped his face with a hand that felt like a block of ice. 'Tell Dietrich he's to rig lifelines before he does anything else.

'Leave it to me, sir.'

'I said Dietrich.'

'But he's attending to Hautpmann Kleist, sir,' Best protested stubbornly.

'You are to relieve him,' Hartmann said tersely. 'That's an order.'

Much as he disliked it, there were times when a captain had to play God. He had nothing against Dietrich. On the contrary, the second watch officer was a very likeable young man with some promise, but Werner Best was the more experienced and he couldn't afford to lose his second-in-command. It was as simple as that.

U 195 stayed on the surface for exactly three hours before submerging again at 2230, her batteries fully recharged. The RAF did not molest them, but a price was extracted for their impudence. As the lookouts and gun crews were called below, a huge wave surged over the upper platform and swept gunner's mate Joachim Richter overboard a split second after he had detached himself from the lifeline. He was the first man Hartmann had ever lost at sea.

CHAPTER 13

New York

Tuesday, 28 November 1944

Usually the squad room was pretty crowded, but for once Delgado had the place to himself. The unexpected peace and quiet were exactly what he needed to catch up on the paperwork connected with the Ziggermann holdup. Although Eltsberg and Kalmbach had been arrested in Brooklyn late on Saturday night, he wouldn't have a case unless Novak gave evidence for the prosecution. Kalmbach and Eltsberg weren't talking, and the ex-prizefighter had been clean when the Brooklyn police had picked him up. Neither Jacob Levy, who'd managed the outfitters for

Passaretti, nor the assistant could identify either man, and while Delgado was damn sure Kalmbach had done the shooting, it was a mite hard to prove without a murder weapon.

Novak was the key. If the Assistant District Attorney hadn't tied one hand behind his back, he could have used Larry to drive a wedge between the two men. The Assistant DA, however, was not prepared to waive the conspiracy charge against Novak, apparently because it was against his principles to make a deal with a known felon. He had hoped that either Lieutenant Caskey or Captain Burns could persuade the stupid son of a bitch to see reason, but so far they hadn't succeeded in budging him one inch. As a result, Delgado had spent the whole of Monday pounding up and down Eleventh Avenue and West 48th hoping to find a witness who could help him nail Kalmbach and Eltsberg. All he had to show for it was a mass of shorthand notes that now had to be typed up for Caskey's benefit.

The extra work would serve no useful purpose. If the Assistant DA refused to change his mind. Kalmbach and Eltsberg would be released on bail and the case against them would eventually go by default. Things hadn't been going too well for Delgado lately and that would be another blot on his copy book. He had too many unsolved cases already. For instance, there was Mr. Ambrose, the outraged bank clerk who'd had his wallet lifted. The special antipickpocket squad had had a bonanza on Thanksgiving Day, but they hadn't netted the guy who'd done Ambrose, which made for one very aggrieved citizen. Ambrose was also sour because the Office of Price Administration was being difficult about the gas coupons he'd lost, and he appeared to blame Delgado and the entire Police Department for that.

A telephone disturbed the peace and quiet. It rang several times and then stopped, but after a brief interval another phone trilled in its place. By a process of elimination, the caller finally got around to the extension on Delgado's desk.

Answering it, he heard the desk sergeant say. 'It's me –

128

Frank Toomis. Where the hell is everybody, Ben?'

'Out,' said Delgado.

'I already know that. What are they doing? Drinking in a bar someplace?'

'Don't you ever read the newspapers, Frank?' Delgado said wearily. 'There was an epidemic of safecracking in Manhattan and the Bronx over the weekend. More than thirteen grand was taken from seven different safes. One of them happened to be in our area.'

'And it takes the whole squad to investigate one lousy break-in?'

Ganley was out doing a follow-up on West 48th and the other detectives had a full case load, but it was futile to explain that to Toomis. Frank Toomis had come up from patrolman and was within two years of retirement. It was a sore point with him that early on in his career, somebody had decided he would never make a detective. As a result, he never missed an opportunity to take it out on anybody who had.

'All right, Frank,' said Delgado, 'you've had your little joke. Now tell me what's bothering you.'

'I've got a British naval officer here by the name of Anderson. He's asking for that Limey soldier we picked up last night.'

'So?'

'So he's kind of ruffled because we no longer have the jerk.' Toomis lowered his voice until it was barely audible. 'Do me a favour, Ben, explain the situation to him. I only know half the story. Lieutenant Caskey took this Yates guy down to the 14th Precinct, but he neglected to tell me why.'

Suddenly Toomis began to make sense. Yates was an anti-aircraft gunner serving with a detachment on board the SS *Queenstown Bay*, a British merchantman that had sailed in convoy on Saturday. He had been posted as a deserter after the ship had left New York, and the naval authorities had asked the Police Department to keep an eye out for him.

'I think you ought to see Anderson, Ben. After all, it was your head man who fouled up the situation.'

The desk sergeant had an unhappy knack of rubbing everybody the wrong way, but Delgado had learned to live with it and keep his temper. 'Okay then, you'd better send Anderson up to me,' he said tersely. 'Maybe I can straighten things out with him.'

Delgado put the phone down and looked at the battered coffee percolator which he kept in the bottom drawer of his desk. Measuring two heaping spoonfuls of ground coffee into the percolator, he filled the pot from the water cooler and then placed it on the electric ring, the most valuable and most used piece of equipment the squad possessed.

Anderson? The name rang a bell. Delgado snapped his fingers: Wednesday night at the Polyclinic Hospital when Ganley had dragged him from home to see Shaffer's body. He remembered Ganley telling him that one of the witnesses to the traffic accident had been a Lieutenant Commander John Anderson of the Royal Navy. It had to be the same guy.

'Detective Delgado?'

'That's me.' Delgado turned and faced the newcomer with a smile. 'And you must be Lieutenant Commander Anderson. Right?'

He liked the look of what he saw. Anderson was about the same height as himself, an inch under six foot. His face, while not exactly handsome, looked strong and seemed to match his firm handshake. Delgado had a theory that you could tell what a person was like by his handshake; if a man offer you a limp hand, he probably had a weak character to go with it.

'Would you like a cup of coffee? It'll have to be black – I'm out of cream.'

'Black will suit me fine,' said Anderson.

'Good. Sit yourself down.' Delgado moved the typewriter to one side and brought another chair up to his desk. 'This isn't the first time you've been here, is it, Commander?'

Anderson looked surprised. 'You must be confusing me with someone else.'

'Weren't you a witness to the traffic accident on Eighth Avenue last Wednesday night?'

130

'Yes, I was there with Lieutenant Canford. One of your policeman took our names and addresses. He said an officer would call round to Battery Place and take a statement from us. That was the last we heard about it. I presume somebody decided that three eyewitnesses were sufficient.'

'Three?' Delgado asked sharply.

'The cab driver and the two passengers – a man and a woman.'

Delgado frowned. He was pretty sure Ganley had only mentioned one fare – a Captain Paul Webber of National Eastern Airlines. Not that a missing witness was either here or there. The traffic department had already cleared the cab driver of blame and the case was dead and buried along with Shaffer. Nevertheless, he made a mental note to look into it, if only to satisfy his curiosity.

'About Gunner Yates ...' said Anderson.

'Oh yeah, the soldier. You want to take him into naval custody?'

'That's why I'm here. I've got two escorts downstairs.'

'Well, I'm afraid it's not that straightforward, Commander. It just so happens you're not the only one who wants him.'

'I see. What's he done?'

'We may know the answer to that after the lineup.' Delgado walked over to the cooler and removed two paper cups from the dispenser. The coffee was not boiling yet, but the diversion gave him time to consider how he was going to smooth things over with Anderson. 'How much does your army pay a guy like Yates?' he asked.

'Four shillings and sixpence a day.'

'What's that in dollars?'

'About ninety cents,' said Anderson.

'Ninety cents, huh?' Delgado whislted softly. 'You know something, Commander? When our guys searched him, Yates had a little over seventy-five dollars in his pockets.'

'Well, he certainly didn't come by that honestly.'

'He has a record then?'

'As long as your arm. Yates did two spells in Borstal before he was sixteen. That was followed by six months' imprisonment for theft and one of two years with hard labour for grievous bodily harm.'

'What exactly is Borstal?' Delgado asked.

'Reform school,' said Anderson. 'Yates was released from prison in 1941. That was when the army got him, which they've probably regretted ever since because he's a bloody awful soldier.

That was something of an understatement. Yates had spent more time in the brig than he had on the barrack square. His regimental conduct sheet ran to several pages and included nearly every petty crime in the Manual of Military Law. He was the kind of man commanding officers were anxious to get rid of at the first opportunity, and the records showed that he had been transferred from one unit to another until finally some bright spark had wished him on to the Marine Artillery Regiment.

'So why didn't your army give him a dishonourable discharge?'

'Because I imagine they believed that that was just what Yates wanted,' said Anderson.

'Yeah, well he's still a load of grief. One of our patrolmen picked him up for being drunk and disorderly.'

'Yes, so I heard.' Anderson smiled. 'Don't you think it's time you stopped pussyfooting around and get to the point?'

'The point is that a couple of pansies got rolled late on Saturday night within a block of Sixth Avenue and 18th Street. Yates could be the guy who worked them over. Anyway, Lieutenant Caskey took him down to the 14th Precinct so that they could put him in a lineup.' Delgado poured out the coffee and returned to the desk with a paper cup in each hand. 'I'm afraid you've had a wasted journey. Commander, because nobody here thought to inform the navy. It wasn't very smart of us and you've every right to be sore with the Police Department.'

There had been a fuck-up and Anderson knew it wasn't Delgado's fault. The detective was taking the flak on behalf of his superiors, but unlike others Anderson had met in similar situations, he hadn't attempted to dissociate

132

himself from blame. Instead, he had been frank and open about it, shouldering a responsibility that wasn't his. Anderson liked him for that.

'Our image must be pretty tarnished as far as you're concerned,' Delgado said casually. 'I mean Frank Toomis didn't make you feel exactly welcome, did he?'

'Toomis?'

'The desk sergeant downstairs.'

'Oh, him. Well, I've met .abrasive characters like Sergeant Toomis before. They don't bother me.'

The faint smile didn't soften the steely glint in Anderson's eyes and Delgado sensed he was not a man to cross swords with unless you were aching for trouble. He had a distinct feeling that Anderson would not have hesitated to make life unpleasant for Frank Toomis had the desk sergeant gone too far.

'And then there was the traffic accident.' Delgado raised the paper cup to his lips and drank a mouthful of coffee. 'I mean, it isn't often we find members of the public who are willing to help the police. The least we could have done was let you know we didn't need a statement from you and Miss Canford.'

'There's no need to feel bad about that. It's possible I misunderstood the officer. He could easily have said that somebody might call round to Battery Place.'

'I don't think your memory is at fault, Commander.' Delgado finished his coffee and dropped the empty cup into the wastebasket. 'You were pretty definite about the number of witnesses – the cab driver, the man and ... the woman.'

The slight pause suggested that Delgado thought he could have been wrong about the woman, and immediately Anderson launched into a description of her, recalling that she'd been wearing a navy blue coat cut on military lines but that he was unable to describe her face because she had been looking the other way. Her hair was probably light brown but he couldn't be certain about that, because it had been combed back and was largely hidden by a peaked cap similar in style and shape to the Wac's. At a rough guess, he said he thought she was in her mid-thirties.

Delgado said, 'That's not a bad description considering you only caught a glimpse of her.'

'She's not a figment of my imagination.'

'Did I say she was, Commander?'

Delgado hadn't, at least not in so many words, but he'd certainly implied as much. Anderson wasn't sure what to make of his attitude. A few minutes ago the detective had gone out of his way to encourage him to describe the girl, whereas now he seemed totally disinterested in her.

'I'm sorry we wasted your time.' Delgado smiled and slowly got to his feet. 'But I promise we'll keep you posted about Yates from now on.'

'I'd sooner you got in touch with the executive officer at the escort base on Staten Island.' Anderson downed the rest of his coffee and moved his chair back. 'He's the man who's really interested. I only came her to collect Yates as a favour.'

'That's always the way, isn't it?' Delgado said cheerfully. 'You do some guy a good turn and end up regretting it.'

Following Anderson out into the corridor. Delgado shook hands again, said what a pleasure it had been to meet him and then returned to his desk. The notes he'd been typing for Lieutenant Caskey would serve little purpose, but being a methodical man, he doggedly completed them before asking the clerical office for the report on the traffic accident. Although the conncection between the woman Anderson had described and the Ziggermann case was both remote and somewhat irrelevant, he knew he wouldn't rest until his curiosity had been satisfied.

As it turned out, the report was inconclusive. The only woman to appear among the witnesses was Lieutenant (j.g.) Virginia Canford, but that didn't prove Anderson had been mistaken. If Anderson was right, as Delgado believed he was, then Webber had certainly acted very strangely. He wondered what his wife, Gina, would make of his behaviour. It was a standing joke in the family that Gina was the one who should have been the detective. With her intuition, she had an uncanny knack of pointing him in the right direction, even if she didn't come up with the solution.

Lifting the phone off the hook, he called Gina at the office where she worked and arranged to meet her for lunch at the Hickory House on East 48th.

Hickory House was a convenient place to meet Gina because she was employed by a firm of advertising agents whose offices were in Rockefeller Centre. It wasn't far out of his way either, but they rarely met for lunch. Different working hours saw to that.

Arriving a little early, Delgado found a corner table near the cashier where he knew she couldn't miss him and settled down to wait. Barely five minutes later and punctual as always, Gina walked into the restaurant and greeted him with a warm smile.

'This is a lovely surprise, Ben,' she said. 'We ought to meet for lunch more often.'

'I wish we could, honey, but you know how it is with me. I never know from one day to the next what I'll be doing.' Delgado handed her the menu. 'What do you fancy?' he asked.

'Oh, something light – a cheeseburger with a side salad. I have to watch my figure.'

'Me too,' said Delgado. 'I think I'll have a club sandwich.'

Gina smiled. 'All right, Ben,' she said indulgently, 'let's hear it.'

'Hear what?'

'You've obviously got some problem that's bugging you.'

'How well you know me.' Delgado gave their order to a waiter and then turned to face Gina again. 'It's the Ziggermann case,' he said. 'I've run up against a brick wall and now I think I'm going down a blind alley.'

As briefly as he could, he told her about Anderson and the mix-up over the number of witnesses. He also said that he thought Webber had behaved very strangely and then waited for her reaction.

'I think you're making a mountain out of a molehill, Ben. If you want my opinion, Webber is probably having an affair with a married woman, and he couldn't afford to have their names appear in the newspapers in case her husband saw the report. That's why he told her to disappear.'

'What about the cab driver?'

'I daresay Webber made it worth his while to forget she was there. That's what I would have done in his place.'

Gina could be right; certainly her theory fitted all the facts, such as they were. Yet, for all her undeniable logic, Delgado didn't buy the explanation. There was nothing he could put his finger on, but, although it was wholly irrational, a gut feeling told him there was more to the incident than met the eye.

'You want to know something, Ben?'

Delgado looked up and smiled blankly at Gina, unable to follow the drift of her conversation.

'You're working too hard. We hardly ever go out these days because you're always so beat when you come home. For instance, when did we last see a movie?'

'You tell me,' he said.

'That's just it, I can't remember.'

'Is there anything worth seeing?'

'*Meet Me in St. Louis* opens at the Astor tonight. Judy Garland's in it and she's your favourite movie star.'

'Okay – you've talked me into it. Let's get a baby-sitter in and go tonight. How about that?'

Gina told him a baby-sitter wasn't necessary. Francesca was thirteen years old and quite capable of looking after Matthew. Furthermore, she would resent it if the job was given to a girl not much older than herself.

One domestic problem had been solved, but it seemed there were others Gina wanted to talk about. Among other things, she was keen to know if he'd given any thought to what presents they should give the children for Christmas. Delgado tried to be helpful but he found it difficult to keep his mind off Webber. Although Gina's explanation would have satisfied most people, he couldn't accept it. Caskey wouldn't thank him for delving into the traffic accident, but as soon as time permitted, he intended to look up the cab driver and have a few words with him. What was his name?

Janowski? Delgado smiled. Yeah, that was the guy, Leon
Janowski.

'You thought of something, Ben?'

'A train set,' Delgado said hastily. 'Matthew would like
that.'

'I was talking about Francesca,' Gina said with a sigh.

CHAPTER 14

Latitude 59 degrees 13 minutes north
Longitude 11 degrees 45 minutes west
Approximate position at noon,
510 naturical miles SSE of Reykjavik, Iceland.

Thursday, 30 November 1944

Of the five crosses Hartmann had marked on the chart in
pencil, only one denoting the position of U 195 was an
accurate fix. With one exception, the others were an
educated guess based on information received from the
Beobachtungs-Dienst, the signals intercept service of the
Kriegsmarine. The exception was U 234, the converted
type XB minelayer which had sailed from Trondheim on
Thursday, 23 November, exactly twenty-four hours
ahead of U 195. The sealed orders Hartmann had received
from Kapitän zur See Wirth merely indicated where and
when they were to rendezvous with the 'milk cow', but
unlike him, the commander of U 234 had not imposed
wireless silence. Yesterday, shortly before midnight, they
had picked up a brief transmission from U 234
acknowledging the B-Dienst intelligence report and, as a
result, had obtained a bearing on her. Although the bearing
gave only a rough indication of her position, Hartmann
deduced that U 234 had sailed due west from Trondheim to
pass south of the Faroes before turning southwest.

'I reckon our "milk cow" is now approximately fifty
nautical miles to the west of us and roughly on a parallel

course.' Hartman glanced at Galen who was sitting on his left. 'However, I wouldn't like to swear to that. There are too many imponderables to fix her position with any real accuracy.'

'And the other three crosses, Erich?' Galen described a circle on the chart with his index finger. 'Are they also equally uncertain?'

'I've had to guess the enemy's course and speed from the information supplied by the B-Dienst.'

'Nevertheless, you're fairly sure that we are on a collision course with two eastbound convoys and a naval task force?'

'No,' Hartmann shook his head, 'No, that isn't quite correct. We can forget the second convoy. That's SC 189, a slow eastbound which departed from New York on the twenty-fifth of November, and it's most unlikely that our paths will cross.'

'Even so, it's not exactly a comforting picture, is it?'

'We'll need to watch out step.'

Galen rubbed his chin, feeling the week-old beard, The water supply was rigidly controlled and the amount they were allowed each day was just sufficient for a man to wash his face and hands. Shaving was a luxury not even a field officer was permitted to enjoy, as Hartmann had pointed out to him with some vehemence when he'd complained about the meager ration.

'Can you rely on the information provided by the B-Dienst, Erich?' he asked presently.

While the signals intercept service was not infallible, it was the most efficient branch of the Kriegsmarine. From the Tirpitzufer in Berlin, some forty-five teleprinters received transmissions picked up by listening stations as far afield as Hammerfest in northern Norway to Seville in Spain, a secret post that the Franco government conveniently ignored. In an average month, some two thousand messages would be logged and decoded by the cipher experts. Occasionally, the volume of work was such that a signal was overlooked, but never a Munich Blue. A Munich Blue was the nickname given to a particular type of code used by the British to order a convoy to change course

138

and warn them of known U-boat positions. There were three other main ciphers which, although referred to as Cologne, Frankfurt and Munich Red by the B-Dienst, conveyed little or nothing to Hartmann.

Hartmann said, 'I've never known the signals intercept service to be wrong yet, Reinhard.'

Galen made no comment. Instead, he pointed to one of the crosses and said. 'How far are we from that particular convoy?'

Using a pair of dividers, Hartmann measured the separation distance. 'Roughly three hundred and seventy-five naturical miles.'

'Then what the hell are we worried about?' Galen demanded angrily.

'U.S. Navy Task Force 223.' Hartmann jabbed the dividers into the chart, skewering it to the table underneath. 'According to intelligence, that hunter-killer group consists of the destroyers *Pillsbury, Pope, Flaherty, Jenks* and *Chatelain* plus the aircraft carrier *Guadalcanal.*'

'Then I don't envy the crew of U 234.'

Galen appeared to draw some comfort from the knowledge that the 'milk cow' was between them and the enemy, but to see U 234 in the role of a decoy duck was to ignore the facts of life. The surface vessels of Task Force 223 were only a minor threat. Nowadays, the side which had command of the air controlled the seas below. Choosing his words carefully Hartmann explained to Galen just why they would be forced to take evasive action until the danger had passed.

Oberfeldwebel Ernst Meyer clenched his jaws as another spasm gripped his stomach. The pains had started an hour ago, waking him from the first decent sleep he'd had since their departure from Bergen. It had taken him five days to find his sea legs, five long, miserable days of going without food because he couldn't keep anything down. One of the petty officers had changed places with him so that he could have a bottom bunk and they had stuck a pail within easy reach in case he was taken short and vomited onto the deck.

139

Five days when he'd thought he was at death's door and now, just when he was feeling better, the bloody cook had done his best to poison him.

It must have been the cold sausage he'd eaten for breakfast. He remembered thinking at the time that it had tasted sour, but he'd put it down to the aftermath of seasickness. But it was strange that nobody else had been affected. Either they had stronger stomachs or else his sausage had been the only one that had been off. Another spasm gripped his stomach and he rolled over onto his left side.

Hauptmann Kleist was lying on his back in a bunk diagonally across from him on the port side of the boat. Meyer thought the Hauptmann looked as grim as he felt. His face was the colour of old parchment, the skin yellow and stretched tight as a drum across his prominent cheekbones. His eyes were open, almost bulging out of their sockets, as they had been ever since Sunday night when his eardrums had been ruptured. There was nothing anyone could do for Kleist except give him a quarter grain of morphine each day to dull the pain, but if his contorted features were anything to go by, it seemed that even that rough-and-ready treatment wasn't as effective now as it had been.

Meyer felt his stomach grip again and he knew he wouldn't be able to control his bowels much longer. Scrambling out of the bunk, he made his way forward, trying to move quietly so as not to disturb the off-duty men, all of whom were sound asleep. The second officer, Leutnant zur See Dietrich, was on watch in the control room, but he had his nose buried in a technical manual and took no notice of him. Neither did the two hydroplane operators, and while Meyer thought the helmsman muttered something, he didn't catch it. In any case, he was in too much of a hurry to pass the time of day with him.

As he hurried past the captain's cabin, he heard two men talking behind the drawn curtain and immediately recognized Galen's voice. Much as Meyer wanted to, his bowels wouldn't allow him to eavesdrop on their

140

conversation. Reaching the toilet in the bow accommodation room, he locked the door behind him and dropped his pants.

Diarrhoea seemed to be an occupational hazard with the army. Meyer had had several bad attacks during the late spring of '43 when he was serving on the Russian front. He'd been a field gunner back in those days, a sergeant in an artillery battalion equipped with the type 18 light howitzer. Mobility was supposed to be the keynote of war, but their guns had been horse-drawn artillery against T34 tanks and SU guns. He hadn't fancied their chances at Kursk and getting wounded by a shell splinter had been a lucky break for him. It had kept him out of Operation Citadel, the offensive which was intended to eliminate the Russian salient at Kursk, but had resulted in a death ride for the Panzers and the total annhilation of his artillery battalion.

Discharged from the hospital, he'd faced the prospect of returning to the Eastern front with a grim resignation when, to his utter amazement, he was selected to attend a V1 conversion course run by the 155th Flak Regiment. Meyer had thought his transfer to the long-range bombardment organization the best thing to have happened to him since joining the army, but now he wasn't so sure. Apart from the fact that he wasn't cut out to be a sailor, he was also convinced that Double Griffin was just about the craziest and most hazardous operation of all time.

Meyer adjusted his clothing and turned about to find himself confronted with two levers. He remembered Obersteuermann Frick telling him that U 195 was one of the few boats to be equipped with a high pressure 'thunder box', a somewhat complicated mechanism designed to overcome the problem of flushing the toilet when they went below a depth of twenty-five metres. He also recalled that Frick had said the levers had to be pulled in a certain order, otherwise there would be an unpleasant accident. The chief helmsman had claimed the system was so damned tricky that only somebody who'd been on a special course was capable of operating it, but that sounded like a tall story to him.

Meyer stared at the two levers and wondered if he should seek advice. Deciding he would never hear the last of it if he did, he made a rapid choice and pulled the left hand one. A powerful jet of water struck him in the chest with such force that he staggered back against the door. Reacting swiftly, he made a frantic grab for the other lever, hoping to correct the error before they were flooded out, but for some reason it had the reverse effect. The flood continued unabated and within a matter of seconds the toilet was ankle deep in water. Backing out of the head, he ran aft toward the control room to get help.

For Leutnant Dietrich, the opportunity to prove himself in Hartmann's eyes had arrived sooner than he could have hoped. There was no need for Meyer to explain anything. Observing the stream of water spreading across the deck of the bow accommodation room, Dietrich guessed what had happened and immediately ordered the hydroplane operators to take the boat up to periscope depth. It was the only thing he could do in the circumstances. With U 195 lying at a depth of eighty metres, he knew it was impossible to close the valves until the high-water pressure had been relieved.

Hartmann waved a hand in Galen's face, silencing him in midsentence. A few moments ago, somebody had run past the cabin and now he could hear Dietrich shouting in the control room. Suddenly, there was a surge of power from the electric motors and then a pencil started to roll down the chart in front of him.

'He's altered our trim.'

'Who had?' demanded Galen.

'Dietrich.' Hartmann struggled to his feet. 'He's taking us up to the surface.'

Galen drew back the curtain and stepped out into the passageway to make room for him. From somewhere up forward a seaman was cursing in a voice loud enough to wake the dead. Other voices joined in, raising a howl of protest that Galen found incomprehensible, until glancing down at his jackboots, he saw to his horror that the deck was awash.

By the time Hartmann and Galen entered the control room, Dietrich had already taken what steps he could to rectify the situation. The engine room had been alerted and two mechanics were standing by to shut the valves as soon as they reached periscope depth. There were, however, certain factors that were beyond anybody's power to control. The forward battery room was directly below the head and the decking between the two compartments consisted of a number of steel plates riveted to cross members. They were still sixty metres below the surface when the overspill from the toilet began to seep through the joints.

Hartmann was the first to notice the acrid smell, the first to realize that the saltwater dripping onto the batteries was reacting with the sulphuric acid to produce a chlorine gas. Whirling round, he ordered the two mechanics into the bow compartment and then closed the watertight door behind them.

'Stand by to surface,' he rapped. 'Blow tanks one, two and three.'

Dietrich stared at him, his mouth open as if he were having difficulty breathing through his nose. The decisiveness he'd shown earlier had evaporated and there was a danger that his uncertainty would be communicated to the others.

'Blow tanks one, two and three.' Peiper repeated the order as he entered the control room and immediately opened the direct flow valves to blow the diving tanks with compressed air. As far as he was concerned, when Hartmann gave an order you obeyed it, because there was only room for one captain on a U-boat.

Hartmann breathed a sigh of relief. Thank God for August. When faced with a crisis you needed men like him around, men you could depend on. Pushing Dietrich aside, he switched on the tannoy.

'Attention all hands,' Hartmann said calmly. 'This is the

143

captain speaking. Those of you who are forward will know. that the head has been flooded. Some of the saltwater has found its way down to the battery room and is producing a chlorine gas. There is no – repeat no – need to be alarmed. We are about to surface in order to ventilate the interior.'

Hartmann drew a deep breath. So far so good. By explaining the situation to the crew, he had stilled their worst fears and they were unlikely to give way to panic. Now he could begin to think more positively. Lookouts would have to be posted, the 20mm flak guns manned and the radar too. Once the valves had been closed, they could open the lower hatch and allow the gas to disperse. As soon as the concentration had dissipated. Peiper would then have to check the batteries to see how many had been destroyed or damaged. Still using the same measured tones, Hartmann briefed each department in turn, telling them exactly what he wanted done.

U 195 surfaced at 1318 hours. Unclipping the lower hatch, Hartmann climbed into the pressurized cabin and, opening the second hatch, went on up to the bridge, Dietrich, Galen and four lookouts were hard on his heels.

A torpedo mechanic emerged from the fore hatch and stumbled aft toward the conning tower. One by one, the remaining thirty-five men in the bow compartments spilled out onto the foredeck and formed up in line, coughing and retching from the effects of the chlorine gas.

Led by the senior petty officer, the gun crews poured out of the galley hatch behind the conning tower to man the upper and lower platforms. Urged on by Dietrich, it took them exactly two minutes to remove the travelling plugs, break open the watertight ammunition containers, load, cock and elevate the 20mm cannons.

Up on the bridge, Hartmann swept the sky with his powerful Zeiss bincoulars. He thought conditions were favourable, all too favourable for the enemy. The cloud base was fairly high and the visibility moderate-to-good. Turning slowly in a complete circle, he scanned the horizon, looking for a wisp of smoke that would indicate they had company. A breeze was blowing, strong enough to

144

ruffle his hair and raise whitecaps on an otherwise grey and empty sea.

Hartmann lowered his binoculars and removed the cover from the voice pipe. Calling up the helmsman, he checked that they were still on course and then rang 'full ahead' on the telegraph.

'What happens now?' Galen asked him.

'We keep our fingers crossed ...'

Hartmann left the sentence unfinished. The lookouts knew the U-boat was a sitting duck for any marauding aircraft, but no useful purpose would be served by ramming the point home. The atmosphere on the bridge was tense enough without him making the lookouts even more jittery than they already were.

Making a determined effort to appear cheerful and unconcerned, he said, 'However, as the English will have it, every cloud has a silver lining. We're cruising at twelve knots, which will help to put us right back on schedule. We can also charge the batteries in the stern compartment and refill the cyclinders/with compressed air. That should save us a job later.'

'In other words, you're saying that it will take approximately three hours to ventilate the interior and clean up the mess.'

Hartmann glared at Galen. A little knowledge was always a dangerous thing. Galen had learned that it took three hours to recharge the batteries using the snorkel, and from that starting point had proceeded to draw the wrong conclusion.

'Don't put words into my mouth.' Hartmann said in a cold, hard voice. 'It'll take an hour to an hour and a half at the outside.'

Perhaps that was a trifle optimistic, but once the valves had been closed, the bilge pumps would be able to cope with the overspill. Although there was undoubtedly a heavy concentration of chlorine gas in the battery room, that would rapidly disperse when the lower hatch in the bows was opened.

A shrill whistle interrupted his train of thought.

145

Removing the cover from the voice pipe again, Hartmann said, 'Bridge.'

'Control room, Bridge. Radar contact bearing green zero seven five.' Oberleutnant Best swallowed in an attempt to remove the tremour from his voice. 'Range one hundred kilometres, sir.'

Hartmann acknowledged the report and closed the voice pipe. Only simple arithmetic was needed to calculate that the aircraft would be overhead in twenty minutes.

'It could be one of ours,' Galen suggested.

Hartmann thought it extremely unlikely. The Focke Wulf Condors had been withdrawn from the Atlantic following the loss of the U-boat bases in France.

'Maybe the plane will veer away from us, Erich.'

That too was a very remote possibility. The aircraft was either on its way to shadow the fast eastbound convoy or was returning to base. Whatever its mission, the ASV radar would have picked them up and the pilot was certain to make a detour to investigate the contact.

At 1345 hours, Best reported that the aircraft was sixty kilometres away and closing fast. At 1353 hours, Hartmann thought he could see a faint speck on the horizon. Kapitän-leutnant Schlitt had lost U 1206 because somebody had pulled the wrong levers in the high pressure toilet. Now it seemed that history could be about to repeat itself.

CHAPTER 15

Approximate position at 1357 hours,
526 nautical miles SSE of Reykjavik, Iceland.

Thursday, 30 November 1944

Hartmann lowered his binoculars. The Liberator looked as if it was manoeuvring into a favourable attacking position, and he had less than three minutes to decide what he was going to do. With chlorine gas still escaping from the fore

146

hatch, making a crash dive was out of the question. Sooner or later they would have to fight it out, but right now it was essential to gain as much time as they could. That was something which could only be achieved by bluff. Leaning over the bridge, he ordered the seaman on the foredeck casing to wave and shout for all they were worth.

'Are you crazy? What on earth do you think you're doing?'

Galen had seized his arm but Hartmann shook him off and crossed the bridge in a few strides.

'All right, Leutnant Dietrich,' he snapped, 'get your men off the gun platforms.' His voice was sharp and decisive, brooking no questions or interference. 'And be quick about it.'

'Stand fast.' Galen slapped the palm of his hand against the surface attack periscope. 'That's an order, Leutnant Dietrich.'

The outburst confirmed what Hartmann had always suspected. Given their widely different personalities, it was inevitable that Galen would eventually see fit to challenge his authority. It was also perhaps inevitable that he should choose the worst possible moment to do so. There was no time to reason with him; he had to act swiftly and decisively. Galen was standing to one side and slightly behind him. Timing it perfectly. Hartmann jabbed and elbow into his stomach. The blow caught Galen under the heart with enough force to leave him winded.

Hartmann said, 'You heard me, Leutnant. Clear the platforms but have your men ready to man the guns again as soon as I give the word.'

Dietrich hesitated, unable to decide which command to obey. Despite what Hartmann had said, he seemed reluctant to fight it out, and that was the first duty of a U-boat captain. In the end, his dilemma was resolved by the senior gunner who climbed down from the lower platform and was quickly followed by the rest of the men.

Hartmann retraced his steps, rang 'Slow ahead' on the telegraph and then whistled up the control room on the voice pipe. Keeping a tight rein on himself, he ordered

147

Werner Best to trim the boat down by the sterm.

'By the stern, sir.'

Hartmann wasn't sure whether Best was merely repeating the order or querying it. 'That's right, Werner – by the stern. I want them to think we're in trouble. But watch what you're doing. I don't want the bows sticking up out of the water, nor do I want the sea pouring in through the galley hatch. Do I make myself clear?'

'Yes, sir. Should I also tell the helmsman to steer an erratic course?'

'That would certainly add to the realism,' Hartmann said drily.

'My apologies, Erich. I see now that I was completely mistaken.' The apology was halfhearted, Galen barely raising his voice above a whisper.

'Forget it. We were both under a strain.' Hartmann raised his binoculars again and followed the Liberator as it banked away and began to circle them out of range.

'Well, anyway, it would seem your ruse has had the desired effect.'

The Liberator had broken off the attack at the last minute, but it was doubtful whether he deserved all the credit for that. The RAF had changed their tactics after the U-boats had been up-gunned. Nowadays it was only on rare occasions that a single aircraft pressed home an attack in broad daylight. Normally, the pilot kept a surfaced U-boat under observation while he summoned up a second plane or the nearest surface vessel.

'Pilots vary, much the same as U-boat captains do,' said Hartmann. 'Some are bold, some are cautious, many are green and inexperienced, a few are downright reckless. Whatever their individual characteristics, all of them would like to emulate the Hudson pilot who captured U 570.'

They had gained a breathing space, but for how long? The Liberator would have already sent a sighting report to RAF Coastal Command and the British Admiralty. Task Force 223 and the fast eastbound convoy were probably information addressees, but even if they weren't, the Admiralty would certainly have repeated the signal to them by now. Task Force 223 could be anywhere from two to four hundred nautical miles away. Their position, which he'd marked on the chart earlier that morning, had been no more than an educated guess, but whether the separation distance was two or four hundred was irrelevant as far as the destroyers were concerned. They weren't a threat because even if they steamed at thirty knots, it would still take them a minimum of seven hours to reach U 195. No, it was the *Guadalcanal* that worried him.

Hartmann wished the B-Dienst had been a little more specific about the *Guadalcanal*. It would have been very helpful if they had been able to tell him what type of aircraft she was carrying. Air speed was a vital factor when you were trying to calculate how long it would take the Americans to respond. No matter; it was safe to assume that the carrier would have a number of planes on immediate stand-by, bombed up and ready to go at a moment's notice. Taking the worst case, he thought it would be at least an hour before any planes from the *Guadalcanal* arrived on the scene.

An hour? Hartmann recalled reading an intelligence summary a year or so ago which stated that it was usual for a carrier to be protected by a combat air patrol. But it seemed unlikely they would have one up; Göring had withdrawn his precious Focke Wulf Condors from the Atlantic. On the other hand, the Americans could be playing it safe. The Condor had a maximum range of thirty-five hundred kilometres and there was a squadron of Kampfgeschwader 40 operating out of Stavanger. From this base in southern Norway, it was just possible that the Condors could reach Task Force 223.

If the four planes of the combat air patrol joined forces with the Liberator, they would be in real trouble. Suddenly, an hour seemed a very optimistic assessment; suddenly, Hartmann had a feeling that his plan was going to misfire. Success or failure depended on how fast Peiper dealt with the flooded compartments. Although tempted to urge the chief engineer to get a move on, he resisted the impulse. August was an old hand; this was their thirteenth patrol together and he knew what they were up against.

Peiper eased the clip from his nose and took a cautious sniff. The breathing apparatus which he and the chief electro mechanic had put on before entering the battery room was the next best thing to a gas mask. It resembled a life jacket and could be used as such, but its primary function was to enable the user to escape from a sunken U-boat. Basically, it consisted of an oxygen cylinder, an air bag and a tin filled with soda lime crystals to absorb carbon dioxide. The oxygen was inhaled through the mouth via a breather tube that was fitted with a valve to regulate the flow.

Peiper took another sniff and then clapped the chief electro mechanic on the shoulder. 'It's all right now,' he said in a cheerful voice. 'You can take the clip off your nose.'

Things were definitely looking up; the valves had been closed, saltwater was no longer dripping down from the head and the chlorine gas had finally dispersed. Some of the batteries would never be the same again, which would reduce their radius of action when submerged, and that would cause a few long-term problems for Hartmann. But he would find a way of solving them; Erich was a resourceful captain, one of the reasons why the crew had so much confidence in him.

'There's nothing more we can do here,' said Peiper. 'Time to let them know up top that we're ready as we'll ever be.'

'That's the best news I've heard today,' said the mechanic.

The Liberator was still circling, going round and round like a carousel at a fairground. The simile wasn't altogether appropriate, because this was one merry-go-round that wouldn't stop until one of them had been destroyed.

Hartmann picked up the signalling lamp and handed it to one of the lookouts. 'Flash the pilot a message,' he said in a deadpan way. 'Ask him if he'd mind going round the other way for a change because he's making us dizzy.'

It wasn't a very funny joke, but somebody summoned up a laugh and the air of tension eased a little. It eased even more when Werner Best called the bridge over the voice

150

pipe to report that they could now dive below the surface.

'Thank you, Werner,' Hartmann said quietly. 'Please tell the chief engineer we're all very grateful.'

The next move was going to be tricky and could only be accomplished by sleight of hand. If the Liberator pilot knew his business, he would time his bombing run to catch them just after the sea closed over the conning tower, the moment when they would be most vulnerable. Although unmanned, the latent threat posed by the eight 20mm flak guns had deterred the Englishman from coming too close so far, and there was no reason why they shouldn't continue to do so. Acting on that assumption, Hartmann ordered the thirty-five men on the foredeck casing to get below.

It was the first tentative step in the right direction. Watching his seamen and the army detachment as they disappeared through the fore hatch one by one. Hartmann could imagine the reaction among the crew of the Liberator. At first there would be bewilderment, then anger at being tricked, which in turn would give way to a cold resolution to destroy the U-boat when the time was ripe. Before that happened, the wireless operator would tap out yet another message to RAF Coastal Command and the Admiralty. He wondered how many reports they had sent already, wondered too if Galen realized that the British Admiralty had probably been informed about the V1 ramp on the bows of U 195.

Hartmann waited until the last man had closed the fore hatch behind him and then turned to Galen. 'All right, Reinhard,' he said crisply, it's your turn now.'

'I would prefer to stay with you, Erich.'

Hartmann thought it typical of Galen that he should want to be one of the last men to go below. It was part of his blood and iron image, one of the essential qualities of leadership demanded of every true National Socialist by their beloved Führer.

'I can understand your feelings,' said Hartmann, 'but the fewer people there are on the bridge, the better off we'll be.'

'Then send one of the lookouts below and let me take his place.'

Hartmann didn't like it but any compromise was better than a total stalemate at this stage of the game. Deciding that two lookouts would be sufficient, he detailed Galen to watch the starboard side and sent the other three men below.

Although the Liberator was still out of range, he thought the plane had moved in closer, ready to pounce on them as soon as the right opportunity presented itself. In the circumstances, it would be suicidal to attempt a crash dive. Somehow or other, he would have to provoke the Englishman into making the wrong move, to draw him on to the 20mm cannons.

To man all three gun positions would be a mistake. First, the Englishman would never come near them if they did, and second, he would have too many men up top. If the flak didn't get the Liberator at the first attempt, they would have to go down fast before the plane turned and came in at them again – assuming of course they survived the initial attack. That was a pretty large assumption, but it was necessary to think ahead and plan for every eventuality.

When a U-boat was running on the surface, it took upward of half a minute to submerge to a depth of ten metres. While under training, his crew had succeeded in clipping a full two seconds off the existing record, but they would have to better than that today if they were to survive. In a quiet but authoritative voice, Hartmann spelt out to Lieutenant Dietrich exactly what he wanted done.

Like Galen, Dietrich also wanted the world to know that he was a man of blood and iron, but, unlike the artillery officer, he lacked both the nerve and the necessary seniority to plead his case. He could see that it made sense to man only the lower platform, and while he acknowledged that Petty Officer Ulex was undoubtedly the best gunner, he still wished Hartmann had placed him in command of the gun crew instead. However, an order was an order, and with great reluctance he led the other two gun crews below.

Hartmann felt naked and exposed. The bridge was open and the conning tower would offer little protection against the .50 calibre machine guns of the Liberator. He supposed he could always take cover behind the ventilating shaft but not while Galen was standing upright like some bloody guardsman on a parade ground.

'Come on, you bastard,' he muttered. 'What the hell are you waiting for?'

The answer to his question came from the Metox receiver. The radar set did not always respond in the same way when it picked up an intruder. Sometimes it made a buzzing noise, while on other occasions it had been known to give out a hair-raising whistle. This time it positively screamed at him. The noise was so deafening that Hartmann had great difficulty in hearing Werner Best when the first watch officer reported that four more blips had also appeared on the Hohentwiel screen.

'Five to one,' Galen said calmly. 'I daresay we won't have to wait much longer.'

Galen was right about that. The Liberator turned sharply, rapidly lost height and came straight for them, the .50 calibre machine guns in the nost turret sending a stream of tracers arcing toward the bridge. As Hartmann ducked below the lip of the conning tower, he heard several loud clangs and a jagged piece of metal almost parted his hair. A split second later, Petty Officer Ulex opened fire.

Each 20mm cannon was capable of two hundred and fifty rounds a minute and, in a fifteen-second burst, nearly three hundred empty shell cases sprewed out of the ejection slots on the quadruple mounting. At a range of under fifteen hundred metres, Ulex could hardly miss. Bits and pieces flew off the inner port and starboard engines and the Plexiglass nose turret disintegrated.

For a moment or so, Hartmann had a nasty feeling that Ulex had left it too late, but then suddenly the four-engined bomber went into a side slip and fell out of the sky. The starboard wing plunged into the sea and the stricken plane turned a complete cartwheel and exploded in a huge gout of flame. As the column of oily black smoke drifted skyward, four meancing black dots appeared on the horizon.

'Dive – Dive – Dive!' Hartmann thumbed the Klaxon, closed the voice pipe and then shoved Galen toward the hatch, ahead of the lookout. The battle of seconds had started and they slithered down the ladder, their feet scarcely touching the steel rungs.

The battle of seconds had also begun for Petty Officer Ulex and his gun crew. Of the four crew members, two lay dead, their bodies hideously torn apart and mangled beyond recognition by the .50 calibre bullets of the Liberator. The remaining two men were ashen-faced, so paralysed with shock that they appeared rooted to the spot. With complete disregard for his own safety, Ulex grabbed hold of both seamen and bundled them toward the ladder.

It was the last act of a brave man and selfless petty officer. As he ducked beneath the guardrails to jump down onto the deck, Ulex suddenly lost his footing and fell sideways. The soles of both his shoes were coated with a mixture of blood and grease, and skidding wildly, he went over the side. The last thing Ulex saw was the horrified face of Leutnant Dietrich staring at him before he closed the hatch above the galley. Numb with disbelief, he watched the U-boat disappear beneath the surface to leave him alone and helpless in the empty sea.

The sky, however, was far from empty. Guided by the funeral pyre of the Liberator, the four Grumman Avengers closed in for the kill.

Hartmann scrambled down the ladder and closed the hatch to the pressurized cabin above. The watertight doors leading to the bow and stern compartments had already been shut and the control room was so jammed that there was barely enough space for him to turn around. Apart from Werner Best, the two hydroplane operators, August Peiper and Obersteuermann Frick, their numbers were swollen by the presence of Galen and the lookout. Positioning himself behind the hydroplane operators, Hartmann stared at the inclinometre and depth gauges.

'Are we all accounted for, Werner?' he asked softly.

Best shook his head. 'No, sir, I'm afraid three men are missing – Petty Officer Ulex together with Seaman Leber and Olbricht.'

First Richter, then Ulex, Leber and Olbricht – four good men who had served him well. There would be some bad letters to write when they returned to Bergen. Perhaps 'if' was a more appropriate word.

The U-boat was tilted bows-down at an angle of fifteen degrees but they were still only eight metres below the surface. Hartmann held his breath, his eyes never leaving the depth gauge as the needle crept past nine and went on to ten. It was registering fifteen metres when the first Avenger dropped its depth charges. The resultant underwater explosions rocked the boat from side to side and broke the glass in the gauges. A second pattern followed and the lights went out.

'Torch, somebody,' Hartmann said in a steady voice that belied his fear.

Peiper produced a flashlight from his overalls, trained the beam on the depth gauge and saw that the needle was stuck fast. Hartmann saw it too and started counting, his lips barely moving. They went on down, deep, deep into the cellar until, satisfied they were approaching their maximum safe depth, Hartmann ordered the hydroplane operators to level out. Sowly, agonizingly slowly, U 195 steadied herself on an even keel.

Presently, Hartmann asked if anyone would care to bet how many depth charges they would be the target for in the next twenty minutes. There were no takers.

CHAPTER 16

New York

Thursday, 30 November 1944

Anderson could remember when the North Atlantic chart in the Operations Room had resembled a giant-sized pincushion. Back in early '43 when the U-boats had been hunting in wolf packs, the addition of one more flag pin would have been further proof that the Kriegsmarine was slowly gaining the upper hand. Twenty-one months later, it was a different story. With the tide of battle now running so obviously in their favour, the fact that a U-boat had been sighted on the surface in broad dayling was such a rare occurrence that it had caused a ripple of excitement among the duty watch at Eastern Sea Frontier.

The initial sighting report from the RAF Liberator had been sent at 1358 hours Greenwich mean time. Addressed to Coastal Command and the Admiralty, it had been immediately repeated to the fast eastbound convoy, Task Force 223 and Tenth Fleet in Washington. London had omitted the slow convoy, SC 189, from the distribution list for the simple reason that, unlike the fast eastbound, it was still some considerable distance from longitude 35 degrees west, the change of operational control line. Although the convoy and routing section in Washington had wasted no time in relaying the information to the slow convoy, Eastern Sea Frontier had not been accorded the same degree of precedence. Their copy of the initial sighting report had been graded 'Deferred', and as a result, it had reached them at 1530 Eastern standard time, some eight hours after the U-boat had been spotted by the RAF Liberator. As Anderson subsequently pointed out to Virginia Canford, that represented one hell of a delay.

'Well, we're not exactly in the forefront of the battle, are we?' she said reasonably. 'Anyway, what difference does it make? We've received it in good time; the next sailing conference is not until tomorrow.'

Another fast convoy was due to leave New York in forty-eight hours' time, and throughout the day there had been a constant flow of priority signals between Tenth Fleet and Eastern Sea Frontier concerning the proposed route. It was this two-way traffic more than anything else which had delayed the original sighting report and all subsequent messages sent by the Liberator.

'What did Washington have to say about this particular signal?' Anderson pencilled a cross against the relevant entry in the Ops Log before returning it to Virginia Canford.

'Nothing,' she said after glancing at the message. 'Why should they?'

'Because this U-boat, which was observed five hundred and twenty-six miles off Reykjavik, has been specially modified – that's why.'

'You're referring to a contraption on the bows?'

'The pilot said he thought it was some kind of ramp,' Anderson reminded her.

'All right, so it's a ramp. Why should that concern us, John? It's up to Technical Intelligence to figure out what useful purpose it could serve. Anyway, the Navy Department is probably waiting for confirmation from Task Force 223. I don't see how the pilot could be so positive the U-boat had been specially modified, considering what the weather is like.'

'We may be having snow flurries here in New York but the visibility is moderate-to-good off Iceland.' Anderson pointed to an entry in the log. 'It says so, right there.'

'All right, you win. Your RAF pilot has twenty-twenty vision and my memory is rapidly deteriorating.' Virginia frowned. The fact that she hadn't read the signals quite as thoroughly as she ought to have done was no fault of his. So why was she taking it out on him? 'Even so,' she continued in a milder tone, 'I still say the ramp is an academic problem as far as we are concerned.'

'Suppose it's a launching platform for a V1.'

'A flying bomb?' Virginia raised her eyebrows. 'You're not serious?'

He was deadly serious. The U-boat had been positively identified as a type VIIc, which meant its overall length was some two hundred and eighteen feet. The ramp was about ninety feet long, although that was pure guesswork based on the observations of the aircrew, who'd reported that it extended from the conning tower to the bows. While he had no idea whether it was feasible to launch a V1 from a ninety-foot ramp, he assumed the Germans knew what they were doing.

'It would certainly account for the security clamp-down they imposed at Bergen,' he said.

157

'What other surprises do you have up your sleeve?' Virginia smiled, 'I mean, that's not the whole story, is it?'

It wasn't the whole story, but he hadn't really thought beyond the ramp and the obvious purpose it was designed to serve. Of one thing he was sure; as an antishipping weapon the V1 was next to useless. The missile was far too inaccurate, and without a sophisticated guidance system there was not a cat in hell's chance that it could hit a moving target. In any case, trying to sink a merchantman with a flying bomb was a stupendous waste of effort, akin to swatting a fly with a telephone pole. The whole thing smacked of a propaganda exercise; and then suddenly he knew that he'd hit the nail on the head.

'If I were in Goebbels's shoes,' Anderson said slowly, 'I'd want to give the German people the biggest morale booster I could for a Christmas present.'

'Like what?' Virginia asked.

'Like hitting New York or maybe Washington. Either city would make a spectacular target for a V1 attack.'

'New York or Washington,' she mused. 'It's all very reminiscent of Jules Verne, isn't it? However, the question is – what are you going to do about it?'

'I suppose we should take it up with Commander Vandervell.' Anderson tugged the lobe of his right ear. 'He may not be a ball of fire, but he is our immediate superior.'

There was no love lost between them. Richard Luther Vandervell disliked the British and was particularly contemptuous of the Royal Navy; compared to him, Admiral Ernest J. King was an out and out Anglophile. A regular navy man, if was said Vandervell's greatest achievement was making the All-American team while in his final year at Annapolis. Whether or not there was any substance to the jibe, it was a fact that his war had started and ended with Pearl Harbour. Severaly wounded and blown overboard when the *West Virginia* was hit by a two-thousand-pound bomb, he had eventually been invalided home, destined to spend the next two years in a hospital. Discharged from the hospital in January '44 and graded unfit for further combat duty, he had been promoted to

Commander and assigned to a desk job at Eastern Sea Frontier. The fact that he hated the job accentuated his intolerance and prejudices.

'It's your ball game, John,' Virginia said quietly.

Anderson looked up. 'What do you mean by that?' he asked.

'I'm not coming with you. I don't believe my opinion would carry any weight with Commander Vandervell. You know what he thinks of women in uniform.'

They were supposed to be a team and he could have done with some support, but she was right. Vandervell would never listen to Virginia. Nothing riled him more than a woman masquerading as a naval officer – if he'd said it once, he'd said it a dozen times.

'Wish me luck then.' Anderson stood up and moved toward the door. 'I think I'm going to need it.'

'You're going to see Vandervell now?'

'Well, I think it's time I started pitching.' Anderson grinned at her. 'After all, you did say it was my ball game.'

Although his playing days had ended long ago, Richard Vandervell was still in pretty good shape and there wasn't an ounce of spare flesh on his two-hundred-and-ten-pound frame. On the other hand, the photographs of yesteryear, mounted in chromium frames and displayed on a corner shelf in his office, now bore only a passing resemblance to the man seated behind the desk. The happy extrovert, whose mental alertness and cheerful disposition had led his classmates to vote him the cadet most likely to succeed, had become a morose, sullen and embittered officer.

'A V1 attack on New York?' Vandervell pulled a face to show what he thought of the idea. 'That's some crystal ball you've got, Commander.'

'Why is it so impossible?' said Anderson. 'It would bring the war to America's doorstep, and just think of the propaganda Goebbels would make of that.'

'Just suppose you're right – how many flying bombs do you reckon this U-boat would have?'

'Your guess is as good as mine.' Anderson shrugged his

159

shoulders. 'Two, possibly three. Who knows?'

'I thought you were going to tell me.' Vandervell leaned back in his chair and crossed one leg over the other. 'Do you read any of our newspapers, Commander?'

'Yes – the *New York Times* – why?'

'Then you must know that the Technical Service Command of the Army Air Force built a jet-propelled copy of the V1 in sixty days.'

Anderson nodded. 'I also recall that Major General Bennett E. Myers claimed they had developed a better launching ramp.'

'So what? At the end of the day, we're still left with a highly inaccurate weapon which has a two-thousand-pound warhead.' Vandervell clasped both hands behind his neck and looked up at the ceiling as if seeking guidance from the Almighty. 'Now, I'm not an expert on German strategy like you, Commander, but it just seems to me that dropping two or even three tons of high explosive on New York is a waste of time and effort.'

'It could boost their morale.'

'Yeah? Well, it would certainly make our people as mad as hell.'

'With whom?'

'With whom?' Vandervell dragged his eyes away from the ceiling and stared at Anderson. 'With the goddamned Krauts – that's who.'

Anderson said, 'Suppose several hundred civilians were killed in a sneak attack and some newspaperman discovered that we had ignored the threat. How would the American people react to that?'

Vandervell unclasped his hands and sat up. He thought there was a very good chance that some of their wrath would be directed against the Navy Department, in which case a few heads would roll, his own included.

'All right, Commander,' he growled, 'you've made your point. I'll call Washington and see what they think about it.'

Offhand, Delgado couldn't think of one really convincing

160

reason why he should have dropped in on the Ace Cab Company on Eighth Avenue and 43rd Street. The Ziggermann case was sewn up because the Assistant DA had finally agreed to waive the conspiracy charge against Larry Novak, a decision which had prompted Eltsberg to open his mouth and lay everything on Kalmbach. The traffic accident on Eighth Avenue was therefore irrelevant and immaterial, as Gina had been quick to point out to him when he'd brought up the subject again last night. His partner, Jack Ganley, would have agreed with her verdict had he discussed the Webber affair with him, but wisely he'd kept it to himself. Ganley would only have said that he was wasting his time and the Police Department's, that it didn't matter a damn whether or not Webber was playing fast and loose with somebody's wife and that it was none of their business anyway.

'You want to see Leon Janowski?' The despatcher stared at him, unimpressed by the shield Delgado had waved in his face.

'That's right.'

'You the guy who phoned earlier?'

Delgado said he was. He had slipped out of the office to make the call from a pay phone, because he hadn't wanted Ganley and the rest of the squad to know what he was up to.

'I thought the Traffic Department said Leon wasn't to blame?'

'That they did.'

'Then why do you want to see him? Is he in some kind of trouble?'

'Not as far as I know,' said Delgado. 'I just want to talk to him about the holdup on West 48th Street a week ago yesterday.'

'The holdup?'

'Aw, for Chrissakes, where have you been?' Delgado said irritably. 'You couldn't pick up a paper or listen to the radio but what the holdup was stealing all the headlines. Four men took part in that robbery – Shaffer, Mirnick, Kalmbach and Eltsberg.' Delgado ticked off their names on the fingers of his left hand. 'Shaffer had been shot in the back before he was run over and killed by Janowski.'

'So?' The despatcher was still truculent, still pushing for information.

'So we figure Shaffer didn't make it all the way from West 48th to Eighth and 44th by himself. Somebody was with him and we think there's a chance Janowski can give us a description of this accomplice.'

'Yeah, well, Leon should be here any minute.'

Delgado hoped the despatcher was right. It was past six and he'd told Gina that he would be home by five-thirty at the latest. He'd figured that would allow him to put in some overtime on the Webber business after the eight-to-four shift had gone off duty, but he'd stayed on in the office longer than he'd intended. Although Eltsberg and Kalmbach had already appeared in court and a date had been set for their trial, he'd spent the last part of the afternoon going over the evidence again to satisfy himself that the prosecution had a cast-iron case. Ganley had said he was a glutton for punishment, that he was crazy to do the Assistant DA's job for him, but then Ganley didn't have to prove himself. Nobody was going to jump on him if he made a mistake, because he came from the right ethnic background. When you were an Italian you had to be twice as good as anybody else just to get by. It was this conviction that he couldn't afford to make one tiny slip that had brought him to the Ace Cab Company.

'Why don't you step inside the office and warm yourself by the fire? It beats standing out there in the draft.'

Delgado thought the despatcher had to be kidding. The office was a ramshackle construction built onto one wall of the underground garage. It lacked a roof, was about the size of a henhouse and was warmed by an electric heater with a single bar.

'Thanks all the same, but I'd only be in your way.'

'Suit yourself. If you want to wait inside his cab, it's under the window and pointed to a '42 model Dodge in the far corner of the garage. Both front fenders had been crumpled in the accident, and while some attempt had been made to beat them back into shape, they still looked

162

unsightly.

'The Dodge is okay,' the despatcher said, as if reading his mind. 'I mean it's roadworthy.'

'The tyres look kind of smooth to me.'

'There's a shortage and we have to get by as best we can.'

'Yeah, I know – there's a war on.' Delgado heard footsteps and turned toward the exit ramp. 'Is this him coming now?' he asked.

The despatcher leaned forward and poked his head out of the window. 'Uh huh,' he said, 'that's Leon.'

Janowski was a short, slightly built man in his mid-forties whose long, craggy face was a good deal more lined than it should have been at his age. He was wearing a pair of black pants that flapped above his ankles and a brown leather jacket lined with fleece. As he came toward the office, Delgado noticed that he walked with a peculiar gait, his feet splayed outward like a penguin.

'Mr. Janowski?' Delgado produced his badge from the inside pocket of his overcoat. 'I'm Detective Delgado,' he said politely. 'I'd like to ask you a few questions.'

'Yeah?' Janowski collected the car keys from the despatcher. 'What about?'

'The accident you had a week ago.'

'Oh, Jesus, not that again.' Janowski looked disgusted. 'I thought you guys were satisfied it wasn't my fault.'

'You're on the wrong track.' Delgado told him. 'This had to do with the Ziggermann case. The guy you knocked down was involved in the holdup.'

'Shaffer.' Janowski nodded. 'Yeah, I read about him.'

'Right. Now we've had a tip-off that somebody was with him a few moments before he stepped in front of your cab.' Delgado steered him towards the Dodge sedan. 'It's possible you might have seen this person. That's something we can talk about on the way to East 92nd.'

'What are we going there for?'

'It's were I live.' Delgado opened the door. 'Don't worry, I'm not after a free ride.'

'Who's paying? You or the Police Department?'

'Me,' said Delgado.

'Good, Janowski got in beside him and started the engine. 'It's my experience the Police Department don't like parting with their money.' Shifting into first, he pulled out of the parking slot, drove up the ramp and headed west as far as Ninth Avenue before tuning south to double back on 42nd Street. 'It's one hell of a lousy night,' he said presently.

Delgado agreed. The weather had been terrible all day, with rain and snow showers made worse by a bitterly cold wind. Right now, the rain had given way to another flurry of snow, the gusting sixty-mile-an-hour gale driving the flakes against their windshield. As they crossed Broadway, Delgado noticed that the emergency crew of six electricians were still working on the scale model of the Statue of Liberty in Times Square. The flambeau atop the right arm had been swaying so much in the high winds that City Hall had decided the torch should be secured with heavy wire cables, which was no easy job since the electrically powered flame was fifty feet above the ground.

'Do you have a description of this person you're looking for?' Janowski asked after a long silence.

Delgado thought he detected a slight edge to his voice. If you believed a man had something to hide, it often paid to plant the idea in his mind that you knew what it was. If you then left him to stew on it long enough, there was a good chance he'd crack.

'We want to trace a male Caucasian aged twenty to thirty.' Delgado launched into a description that existed only in his imagination and then waited to see how the cab driver would react.

'I can't say I remember seeing the guy,' said Janowski.

'That's a shame. We thought we were onto a good lead.' Delgado lit a cigarette. Janowski hadn't fallen into the trap he'd set for him, which could mean one of two things. Either the cab driver was a lot smarter than he'd allowed for or else he had nothing to hide. 'We're also pursuing another line of inquiry ...' Delgado paused to let it sink in, and then said, 'A young woman was observed hurrying away from the scene.'

'A young woman, huh?' Janowski overtook a car on the inside and turned into Fifth Avenue. 'I can't say I remember seeing her either.'

'I don't suppose Captain Webber shared the cab with anybody, did he?' Delgado blew a smoke ring toward the roof. 'I mean, people do in wartime.'

'Well, he didn't.'

'I see. Where were you taking him?'

'Some hotel – the President or the Paramount – I can't remember which. Is it important?'

'I don't know,' said Delgado. 'Did he have any luggage?'

'I think he had a small bag, the kind airline pilots use.' Janowski tightened his grip on the steering wheel. 'He didn't talk a lot, but I got the impression he was meeting somebody for a drink or maybe it was dinner.'

'Well, I guess that about wraps it up.' Delgado put on a rueful expression. 'I had hoped you might have seen this woman, but that's the way it goes. Sometimes you get lucky, sometimes you don't.'

Janowski didn't actually heave a sigh of relief, but he became visibly more relaxed, which alone was enough to convince Delgado he'd lied about the woman. Proving it would take time, but it wasn't an impossible job. As soon as he had a spare hour or so, he could call at the two hotels Janowski had mentioned and ask to see the register. If he drew a blank at both the President and the Paramount, he would forget the whole thing and accept the fact that Gina had been right about Webber all along.

Webber thought Cynthia Langdon was a good deal less subtle than her mother. Whenever Mrs. Langdon intercepted him on the landing, she managed to make it seem like a chance encounter, whereas Cynthia was already there waiting for him as he climbed the staircase to his apartment. Although the last person he wanted to see, he managed to hide his feelings behind a smile when she greeted him.

'You look all in, Paul,' she said solicitously.

'I'm bushed.' he admitted. 'The return flight from

165

Washington was lousy. Crosswinds all the way – rain – snow – ice. You name it, we had it.'

There had been other things to worry him besides the weather. Christel Zolf had given him plenty to think about after he'd met her in a coffee shop on Pennsylvania Avenue. A third party was about to make an entrance, some faceless character who had travelled thousands of miles to deliver a vital package. The time and the place for the rendezvous had still to be fixed, but the stranger knew how to get in touch with him.

'Are you free that evening, Paul?'

'I'm sorry, Christel.' Webber pinched his eyes. 'What did you say?'

'I said my boss has given me two tickets for *Carmen Jones*. He was expecting a couple of buyers from out of town but they've cancelled their trip.' She hesitated and then, pink with embarrassment, added, 'I just wondered if you were doing anything on Saturday?'

'Saturday?' Webber muttered, groping for excuses. 'Well, I don't know – I'm flying to Detroit and with the weather the way it is. I can't be sure what time I'll be back.'

'Who's Christel?'

'What?' Webber stared at her, a sinking feeling in the pit of his stomach.

'You called me Christel.'

'I'm sorry,' Webber swallowed. 'It was a slip of the tongue. Christel is an air hostess. We often fly together.'

'Is she attractive?'

'Very.' Webber saw the hurt look in her eyes and quickly added, 'She's engaged to another pilot. I believe they're getting married in January.'

'Oh, that's nice.'

Her relief was plain to see and, in spite of himself, he felt sorry for her. 'Look,' he said, 'I'm dying for a drink. Why don't you keep me company?'

Webber knew the risk he was taking. At thirty-two, Cynthia Langdon was getting desperate and he was perhaps her last hope. She had certainly made it very clear that she was interested and was willing to go all the way to

166

attract him. That had been evident last Saturday when they'd parted on her dootstep. He had meant to give her a peck on the cheek but she had pressed her lips against his and opened her mouth. Inviting her into his apartment could lead to complications, but Webber couldn't see that he had any alternative. He'd let the cat out of the bag and he figured being nice to Cynthia was the only way to make her forget he'd ever mentioned Christel's name.

Webber unlocked the door to his apartment, left his trench coat and peaked hat in the hall and ushered her into the living room.

'Well now,' he said with forced cheerfulness, 'what can I get you to drink?'

'Do you have any scotch?'

'I have a bottle of Canadian Club,' he said, surprised. 'How do you like it?'

'Neat, with ice.' The words came out clipped, like a child accepting a dare.

'Me too.'

Webber found two glasses, poured a double into each one and then went into the kitchen to get the ice cubes. When he returned, he saw that Cynthia had plumped herself down on the couch and was trying hard to look demure and yet seductive at one and the same time. She was wearing a dark grey skirt and a white polo-neck sweater which, although a size too small, in no way improved her flat chest.

'Cheers.' he said, raising his glass.

'Happy days,' she replied, giving him a coy smile.

There was an awkward silence while he tried to think of something to say, and then they both started to speak at once.

'You first,' he said, after she had succeeded in muzzling her laughter.

'I was about to suggest you took the weight off your feet, Paul.'

Cynthia didn't have to pat the couch; her eyes made it clear enough that she was hoping he would sit beside her. As he hovered, uncertain what to do, the telephone rang.

Answering it gratefully, he heard a strange voice say,

'Captain Webber?'

'Yes,' he said. 'Who's calling?'

'It's Leon Janowski.'

'Janowski?' he repeated blankly. 'Do I know you?'

'The cab driver. I'm the guy you gave ten bucks to, remember?'

'Oh, yeah.' Webber turned his back on Cynthia and held the phone closer to his mouth. First Christel, now Janowski – everything was coming apart at the seams. 'What can I do for you?' he asked in a low voice.

'Nothing. I just hought you should know the cops have been on to me again. A detective by the name of Delgado. You know him?'

'No. Why should I?'

'He lives in the next street to you. Anyway,' Janowski continued, 'it seems somebody told him about your girl.'

'I don't like the sound of that.'

'Me neither, but you don't have to worry; I played it dumb.' Janowski cleared his throat. 'I think maybe you're off the hook, but I can't swear to that. Delgado is the stubborn kind – he might come back at me. If he does, you'll have to see me right. I mean, I could lose my licence over this. You follow me?'

Webber said he did and waited for Janowski to name his price. There had to be one – why else would the bastard have called him?

'Good,' said Janowski. 'If this Delgado gives me anymore trouble, I'll get in touch with you again – okay?'

The son of a bitch intended to make him sweat it out, but that was his big mistake. He would string him along, playing for time until he was ready to deal with the threat. Janowski lived downtown, on Oliver Street; he remembered the patrolman making a note of his address when he took down the cab driver's statement. It was just a question of looking the place over and picking the right moment.

'You do that,' said Webber and hung up.

He had never contemplated killing anyone before, but there was always a time for everything. And maybe he wouldn't even have to do the job himself. Maybe this faceless character he was due to meet in a few days would do the job for him.

'Something wrong, Paul?'

'What?' He turned to face her.

'You are worried,' said Cynthia. 'I can see it in your eyes.'

'Oh no, it's nothing.' Webber topped his glass up, walked over to the couch and sat down. 'Just some minor problem about the schedules.'

'You sounded cross.' Cynthia tucked one leg under her rump and contrived to move a little closer to him. 'In fact, I'd say you were very cross.'

'Was I? Well, they want me to switch flights with another captain and I don't want to stop over in Chicago.'

'That's got to be one for the Marines.' She smiled and moved a knee into his thigh. 'But I believe you.'

She was obviously flirting with him but there were other questions forming on the tip of her tongue, questions he might find it hard to answer and didn't want to hear. Removing the glass from her hand, he set it on the table beside his, and then kissed her. As he did so, Cynthia opened her mouth and pushed her tongue between his lips. It was very clear to him that he was expected to make love to her, and somewhat to his surprise, Webber found himself getting an erection.

Anderson was having a quiet drink in the wardroom when one of the stewards told him that he was wanted on the telephone in the Mess Secretary's office.

Taking the call, he heard the operator say, 'He's on the line now, Commander,' and then Vandervell came through.

He said, 'remember that U-boat we were talking about late this afternoon? Well, it's now lying at the bottom of the ocean, sent there by the USS *Pope*.'

'I'd say that was very good news.''

'I can tell what you're thinking, Anderson. U-boats have been known to discharge oil through their torpedo tubes.'

'It has happened.'

'But never human offal, right?'

'Human offal?'

'Intestines – arms – legs – that kind of thing. The *Pope* has collected several bucketfuls of the stuff.' There was a brief pause and then Vandervell said, 'You realize what this means?'

'Yes,' said Anderson, 'it means the threat no longer exists.'

'You're damned right, it doesn't,' said Vandervell, and put down the phone.

PART II

DARK DECEMBER

CHAPTER 17

Latitude 58 degrees 17 minutes north
Longitude 20 degrees 8 minutes west

Sunday, 3 December 1944

Hartmann stirred fitfully in his sleep and then sat bolt upright, his heart beating faster than normal, his body cold yet clammy with sweat. Uncertain at first where he was, the chart lying on the table beside the bunk and the faint, distant noise of the electric motors in the engine room eventually reassured him and he began to slowly unwind.

Trying to forget the recurrent nightmare was never easy. The details were too sharply etched in his mind for that. Even now, he could still see the small cobbled square and the tri-colours hanging from every balcony. Even now, he could still hear the jeering crowd hurling insults at the group of frightened young women who were standing in line, waiting their turn at the barber's chair. In the dream, one girl always stood apart from the rest, her shaven head bowed, her eyes downcast as if trying to read the placard that had been pinned to the front of her dress. In the dream, she always raised her face to stare at him with loathing while pointing to the placard which proclaimed that she was Jeanne Verlhac, the whore who was carrying the child of a German naval officer.

Work was the only antidote, the only known cure for the malaise that gripped him whenever his thoughts turned to Jeanne. Seating himself at the table, Hartmann studied the figures showing their daily consumption of fuel which Peiper had produced for him earlier.

They had left Bergen with a hundred and fourteen tons of diesel oil and it could be they would have to get by on that. He hadn't mentioned this possibility to August and the others. There had been no need to. They knew that

173

U-234 had ceased to acknowledge the daily weather forecast and the B-Dienst intelligence report, and could draw their own conclusions. The ominous silence from the 'milk cow' dated from midnight on the thirtieth of November, some ten and a half hours after they had been attacked by the RAF Liberator and the four Grumman Avengers from the USS *Guadalcanal*. Unless the captain of U 234 had suddenly decided to impose wireless silence, which seemed unlikely, there was a very strong probability that the converted minelayer had been sunk.

Hartmann could only guess how this had happened. According to his calculations, the 'milk cow' had been roughly fifty nautical miles due west of U 195 on the thirtieth of November, and provided U 234 had remained in the cellar during the hours of daylight, she could not have been detected from the air. On the other hand, once it was dark, she would undoubtedly have used her snorkel to recharge the batteries and it was just conceivable that the destroyers of Task Force 223 had picked up the air mast on their short range radar as they steamed toward the last known position of U 195. However, from a subjective, if callous point of view, the manner of her destruction was entirely irrelevant. Of far greater importance to Hartmann was the effect it would have on them.

In theory, they had just about enough fuel to reach the target area and return to Bergen provided they didn't exceed ten knots. But they had a deadline to meet. They still had thirty-two hundred miles to go and the order to execute Double Griffin could be signalled to them anytime from the twenty-third of December onward. By the time it was safe enough to cruise on the surface by night, they would have exactly nineteen days to reach the target area by the required date. They would therefore have to go flat-out during the hours of darkness. At high speed, their consumption of diesel oil rose drastically, so drastically that Hartmann calculated they would run out of fuel on the return leg somewhere in the vicinity of the Flemish Gap at longitude 40 degrees west.

Just what Kapitän zur See Wirth would do in the circumstances was hard to predict. In view of the silence from U 234, it was reasonable to assume that he too realized the converted minelayer had been sunk. How soon he could despatch another 'milk cow' was entirely dependent on availability. Whether he would send a second resupply boat was a different question altogether. Much depended on his reading of the situation and the inference he drew from the wireless silence U 195 had maintained since leaving Bergen. Since he had not recalled the 'milk cow' to base, Hartmann believed that until as late as Thursday night, Wirth had refused to believe that U 195 was missing. Since then, however, there was a very real possibility that he had changed his mind. If such was the case, Wirth would do nothing unless action was taken to make him think again. Although they were not clear of the shipping lanes yet, Hartmann decided he would have to change his policy. Tonight, for the first time in ten days. U 195 would break silence. It might not resolve their fuel problem, but at least it would make Galen happy, if such a thing were possible.

At Galen's insistence, the stern accommodation had been divided off by a curtain, with the result that he and the other three officers who occupied the two double-tiered bunks nearest the control room now enjoyed a certain amount of privacy. The odd man out in this arrangement was August Peiper, who had preferred to remain with his chief engine room artificers, a choice that had met with Galen's wholehearted approval. The chief engineer practically worshipped Hartmann and it was obvious to Galen whose side he would be on in the event of a showdown. Inevitably there would be a showdown. Despite the brilliant way Hartmann had outwitted the Liberator pilot, Galen still didn't trust him and was convinced it would be necessary to remove him from command before very long.

From the outset, Hartmann had shown precious little enthusiasm for the operation. Granted they had to

175

proceed with caution until they were clear of the shipping lanes, but it was questionable whether he would even try to make up the lost time when eventually the situation allowed. Although his war record was extremely impressive, his attitude now bordered on the defeatist, which alone was enough to render him unfit for command. But removing Erich wouldn't be easy. Oberleutnant Best would have been the logical choice to succeed him. However, from observation, Galen knew the first watch officer was utterly loyal to Hartmann. Even if ordered to do so, Werner Best would undoubtedly refuse to take over command. However, Karl-Hans Dietrich was a different kettle of fish altogether.

The young Leutnant zur See was ambitious and Hartmann had wounded his vanity on two occasions that Galen knew of. When they were caught in the storm off the Shetlands, he had said point blank that Dietrich lacked the necessary experience to take command in an emergency. Ordering Petty Officer Ulex, the senior gunner, to take charge of the quadruple 20mm was another rebuff that had humiliated Dietrich. Even more significant was the fact that the second watch officer had been on the point of refusing to obey an order when it had seemed to him that Hartmann was about to surrender. Neither Best nor Peiper would dream of questioning Erich's authority, but with Dietrich the battle was already half won.

Although Dietrich was still asleep, Galen judged the moment ripe to have a talk with him and climbed down from the top bunk. Werner Best had the watch and was on duty in the control room along with Frick, the chief helmsman. There remained Hauptmann Kleist and Oberfeldwebel Meyer who occupied the lower starboard berth on the other side of the curtain. With his ruptured eardrums, Kleist was physically incapable of overhearing them, and Meyer was easy to deal with. Drawing the curtain aside, he woke the Oberfeldwebel and sent him forward, ostensibly to rouse the detachment and set them to work cleaning their personal weapons. That the double-tiered bunk directly opposite was vacant was no surprise to Galen. He had known beforehand that both petty officers would still be hard at work replacing a big end bearing in the port diesel engine that was in danger of seizing up.

Once Meyer was safely out of the way, Galen woke Dietrich, shaking him by the shoulder until he came to and opened his eyes.

'Herr Major?' Dietrich looked puzzled and then, thoroughly alarmed, started to get up. 'My God,' he whispered, 'I'm late. What time is it?'

'I don't know.' Galen lied. 'I was about to ask you the same question.'

Still befuddled, Dietrich reached under the pillow for his wristwatch and stared at it blankly. 'It's only 1605,' he mumbled. 'It won't be dark up top for another half hour yet.'

'How unfortunate – I've just told Meyer to wake the detachment.' Galen pulled a wry face and sat down on the bunk beside him. 'I'm not cut out to be a sailor. I can't get used to the routine. Of course, it's different for you. You're an old hand at the game, Karl.'

'I suppose so. This is my fourth patrol.'

'Your fourth?' Galen tried to sound impressed.

'Well, perhaps it would be more accurate to say three and a half.'

'What an odd number. How do you arrive at that figure?'

'We tried to stop the Allies landing on D-day,' said Dietrich.

U 195 had sailed from Brest on the sixth of June with ten other boats from the 9th Flotilla, in what had been the most disastrous operation ever. Within seventy-two hours, four U-boats had been sunk and three had been forced to turn back. Of the remaining four, only Hartmann had achieved anything, if sinking a frigate and one tank landing ship could be rated a success.

'The T5 accoustic torpedo was supposed to be the answer to all our prayers.' said Dietrich, 'but nine times

177

out of ten it detonated prematurely. Two hits from fourteen torpedoes – what could have been more futile than that?'

Their talk wasn't going as well as Galen had hoped. Far from criticizing Hartmann, the junior officer seemed determined to find excuses for him. 'I can understand why that particular operation didn't count as a full patrol,' he said after some thought.

'Oh, but it did,' Dietrich said vehemently. 'You see, we'd fired all our torpedoes. It was the move to Bergen that didn't count. We left Brest with a full complement of torpedoes and we still had all fourteen T5s when we arrived at the other end.'

'Were there no merchantmen to be had?'

Dietrich scowled. 'We didn't look very hard. The Herr Korvettenkapitän told us we were under orders to proceed to Bergen with utmost despatch. Utmost despatch.' Dietrich grunted to show his disgust, 'that's an English expression.'

'I didn't know your captain was an Anglophile,' Galen said mildly.

'He respects them, if that's what you mean.' Dietrich frowned. 'I don't see what good it does to respect your enemy. In fact, I believe it's a sign of weakness.'

Most officers who failed to respect the enemy usually made the mistake of underestimating them and ended up with a bloody nose as a result. Galen had learned that lesson from bitter experience on the Eastern front, but he wasn't about to enlighten Dietrich. Their conversation was now coming along nicely and he wanted to lead the junior officer on, not shut him up.

'Personally, I've no time for people who profess to have a healthy respect for the enemy. It's a refuge for the faint-hearted, the kind of excuse used by a leader who's afraid to press home an attack.' Galen waited, allowing time for the innuendo to sink in and then continued in a different vein but developing the same theme. 'Still, I expect your last patrol was much more successful.'

'Hardly,' said Dietrich. 'Our total bag was one small

collier which we intercepted off Newcastle upon Tyne.'

'How times have changed,' said Galen, clucking his tongue.

'They certainly have, Herr Major. Things were so very different fifteen months ago when I joined U 195 fresh from the Baltic training flotilla. I'll never forget my first patrol as long as I live.' Dietrich faced him, his eyes burning with excitement like two coals of fire. 'The B-Dienst gave us a fix on this convoy which was nine days out of Halifax and we came up behind it. There was a thick mist and you couldn't see above a thousand meters. We were running on the surface in daylight, which apparently was pretty unheard of because the Allies had closed the air gap in mid-Atlantic early in '43. But this didn't seem to bother the captain. Anyway, we'd been tailing the convoy for about an hour when the rearmost escort put about and came after us. I thought the captain would take us down into the cellar, but he did nothing of the kind. Instead, he chose to run before the escort, drawing her away from the convoy. A frigate would have caught us but he was gambling that we were up against a corvette, and he knew we had the edge on that class for speed. The captain also knew the escort would have to turn back sooner or later because the rear end of the convoy was wide open to attack, except that none of the other U-boats in the pack had made contact at that stage.'

The monologue went on and on. Galen listening with mounting impatience as Dietrich described how the escort had eventually turned back and how they had followed suit. Hartmann had continued to run on the surface, making a wide outflanking movement to slip in behind the escort guarding the starboard quarter of the convoy. He'd adopted the Hundekurve maneuver, the so-called 'dog's curve,' an attack path which enabled a U-boat to present the smallest possible profile to the enemy throughout.

'The lookouts were sent below.' Dietrich continued, 'but I was allowed to remain on the bridge with the captain while he called off the range and bearing on an eight-thousand-ton freighter. We let go with both torpedo tubes, and then we were off the bridge and diving so fast it made my head spin.'

At close range they could hardly miss the target, but all the same, it had seemed an age before they heard the torpedoes strike. Some two or three minutes later it had been their turn to be on the receiving end. One of the escorts had dropped a total of twenty-five depth charges, but only the first pattern of five had been anywhere near them. As Dietrich explained it, things would have been very different had the British been able to spare two corvettes, because one would have shadowed while the other attacked. That way they wouldn't have lost sonar contact and Hartmann would never have been able to outfox them.

'As soon as the danger had passed, we reloaded the torpedo tubes, which is no easy job. In fact, it takes upward of twenty minutes and even with the boat trimmed slightly heavy at the bows, it's still damned hard work. U 195 belongs to a particular class of six that only has two bow tubes. Some type VIIc's don't have a stern tube, but at least they all have four up front where it counts. We've never been able to fire a spread, which is one hell of a handicap.' Dietrich broke off momentarily to scratch a prickly heat rash under his chin. 'Anyway, once we'd reloaded, we went after the convoy again. It took us the best part of seven hours to catch up and get ahead of them. I thought they had changed course and we'd lost them in the mist, but the captain had anticipated their every move. It was uncanny, almost as if he possessed a sixth sense.'

Galen tried to conceal his irritation. Hartmann's charisma was such that it seemed even Dietrich was moved to eulogize him. The second watch officer was his only potential ally among the crew, and somehow he had to find a way to win him over.

'We picked off a fifteen-thousand-ton oil tanker shortly after dusk and you've never seen a fireworks display like it. The following morning we knocked off a straggler, one of those Liberty ships the Americans are said to build in

180

ninety days.' Dietrich sighed, a wistful expression on his face. 'I wish the other patrols could have been the same, but our luck simply ran out.'

Galen saw an opening at last and made the most of it. 'That is too simple an explanation for me, Karl,' he said.

'You think so, sir?'

'I'm certain of it. A bold man makes his own luck. Erich was a great captain in his day but he has become tired and war weary. I tell you, his heart is not in this mission and that's a great pity, Karl, because Double Griffin is part of a much larger operation which will change the course of the war. Our enemies think we are on our knees, but they are mistaken. Believe me, in the Sixth SS Panzer, Fifth Panzer and Seventh Armies, Germany has the means to strike the Anglo-Americans a blow from which they will never recover.'

'Does the Herr Korvettenkapitän know this?'

'No, it's for your ears only, Karl.' Galen squeezed his shoulder, a gesture that was meant to be a sign of friendship between comrades. 'I know what you are going to say – Erich would see things in a different light if he knew about this forthcoming offensive – but you're wrong. It may shock you to hear this, but Erich has told me he believes the war is already lost. Of course, he will continue to do his duty as he sees it, because that's the kind of man he is.'

Galen could see from the disapproving expression on the younger man's face that in the space of a few minutes he had managed to tarnish Hartmann's image. The constant and deliberate use of his Christian name had helped to diminish his authority, so that the Korvettenkapitän was no longer quite the awesome figure Dietrich had previously felt him to be. All he had to do now was convince him that Hartmann needed their help.

'On his past record alone, Erich should have been appointed to command a flotilla long ago. It's certain he will be promoted if this operation is a success, and God knows he'll have deserved it. Unfortunately, at the moment he lacks the will to see it through unaided. You

181

and I must therefore stiffen his resolve and, if necessary, we must be prepared to act in his name should Erich show signs of faltering.'

'Wouldn't that be tantamount to mutiny?' Dietrich asked in a whisper.

'As officers, we've all sworn a personal oath of loyalty to the Führer. It's my job to see that his plans are fulfilled. That's why I was assigned to this operation.' Galen stood up, turned his back on Kleist and removed his jacket. Unbuttoning the right sleeve of his shirt, he rolled it up to show Dietrich the blood group tattooed on the inside of the upper arm. 'If you're in doubt, here's my authority.'

It was a touch of theatre, a dramatic gesture which, although not without risk, was necessary to bind Dietrich to a common purpose.

'You're a member of the SS.'

The awe in Dietrich's voice was just what Galen had wanted to hear, and from that moment he knew he had the second watch officer in the palm of his hand.

'What do you want me to do?'

The question was breathless yet eager. It marked the first step in their conspiracy and was something Galen could build on.

'That depends on the attitude Erich adopts when we reach longitude 70 degrees west.'

'I don't understand.'

'It's the change of operational control line.' Galen buttoned the shirt-sleeve and donned his jacket again. 'The point where your captain is required to defer to my instructions except in matters of seamanship. Until then, you have no need to do anything.'

It was evident his reply had failed to satisfy Dietrich's curiosity, but the sudden piping of 'all hands to duty stations' absolved him of any further explanation for the present.

At exactly 2359 hours, U 195 broke wireless silence for the first time in ten days to acknowledge the B-Dienst report and weather forecast. Although this change of policy surprised Galen, it in no way altered his conviction that eventually Hartmann would have to be forcibly removed from command.

CHAPTER 18

New York

Tuesday, 5 December 1944

For the second day running, Delgado decided to forego lunch in order to satisfy his curiosity about Webber. Yesterday he'd dropped by the President Hotel on West 48th Street; today he would try his luck with the Paramount. If he drew a blank there, as he had at the President, Delgado intended to call a halt. According to his reckoning, there were about sixty-eight hotels on the West Side and he simply didn't have the time to check out each one, looking for the mystery woman Anderson had described.

He didn't like the idea of quitting, but finding this missing witness was a job that could only be tackled when he had a spare moment, and lately he'd had precious few of those. After talking to Janowski on Thursday night, he'd hoped to make a start the following day, but instead he'd been dragged into the investigation of a somewhat bizarre holdup. The victim was a lawyer who'd dropped his wife off at the Barrymore Theatre and was looking for somewhere to park, when a youth had opened the door and scrambled into the car while he was held at a light. The kid had stuck a gun into his ribs, had muttered something about this town being too hot for him and had then ordered the lawyer to take him to Jersey City. Two miles the other side of the Holland Tunnel, the lawyer had been forced to pull off the road onto a vacant lot, where he'd been relieved of the car keys and told to hand over his wallet. The lawyer was the kind of man who preferred to use a checkbook, and at first the robber had refused to believe that ten dollars was all the cash he had on him. When the lawyer did manage to convince him that this was indeed the case, the gunman had returned two dollars for the cab fare back to New York and had then made off with his car. Declining to accept the gunman's advice that he could still catch the second half of the show, the lawyer had gone straight to the Jersey City police, with whom he spent most of Thursday night. On their instructions, he reported to the 18th Precinct the following morning, where Delgado had taken down his statement before giving him the mug shot file to look through.

The quixotic behaviour of the gunman suggested to Delgado that he was a rank amateur with no previous record, an opinion which was confirmed when the lawyer had been unable to identify his assailant among the photographs of convicted criminals. The fact that the Jersey City Police Department had since recovered the stolen car had mollified the lawyer to some extent, but it hadn't let either Ganley or himself off the hook. The crime had been committed in the 18th Precinct area, and consequently it was still their baby.

Delgado thought it unlikely that he and Ganley would solve the case, but they had to go through the motions. Going through the motions entailed checking every bar in the theatre district to see if they could find a witness who remembered seeing anyone resembling the gunman's description on the night of the thirtieth of November. The case was now in its fifth day, and despite all the legwork they'd done, they had got nowhere. The number of man hours they had spent so far had reached a staggering total, and Caskey was already making noises about it being a waste of time to continue the search. Before the day was over, the lieutenant would probably tell him to drop the case, and that would be yet another unsolved crime on his record. Putting that depressing thought behind him, Delgado entered the lobby of the Paramount Hotel and walked over to the reception counter.

The desk clerk was in his early twenties, had dark, sleek

184

hair, looked painfully thin and was clearly 4F. The welcoming smile on his face became somewhat apprehensive the instant Delgado produced his badge and told him what he wanted.

'A Mr. Paul Webber?' The desk clerk leafed through the register. 'On Wednesday, the twenty second of November?'

'That's right,' said Delgado. 'He might have signed, himself in as Captain Paul Webber. He's a pilot with National Eastern Airlines.'

The clerk nodded, found the appropriate day in the register and ran a finger down the page. Stopping halfway, he reversed the book so that Delgado could see the entry he'd marked with his nail. 'Room 311,' he announced.

Delgado saw that Webber had given his address as care of National Eastern Airlines, which struck him as somewhat curious. 'Is that a single or a double?' he asked.

'Single.'

Room 312 had been occupied by a Mr. and Mrs. Arthur J. Phelps of Boston. 310 was obviously a single room but the signature was practically indecipherable. The Christian name consisted of the letters 'Ch' followed by a straight line with a dot above it, which seemed to indicate an 'i,' and ended with an 'e' or an 'l.' The surname was shorter in length and began with a 'Z' and finished with either an 'f' or a letter 'b' without the top loop. Although not a handwriting expert, Delgado thought it showed a feminine touch.

'Who was the woman in 310?'

The clerk leaned across the counter, craning his neck to look at the entry. 'Home address – Georgetown, Washington,' he said and sucked on his teeth. 'I can't make out the name.'

'Neither can I.'

'Are you sure the signature belongs to a woman?'

'I'm sure,' said Delgado. 'Maybe you weren't here when she checked in? She would have arrived between seven and seven-thirty in the evening.'

'I finish work at six.' The desk clerk smiled apologetically. 'You could try asking my relief. It's possible he may remember her.'

He might, and then again he might not. The Paramount wasn't exactly a small hotel and, like Webber, the mystery woman had stayed only the one night. With guests coming and going all the time, it seemed unlikely that the night clerk would remember her name, but even if he could, it didn't necessarily follow that she was Webber's girl friend.

'How was the reservation made? I mean, did she write a letter of make a phone call?'

'I don't know, sir. I could ask the accounts office.'

'Suppose you do that.' said Delgado.

Two minutes and one internal call later, the desk clerk was able to tell him that both rooms had been booked and paid for by Webber. Unfortunately, accounts didn't have the name of the woman in 310 but, as far as Delgado was concerned, he had proof of her existence, even though she remained a shadowy figure with an indecipherable signature.

Virginia Canford looked up. The sound of Anderson's footsteps in the corridor outside her office was unmistakable. Most Americans tended to amble, but he always walked purposefully, as if in a hurry to get from one place to another. It was even possible to judge what sort of mood he was in from his measured pace, and listening to the loud clack of his heels on the floor, Virginia could tell he was angry.

No special insight was required to guess the reason why. Alone among the staff of Eastern Sea Frontier, Anderson wasn't wholly convinced that the USS *Pope* had sunk the same U-boat as had shot down the RAF Liberator. He'd tried his theory out on her before tackling Commander Richard Vandervell, and while she was not qualified to pass judgment, his argument had sounded pretty convincing to her. Vandervell had thought otherwise and had said so in no uncertain terms, displaying his customary hostility toward the Royal Navy.

Most people she knew would have dropped the hot potato there and then, but not John Anderson. She had learned from previous experience that once he got the bit between his teeth, nothing would persuade him to let go. Following the sharp rebuff from Vandervell, he'd decided to take it up with the Senior British Liaison Officer at Navy District. The way he slammed the door behind him when he entered the office was a sign that he'd had no joy there either.

Unsure of the sort of reception she would receive, Virginia tapped on the communicating door and then walked into the adjoining room.

Anderson was standing near the window, his back toward her, both hands clasped behind him.

'You know something, Ginny?' He turned about and gave her a wry smile. 'If I lived to be a hundred, I would never make a lawyer. I lost the case by default.'

'What did he say?'

'Much the same as Vandervell – that a difference of seven nautical miles was inconclusive, given the time gap between the two sightings.'

Even if the liaison officer had agreed with him, Virginia doubted that it would have made any difference. Vandervell was, and always had been the key, the man who had to be convinced. For all that he was anti-British, Vandervell was no fool. If Anderson hadn't rubbed him the wrong way, she thought, Vandervell might have been more receptive. In the circumstances, it had been less than diplomatic of John to remind him that the U.S. Navy was not infallible when he was still brooding over Saturday's game in Baltimore which the Army had won 23 to 7.

'But you still don't agree?'

Damn right he didn't. According to the 'After Action Report' from Task Force 223, the long range Liberator had made radar contact with a U-boat on the surface of latitude 59 degrees 13 minutes north, longitude 11 degrees 45 minutes west. The U-boat had then remained on the surface for about an hour and a half, steering an erratic course at an estimated speed of six knots before

187

submerging. At that point in time, the last fix sent by the pilot of the Liberator, before he was shot down, had tallied almost exactly with that given by the flight commander of the four Grumman Avengers from the USS *Guadalcanal*. Some five hours later, the USS *Pope* had picked up a U-boat on her radar exactly forty-seven nautical miles due west of the last known position.

'It doesn't add up,' said Anderson. 'The maximum underwater speed of a type VIIc is eight knots. Anyway, it's extremely unlikely that a captain who'd just survived an aerial attack would have been caught napping again within the space of five hours. I don't see him running toward the enemy either.'

'How would he have known where Task Force 223 was?'

'The Avengers were on the horizon when he crash-dived. He would have seen them approaching from the west. The *Pope* sank a U-boat all right, but it wasn't the same one, Ginny.'

'So what are you going to do?' she asked.

'I don't rightly know. At the moment, I don't think there's much point in taking it any further. If I can't convince Vandervell, nobody in Washington is going to listen to me.'

Virginia thought it was a wise decision, but for a very different reason. She knew that if he had a mind to, Vandervell could wreck his career. There was no need to initiate an adverse report; a phone call to one of his former classmates in Washington would suffice. Vandervell had only to say that Anderson was being difficult and uncooperative and John would be removed under a cloud. A blot like that on his copy book would be enough to ensure his name never appeared in any future promotion list.

'Remember Gunner Yates?' she said, glad of an opportunity to change the subject.

'What's he done now?'

'Nothing. A Sergeant Toomis phoned to say that the police are releasing him into naval custody.'

The news didn't exactly thrill him, but Delgado had kept his word. He'd respected the detective for his frankness when they'd met, but now Delgado went up even further in his estimation.

'It seems the two men he rolled couldn't identify him after all,' she added.

'So when do I have to collect him?'

'You don't. I passed the message on to the escort base and told that smooth-talking Canadian exec that Yates was strictly his problem.

Anderson raised an eyebrow. 'And he didn't argue the toss?' he asked incredulously.

'He took it like a lamb.'

'Words fail me. Ginny. I'm lost in admiration.' Anderson smiled. 'How about having dinner with me tonight?'

'Why? Because I did you a favour?'

'Of course not. It's just that I can't think of a nicer way to spend an evening.'

'Who's kidding who?' she said lightly.

A pair of strong hands seized her wrists and pulled her toward him and before she had time to ask him what he thought he was doing, his mouth closed on hers.

'Does that convince you?' he said later.

'You bet it does,' she murmured.

'I can't think what's come over you, Ben,' said Gina. 'This is the second time in a week you've arrived home early.'

They were sitting in the kitchen, the supper dishes drying off in the plate rack. The door to the living room was ajar and from the noise of gunfire coming from the radio, Delgado assumed his son was listening to *The Lone Ranger*.

'Why this new leaf all of a sudden?'

'Does there have to be a reason?' he countered.

'You've got a guilty conscience about something, Ben.'

'Like what?'

'I don't know,' said Gina. 'I'm waiting for you to tell me.'

Delgado sighed, fished a crumpled scrap of paper from his pocket and pushed it across the table. 'Well, as it happens, there is another woman,' he said jokingly. 'But I haven't met her yet.'

'Webber's lady friend?'

'Who else?'

Gina stared at the illegible scrawl, her forehead wrinkling in a puzzled frown. 'What's it supposed to be?' she asked. 'Egyptian hieroglyphics?'

'It's supposed to be a facsimile of her signature.' Delgado twisted round, opened the refrigerator and helped himself to a can of beer. 'I thought maybe you could make out her name.'

Gina held the scrap of paper at arm's length, turning it this way and that while he opened the can and drank from it.

'There's a glass in the cupboard, Ben,' she said patiently.

'A glass, huh? Why don't you come right out with it, honey? Why don't you tell me straight that you don't like me drinking out of a can?'

'All right, Ben. I don't like you drinking out of a can.'

'Well, okay,' said Delgado and grinned. 'I'll get a glass then.'

'Her first name could be Christine.'

'That's what I figured.' Delgado poured his beer into a glass and returned to the table. 'What about the surname?'

'Zoel? Zulb? I've really no idea.' Gina handed the scrap of paper back to him. 'Does it really matter who she is, Ben?'

'Webber made the reservations and they had adjoining rooms. The address he gave was care of National Eastern Airlines instead of his home on East 92nd, and the woman came from Georgetown, Washington. Now, don't you think the whole thing is kind of odd? I mean, why didn't he take her back to his place?'

'Perhaps Webber has someone else in tow as well and he didn't want to risk them meeting face to face. He may

190

well be a philanderer, but that doesn't make him a criminal.'

'Janowski lied to me.'

'So what? Webber simply bribed the cab driver so that her name wouldn't appear in the newspapers.' Gina cupped her face in both hands, her elbows resting on the kitchen table. 'Why do you have this fixation about Webber, Ben?'

'I don't know – there's something about him that keeps bugging me, something I can't put my finger on.'

'I would have thought you had enough to do without chasing shadows, but of course you know best.'

'You think I should drop it?'

'It's not for me to say,' Gina said quietly.

Delgado stroked her hair with a finger. 'I'd still like to hear your opinion,' he said.

Gina hesitated, reluctant even now to say what she thought, despite what Ben had said. A murmured 'please' finally convinced her he meant it.

'What you do in your spare time is your affair, but I don't think this particular bit of overtime would go down well with Lieutenant Caskey. It's a blind alley – you told me so yourself.'

He had, too, a week ago when they'd met for lunch at the Hickory House, and nothing had changed since then.

'You're absolutely right,' he said. 'There's no percentage in pursuing the Webber affair.'

All the same Delgado shoved the crumpled piece of paper into his pocket. Tomorrow, when he walked into the squad-room, he would push it under the sheet of glass on his desk where he kept all the other memos to himself.

'Good.' Gina nodded emphatically. 'Now maybe we can talk about something else for a change. Do you realize there are only sixteen shopping days to Christmas?'

He hadn't, nor had he realized just what was involved. As well as a host of relatives on either side of the family, it appeared they still hadn't got anything for his parents and Gina wanted some suggestions from him. Resolutely switching his thoughts away from Webber, Delgado turned his mind to the problem of Christmas gifts.

The man who entered the phone booth in Harry's Soda Fountain and Drugstore on Astoria Boulevard in Queens was in his late thirties, had a pockmarked, sallow face, was a shade over five feet ten inches and was lean with it. According to his social security and draft exemption cards, his name was Henry Osprey.

Following an absence of seven years, Osprey had returned to New York, travelling four thousand miles to make a very special delivery. He had sailed from Kiel in U 1230 with two other companions some three weeks before the meeting between Kapitän zur See Wirth and Sturmbannführer Otto Skorzeny took place at Oranienburg. Forty-eight days later, on Wednesday the twenty-ninth of November, the U-boat had entered Frenchman Bay on the coast of Maine. Passing between Bar Harbour and Winter Harbour, U 1230 had proceeded up the bay to Hancock Point where Osprey and his two companions had then made their way ashore in an inflatable assault boat, landing shortly after 2300 hours Eastern standard time. After burying the boat in a wood, the three men had split up, Osprey travelling to Boston by Greyhound bus the following morning. He had spent four nights at the home of a Nazi sympathizer in Boston, where he'd received a detailed briefing on the American scene and the changes that had taken place in his absence, before moving on to New York.

For Osprey, this was now the moment of truth. Lifting the phone off the hook, he dialed the number he'd memorized weeks ago in Berlin. After a long delay, the man he'd travelled four thousand miles to see finally answered the telephone.

'Mr. Webber?' he said. 'My name's Henry Osprey. You won't know me, but we have a mutual friend – a Mrs. Amy Butcher.'

The response he got from Webber was cautious, but no more than he'd expected.

'I ran into her the other day in Boston,' Osprey

continued, 'and she said to be sure and look you up when I was in New York. As a matter of fact, Amy asked me if I'd mind delivering a new suitcase to you. I understand she borrowed one of yours for the summer vacation and it got damaged.'

Webber caught on fast, agreed that was so and then enlarged on the story to make their conversation seem more natural before suggesting where and when they should meet.

'Tomorrow evening will suit me fine,' Osprey said presently. 'I'll look forward to meeting you at six-thirty, Mr. Webber.'

Osprey hung up and left the booth feeling vaguely uneasy. Berlin had led him to understand that his job was finished once the delivery had been made, but Webber had hinted there was something else in the wind, a favour he wanted doing. Osprey didn't like the sound of that, not one bit.

CHAPTER 19

New York

Wednesday, 6 December 1944. Evening.

Webber strolled toward the far end of the curved island platform. The evening rush hour was over, and apart from himself, there were just five other men and two women waiting for the next downtown train to arrive at Chatham Square. The men were all dressed alike in dark overcoats and black fedoras, a uniformity which suggested they were civil servants from the nearby Municipal building. Four of them had their noses buried in newspapers while the fifth was deep in conversation with a middle-aged woman. Near the couple, a pretty blond in her early twenties with a Veronica Lake hairstyle was staring at a billboard which advertised the fact that *Laura*, starring Dana Andrews,

Gene Tierney and Clifton Webb, was now showing at the Regent.

Webber reached the far end of the platform and, gazing up at the domed roof of the World Building, wondered if it would still be there in a year's time. That was the trouble with New York; its face kept changing, and once-familiar landmarks had a habit of disappearing almost overnight. The old Ninth Avenue elevated had been dismantled back in 1940, and before the decade was out, there wouldn't be a single el left in the city. Of course, it was absurd to feel upset about the changes that were taking place, especially as he would be instrumental in wreaking death and destruction on the metropolis, but he couldn't help it. The streak of sentimentality that was part of his Teutonic character was never far below the surface.

A rhythmic drumming noise captured his attention, and glancing to the right, Webber saw a pinpoint of light in the distance. The light grew larger, the drumming sound changing to a loud clatter as the outline of a downtown local became visible. Approaching the curve, the motorman applied the brakes, adding a harsh, nerve-grinding squeal to the cacophony of noise. Gradually slowing to a halt, the four-coach train drew into the island platform.

Twelve passengers left the train. Among them, Webber spotted a man carrying a small suitcase in his left hand who answered to the description Christel Zolf had given him when they'd met in Washington a week ago. As soon as he was satisfied that Osprey was not being followed, Webber caught up with the courier and fell in step beside him.

'How's Amy Butcher feeling these days?' he murmured.

'Amy's fine. Mr. Webber,' Osprey said casually. 'She sends her warm regards. I haven't kept you waiting, have I?'

'No, you're right on time. My car's parked outside the station.'

They went on down the steps to the street below, where Webber opened the trunk of his Studebaker two-door sedan and invited Osprey to dump the suitcase inside. Without apparent haste, both men then got into the car, Webber checking in the rearview mirror before pulling out from the curb to turn on to East Broadway.

'All right,' he said presently, 'let's hear it.'

'The transmitter is built into the suitcase. It has ground crystals, is preset to the correct frequency and has a maximum range of one hundred and fifty miles when tapped into the mains.' Osprey dug out a crumpled packet of Lucky strike, saw there was only one cigarette left, thought about offering it to Webber and then, with an apologetic smile, kept it for himself. Using the cigarette lighter in the dash, he lit up and inhaled. 'The dry cell batteries are an alternative source of power for use in an emergency. They have a working life of eight hours, but produce a much weaker signal that won't carry above eighty miles.'

There was more to come. Apart from operating procedures, schedules and call signs, Webber was required to memorize a list of code words relating to Operation Griffin.

'Contact will be established at 2240 our time on Saturday the twenty-third,' Osprey continued. 'If the strike is to take place within the next twenty-four hours, you'll be asked for a weather forecast.'

'Just like that,' Webber said drily.

'I don't see why it should be difficult. You're a pilot with National Eastern Airlines and there's a Met section at La Guardia. All our people are interested in is the direction and speed of the prevailing winds from ground level up to six thousand feet.'

If he wasn't flying that day, the weathermen might think it odd that he should want a forecast, but Webber let it pass. Leaving East Broadway, he cut through Clinton, turned left on Grand Street and headed toward the Bowery.

'What else do you have for me?' he asked.

'A homing beacon for the V1,' said Osprey, producing a small flashlight from the pocket of his overcoat. 'You

195

push the switch forward and it starts transmitting.'

'Can the signal be detected?'

'Not by the public.' Osprey placed the beacon on the bench seat within reach of Webber. 'You'd need a High Frequency Direction Finder to pick it up and NYPD doesn't have one.'

'You're forgetting the navy.'

'I can assure you we haven't. The shore-based installations will be looking out to sea, and you can forget the escort vessels – they'll be on harbour routine, which means their sets will be switched off.'

'Maybe, but I wouldn't bet my shirt on it.'

'I can see what you're worried about.' Osprey opened the ashtray in the dashboard and stubbed out his cigarette 'Once you've placed the homing beacon in the target area, you can walk away from it.'

'Assuming I'm still around when the time comes.'

'What do you mean by that?' Osprey asked in a sharp voice.

In a few brief sentences, Webber told him about Janowski and Delgado and how he thought they should deal with the cab driver. By the time he'd finished, they were on Third Avenue and heading north.

'You're crazy,' Osprey said fiercely. 'Killing Janowski is plain stupid.'

'You think I should buy him off?'

'Hell, no. In your place, I'd sit back and do nothing. Janowski's bluffing – he won't go to the police.'

'It'll be the other way around. This Delgado is a very nosy character. I don't know why the bastard is so damned interested, but he is, and Janowski knows too much. He's got to be taken out.'

'That's a surefire way to draw attention to yourself.'

'Not if you make it look like an accident.'

'Oh no.' Osprey shook his head vehemently. 'I'm not about to kill anybody. I've made the delivery and that's it. Besides, the longer I stay in New York, the bigger risk I become for everyone concerned – you included.'

'When are you leaving?' Webber asked insistently.

'That's my business.'

'I know where Janowski lives. I can tell you what he does during the day before he goes on night shift. I've planned the whole thing?'

Osprey cut him off in midsentence. 'I don't want to know,' he said loudly. 'Just pull over to the curb and let me out – right here, right now.'

It was said with force and in a way that preempted any further argument. Webber could see that nothing he said would persuade the other man to change his mind. He had met with a blank wall and the only thing he could do was back off and take a fresh look at the problem.

'All right,' he snapped, 'keep your shirt on. I've got the message.' Gliding over to the curb, he pulled up outside a fruit and vegetable store and shifted the gear lever into neutral.

'I hope you have.' Osprey turned to face him, one hand on the door handle. 'Just take it easy and you'll be okay.'

The courier punched him lightly on the arm to emphasize the point he had made and then got out of the sedan. The entrance to the Third Avenue El 59th Street station was no distance from the fruit and vegetable store. Reaching it in a few strides, Osprey climbed the covered walkway to the track above and disappeared from view.

A month ago, when Tom Sullivan had introduced them to each other, Anderson had rapidly decided that, although undoubtedly attractive, Lieutenant (j.g.) Virginia Canford was just about the most arrogant, stuck-up young woman he'd ever met. She had also made it clear that she didn't think much of him either. Thirty days later, it was a very different story. From being coldly polite to one another, they had gradually come together, seeing more and more of each other when they were off duty. Yesterday evening he had taken her to the Astor, blowing most of his pay for the month; tonight she had invited him to her place for dinner. To use an American expression, he supposed their relationship had reached the point where it could be said they were now going steady.

197

'That was good, very good.' Anderson placed the spoon and fork together on the plate and wiped his mouth on a napkin. 'Is there anything you can't do, Ginny?'

'I hate to disillusion you, but I can't even boil an egg.'

Anderson laughed. 'But you can cook a three-course dinner?'

'Well, the truth is that my roommate, Judy, cooked the chicken before she went out. The soup and the apple pie only needed warming up. One thing I am good at though is getting other people to do the domestic chores.' Virginia smiled. 'You want to help with the dishes?'

'It's hard to resist an appeal like that,' he said.

The kitchen was much tidier than she'd led him to expect. The saucepans had already been emptied and neatly stacked on the draining board and the gravy pan left to soak in the sink. Donning an apron and a pair of rubber gloves, Virginia set to with the same kind of efficiency she showed at the office.

'Some man is going to be very lucky,' he observed mildly.

'You think so?' Virginia handed him a soapy plate to dry.

'Well, if you really want to know, I don't happen to believe a woman's place is in the kitchen.'

First she couldn't cook; now it seemed she loathed housework. Anderson wondered if he was being warned off or whether she was merely telling him the score.

'Nor do I think keeping house for a man should be her ultimate ambition.'

'You don't intend to get married then?'

'I didn't say that. The trouble with most men is that they tend to see a woman as some sort of prized possession. The more attractive she is, the more likely they are to treat her like a clotheshorse. They want other men to admire her because it flatters their ego.'

He thought Ginny probably had a point, although she wasn't averse to admiration herself. She hadn't been exactly displeased when he'd said how much he liked the green velvet dress she was wearing.

'It's just that you're not ready to settle down yet,' he suggested.

'I've had a very expensive education, John. I want to make the most of it. In three of four years' time, I may feel differently.' She shrugged her shoulders. 'Who knows?'

Anderson got the message. Virginia liked him well enough, but she valued her freedom more.

'Anyway, I doubt if I will ever really settle down in the way you mean.' Virginia picked up a scouring pad and vigorously attacked the gravy pan. 'I don't see myself running a home for the rest of my days. Neither do I see myself becoming an active member of the Daughters of the American Revolution or whatever.

There were a lot of things she wanted to do with her life. It seemed the *Saturday Evening Post* had published two of her short stories and *Esquire* had accepted another shortly before she was posted to Eastern Sea Frontier. There was also a novel she intended to write one day. Other people had said much the same thing to him, but in her case Anderson knew she would do it and succeed.

'I hope you'll send me an autographed copy,' he said.

'Oh, I certainly will.' Virginia emptied the dishpan and removed her apron and rubber gloves. 'What are you going to do when this war is over?'

'I'll stay on in the navy and earn my pension.'

Put like that, it sounded dull and mundane compared with her plans for the future, but it was the career he had chosen to follow. He just hoped he wouldn't become bitter and disillusioned like Vandervell.

'Anyway, what do you want to do right now?' he asked swiftly. 'Go to the movies?'

'Why do that when we've got the apartment to ourselves?' She caught hold of his hand and led him into the living room. 'I've got a much better idea. Let's have a drink and just sit and talk. When we get tired of doing that, we can always play a few records.'

The record player was destined to remain silent. For the first time since he'd known her, Virginia really opened up and talked about herself. She told him how happy she'd been at Shipley and later at Bryn Mawr; about her first date and the time she broke her wrist while skiing in Vermont, and about her parents and the family home in East Hampton.

'I'm going there this coming weekend,' she said. 'Commander Vandervell has given me a forty-eight hour furlough starting Friday night.'

'How very decent of him.'

'Why don't you come too? I'll borrow Dad's car and meet you at the train Saturday morning.

The invitation was proffered almost as a casual afterthought, and he accepted with the same kind of nonchalance.

Webber entered the hallway of his apartment with a feeling of relief and closed the door quietly behind him. From the moment he'd turned into East 93rd Street, no thief in the night could have been more furtive. While still a good fifty yards from the house, he'd switched off the headlights and engine to coast the rest of the way in neutral. Before opening the trunk, he'd checked the Langdon's apartment to make sure the curtains were drawn and that nobody was watching him from the window. Once inside the house, he'd avoided every loose floorboard on the staircase and had crept along the landing with the stealthiness of a cat stalking a bird.

A cat stalking a bird? On reflection, Webber thought the simile was inappropriate. He was more like a fly caught in the web that Cynthia and her mother had spun for him. He'd become entangled because of a momentary lapse of concentration which had led to a careless slip of the tongue. Who's Christel? Cynthia had asked, and he had said that she was an air hostess, but the explanation hadn't sounded very convincing to his ears and he'd panicked. Inviting Cynthia in for a drink had been a stupid mistake, but making love to her had been an act of folly bordering on the insane. She had shed her inhibitions, displaying an animal-like ferocity that had alarmed him, crushing his ribs with her thin bony legs and raking his back with sharp fingernails, her teeth bared in a snarl. He had seen the hungry possessiveness in her eyes and had had an inkling of what was to follow, but even so, the depth and persistence of her questioning had been a harrowing experience and he'd needed to have all his wits about him. Her curiosity was insatiable. If Cynthia had waylaid him on the landing a few minutes ago, she would have made some comment about the luggage he was carrying and he would have had a hard time explaining that away.

Shedding his overcoat, Webber removed the homing beacon from the pocket and took the suitcase into the living toom where he examined it over a large scotch. The transmitter was concealed under a false bottom, together with the headphones, Morse key and a flexible thirty-foot wire aerial. On closer inspection, he noticed that the power lead had been fitted with the wrong type of plug, but that was a small problem and easily remedied.

Although the suitcase looked innocent enough, it was a potent and visible reminder of what he'd let himself in for when he'd offered his services to the German consular official in San Francisco ten long years ago. Up to now, he had always called the tune, deciding where and when he and Christel Zolf should meet. Up to now, the risks had been negligible. But all of a sudden, the whole business was no longer an enthralling game that made the adrenalin flow; it was a matter of life and death. Closing the lid with a snap, he took the suitcase into the bedroom and hid it in the closet.

Returning to the living room, Webber topped his glass from the bottle of Canadian Club on the sideboard and flopped into an armchair. Osprey had advised him to leave Janowski well enough alone, but he wasn't on the firing line. If he sat back and did nothing, the cab driver might open his big mouth and then he would have Delgado on his back, which was the last thing he needed. Janowski had said Delgado was the stubborn kind, which probably meant he was the sort of cop who was prepared to bend the rules if it means solving a case. A man like that wouldn't hesitate to break into his apartment if he suspected he had something to hide.

He had known all along that Janowski was the danger man, the human time bomb that had to be defused sooner or later. He had spent a lot of time figuring just how his death could be made to look like an accident, and he knew his plan would have gone like clockwork. Osprey had been tailor-made for the job too, a natural who would have merged into the background like a chameleon. With the right garb, he could have slipped into the tenement building on Oliver Street and left again without any of the neighbours taking much notice of him. Osprey could also have gotten close to Janowski without the cab driver smelling a rat as soon as he opened the door. With him it was different; Janowski knew his face and the alarm bells would start ringing the moment he saw him on the doorstep.

The right garb? Well, sure, he needed to wear something that didn't make him conspicuous in the neighbourhood, something people would immediately accept. At the same time, he needed something to make them look hastily the other way, something that would hold Janowski's attention for those few vital seconds.

The idea came to him suddenly and was so obvious that he wondered why he hadn't thought of it before. Leaving his drink on the table, Webber got out the telephone directory for Manhattan and started leafing through it, looking for the name and address of a theatrical costumer.

CHAPTER 20

East Hampton, Long Island

Saturday, 9 December 1944. Afternoon.

The house was called Glendales. Anderson reckoned the movie moguls could have saved themselves a small fortune in stage sets had they asked to film it when they made *Rebecca*. It resembled Sunnyside, the home of Washington Irving at Tarrytown on the Hudson, but was twice as big. Built in 1858 in the style of an Elizabethan manor, its stone face was covered in ivy, which added a certain maturity and made the house look much older than it was. The estate comprised forty acres landscaped with copper beech, silver birth, elm and oak trees. There were two lawn tennis courts, a heated outdoor swimming pool and a large stable, part of which was used to garage a Cadillac Fleetwood sedan, a Lincoln Continental Cabriolet and a Pontiac Torpedo Six. The Pontiac belonged to Virginia and had been jacked up on blocks for the duration.

Glendales had three reception rooms, an oak-panelled dining room, a study, a library and a billiard room on the ground floor. From the large entrance hall, an imposing staircase made three right-angled turns to reach a broad landing that was used as a portrait gallery. Anderson's room was in the crenellated tower of the east wing, from which aspect he had a magnificent view of the Atlantic Ocean. That it was also far removed from Virginia's bedroom was, he thought, not without some significance.

Her parents, though charming, were somewhat intimidating. Howard Canford, a slightly taller and more broad-shouldered version of Governor Thomas Dewey, was in his mid-fifties, but looked no older than his wife who was eight years younger. Mother and daughter were so alike that there was never any doubt from whom Virginia had inherited her good looks and occasionally regal manner.

Lunch was served in the oak-panelled dining room. The china was Crown Derby imported from England before the war, while the silver, he was proudly informed, had been specially made for Virginia's great, great, great grandfather before King George the Third had ascended the throne.

The conversation ranged far and wide, from the war to the latest shows on Broadway, but mostly it concerned Anderson. How long had he been in the Royal Navy? Where did he come from? And what did his people do? Questions that were put to him in the nicest possible way by Mrs. Canford, whom he wryly thought would have made a first-class interrogator.

Coffee was served in the rose salon, a large room with rose-coloured velvet drapes in the windows, matching easy chairs covered in the same material and a grand piano on which there were several photographs of Virginia in silver frames. Virginia in gown and mortarboard on Graduation Day, in riding habit, and looking singularly determined in a white blouse and tennis shorts that showed off her long, suntanned and very shapely legs.

Tennis, it transpired, was her favourite sport and she had taken part in the National Championships in 1938 at the age of eighteen, progressing as far as the third round before she was eliminated. It was all rather deflating for the male ego and, not for the first time, Anderson wondered if there was anything she couldn't do superlatively well. His opinion that Virginia was a very single-minded young woman was reinforced when he learned that she had given up competitive tennis a year later, having decided she wanted to be a lawyer and that the two didn't mix. 'Besides, I knew I didn't have the talent to become a champion,' she had said with typical candor, and had then dashed off to her room to change into something more suitable for the beach.

Something more suitable was a pair of tan-coloured slacks, a floppy polo-neck sweater, a fleece-lined jacket and a pair of sneakers. Slipping on the duffle coat which he'd left in the hall, Anderson followed her out of the house. In contrast to yesterday's rain and sixty-mile-an-hour gale which had led to the cancellation of seventy-five flights at

204

La Guardia, the weather was much kinder even though there was a sharp nip in the air.

'You're very quiet,' Virginia said presently.

'My draft chit arrived this morning.'

'Your what?'

'A signal from the Admiralty appointing me to HMS *Aden* as first lieutenant.

'Oh.'

Her voice sounded flat, on a par with how he'd felt when the Senior British Liaison Officer had given him the news over breakfast in the wardroom. Although the seagoing appointment was what he wanted, Anderson reckoned it was due entirely to the whims of their lordships at the Admiralty rather than the culmination of the fourteen-month campaign he had waged. Certainly his latest application submitted only a fortnight ago could not have done the trick; unless it had gone by airmail, it was still somewhere on the high seas. There was another reason why he had received the news with mixed feelings, one that had to do with his growing attachment to Virginia Canford. She had come to mean a lot to him, and lately he thought she felt the same way. But, in more rational moments, he'd always known it was an impossible situation. Now, having met her parents and seen Glendales, he was quite certain that the overwhelming disparity of their respective backgrounds was an insurmountable barrier between them.

'It's not a rush move,' he said. 'I don't have to report to San Francisco until the fourth of January, and even then, there's no telling when I will be allocated a seat on a plane. I'm not sure where HMS *Aden* is at the moment, but she's part of the British Pacific Fleet.

Virginia slipped her arm through his. The fourth of January was less than a month away, but any kind of reprieve was better than no reprieve at all. 'What exactly is a first lieutenant?' she asked.

'You'd call him an exec. The *Aden* is a six-inch-gun cruiser, so it's a plum appointment.'

'They should have given you a command,' she said firmly.

It was nice of her to say so, but Virginia knew next to nothing about the career structure of the Royal Navy.

'I commanded HMS *Magenta* before I was posted to New York. She was a Flower Class corvette built on the lines of a whalecatcher.' Anderson stooped down, picked up a pebble and sent it skimming across the water. 'I tell you the old *Magenta* was a pretty lively ship even when conditions were relatively calm. We reckoned she would have rolled on a wet sponge.'

She had also been an uncomfortable ship in other ways. Designed as a coastal escort, there had been no facilities for baking bread, and lacking a refrigerator, food had to be rationed after ten days at sea. Just to make life even more difficult, the galley was aft, so far removed from the crew's accommodation in the fo'c'sle that they rarely got a hot meal.

'For us, the North Atlantic was the real enemy, especially in winter. Looking back, I can't remember a time when we weren't cold, hungry, tired or soaked to the skin. Yet, for all the hardships and discomfort, we were proud of the *Magenta* and every time we brought a convoy into Liverpool, there was immense satisfaction in knowing that you were doing a vital job in keeping the lifeline open. And when we sank that U-boat back in 1941 – well, that was the icing on the cake.'

There had been an element of luck about it. In those days, the navy was still using the old Mark VII depth charge which had a maximum setting of five hundred feet, and since the U-boats were capable of diving well below that, their chances of survival were usually better than good.

'It was unbelievable. We were on our way to rendezvous with an eastbound convoy when this U-boat began to surface dead ahead of us. The range was five thousand yards and we were making sixteen knots, but even when their lookouts began to spill out of the conning tower, we still held our fire. I wanted to be sure of a first-round hit with the four-inch gun on the fo'c'sle and to close the distance as much as possible before they spotted us. When

they did, we opened up and damn near parted their hair.
The gun crew got off another two rounds before the U-boat
crash-dived and then the asdic started pinging. We knew
we had him because there was no way that U-boat could get
below five hundred feet before we dropped our depth
charges. The sea erupted behind us and five boiling geysers
soared into the air. Soon afterward the asdic lost contact,
but as we came about, the sub slowly rose to the surface. I
don't know how many of the crew managed to jump
overboard before she went down stern-first, but we only
picked up nine survivors. One year later, we met with the
same fate.'

The war at sea had just entered a new phase, one in
which the U-boats were hunting in wolf packs. Apart from
themselves, the close escort group which had rendezvoused
with the fast eastbound convoy at the midocean meeting
point had consisted of one antisubmarine trawler, an
elderly sloop of World War I vintage, a Hunt Class
destroyer and two other corvettes. The sloop had developed
engine trouble the following morning and had been forced
to leave them and make for Reykjavik. Shortly after her
departure, a wolf pack had attacked and by nightfall they
had sunk two freighters and a refrigerated cargo liner. In
every case, the merchantmen detailed to act as the rescue
ship had refused to stop for survivors and they had to do the
job instead.

'The ship's complement was eighty-five officers and
men,' said Anderson. 'When the oil tanker was torpedoed
around midnight, we had double that number on board.'

The tanker had burned like a torch to silhouette them
against the dark horizon, and there wasn't a man who
hadn't cursed the survivors as they swam toward the
corvette.

'They were coated in oil and few of them had the strength
to climb the scrambling nets we'd put over the side. One
man literally slipped through our fingers and fell back into
the sea and that was the last we saw of him.'

The *Magenta* had been a sitting duck, but incredibly they
had got away with it. 'I always knew she was a lucky ship,'

the coxswain had said, but their reprieve had lasted exactly one hour. They were doing sixteen knots, going flat-out to catch up with the convoy, when the torpedoes ripped into the hull.

'One hit the bows, the other struck us amidships on the port side. We only had time to launch one of the life rafts before she started to keel over. After that, it was a case of every man for himself.'

All the merchant seamen, together with a large proportion of the ship's company, had been belowdecks at the time and they had gone down with the *Magenta*. He and the bo'sun's mate had spent the rest of the night swimming round and round in circles, herding the survivors toward the life raft where they had hung on to the lines. And then they had died one by one, some rapidly succumbing to the intense cold, others hanging on, clinging to life with great obstinacy until the very last minute. A few had cursed and screamed, but most of them went quickly and with great dignity.

'Only seven of us were still alive by the time HMS *Dainty* arrived on the scene.'

It was a simple statement of fact delivered without a trace of emotion, and it send a cold shiver down Virginia's spine.

'First the *Valhalla* mined in the Thames Estuary and then the *Magenta* torpedoed in mid-Atlantic.' Anderson paused in midstride, aimed a kick at a rusty can half buried in the loose sand and booted it into the air. 'Let's hope I'm not a jinx,' he said cheerfully. 'The *Aden* has come through this war without a scratch so far. It would be ironic if she were to be hit by a kamikaze soon after I joined her.'

'Don't talk like that,' Virginia said angrily.

'It was meant to be a joke, Ginny.'

It was less than funny and she didn't believe him. He had had two narrow escapes and she thought that, in a roundabout way, he was expressing a secret fear that his luck might run out if it happened a third time.

Grabbing hold of his arm again, she steered him away from the sea. 'Come on, John,' she said, 'there's something I want to show you.'

'Oh yes? What's that?'

At that previse moment, Virginia hadn't the faintest idea. All she knew was that the beach was no longer the idyllic place it used to be. The sea looked menacing and cruel, and she felt a compulsion to tear him away from it. Branching off to the right, she followed a well-worn path that led past the lily pond toward the summerhouse at the far end of the rose garden.

'I get it,' he said presently. 'You're taking me on a mystery tour of the grounds. Am I right?'

'Not quite,' she said. 'Look, there it is – my retreat.'

Anderson followed the line of her outstretched arm. The summerhouse was octagonal in shape and built of stone, with four stained-glass windows in leaded frames. The walls were covered in a mass of ivy which had begun to establish a stranglehold on the sloping roof, its tentacles creeping toward the weathercock on top. The evergreen bushes and the hedge behind it were overgrown and the whole place looked neglected. Before the war, Mrs. Canford had told him, there had been four gardeners, whereas now there were only two – an old man and a boy who intended to join the marines as soon as he turned seventeen.

'Race you,' said Virginia.

'Where to?'

'The summerhouse, of course.'

She took off, her long legs covering the lawn in effortless strides, to steal a lead on him that Anderson suspected he would be hard-pressed to make up. That Virginia had all the style and power of a natural athlete became very evident as he tried to close the gap between them. At the halfway point she was still holding off his challenge, but then she began to tire and with twenty yards to go, he managed to forge slightly ahead to beat her to the door by a couple of strides.

'All right, you win,' she said breathlessly and lurched inside the summerhouse to collapse onto a bench. 'I'm out of condition.'

'I'm not exactly a hundred percent fit either. 'He tried

not to gasp, but the effort wasn't altogether successful. A stitch was lancing into his left side and both legs felt like they were made of lead.

'Well, what do you think of my retreat?'

'It's certainly secluded.' Anderson pointed to a solid-looking refectory table which, apart from gathering a lot of dust, took up most of the available space. 'Is this where you wrote the short stories for the *Saturday Evening Post* and *Esquire*?'

'Among other things.'

'Such as?' he prompted.

'Oh, this and that,' she said vaguely. 'Reading a book or just daydreaming. Usually I came here when I wanted to be alone.'

'Like Garbo.'

She smiled briefly and shivered, recalling the night of her coming-out party and how she'd had to fend off the latest eligible young man her mother had picked out for her. 'I know you will like him, darling,' she had said, 'he's very nice and intelligent too. Believe me, he will go a long way.' He had certainly done his best to convince her of that, though not quite in the way her mother had meant. Once he had lured her down to the summerhouse, his version of going a long way had been entirely directed towards a determined effort to remove her underwear.

'I think it's time we were moving on.' Anderson felt her forehead. 'You were in a muck sweat a few minutes ago and now you're shivering.'

'I'm not cold, really.'

'Well, I am. It's bloody chilly in here and we don't want you catching cold, do we?'

Virginia was touched. None of her previous boyfriends had shown such concern for her well-being, and jumping to her feet, she put her arms around his waist and kissed him warmly. What had started as a spontaneous gesture of affection became more ardent and she pressed herself against him, her mouth opening in eager anticipation. Presently, she rested her head on his shoulder and leaned against him while he unbuttoned her jacket and slipped his

210

hands inside. She made no move to stop him when he raised the sweater but then, as he fumbled with the bra, his cold fingers touched her spine and instinctively she broke away and tugged her sweater down.

'My God,' she breathed, 'you're ice cold.'

'Like someone else I know.'

'What do you mean by that?' she snapped.

'Oh, forget it,' he said wearily. 'You're a nice girl, Ginny, and I got the wrong idea. Let's leave it at that.'

'Good.' She tossed her head angrily. 'It's the only sensible thing you've said all afternoon.'

Her head up, her chin at a defiant angle, Virginia walked out on him, and without a backward glance made off toward the house. But before she had gone a hundred yards, contrition set in. Trying not to make it too obvious, she slowed her pace until he caught up with her.

'I'm sorry,' she murmured. 'I lost my temper.'

'You had every right,' he said quietly. 'But don't worry – it won't happen again.'

Together, yet apart, they crossed the lawn and entered the house.

CHAPTER 21

New York

Sunday, 10 December 1944. Evening.

Webber opened the closet and checked his appearance in the full-length mirror. The uniform, which he'd hired from Dayburn's Theatrical Props and Costumes on East 35th Street, fitted him like a glove and looked authentic. Someone with a professional eye for detail might notice that the nightstick wasn't the correct regulation length and that the angled crown of his peaked cap was a shade too big, but that didn't bother him too much. Before entering the tenement building on Oliver Street, he intended to make

211

damn sure the neighbourhood patrolman wasn't in the vicinity.

Convinced that he looked the part, Webber went into the bathroom and took out a package of cotton from the medicine cabinet. Pulling off two pieces, he rinsed them both under the tap and then inserted them into his mouth. Carefully wadding the pads along his gums, he filled them out, distorting his features so as to give himself a round, moon-shaped face. The cap would conceal his hair and, if worn at the right angle, he reckoned the peak would make it difficult for anyone to get a close look at his nose and eyes. Satisfied with the changes made to his face, he wondered how his voice would sound. Gazing at his reflection in the shaving mirror, he said, 'Are you Leon Janowski?' His speech was slurred, the accent not exactly Lower East Side but good enough to pass muster.

Leaving the bathroom, he went into the kitchen and switched on the portable radio. If his wristwatch was correct, the six o'clock newscast from station WMCA would be on the air two minutes from now. The schedule he'd worked out was pretty tight, but provided everything went according to plan, he should be back in time to catch the seven-thirty bulletin. A lot could happen in ninety minutes though, and Webber just hoped that nobody would telephone while he was out. He wasn't expecting anyone to call, but the possibility existed that Cynthia Langdon might take it into her head to ring him. Leaving the phone off the hook wasn't the answer. The prolonged engaged tone might lead her to think it was out of order, and if she reported the fact to the telephone company, the alibi he intended to establish could well collapse like a house of cards. If worse came to worst, he would have to convince Cynthia he'd been fast asleep at the time and hadn't heard the damn thing. He thought that shouldn't be too difficult, particularly as she fondly imagined that he was in love with her.

The commercials came to an end and then the same brisk voice rattled off the station identification and advised everyone to stay tuned for the six o'clock newscast. Waiting

212

just long enough to hear the time check which preceeded the bulletin, Webber switched off the portable and returned to the bedroom.

Like the rest of the uniform, the closed-neck greatcoat was a good fit. Although the rubber hose filled with lead shot made a slight bulge in one pocket, Webber figured no one would notice it in the dark, provided he kept his right arm close to his side. However, leaving the apartment house without any of the neighbours seeing him in this get-up was the immediate and far more serious problem he had to consider. He could just picture Cynthia Langdon's expression as her eyes took in the police uniform and his swollen face and could hear the questions she was bound to ask. Questions such as: Why are you dressed like that, Paul, and what's wrong with your face? Questions he couldn't answer without arousing her deepest suspicion. One thing was certain; if ever he needed to be on a winning streak, it was here and now. Tucking the peaked cap under his arm, he walked to the hall door and let himself out of the apartment.

The muted sound of a piano reached him from the Langdons and he guessed they were holding one of their musical evenings. In an unguarded moment while lying naked in his arms, Cynthia had told him that she hated these soirées, but that they were a ritual the family had observed every Sunday since she could remember. For his part, Webber was glad that they were still keeping up the tradition. Silently, and as quickly as he could on tiptoe, he made for the stairs and went on down. Once outside the house, he began to breathe a little easier.

The Studebaker was parked directly opposite the front porch, facing Central Park and some distance from the nearest street-light. Pausing just long enough to make sure no one else was about, Webber left the shadows, unlocked the door and tossing the peaked cap onto the passenger's seat, slid behind the wheel. When cold, the engine was often difficult to start, but on this occasion he gave it just the right amount of choke and it caught first time. Pushing his feet gently down on the accelerator, he pulled away from the

213

curb and turned left on Fifth Avenue.

Between East 93rd Street and Central Park South, he passed no more than a handful of pedestrians, but from that point on it was a very different story. By the time Webber reached St. Patrick's Cathedral the sidewalks were jam-packed, especially outside Saks where the window displays had drawn a crowd eight deep. The sixty-foot Christmas tree in Rockefeller Plaza was another attraction that seemed to have persuaded half the population of New York to turn up en masse to see the sights at a time when he would have been a whole lot happier it they'd stayed at home.

Apart from having to contend with a small army of jaywalkers, every light was against him all the way to 42nd Street. Thereafter, the traffic began to flow more freely, and driving past the Flatiron Building at 23rd Street, he filtered into Broadway. The impulse to put his foot down was strong but he resisted the urge, knowing that a ticket for speeding would be the equivalent of a nail in his coffin. Turning east on 8th Street, he cut across to Fourth Avenue and then headed toward the Bowery.

Oliver Street, a narrow thoroughfare between a hodgepodge of run-down tenements, was close enough to the Brooklyn Bridge to be dwarfed by it. No matter what time of day it was, one or the other side of the street was nearly always in shadow. The sidewalks were poorly lit, and when night came, the shadows merely got darker and became more intimidating. Reaching the T-junction at the bottom, Webber turned left on Madison Street and then stopped one hundred yards farther on.

Although the journey downtown had taken longer than he'd planned, there was still a healthy margin of time. Janowski worked a six-day, fifty-four hour week from Sunday through Friday. On weekdays his shift with the Ace Cab Company ran from six in the evening to four in the morning, but Sunday was different. On Sundays he clocked in at eight o'clock to put in the remaining four hours to midnight.

Jamming the peaked cap on his head, Webber got out of

the car, locked the door and walked away from it. Despite the fact that every pier on the East River was crammed with shipping, there was no sign of life anywhere. This was not altogether surprising, since there was no good reason why any merchant seaman should venture as far as Madison Street in search of a bar when there were popular haunts like Meyer's Hotel on the waterfront. Even so, the atmosphere was electric. In the still night air he could hear the staccato beat of rivet guns at work in the Brooklyn Navy Yard and the distant whine of a crane, background noises that kept his nerves tingling. Willing himself to stay calm, he turned the corner into Oliver Street.

The tenement where Janowski lived was on the left-hand side of the street and roughly fifty yards from the T-junction. More in hope than anticipation, Webber tried the front door, and, much to his surprise and relief, discovered that it wasn't locked. Pushing it open, he stepped inside the dimly lit hallway and almost blundered into an evil-smelling trash can that one of the occupants had left outside his apartment. Somewhere in the house a radio was playing, and he saw little point in walking softly when the walls were so obviously paper thin. Boldly, as if he had every right to be there, he climbed the staircase to the second floor. Boldly, despite the nervous flutter in his stomach, he pressed the bell to summon Janowski to the door.

Getting no response, he pressed the bell again and then hammered the door.

Moments later, a grumpy voice called, 'Aw right, aw right – knock it off – I'm not deaf, for Chrissakes. Who the hell wants me anyway?'

'I'm a police officer,' Webber said loudly. 'Now suppose you button your lip and open the door.'

Janowski did so, but only as far as the security chain would allow. 'Yeah?' he grunted. 'What do you want with me?'

Webber turned his head slightly to the right so that the other man couldn't get a close look at his face. 'Your name's Leon Janowski and you work for the Ace Cab Company?'

'So what?'

'So they lost a whole month's quota of gasoline coupons sometime on Friday night.' Webber jerked a thumb at the apartment across the landing. 'Now, are you going to invite me inside or do you want the neighbours to hear the rest of the story?'

Janowski hesitated. Then, shrugging his shoulders, he released the chain and stepped aside. As Webber slipped past him, he reached inside the right-hand pocket of the greatcoat for the length of rubber hose. Whipping it out, he swung around, raised his arm aloft and smashed the homemade blackjack into the cab driver's skull.

Janowski slumped to the floor and lay still, his head over to one side, his mouth wide open. Stepping over his body, Webber closed the door and turned the key in the lock. So far, everything had gone according to plan, but there was a long way to go yet before he was home and dry. One speck of blood in the wrong place and the police would know that the dead man had been murdered. With that thought in mind, he went into the bedroom to return with a soiled pillowcase, which he used to clean up the mess on the floor before slipping it over Janowski's head. That done, he then dragged the corpse into the kitchen.

The kitchen was little more than a glorified cubbyhole and was infected with dry rot, which had spread upward from the baseboards to attack the walls. The floorboards under the sink had been raised to expose the joists, which were covered with a white fungus that smelled of mushrooms. There were mice droppings everywhere; outside the cupboards, under the kitchen table and around the gas stove. A piece of cardboard had been pinned to the window frames as a crude replacement for a broken pane of glass.

Webber removed the pillowcase and dropped it into the sink for the time being. Then he lifted the dead man under the armpits and banged his lifeless head against the gas stove, to leave a smear of blood on a corner edge of the front burner. Quickly unlacing both shoes, he slipped them off Janowski's feet and rubbed the soles on the dusty floor. To create the impression that the cab driver had slipped and fallen against the gas stove while attempting to change the light bulb, he planted one footprint in the center of the table and faked another on the edge of the kitchen chair. Satisfied with the end result, Webber replaced the shoes on Jonowski's feet and laced them up again.

One look at the untidy state of the kitchen was enough to convince him that looking for a spare electric light bulb in that pigsty would be a waste of valuable time, and going into the next room, he unscrewed the one in the bathroom. Returning to the kitchen, he found a pile of old newspapers on the floor of a closet, which he used to cover part of the table and chair before climbing up to remove the bulb in the ceiling.

From there on, it took Webber less than five minutes to complete the job. Leaving one light bulb on the table, he smashed the other on the floor before dumping the newspapers back inside the closet. Retrieving the bloodstained pillowcase from the sink, he tucked it inside the greatcoat and then overturned the kitchen chair on the way out.

Careful to make as little noise as possible, he unlocked the front door and stepped out onto the landing. To his sensitive ears, the latch seemed to make a very loud click as he pulled the door to behind him, so loud that his heart started thumping. Sick with apprehension, he forced himself to walk down the staircase, and after what seemed an eternity, he finally reached the front hall. From there, it was only a few strides to the street. Even so, his heart didn't stop thumping until he was safely back inside the Studebaker and heading uptown.

Although a number of potantial hazards still lay ahead, Webber had a feeling that everything was going to work out just the way he'd planned. Of course, finding the street door open had been a stroke of luck, but it was no more than he'd deserved. Had it been locked, he would have been forced to rouse one of Janowski's neighbours in the tenement or else climb the fire escape at the front. As relief set in, he decided it was now safe for him to remove the sodden lumps of cotton.from inside his cheeks, and he tossed them out of the car window.

There were several other items he would need to dispose of when a suitable opportunity presented itself. The bloodstained pillowcase inside his greatcoat would have to be destroyed and the uniform too. Naturally, he'd had the foresight to give a false name and address when he'd hired it from Dayburn's, so there wouldn't be any problem from them. Getting rid of the pillowcase would be comparatively simple. He could burn that in the basement furnace when the superintendent wasn't around, but not the uniform and greatcoat. They were too bulky to go in the fire and he would have to bury them someplace.

Entering East 93rd Street from Madison Avenue, Webber switched off the engine and put the gear in neutral. Coasting up to the apartment house, he parked the Studebaker in the same position as before, directly opposite the front porch. As he left the car and made toward the door, a man out walking his dog passed by on the other side of the street. Although the man was a stranger and it was too dark for him to have seen his uniform, the near encounter still gave Webber a nasty turn. He feared it was an omen of things to come, but in fact there were no further mishaps.

Once inside his own apartment, Webber stripped, packed the uniform and greatcoat into the boxes supplied by Dayburn's and then changed into sports clothes. At seven-fifty, some twenty minutes behind the schedule he'd planned, he picked up the telephone and called Cynthia. In no time at all, her mother answered the phone.

'Good evening, Mrs. Langdon,' Webber said, 'it's me – Paul. Do you think I could have a word with Cynthia, please?'

Of course he could. Mrs. Langdon wasn't about to stand in his way. In her fond imagination, she saw herself as the matchmaker who'd brought the two of them together. When Cynthia came on the line, she sounded breathless and eager, just how he wanted her to be.

'I meant to call you earlier,' he said, 'after I'd had a nap.

218

Unfortunately I overslept. How would you like to come over for a drink?'

A seductive tone of voice made it clear that a drink wasn't the only thing he had in mind. In accepting the invitation, Cynthia gave a broad hint that she'd got the message. From that moment on, Webber knew it would be easy to establish an alibi.

CHAPTER 22

North Western Atlantic Basin
Latitude 45 degrees 3 minutes north
Longitude 36 degrees 9 minutes west

Monday, 11 December 1944

'We surfaced at 1900 and for the past three hours have maintained a cruising speed of ten knots. This is the first time we have been able to do this since the twenty-sixth of November. On that occasion, we took advantage of the severe weather conditions off the Shetlands to recharge our batteries. The difference between then and now is that I intend to remain on the surface until just before first light, assuming of course the enemy continues to leave us in peace. The change of routine has also provided us with the first opportunity we've had to dump our accumulated rubbish over the side. As a result, life on board has become much more tolerable now that our nostrils are no longer assailed with the smell of potato peelings and rotting cabbage leaves.'

Hartmann laid his fountain pen aside. Although it was strictly against regulations to keep a diary in wartime, he had never observed the order. In fact, his first act on assuming command of U 195 had been to open a private journal for the purpose of enlarging upon the entries recorded in the ship's log. Unlike the log, the journal gave the whole story and was a sort of unofficial history. It was also a safety valve which allowed him to blow off steam, something he couldn't do in front of the crew without it having an adverse effect on their morale.

Operation Double Griffin was a case in point. If the men knew that he thought it was going to be the biggest fiasco of the war, their morale would go overboard with the rubbish. Although Kapitän zur See Wirth had despatched a second 'milk cow' to meet them on the return leg, Hartmann still wasn't sure whether they would have enough fuel to reach the rendezvous. Of course, he was assuming they would still be in one piece by then, which was pretty debatable in view of the hazards that lay ahead.

They would be living on borrowed time the moment they surfaced off New York. Both VIs were stored below the bow torpedo room and before the first missile could be winched up on deck, the jumping wire which stretched from the conning tower to the bows would have to be unshackled. Since each flying bomb had been stripped down, Galen's men would have to replace the Argus duct engine and the short stubby wings, a job that could only be tackled after the missile had been positioned on the ramp. Once that task had been completed, they could then think about servicing and preparing the VI for launching. From the word go, Hartmann reckoned the launch programme would take all of two hours, even if the sea was as calm as a millpond. And two hours was a hell of a long time to be on the surface when, less than two hundred miles away, there was an anitsubmarine squadron of the USAAF at Fort Dix, New Jersey.

As Hartmann took up his pen again, somebody outside his cabin coughed discreetly to attract his attention.

'Yes?' he said tersely. 'Who is it?'

'Obersteuermann Frick, sir.' The chief helmsman shuffled his feet nervously. 'May I have a word with you, sir?'

'Yes, of course.' Hartmann closed the journal and, stretching out a hand, drew back the curtain. 'Come in and sit down.'

Frick stepped inside the tiny cabin and, edging his way around the table, sat down on the bench seat. Uncertain what to do with his large hands, he finally clasped them together on his lap.

'Well now,' Hartmann said cheerfully, 'what's the problem?'

Fricks problem was that he didn't know how or where to begin. Until a few minutes ago, he had known exactly what he was going to say, but now that they were face to face, his confidence had simply evaporated. Approachable as the captain was, there was still an unbridgeable gulf between officer and enlisted man. Then, too, officers had a habit of sticking together, and Hartmann would probably bite his head off if he tried to open his eyes about Leutnant zur See Dietrich. That being the case, he would have to tread warily and go at it in a roundabout way.

'It concerns the armoury, sir,' he said finally.

'The armoury,' Hartmann repeated in a dry voice. They had six Mauser automatic pistols and seven rifles on charge, a hangover from the early days of the war when it had been policy to stop and search neutral merchant ships on the high seas. By the time U 195 was commissioned, boarding parties were already a thing of the past, even though the Kriegsmarine apparently hadn't accepted that simple fact. 'What about the armoury?'

'Major Galen has taken charge of the keys, sir.' Frick lowered his eyes and looked down, his face slowly turning red until it almost matched the colour of his beard. 'I just thought you ought to know, sir,' he mumbled.

Hartmann stared at him thoughtfully, puzzled to know why Frick should concern himself about the armoury when Dietrich was in charge of that department. The chief helmsman was anything but a troublemaker and there had to be more to it than met the eye. 'Have you raised the matter with Leutnant Dietrich?' he asked quietly.

'Yes, sir. He said that as the army detachment mustered for rifle inspection, it would be much more convenient if Major Galen had charge of the keys.'

'That would seem a sensible arrangement.'

'Yes, sir.' Frick bit his lip. 'It's just that it would be easier all around if Oberfeldwebel Meyer had them. I mean it would be less embarrassing for the men.'

'You'd like me to have a word with Major Galen?'

'The men would appreciate it, sir.'

'Yes, I'm sure they would,' Hartmann said drily. 'Is there anything else you'd like to get off your chest while you're about it?'

There most certainly was, but Frick decided he'd said enough for the time being. He had pointed a finger at Leutnant Dietrich and the rest was up to the captain. Provided Hartmann kept his ears and eyes open, he would soon become aware of the fact that Galen and the second watch officer were as thick as two thieves and might wonder about that.

'No?' Hartmann smiled. 'Well, in that case ...'

Frick stood up, clicked his heels together and then left the cabin, only too relieved that Hartmann had not pressed him into a corner.

Although Werner Best couldn't put his finger on it, there was something about Hauptmann Kleist that made him feel vaguely uneasy. Judging by the way they kept fidgeting, it was quite obvious that Kleist had much the same effect on the lookouts, and he wished the artillery officer had stayed below instead of joining them up on the bridge. The poor devil couldn't help it, but he looked and acted like a zombie. Best supposed that was hardly surprising considering the agonies Kleist must have suffered in the past two weeks. In fact, it was a wonder he hadn't lost his sanity. Although they had been giving him a quarter grain of morphine each day, it had only dulled the pain, not killed it. You only had to look into his eyes to know that.

'How are you feeling now, Martin?' Best laid a hand on Kleist's shoulder. 'All the better for a breath of fresh air?'

The artillery officer stared at him and then pointed to his ears, a contemptuous expression on his face.

'That's right,' said Best. 'I'm a goddamn fool. You can't hear a thing, can you?'

Kleist hadn't been exactly the easiest person to get along with even before his eardrums had been ruptured. He was the kind of man who preferred his own company and never said a word to anyone unless he had to. Best recalled how reticent Kleist had been the night he and Dietrich had been introduced to him in the officer's mess at Bergen. Every question they'd asked had received a one-word answer, except of course when Kleist had told them that he came from Dortmund. In disclosing that piece of information about himself, he'd been quite loquacious, actually stringing a whole sentence together. The only time he'd really come to life had been when old August Peiper had made some caustic remark about the documentary film they'd seen in the mess hall earlier that evening. Kleist had taken it as a personal slight, and rounding on Peiper, had launched into a high technical assessment of the VI, the gist of his argument being that the flying bomb made every other weapon system obsolete. In truth, that had been the one point they had grasped, the one pearl of wisdom that had emerged from the scientific gobbledygook.

Kleist might not be the most entertaining companion in the world but he was indispensable. Galen had provided proof of that as recently as last Thursday, when he'd suddenly decided that Kleist could not be allowed to waste away. Up until then, he had lain on his bunk refusing to eat anything, but the major had soon changed that. You might be as deaf as a post, but when Galen said eat, you ate. And when the major decided that you needed to get some fresh air into your lungs, you left your bunk and climbed up to the bridge.

Best raised the binoculars to his eyes and swept the dark horizon. Major Reinhard Galen: Now there was an officer he wouldn't like to cross. He was about as trustworthy as a rattlesnake and twice as deadly. Pure supposition? Possibly, but any man who bore such a striking resemblance to the late Reinhard Heydrich, the former chief of the Reich Security Main Office and Protector of Bohemia-Moravia, had to be cast in the same mould. Just why such an arrogant and poisonous bastard should go out of his way to be pleasant to Karl-Hans Deitrich was beyond his comprehension. They had nothing in common except

223

an unshakable belief that under the Führer's inspiring leadership. Germany was bound to win the war in the end. Whatever the reason, theirs was a decidedly odd friendship.

Best lowered the glasses and turned about to find that Kleist had vanished. He told himself that there was no need to be alarmed, that there was probably a rational explanation for his disappearance, but a fearful premonition that something was terribly wrong persisted.

'Where did he go?' he said hoarsely.

'Who, sir?'

The starboard lookout sounded bored, his tone almost insolent, it seemed to Best.

'Hauptmann Kleist, you goddamn idiot,' he snarled. 'That's who.'

'Yes, sir.' The seaman looked round the bridge, visibly shaken. 'Perhaps he's gone below, sir?' he suggested hopefully.

Best thought there was only one way to find out. Removing the cover to the voice pipe, he whistled up the control room. One brief question, one equally short reply, and the premonition became a stone-cold certainty. 'Very good,' he said in a numbed voice. 'Pass the word – captain to the bridge, please.' Then, moving to the telegraph, he rang for slow ahead.

It wasn't difficult to put two and two together. While their backs had been turned, Kleist must have climbed down onto the lower gun platform and from there had made his way aft. There had been nothing to deter him from jumping overboard. In fact, he didn't have to jump. With U 195 low in the water and the stern awash, he could walk straight into the sea.

Best groaned. He should have known what was in his mind. God knows there had been enough warning signs, and it wasn't as if Kleist had been the only potential suicide he'd met. There was the communications officer he'd met in the hospital at Wilhelmshaven two years ago last January. On that occasion, Best had been admitted to the hospital with mild concussion after slipping on a patch of black ice and, while being kept under observation, had

224

found himself sharing a room on the officer's ward with an elderly Leutnant zur See who was apparently suffering from insomnia. Their room had been on the fourth floor and that same night, in the middle of a snowstorm, the communications officer had walked out onto the balcony. As the minutes dragged by, he had become more and more apprehensive and had been on the point of summoning the night nurse when the officer finally stepped back inside the room. The following morning, taking advantage of the man's temporary absence, Best had told the ward sister that he suspected the elderly officer was on the verge of a nervous breakdown, and had been soundly rebuked for his pains. How could he possibly know what he was talking about? He wasn't a doctor, was he? That he wasn't, but all the same, less than twenty-four hours after he'd been discharged from hospital, the Leutnant zur See had blown his brains out.

'What the hell's going on?'

The harsh voice of the captain jerked him back to the present and he spun round to face Hartmann. 'It's Hauptmann Kleist, sir.' Best swallowed nervously. 'He's missing. I think he's jumped overboard.'

'You think?'

'I mean, I've checked, sir. He's not below.'

'I see.' Hartmann rubbed his jaw. 'How long has Kleist been missing?'

'Ten, perhaps fifteen minutes.' Best said miserably.

The arithmetic was simple. Until a few moments ago, they had been cruising at ten knots and in fifteen minutes would have covered two and a half nautical miles. Looking for Kleist in the dark would be like trying to find a needle in a haystack. But at least they must try.

'And our present course?'

Best checked the compass. 'Two three eight degrees, sir.'

Hartmann bent over the voice pipe. 'Bridge – control room,' he rasped. 'Steer zero five eight.'

From below, the duty helmsman repeated the new course and then operated the push buttons controlling the rudder to bring them round. Moving to the telegraph, Hartmann rang for full ahead.

At 2305 hours, they reached the approximate position where Kleist was thought to have jumped overboard. For the next forty-five minutes they then conducted a methodical search of the area, illuminating the night sky with one signal cartridge after another in a vain attempt to find him. Even so, it was only after Best had reported that they were about to run out of illuminating cartridges for the signal pistols that Hartmann reluctantly decided to abandon the search.

CHAPTER 23

Ziegenberg near Frankfurt

Tuesday, 12 December 1944. Night.

Although Kapitän zur See Wirth had lost all sense of direction, he was pretty sure they had been driving around in circles for the last half hour. The bus ride in the dark was the final stage of a journey that had taken him from Kiel to the B-Dienst department at the Tirpitzufer in Berlin and then on to Field Marshal von Rundstedt's headquarters, where he had been searched by an Unterscharführer. That senior officers should have to submit to that kind of treatment at the hands of a grubby little corporal in the SS was nothing less than a monstrous outrage. He had said so in no uncertain terms to von Rundstedt's deputy chief of staff but of course the staff officer had been powerless to do anything about it. The order had come from the Führer himself and nobody was excempt. It applied equally to Field Marshal Model, General Hasso von Manteuffel and SS Oberstgruppenführer Joseph Sepp Dietrich, all of whom had had their briefcases and sidearms removed before they were shepherded onto the bus.

Wirth leaned back in the seat and closed his eyes. The

warm atmosphere inside the bus made him feel drowsy and it had been a tiring journey as well as a tiresome one. He had never been one for dozing off, but there was little point in trying to stay awake when the windows were blacked out with masking tape. Although in the aftermath of the July bomb plot it was only to be expected that the SS would take rigorous precautions to protect the Führer from any would-be assassin, this night mystery tour was carrying security to insane lengths.

But then, of course, the Führer was insane. There were enough factual stories going the rounds to convince Wirth of that. It was an established fact that after Field Marshal Witzleben and Generals Steiff, Hoeppner and Fellgiebel had been sentenced to death by the People's Court for their part in the bomb plot, their subsequent execution by hanging had been filmed on the express orders of Adolph Hitler. That anyone could bear to witness the slow death struggles of the half-naked sixty-three-year-old Field Marshal, and to actually enjoy the spectacle as the Führer had, was beyond belief. The film was to have been used for propaganda purposes, to inspire loyalty through fear, but the idea had been dropped after the officer cadets at Gross-Lichterfelde had walked out in protest when it was screened for their benefit.

The bus driver dropped into third gear, made a sharp right-hand turn and then gradually slowed to a halt. As Wirth came to, their NCO escort, a Scharführer in combat smock and baggy trousers, opened the door and got out. A colonel of the General Staff, immaculate in dress uniform, then boarded the bus, and having introduced himself to Field Marshal Model, invited everyone present to follow him. One by one, the officers rose to their feet and trooped off the bus like so many sheep..

A fatigue party had cleared and gritted a footpath in the snow which led to a large underground concrete bunker. Inside the entrance, two SS men stopped Wirth to check his identity card once more before allowing him to join the other officers in the conference room at the far end of the corridor.

The seating in the conference room had been arranged on the lines of a theatre, with six rows of chairs facing the podium. Those at the front enjoyed the comfort of leather armchairs, while the lesser fry at the back had to sit on wooden benches borrowed from the enlisted men's cookhouse. A seating plan displayed on a bulletin board inside the entrance disabused Wirth of any notion that he might be senior enough to be numbered among the elite. Consoled by the thought that out of sight was out of mind, he took his place in the back row, to find himself sitting directly behind Otto Skorzeny. Unlike the other junior officers from all three services, the Sturmbannführer had been allocated an easy chair, proof that some people in the Third Reich were more equal than others.

'Welcome to Ziegenberg, Christian.' Skorzeny twisted round to face him. 'I was beginning to think your bus driver had got himself lost.'

'Well, I'm not at all sure he knew the route either.' Wirth took out a handkerchief and blew his nose. 'It was my impression we were going round in circles.'

'An old trick, Christian.'

'I beg your pardon?'

'To ensure you were thoroughly disorientated. You could have walked here in half the time.'

The immaculate colonel, who'd let them off the bus, mounted the podium, unveiled a map of Belgium and the Low Countries and then returned to his chair in the front row. Before he could sit down, a door opened at the back of the hall and a stooped figure shuffled onto the stage. As one man, the audience rose to their feet, a forest of arms extended in the Hitler salute.

Observing the Führer as he hobbled toward the lectern dragging one leg behind him, it was plain to Wirth that their leader was a very sick man. His face looked puffy and deadly white, the hands clutching the lectern trembled and his left arm was afflicted with a violent twitch which he did his best to conceal. His spirit, however, was as fiery as ever.

Glaring at the audience, Hitler said. 'Never in history was there a coalition like that of our enemies, composed of

228

such heterogeneous elements with such divergent aims. Ultra-capitalist states on the one hand; ultra-Marxist states on the other. On the one hand a dying empire, Britain; on the other, a colony bent upon inheritance, the United States.'

Wirth felt his jaw drop. Like everyone else in the room, he had expected to be briefed on the forthcoming offensive in the West. Instead, it appeared the Führer was determined to make a political speech, using the kind of oratory that had fired the Nuremberg rallies and delighted the party faithful in the Munich beer halls.

'Each of the partners went into this coalition with the hope of realizing his political ambitions. America wishes to become England's heir, Russia wants to gain the Balkans, and England? Well, she wishes to retain her possessions in the Mediterranean. Even now these states are at loggerheads and he who, like a spider sitting in the middle of his web, can watch developments, observes how these antagonisms grow stronger and stronger from hour to hour.'

Was the Führer hoping to drive a wedge between the Allies then? Wirth stared at the broad arrows on the map, one pointing toward Brussels, the other toward Antwerp. Maybe there was some point to his speech after all.

'If now we can deliver a few more blows, then at any moment this artificially bolstered front may suddenly collapse with a gigantic clap of thunder. Provided ...' The Führer pointed a finger at the audience and wagged it as if admonishing a class of unruly schoolboys. 'Provided always that there is no weakening on the part of Germany.'

Hitler ranted on, working himself up into an uncontrollable rage as he neared the end of his speech. To Wirth it seemed the Führer was literally foaming at the mouth like a rabid dog.

'It is essential to deprive the enemy of his belief that victory is certain,' he raved. 'Wars are finally decided by one side or the other recognizing that they can't be won. We must allow no moment to pass without showing the enemy that, whatever he does, he can never rely on capitulation.

The Third Reich will never capitulate. NEVER NEVER ...' He pounded the lectern with a clenched fist. 'NEVER' NEVER NEVER.'

On that note, and without saying another word, the Führer left the podium and limped out of the conference room. Although most of the audience were astounded by his sudden and inexplicable exit, Field Marshal Model and the generals accepted it with something approaching equanimity. Calmly, as if what had happened was an everyday occurrence, they rose to their feet and strolled toward the exit.

Wirth couldn't believe it. He had spent sixteen hours on the road to attend what Admiral von Friedeburg, the C-in-C of the U-boat fleet, had said would be the most important conference of the war, and instead of the detailed briefing he'd anticipated, had received a political pep talk. If what he had witnessed was a typical Führer conference, he thought it was no wonder that Germany was losing the war.

'What's the matter, Christian?' Skorzeny clapped him on the shoulder. 'Still in a daze? Well, I'm not surprised – the Führer does have an hypnotic effect on some people.'

Wirth looked about him. 'Everybody's gone,' he said in a flat voice.

'Why would they stay on? The conference is over.'

'But what about the offensive? Has it been cancelled?'

'Of course it hasn't. The generals received their orders weeks ago. As a matter of fact, I was first told about the plan on the twentieth of October, soon after I returned from Budapest.' Skorzeny moved out into the aisle, waited for the other man to join him and then led Wirth toward the podium and the large-scale map displayed on the wall behind the platform. 'When I see how the Allies have deployed their armies,' he said, 'I am reminded of a woman with a large bust, a narrow waist and childbearing hips.

'I'm afraid the analogy is lost on me.' With masked his distaste for the Sturmbannführer's crudity behind a feeble smile. 'But then I don't know what the various military symbols stand for.'

'Why should you? You're a sailor not a soldier.' Skorzeny

230

grabbed the pointer staff which was leaning against the lectern and approached the map. 'Look at it this way,' he said. 'Up here in the north on a line from the Schelde through Nijmegen and on to the Aachen, we have the First Canadian, the Second British and the Ninth American Armies. They are the large bosom. Down here in Luxembourg, we have the broad hips of Patton's Third Army. In between, there is the American First Army covering the Ardennes with just five divisions strung out over a front of one hundred and thirty-six kilometers. They are the narrow waist, and that's where we are going to hit them in three days' time.' The pointer staff became a lance to illustrate the main thrust lines. In the north, Sepp Dietrich and the Sixth SS Panzer Army would advance on Liège with Antwerp the final objective; while in the south, Hasso von Manteuffel and the Fifth Panzer Army would drive on Houffalize, cross the Meuse at Dinant and then swing north, capturing Brussels on their way to Antwerp and the final linkup. 'My brigade will spearhead the advance, dressed in American uniforms.' Skorzeny returned the pointer staff to the lectern. 'We shall seize the bridges over the Meuse and create the maximum confusion in the rear areas.'

'It's certainly a bold plan.' Wirth said drily. 'But do we have the necessary resources to carry it out?'

It seemed they had. By scraping the bottom of the barrel, the Führer had collected nearly two thousand five hundred tanks and assault guns and had assembled some twenty-eight divisions, of which nine were Panzers. In addition, a further six division were available for a secondary offensive in the Alsace after the breakthrough in the Ardennes had been achieved. Göring had also promised to supply three thousand fighter planes, though Skorzeny did not appear to have too much faith in the Reichmarshal's ability to deliver the goods.

'Four of the five American divisions facing Field Marshal Model's Army Group B are understrength and we shall go through them like a knife through butter. Antwerp is Eisenhower's main supply port, and once we've split their

231

armies in two, the Anglo-Americans will be in no position to launch another offensive against Germany. We will then be able to turn against the Russians.'

They had robbed Peter to pay Paul, withholding reinforcements from the German forces in the East to form Model's striking force. Guderian, the Chief of the General Staff, had protested about it, but the Führer had refused to listen to him. He didn't need Guderian's advice; he had been commanding the German Army in the field for the past five years and had more practical experience in these matters than any officer of the General Staff could ever hope to have. He'd studied Clausewitz and Moltke and had read all the Schlieffin papers, so there was little he didn't know about the art of war, thank you.

'Just think, Christian, there are two hundred and fifty thousand men tucked away in the Eiffel, waiting in their assembly areas for the word go. What wouldn't I give to be with the spearhead.'

'I thought you said your brigade was leading the advance?'

'So it is, but I am forbidden to go with them.' Skorzeny pulled a face. 'Orders from the Führer.'

'You must be very disappointed,' Wirth murmured.

'Yes, I am. Still, I'm not the only one. I imagine you wish you were in command of U 195 instead of Hartmann.'

Wirth had no desire to be in Hartmann's shoes. Double Griffin was virtually a suicide mission. If the enemy didn't sink him first, he thought there was a very good chance that Erich would run out of fuel before he rendezvoused with the resupply boat from Trondheim.

'Yes, I do rather envy him,' he said, knowing it to be rank hypocrisy.

'That's what I thought you'd say. However, I know one person who isn't very enthusiastic about the operation.'

'Who?' asked Wirth.

'Von Rundstedt. It was suggested the offensive should be named after him.' Skorzeny stepped off the podium and moved toward the exit. 'Do you know what the old gentleman said when he heard about it?'

Wirth shook his head.

'He said that as the Führer had planned the offensive, he should take the credit.' Skorzeny threw back his head and laughed uproariously.

Wirth was damned if he could see the joke, but he thought it only politic to appear amused.

CHAPTER 24

New York

Thursday, 14 December 1944

'This is station WNYC, New York,' the newscaster continued. 'On the home front, Mayor La Guardia said yesterday that he wouldn't hesitate to declare a state of emergency in the city if the meat retailers went ahead with their threat to shut down their shops starting Christmas Day. It seems Mayor La Guardia also made the headlines in Germany. Referring to his speech on Sunday in which he declared "that the people of New York would have no business relations with Naziland for a hundred years if their defenceless city were bombarded by V2 rockets." Captain Ludwig Sertorious of the German Transocean News Agency is quoted as saying: "Apparently it is quite acceptable for the Americans to bomb Turin, Milan, Ravenna, Colgone, Munich or Vienna whenever they so choose, but it is a deadly sin to harm New York."

'With nine shopping days to go, Macy's mail order department reports that the majority of servicemen are buying hope chests for their fiancées and music boxes playing Irving Berlin's "Always" and Brahm's "Lullaby." Still on Christmas, the window display at Schulte's Fifth Avenue and 42nd Street store provoked mixed emotions from the onlookers yesterday. Three laughing Santas are surrounded by posters of a popular brand of cigarette with the centre one disappearing, clutching a carton. One

233

disappointed purchaser was heard to ask, "Is he laughing at us or with us?" Indications are that the current shortage of cigarettes is likely to become worse because of continuous high demand.

'There is still no sign of the barrage balloon which disappeared in the high winds shortly before dawn on Tuesday after it had been hoisted over Broadway to advertise the movie *Winged Victory*, proceeds from which are going to Army Relief. The world premiere of *National Velvet* starring newcomer Elizabeth Taylor starts today at the Radio City Music Hall. For a preview of the movie, here is ...'

Webber switched off the radio and poured himself another cup of coffee. Things were looking good, he thought. The early morning news was largely a rehash of yesterday's, but for the fourth consecutive day there had been no mention of a suspected homicide on Oliver Street. Better still, Janowski's name had yet to appear in the newspapers. It seemed that, in death as in life, the cab driver was destined to remain an anonymous figure, just one of seven and a half million people who happened to live in New York.

Perhaps nobody had found the body yet? Webber dismissed the thought as quickly as it had occurred to him. Janowski might have lived alone, but he wasn't a recluse. Somebody was bound to have missed him – the despatcher at the Ace Cab Company for one.

He could forget Janowski. No matter what the autopsy uncovered, there was nothing to connect him with the cab driver. No one had seen him enter or leave the tenement building on Oliver Street and he'd gotten rid of the incriminating evidence. The bloodstained pillowcase had gone into the basement furnace and the patrolman's uniform, along with the murder weapon, were now lying at the bottom of the East River in a suitcase weighted down with bricks.

Webber wished he could do the same with Mayor La Guardia and Doctor Goebbels and his whole damned Ministry of Propaganda. Maybe civilian morale did need bolstering, but allowing Albert Speer to announce that their V2 weapon would be ready for firing against New York by the end of December had been a prime example of the crass stupidity that was losing the war for Germany. Once his claim had appeared in the Swedish press, just about everybody who was anybody in New York had seen fit to make some kind of statement. Deputy Chief Police Inspector Arthur W. Wallender had sought to reassure the population with the assurance that the city's protective forces were ready for every eventuality, while Alfred Africano, former president of the American Rocket Society, had dismissed the threat on scientific grounds. His calculations showed that in order to deliver a one-ton warhead, the weight of the rocket would need to be in the region of two and a half thousand tons and would cost ten million dollars to build.

Webber just hoped things would quiet down before the twenty-third of December. Nine shopping days to Christmas the newscaster had said, but for him it was nine days to zero hour and the first transmission from U 195. Webber frowned: He would have to make sure he was available right through the holiday. Osprey had said the attack would be launched anytime between Christmas Eve and the New Year and he would have to be flexible, whatever the hell that was supposed to mean. He still had two weeks vacation coming to him, but National Eastern Airlines wouldn't take it kindly if he asked for a leave of absence. They were bound to schedule extra flights over the holiday period and would require every pilot they had to be on duty. Flexibility? Well, as a final resort, he supposed he could always report sick.

Webber swallowed the rest of the coffee, rinsed the breakfast things under the tap and then stacked them in the plate rack to dry. Collecting his overnight bag from the bedroom, he put on his trench coat and left the apartment.

With the local weather bureau forecasting strong winds and occasional snow flurries, Webber was glad that he was spending the night in Miami.

235

Janowski's death had not made the headlines, nor had it even rated a mention elsewhere in the newspapers, but this didn't altogether surprise Delgado. A fatal accident in the home was the kind of copy that ended up on the spike after it reached the subeditor. However, his death had become a newsworthy item sometime between Monday evening, when the body had been discovered, and Tuesday afternoon, when the autopsy had been completed. Or at least it had as far as the detectives of the 5th Precinct on Elizabeth Street were concerned. It had now reached a wider audience, because late on Wednesday night somebody in the Chief of Detectives Bureau at Police Headquarters had decided to include it in the daily teletype the following morning.

'What do you make of this, Jack?' Delgado walked over to Ganley's desk and placed the teletype in front of him. 'Right here at the bottom of the page,' he said.

Ganley skimmed through the paragraph, the thoughtful expression on his face rapidly giving way to the faint smile as the memory bank inside his head made the connection. 'Leon Janowski,' he said, 'the cab driver who knocked down Earl Shaffer, right?'

'You got it, said Delgado.

'A case of foul play.' Ganley clucked his tongue.

'That's what the M.E. says.'

'And somebody tried to make it look like an accident. You think a pro did it, Ben?'

'Maybe. It was certainly premeditated.'

'That it was.' Ganley rubbed his chin. 'I wonder what racket Janowski was into? Whatever it was, you can bet it was pretty small beer.'

'How come?' asked Delgado.

'Well, if it was a big operation like the numbers racket and Janowski had been keeping something back for himself, then the killer wouldn't have tried to fake an accident, would he? I mean, the man who marked Janowski's card would want all the other little guys to know what would happen to them if they stepped out of line.' Ganley looked up and smiled. 'I know what you're going to

236

say, Ben – suddenly it's not a pro job anymore.'

'So?'

'So what the hell? It's not our beef, is it?'

'Janowski was tied in with the Ziggermann case.'

'Aw, come on. Ben – that's stretching things a bit far and you know it. What we have here are two entirely separate crimes. The fact that Janowski figures in both of them is purely coincidental.'

Delgado knew that Gina would have made exactly the same point, but he didn't buy it. When you were faced with a premeditated homicide, anybody who had known the deceased was automatically a suspect. In pruning the list, you looked for a motive and then, after you'd narrowed down the field, you examined the question of opportunity. Janowski had covered for Webber and therefore, in his book, that made the airline pilot a prime suspect.

'Don't you agree, Ben?'

'Sure I do.' Delgado said hastily. 'It's just a coincidence.'

The way he saw it, Webber's mysterious lady friend from Georgetown had provided the motive. Either Janowski had tried to put the squeeze on him or else Webber had got it into his head that the cab driver knew too much. Both possibilities were pretty thin, but the woman did exist and Webber had certainly done everything in his power to keep her out of the limelight.

Motive was one thing, opportunity was something else. The teletype did not give the time of death and it was short on background information too. Delgado supposed he could always call the Medical Examiner's Office and speak to Matthew Quincy; they knew each other from way back and Matt would tell him all he needed to know without asking too many awkward questions. But not now; the squad room was too crowded and he didn't want Ganley and the others to overhear his conversation.

For the rest of the morning, Delgado concerned himself with the great cigarette shortage, which an enterprising band of thieves was trying to resolve in its own inimitable fashion. Since last Friday, no less than five cigar stores had been burglarized and it was a question of trying to figure out where they would strike next.

The squad room remained crowded until well into the afternoon. It was bitterly cold outside, and whether by accident or design, it seemed that every detective on the squad had a lot of paperwork to catch up on. Around four o'clock, a somewhat testy Lieutenant Caskey emerged from his office to ask who the hell was out preventing crime in the precinct, an inquiry which had spurred Ganley and two other more or less dedicated cops into action. By four-thirty, their numbers had thinned out enough for Delgado to call Matthew Quincy.

Quincy said, 'To what do I owe this honour, Ben?'

'I figured it was time we got together again and met for a drink somewhere,' Delgado said, smiling.

'There has to be an angle,' said Quincy.

'There is,' Delgado agreed. 'His name is Leon Janowski.'

'The cab driver? I didn't know you'd been transferred to the 5th Precinct.'

'You know me, Matt, I'm just plain nosy. Who did the autopsy.'

'I did.'

'You want to tell me about it?' Delgado asked.

'There's not much to tell. The deceased failed to show up at the Ace Cab Company on Sunday night. When he didn't appear on Monday, the despatcher asked one of the other cab drivers to look him up. By the time I got to see the body, rigor mortis had set in and he was stone cold. I won't bore you with all the medical details, but there was sufficient evidence for me to deduce that death occurred between seven and ten on Sunday night. From the nature of the head wound, it was apparent that the killer had used a blackjack, probably a length of rubber hose filled with lead shot.'

'So you knew right away it wasn't an accident?'

'Well, let's say I wasn't wholly convinced.' Quincy said laconically. 'Apart from the fact that the injury wasn't consistent with the deceased having struck his head against the gas stove, there were a number of other things that

238

didn't add up.'

'Such as?'

'Well, for instance, I found some cotton fibres and feather fronds in the congealed blood around the lips of the wound which suggested that Janowski's head had been wrapped in a pillowcase or cushion cover. Then there were the footprints on the table and kitchen chair. The weight distribution was much too even considering the shoes were worn down at the heels.'

Janowski had a peculiar gait. Delgado could see him now, walking down the ramp toward the despatcher's office, his feet splayed out like a penguin.

'I guess that about covers it,' said Quincey.

'Were there any signs of a struggle?' Delgado asked.

Quincy sighed. 'You want to know an awful lot, Ben, for the price of a lousy beer.'

'Let's make it two beers,' Delgado said cheerfully. 'I'm feeling in a generous mood.'

None of the neighbours had seen anything and there had been nothing to suggest that Janowski had put up a fight. He had simply opened the door to the killer and had then been struck down from behind.

'Now you know as much as I do, Ben.'

'You've been a big help,' Delgado assured him. 'What do you say we meet for a drink at Joe Allen's tomorrow night around six?'

Quincy said he would look forward to it and hung up. Slowly and in a thoughtful frame of mind, Delgado replaced the phone in its cradle.

The information he'd been given had raised more questions than it had answered. As a rule, nine homicides out of ten were committed in the heat of the moment, but Janowski's had been the exception. The killer had obviously given a lot of thought to the problem, but of even greater significance was the fact that he had known exactly where and when to strike with the minimum risk to himself. He wondered how a stranger could have acquired such a detailed knowledge of Janowski's lifestyle. Playing a hunch, he called the Ace Cab Company.

The despatcher wasn't exactly pleased to hear from him again.

'What's with you guys at the 18th Precinct?' he said. 'Haven't you got anything better to do with your time?' First you call, then Sergeant Mulvaney, and now it's you again.'

'Sergeant who?' Delgado asked sharply.

'Mulvaney. He phoned about ten days ago wanting to know what hours Janowski worked. I asked him what business it was of his and he said Traffic wanted to make sure Leon hadn't been half asleep when the accident occurred.'

'And you filled him in?'

'Sure I did,' said the despatcher. 'It's company policy to help you guys any way we can. So – what can I do for you?'

'You already have.' Delgado told him and put the phone down. The fact that the 18th Precinct didn't have a Sergeant Mulvaney was reason enough to convince him that it was time he had a quiet word with some of Webber's neighbours.

He glanced at the crumpled scrap of paper which, along with a whole lot of other memos to himself, he kept under the sheet of glass on his desk. Perhaps it was even possible that somebody might be able to put a name to that illegible signature he'd copied from the hotel register.

Delgado ran a finger down the list of tenants displayed inside the porch and wondered whose bell he should press. The Langdon's? They lived on the same floor as Webber, but maybe it would be better to start at the bottom and work his way up. That would seem the most sensible way of going about it. He would have to call on all the neighbours anyway, otherwise Webber might think it odd that only he and the Langdons had been singled out. The rabies outbreak which had started in October and caused all kinds of panic was now officially under control, but he decided to bend the fact a little. It was the only way he could think of to question the residents without arousing Webber's

240

suspicion. Even so, he would have to play it carefully.

A voice behind him said, 'Can I help you?'

The woman was about thirty years old, was painfully thin and had deep-set eyes that looked kind of predatory.

Delgado produced his badge for her brief inspection. 'I'm a police officer,' he said, careful not to give his name. 'And you are?'

'Cynthia Langdon.'

'Well, Mrs. Langdon, it just so ...'

'Miss,' she said firmly.

Delgado nodded. It seemed the safest thing to do. He thought she would probably take it the wrong way if he apologized for his mistake.

'You were saying, officer?'

'Well, Miss Langdon, I was going to call on you, but now it won't be necessary.'

'Why not?' she demanded.

'Because the victim I'm looking for is a middle-aged man.' Delgado smiled. 'Or at least that's the description we were given by the dog owner.'

'I don't believe it.' Cynthia Langdon opened her handbag, found a bunch of keys and opened the front door. 'I would have thought the police had better things to do with their time than chase after a man who's been bitten by a dog.'

'This dog had rabies,' Delgado said and followed her into the hall. 'Like the other thirty-five that have been destroyed since October.'

'Oh, my God. I thought the Department of Health claimed they had the outbreak under control?'

'They think it could be a fresh outbreak. Anyway, this man was bitten on Sunday evening around six-thirty.'

'Sunday evening?' Her voice rose. 'And now it's Thursday.'

'We weren't informed the dog had rabies until late this afternoon,' he lied.

'That's absolutely disgraceful. I've a good mind to telephone the Department of Health and tell them so.'

Delgado closed his eyes. The NYPD often had cause to be grateful for the assistance they received from public-spirited citizens, but this one was getting to be a regular pain in the ass. If he didn't shut her up, Cynthia Langdon would ask for his name and precinct and then the fat really would be in the fire.

'Lady,' he said patiently, 'if I were you, I'd call the mayor, but right now I'm concerned to trace a middle-aged man. The dog owner said the victim lived somewhere on East 93rd.'

'You're not going to check the whole street by yourself, are you?' she asked incredulously.

'No, but I'm more likely to run him down than the other officers. You see, the victim was on his way home from walking in Central Park when the dog bit him.' Delgado began to edge away from her. 'Now, if you'll excuse me Miss Langdon, I'd better get started.'

'Well, you needn't bother us.'

'Us?' he repeated.

'My parents and I. We were home all evening, officer. And there's no point in calling on Captain Webber either; he's stopping over in Miami tonight.'

'Captain Webber?' Delgado asked innocently.

'He's a pilot with National Eastern Airlines.'

'Thank you for telling me. We'll ask the airline to get in touch with him.'

'You've no need to do that. Captain Webber didn't go out on Sunday.'

'Are you quite sure about that?' Delgado tried to conceal his disappointment. 'I mean, we can't afford to take any chances.'

'I'm positive,' Cynthia said sweetly. 'You see, I was with Paul all evening.'

Suddenly his theory went down the tube, suddenly Webber was no longer the number-one suspect.

A buzzer whirred, tripping the lock. Pushing the door open, Anderson stepped inside the hallway and started up the

242

staircase to Virginia's apartment on the second floor, uncertain what sort of reception he would receive from the invalid. Although Virginia had returned from Glendales looking very peaky indeed, she had reported for duty on the Monday when it had been bloody obvious to everybody that she ought to have reported sick. Thanks to her obstinacy, the severe chill had turned to flu and by Tuesday lunchtime she was in bed with a temperature of a hundred and one. Of course, he'd telephoned Judy Usmar, her roommate, to see how she was, but all the same he should have looked in on Virginia before now. It was stupid to avoid her just because they'd had that spat on Saturday.

Anderson pressed the bell to her apartment and waited. Presently, he heard footsteps in the hall and then Judy Usmar opened the door.

'Well, hello stranger,' she said with a broad smile. 'I know someone who'll be pleased to see you.'

'Still playing the matchmaker, Judy?' he asked as he stepped inside the hall. 'How's Virginia?'

'Feeling a little sorry for herself, but she's coming along.' Judy closed the door behind him and then crooked a finger.

'Come and see for yourself,' she said.

Virginia was propped up in bed, looking wan and listless. Her eyes were heavy and her nose was redder than a stop-light. She was wearing a fluffy bed jacket over a white satin nightdress that was more than a little breathtaking.

'Guess who?' said Judy and pushed him forward.

As Virginia turned her head toward him, her face suddenly lip up with a warm smile. 'John,' she croaked.

'Hullo, Ginny.' Anderson produced a bottle of whisky from the pocket of his overcoat. 'I thought this might help to cheer you up.'

The whisky had come from the wardroom of HMS *Medina*, a River Class frigate undergoing a refit in the Brooklyn Navy Yard. Persuading her first lieutenant to part with it had entailed a certain amount of bribery and corruption. He supposed flowers would have been more appropriate, but somehow he didn't see himself arriving on anyone's doorstep clutching a bunch of roses.

'Johnnie Walker,' she said, reading the label on the bottle, her voice sounding like a rasp.

'Just the stuff to put wool in your socks,' he said cheerfully. 'Do we have any glasses?'

'I'll get them,' said Judy, 'and then I've leave you two lovebirds in peace.'

There was no answer to that; at least he couldn't think of one.

'Judy's incorrigible,' Virginia told him when they were finally alone, 'but she means well.'

'That'll be the epitaph on her tombstone if she doesn't watch it.' Anderson broke the seal on the bottle and poured two doubles. 'How do you want yours?' he asked. 'Neat or with a splash of water?'

'Straight,' she rasped.

'That's my girl,' he said, 'tough as old boots.'

'Why don't you take your coat off?' Virginia cleared her throat noisily. 'I mean, you are going to stay awhile, aren't you?' she asked with a hopeful expression in her eyes.

'Of course I am.' Anderson shucked off his overcoat and draped it over a chair. As he sat down near the bed, a tentative hand moved across the blanket to reach for his.

'How did the sailing conference go today?'

'Oh, I think the convoy will make it downriver,' he said with a smile.

'I'm sorry you had to stand in for me. Still, if nothing else, the U-boat plot was up to date.' She searched his face. 'Wasn't it?'

He nodded. 'I checked all the intercept reports to make sure.'

'And?'

'Everything was okay.'

'You found I'd overlooked something. Come on, admit it.'

'Well, for a while it looked as though we'd mislaid a U-boat. There was a wireless intercept dated the first of December which reported that one was thought to be operating off the coast of Maine approximately two

244

hundred miles southeast of Frenchman Bay. I couldn't find it on the plot.'

'I scrubbed it a few days later because it was unconfirmed. I suppose I should have checked with the tracking room in Washington.'

'Not to worry,' he said. 'No harm done.'

'I slipped up, didn't I?'

She had, but there was no point rubbing it in. The U-boat had obviously changed frequency and there should have been a follow-up. Virginia should have queried the sighting with Tenth Fleet, but somehow it had been overlooked.

'I wonder what it was doing off the coast of Maine?' she said, frowning.

Anderson thought it a good question. No U-boat had come that close to the eastern seaboard for well over a year. Furthermore, no captain in his right mind would choose to go hunting in an area that was swarming with escort vessels. A madman might be running the Third Reich, but as far as he knew, the Kriegsmarine hadn't appointed a lunatic to command one of their U-boats.

CHAPTER 25

Latitude 39 degrees 5 minutes north
Longitude 68 degrees 41 minutes west

Night, Thursday 21/Friday 22 December 1944

The time signal came through loud and clear on the rebroadcast system and was followed a fraction later by the triumphant blare of martial music. Like two animated puppets, Galen and Deitrich immediately looked up at the amplifier above Hartmann's bunk with an expression of rapt attention on their faces. Their reverence no longer surprised Hartmann. They were the disciples of the Third Reich waiting to hear the latest parable from Berlin as they had done ever since the Ardennes offensive had started before dawn on the sixteenth of December.

The Horst Wessel anthem faded out, giving way to the bombastic voice of the newscaster. 'Soldiers, sailors and airmen of the Third Reich,' he crowed, 'you have cause to rejoice. Continuing their irresistible advance, the Sixth SS Panzer Army today captured the vitally important communication center of St. Vith, inflicting heavy casualties on the American Seventh Armoured Division. Farther to the south, the Fifth Panzer Army has seized Houffalize and is tightening its grip on Bastogne, which is expected to fall at any hour. As a result of these and other hammer blows, the 10th Armoured together with the 28th and 106th Infantry Divisions have ceased to exist as fighting formations, and therefore the destruction of Major General Troy Middleton's 8th Corps has now been completed.'

Hartmann examined his fingernails. Fairy tales were all very well for the ears of children, but not for grown men unless their faculties were impaired. Familiar with the techniques employed by the Ministry of Propaganda, he had learned that the louder the voice, the more certain you could be that there was less to crow about. Contrary to what the newscaster had said, the Sixth SS Panzer Army was not an irresistible force, because it had taken them six days to capture St. Vith. True, Hasso von Manteuffel's army was making better progress in the south, but he recalled that for the past three days it had been confidently predicted that Bastogne was about to fall at any moment.

'Bastogne,' the newscaster continued, 'will become the graveyard of the American 101st Airborne Division. Meanwhile, our armoured spearheads have bypassed the town and are pressing on toward the Meuse. Latest reports from the front say that our forward elements are now less than twenty kilometers from Dinant. Thousands of prisoners have been taken and from Stavelot in the north to St. Hubert in the south, the enemy is in full retreat. Confusion reigns everywhere ...'

And not only among the Americans, Hartmann thought. The same place names were being repeated every night, and even though he didn't have a map, it was obvious to him that the offensive was beginning to run out of steam. Army Group B no longer enjoyed the advantage of surprise they had possessed on the sixteenth of December, when the assault waves, ghostly figures in their white combat smocks and supported by an artillery barrage from over two thousand guns, had advanced through the fog to roll through the American outpost line on the snowy heights of the Schnee Eifel. Overwhelmed by superior numbers, the Americans had fallen back in confusion, but very early on it had become apparent that both the Fifth and Sixth Panzer Armies were encountering much stiffer resistance than they had anticipated. To the connoisseur who knew what to look for, references to heavy and bitter fighting were signs that the battle was not going quite according to plan. However, as long as the fog persisted and the Allied planes remained grounded, there was still an outside chance that they could pull it off. So far, the weather had been on their side and it would need to stay that way.

'Onward then, onward to victory,' concluded the voice from Berlin.

The strident noise of the Horst Wessel anthem reverberated through the amplifier again but only for a few bars. As if sensing Hartmann's strong aversion to the march, the radio operator switched off the rebroadcast, terminating it abruptly.

Galen said, 'Your petty officer was unnecessarily quick off the mark, wasn't he?'

'We've heard the news,' said Hartmann, 'we can do without the pomp and circumstance.'

'Quite so. It's best to let the facts speak for themselves. We've got the Americans on the run and there's no need for theatrical embellishments.'

Hartmann refused to be drawn. Galen in an affable mood was twice as dangerous as when he was being his usual unpleasant self. The leopard hadn't changed his spots, merely his tactics. Galen was still probing, still trying to gauge his loyalty to the Führer, this time for the benefit of young Dietrich. Thanks to Obersteuermann Frick, forewarned was forearmed. He had recognised the chief helmsman's complaint about the keys to the armoury for what it was – a discreet hint that Major Galen and the second watch officer were up to something. Until recently, it would never have entered his head to question Dietrich's loyalty. Dietrich had always struck him as a likable if inexperienced young officer. He was perhaps a little too earnest and inflexible, but it wasn't Karl's fault that he lacked a sense of humour. Of course, he was very susceptible to flattery, a flaw in his character that a number of seamen in his division had been quick to exploit, and without a doubt Galen had played on this weakness to suborn him.

It was difficult to gauge the strength of the opposition in the event of a showdown. Whatever else he might be, Galen was no fool. With only nine men under his direct command, Galen would need to be quite certain that he had the support of a sizable minority of the crew before he started anything. Every captain liked to believe that there were no rotten apples in his barrel, but, as a realist, Hartmann reckoned there were bound to be a few malcontents, men he'd disciplined in the past and who still bore him a grudge. However, Galen couldn't be sure that his own detachment would back him to a man in a crisis. Judging by the mutinous expressions he'd observed, the artillery officer wasn't exactly a popular figure, especially with Oberfeldwebel Meyer. Galen had been on his back as a result of the mishap with the high pressure toilet, although since Hauptmann Kleist's death, he had gone out of his way to be pleasant to the warrant officer, probably because he needed Meyer's expertise.

'You're looking very thoughtful, Erich.'

'I was just gazing into my crystal ball.'

'And what did you see?' asked Galen.

'Trouble,' said Hartmann. 'We're just four hundred nautical miles from the American coastline.'

'I have a feeling you're leading up to something.'

He most certainly was. Tomorrow they would cross longitude seventy degrees west, the change of operational control line where he was required to comply with Galen's instructions except in matters of seamanship. Kapitän zur

248

See Wirth should never have agreed to such a preposterous arrangement in the first place, but once having witnessed the animosity that existed between them, he should have taken steps to get the order rescinded. As it was, the dual system of command turned a difficult situation into an explosive one. No matter how much it went against the grain to suck up to Galen, the safety and well-being of his crew demanded that he do his best to defuse the potential time bomb.

'How right you are.' Hartmann managed a faint smile. 'I was about to suggest that we should revert to a more cautious approach. After all, we don't want a repeat of that episode off Iceland.'

'What exactly do you have in mind?' Galen asked coldly.

'After tonight, I don't intend to surface again until we receive orders to execute Double Griffin.'

Galen looked as if he were about to object, but he never got the chance. Before he could open his mouth, the silence was broken by a loud blast on the Klaxon.

From bow to stern, the alarm signal produced an immediate response from the crew, especially in the engine room where the fuel lever was switched to zero and the air intake and exhaust conduits were closed with lightning speed. Within seconds, both diesel engines had been shut down and the electric motors put to work. As August Peiper made his way forward to the control room, Werner Best gave the order to flood and he heard the thundering roar of compressed air escaping from all three diving tanks. Simultaneously and without waiting for orders, the hydroplane operators set the forward plane hard down and the aft plane down. Bow-heavy, U 195 began to sink below the waves, the bilge water rushing forward under the deck plates. By the time Hartmann reached the control room, the sea had already closed above the conning tower.

Best said, 'There's an escort vessel on our starboard beam, sir. The radar must be on the blink – it hardly gave us any warning at all.'

Hartmann nodded, stepped back into the passage and tapped the radio operator on the shoulder. 'What do you hear?' he asked.

The petty officer pressed the hydrophones to his ears. 'Faint noise two hundred and twenty degrees ... ' He moistened his lips. '... two hundred and ten degrees, getting louder ... two hundred degrees and closing ...'

HMCS *Chicahagof* was a Loch Class frigate, two days out of Halifax and proceeding independently to join the antisubmarine squadron at Kingston, Jamaica. At 2230 hours, her type 272 centrimetric radar detected a U-boat on the surface at a range of seven thousand yards on the port beam. At that precise moment in time, it was debatable who was the more surprised, but as the Canadian frigate altered course to port, the U-boat became alive to the danger and went down fast. With that, the bright dot on the display screen of the radar disappeared and the *Chicahagof*'s asdic started pinging.

So far as antisubmarine weapons were concerned, the frigate was equipped with two Squid mortars on the fo'c'sle, two depth charge throwers mounted port and starboard and a chute over the stern. Of this arsenal, the Squids were the most effective. Each three-barrelled mortar had a fixed elevation of forty-five degrees and could be tilted fifteen degrees either side of vertical to compensate for the ship's roll. The barrels were also slightly offset from the weapon's point of aim so that the hundred-pound projectiles were spread to land in a triangle. Closing at twelve knots, the *Chicahagof* opened fire with the mortars at an estimated range of three hundred yards and then immediately altered course in order to maintain asdic contact.

Six violent explosions coming one on top of the other rocked and buffeted U 195, fusing all the lights and breaking the glass plate on the depth gauge that had been replaced after the air attack on the thirtieth of November. There was a brief pause and then four more depth charges arrived, less accurate than the previous salvo but close enough to give them a severe shaking. White cones from a dozen flashlights pierced the darkness, and Hartmann heard Peiper call out for spare fuses in a voice that sounded very shaky. Two, perhaps three minutes later, the overhead lights came on again.

The petty officer manning the hydrophones said, 'Steady on one eight five degrees – propeller noise fading.'

Hartmann ducked his head under the sill and looked inside the control room. The atmosphere was electric and he could smell their fear as well as see it in their faces. Obersteuermann Frick and the two hydroplane operators looked as if they had just seen a ghost. Peiper was bathed in sweat, the perspiration dripping off his nose like a leaky tap, while Best appeared to be mouthing a prayer.

'Change of course to zero five degrees.' The petty officer in the radio shack raised his voice. 'Propeller noise now increasing.'

'The bastard means to have another crack at us,' Best said hoarsely.

'I'd be more surprised if he left us alone.' Frick muttered to himself.

'Hard a-port,' Hartmann said crisply.

'Hard a-port it is,' Frick repeated.

'One ... two ... three ... four ... five ... six.' Hartmann counted the explosions out loud in a voice that was remarkably firm.

HMCS *Chicahagof* dropped five more depth charges in her wake for good measure and then opened the range to fifteen hundred yards before coming about, her asdic still in contact with the U-boat. Reducing speed to one third ahead, she crept forward, her captain eventually stopping both engines as they drew near their prey.

'Can you hear anything?'

'No sir.' The petty officer lifted one of his earphones so that Hartmann could listen to the faint rushing noise of the sea. 'It looks as though we've lost him, sir.'

251

Hartmann thought the petty officer could well be right. Certainly the hydrophones had been silent for the past hour and that was a good sign. Leaving the radio shack, he returned to the control room and ordered Peiper to take the boat up to periscope depth before climbing into the pressurized cabin in the conning tower.

'What's our helm?' he asked presently.

'Rudder thirty-one degrees starboard,' said Frick.

'Depth gauge now showing twenty-five meters, Peiper called from below. 'Now twenty, now fifteen.'

Hartmann raised the periscope.

'Now ten, nine, eight, seven, six ... ' Peiper continued.

The periscope cleared the water. Commencing a three hundred and sixty degree sweep, Hartmann found himself staring at the blurred outline of a stationary frigate. 'Dive,' he shouted, 'all the way down and fast.' His feet barely touching the rungs, Hartmann scrambled down the ladder into the control room.

Working like a man possessed, Peiper flooded the diving tanks, called for full power from both electric motors and then ordered all hands forward to make the boat bow-heavy, a manoeuvre that increased their rate of descent.

Best said, 'I reckon the next few minutes are going to be interesting.'

It was all of that and more. The attack started at 2340 hours and continued unabated for the next hour and twenty-five minutes, the frigate going back and forth, back and forth, to drop one pattern after another. The floor plates vibrated, clattered and jumped under the stress; the lights failed yet again, crockery was smashed to pieces, bits of paint flaked off the ceiling and personal gear that had been carefully stowed away, broke loose and rolled about on the deck. There were leakages everywhere – above the exhaust valves in the engine room, near the stern torpedo tube and in the control room where a jet of water began to spurt from the nozzle of the water gauge.

Hartmann pulled them through. He sat on the jump seat, his back resting against the sky-navigation periscope, his feet crossed at the ankle and propped up on the chart table.

His voice in the intercom sounded casual, almost bored, as he assured everybody that U 195 could take everything the enemy cared to throw at them and then some. He never once raised his voice, nor did he lose his cool when the enemy appeared to outguess and outmanoeuvre him no matter how often they twisted and turned.

And then, at long last, the petty officer reported that he could no longer hear the frigate's asdic nor the sound of her propellers.

Hartmann glanced at his wristwatch. 'Zero two fifty-five,' he muttered.

'Check,' said Best, and then added, 'It seems remarkably quiet upstairs.'

Too quiet, thought Hartmann. The long silence was no guarantee that they had lost the frigate. Her captain had shown that he was prepared to sit it out and time was certainly on his side. Their batteries were damn near exhausted, and sooner or later they would have to come up for air. When they did, like as not, they would find half the United States Navy waiting for them.

'All right,' he said crisply, 'tubes one to three stand by for underwater firing. Flood tubes. Open torpedo doors.'

'Do you think he's still waiting for us, sir?' Best said.

'It's possible,' said Hartmann. 'Anyway, I don't intend for us to be caught with our trousers down. We've got two fish in our bows and a sting in the tail. With any luck, we won't have to manoeuvre into a firing position.' He turned to Peiper. 'You can cut the E motors, August.'

'We'll lose our neutral buoyancy, sir.'

'That's the whole idea,' said Hartmann. 'Hopefully, we'll bob up like a cork. Desperate situations call for desperate measures, and you'll just have to balance the boat as best you can.'

It was a tall order, but if anyone could do it, the chief engineer was the man for the job. Slowly, Hartmann climbed the ladder leading to the pressurized cabin above and settled himself at the attack periscope. Slowly, as if reluctant to leave the deep where she was safe, U 195 began to rise to the surface.

Hartmann raised the periscope and within a matter of seconds renewed their acquaintance with the frigate. 'Range four thousand meters,' he snapped. 'Go to zero, half speed ahead. Enemy position bow right. Werner, angle sixty. Enemy stationary – correction – now moving estimated speed five knots and increasing.'

'Sonar bearing two four three degrees,' the petty officer called from the radio shack.

'Check,' said Hartmann. 'Enemy speed now twelve knots, torpedoes to five meters – hydroplane station bow right – angle now six three degrees.'

Best repeated the periscope directions and transmitted the data to the T5 acoustic torpedoes in the bow tubes.

Hartmann said, 'Fire one. Fire two.' Then he gave the order to dive.

The torpedoes ran straight and true, to explode within seconds of one another. The general consensus was that both fish had found the target, but Hartmann, taking a more cautious view, ordered the torpedo mechanics to reload, a task that took them forty-five minutes to complete.

At 0417 hours, he again took the boat up to periscope depth. Finding no sign of the frigate, he decided to recharge their batteries, using the snorkel. At 0603, just under two and a quarter hours later, the Metox receiver started to warble and they were obliged to make another hasty descent. That the marauding aircraft did not molest them was the biggest and most pleasant surprise they'd had all night. It was, said Galen, a good omen for the future success of the operation. Peiper just hoped he was right for once.

CHAPTER 26

New York

Saturday, 23 December 1944

The sky was a slate grey and there were signs that they could expect a light fall of snow before the day was out. The barometer in Vandervell's office was still registering sixty-five degrees Fahrenheit, but as he continued to expound his theory, it seemed to Anderson that the temperature was rapidly dropping to zero.

'I know it may strike you as improbable,' he said, 'but I believe the U-boat which sunk the *Chicahagof* in the early hours of yesterday morning is the same one that shot down the RAF Liberator on the thirtieth of November.'

'You've got a one track mind, Commander,' Vandervell growled.

'It's also the same U-boat spotted by the Chance Vought Kingfisher from the USS *Lovel* at 0600 hours, when the seaplane was looking for survivors from the Canadian frigate.'

'Now, there I'm inclined to agree with you. The sub wasn't all that far from the last known position of the *Chicahagof*.'

At last they were getting somewhere, thought Anderson. *Chicahagof* had been torpedoed at 0310, at which time the USS *Lovel*, the latest cruiser of the Indianapolis Class, together with her attendant destroyers, had been exercising off Nantucket about one hundred and sixty miles to the north-west. In the search and rescue operation that had followed, the cruiser had launched her seaplane to scout ahead of the task force.

'I know the Kingfisher's observer said he thought there was some kind of structure on the bows, but I don't buy that.' Vandervell rested both elbows on the desk and leaned forward, his short bull neck disappearing between the hunched shoulders. 'The goddamned sub was running at periscope depth.'

'It was snorkeling.'

'All right, Commander, have it your way – it was snorkeling. But, unless the Almighty gave that observer X-ray eyes, he couldn't have seen anything apart from the air mast. He saw the turbulence it caused in the water and allowed his imagination to run riot, like someone else who ought to know better.'

Meaning me, thought Anderson. 'Are you saying he was mistaken?'

'Damn positive he was, Vandervell snorted.

'I'm not so sure. In the North Sea it's possible to see a submarine ten feet below the surface and there have been a number of instances in the Mediterranean Theatre where a plane has stopped and attacked a U-boat at a depth of over thirty feet. How far you can look down depends on the height of the aircraft, the prevailing weather conditions, the amount of daylight and the type of seabed. In this instance, the Kingfisher was flying at five hundred feet when the observer spotted the air mast. At that altitude they would have come in under the radar and caught the enemy napping. According to the pilot, their air speed was a hundred and seventy-five knots., which means they would almost have been on top of the U-boat before she went down into the cellar.'

'I think you're making too much of the incident,' said Vandervell. 'Maybe it has escaped your notice, but they're a pair of greenhorns fresh out of training school.'

'Nevertheless, I still say we can't afford to ignore their report. New York is a defenceless city – Mayor La Guardia said so and, from the German point of view, there was never a better time to launch a sneak attack.'

Vandervell was not unaware of the force of this argument. The counterstroke in the Ardennes had come like a thunderbolt out of the blue, especially to the people at home who had been led to believe that the German Army was on its last legs. Eisenhower's staff had tried to impose what amounted to a news blackout, and only now, a week after the offensive had started, were the American people beginning to realise how badly the Battle of the Bulge was going. Even so, Anderson was wrong in thinking a VI attack on New York was a good military proposition, and what's more, he could prove it. Opening the top drawer in his desk, Vandervell took out a sheet of paper.

'I have a few facts and figures here provided by the British Information Service which might interest you, Commander,' he said. 'From June through to August, a total of eight thousand six hundred and seventeen flying bombs were directed against London from launching sites in northern France. Of this total, only two thousand three hundred and forty reached the capital, killing five and a half thousand civilians. In short, each bomb that landed in the target area only inflicted two fatal casualties.'

Vandervell was thinking like an economist ironing out the peaks and troughs so that in the end he simply measured the yield against the total investment. Death and destruction were reduced to merely plus and minus figures on the balance sheet.

'I seem to recall there were several major incidents,' Anderson said in a voice cold with anger.

'Sure there were.'

Vandervell went back to his facts and figures again. A hundred and twenty-one people had been killed when a flying bomb had struck the Brigade of Guards chapel in Birdcage Walk; a hundred and twenty-four in Chelsea, and a further one hundred and ninety-eight when one of the Air Ministry buildings in the Strand had been hit on the twenty-eighth of June. The worst incident had occurred on the twenty-third of August when two hundred and eleven people had died in East Barnet.

Faced with this mass of statistics, Anderson made one last attempt to win Vandervell over to his way of thinking. 'It's Christmas Eve tomorrow,' he said, 'and a hell of a lot of people are going away on holiday this evening. You'd have a major disaster on your hands if a VI landed on Grand Central or Pennsylvania Station.'

Vandervell had an answer to that. The flying bomb was a

highly inaccurate weapon: Of those missiles that were not shot down by the air and ground defences, only one in three had fallen in London.

'If they can miss a city, Anderson, there's a fat chance of them hitting a pinpoint target like Grand Central.' His mouth curled in a derisive smile. 'Of course, it's always possible they might have a radio-controlled version on this elusive sub of yours. As a matter of fact, I'm surprised you didn't make the point.'

'Would it have made any difference if I had?'

Vandervell glared at him, his face becoming even darker, if that were possible. 'Let me ask you a question for a change,' he snapped. 'What's our mission here at Eastern Sea Frontier?'

'The onward movement of all eastbound convoys,' Anderson said, knowing he'd lost the argument.

'You're damn right it is. Evaluating a real or imaginary threat against New York is a job for the Tenth Fleet and we've no business poking our noses into their affairs.'

'In other words, I don't know what I'm talking about?'

'I was beginning to think you'd never get the message,' said Vandervell.

Virginia Canford got the message the moment Anderson walked into her ofice.

'I guess the irresistible force just collided with the immovable object,' she said, and smiled.

'That's one way of putting it.' Anderson perched himself on the window sill above the radiator. 'I thought I had a good case, but our onetime football star had done his homework weeks ago. For every point I made, Vandervell went one better. He had the facts and figures to prove it would be a totally unproductive operation. One can only hope that Adolph Hitler shares his opinion.'

'How much time do we have, John?'

It wasn't the easiest of questions to answer. The VI had a range of one hundred and sixty miles, but latterly this had been increased to two fifty. Taking the latter figure, Anderson thought it likely that they would allow a leeway of about thirty miles to be sure of reaching the target area, which meant that the bomb would probably be launched within a radius of two hundred and twenty miles. The seaplane had sighted the U-boat at latitude 39 degrees 37 minutes north, longitude 69 degrees 2 minutes west, some three hundred and ninety miles east of New York.

'A lot depends on how cautious the captain is, but I don't see him being in position much before ten o'clock tonight.'

'Wouldn't he try to make it earlier than that?'

'I'd have knocked several hours off if Vandervell had asked me.' Anderson grimaced. 'Just to scare the pants off him.'

'What I meant was – I doubt if Grand Central of Penn Station will be all that crowded by then.'

'There are other targets, other nights.'

'Or days?'

Anderson shook his head. 'The U-boat won't surface in daylight. That's one thing I am sure of.'

'And the rest is pure guesswork?'

'You know certain facts, you draw certain conclusions – that's the business of war, Ginny. If your information is high grade, you'll be right more often than wrong.'

'Vandervell is a long way from the top of the ladder,' she said.

'Sure, I could go over his head and take it to the Admiral at Navy District, but how far would it get me? Vandervell's my superior officer and the Admiral is bound to ask his opinion.'

He was right, but they were talking at cross-purposes.

'You need someone on your side who has plenty of clout in Washington,' said Virginia. 'Someone like Uncle Walter.'

It was another reminder that they came from very different backgrounds. He remembered Tom Sullivan telling him that one of her uncles was a member of the Senate Committee for Foreign Relations.

'Would he listen to me?' he asked.

'He will if I ask him,' she said.

That figured. Virginia could twist any man round her

little finger when she put her mind to it.

'Of course, Vandervell does have a point,' said Anderson. 'The VI is a highly inaccurate weapon. Unless it was radio controlled from the ground, there's no way they could hit a pinpoint target.'

From the ground? By an agent inside the target area? As Virginia would have observed, it was all a bit like Jules Verne. But was it all that improbable? In June 1942 two groups of saboteurs totalling eight men had been put ashore on Long Island and the Florida Keys. Their mission had been a complete failure, but there was no reason to suppose German Intelligence wouldn't try again. And maybe they had. There was that wireless intercept just over three weeks ago, which reported that a U-boat was thought to be operating approximately two hundred miles southeast of Frenchman Bay. What was it Ginny had said? I wonder what it was doing off the coast of Maine? Well, it could have been that the U-boat had either been about to put an intruder ashore or had already done so.

'Can you hold the fort for me, Ginny? he asked.

'Sure I can. Where are you going?'

'The Brooklyn Navy Yard,' he said. 'I want to have a word with the captain of HMS *Medina*.'

'The *Medina*?' She frowned. 'That sounds familiar.'

'She's a River Class frigate. I managed to persuade her first lieutenant to part with a bottle of whisky when you were down with the flu.'

A bottle of Johnnie Walker as she recalled. Just the stuff to put wool in your socks, he'd told her cheerfully, and it had too. She couldn't remember that evening too clearly; it had passed in an alcoholic daze, but two days later she was up and about again as bright as a new penny.

'Will you thank him for me and say it did me a power of good?'

'Yes, of course.' What a pity he didn't have a snapshot of Ginny in a swimsuit; the first lieutenant would probably have fallen over himself to produce another bottle.

'When do you think you'll be back?' she asked.

Anderson glanced at his wristwatch. 'Not before lunch,'

he said.

'Okay. If I raise Uncle Walter before then, I'll phone through to the Navy Yard.'

Anderson nodded, his thoughts elsewhere. Maybe there was no such thing as a radio-controlled VI, but unless they were prepared to launch the missile blind, they would need an accurate local weather forecast. And only someone who had been planted in New York could give them that.

HMS *Medina* was berthed in the shadow of a giant crane, the behemoth of the Brooklyn Navy Yard which could lift two hundred and fifty tons with ease. As a fighting ship, the frigate was now a sorry sight, and if he hadn't known better, Anderson would have said she was being broken up for scrap. Her decks were filthy, covered in grease, and a whole army of caulkers, joiners, welders and electricians seemed to have taken root in her bowels.

Her captain was a lieutenant commander in the Royal Naval Reserve who, in peacetime, had been a first officer with the Peninsula and Orient Line. The first lieutenant had been an insurance clerk, one of the many weekend sailors who had joined the Royal Navy Volunteer Reserve before the war. There used to be a saying that RNRs were seamen trying to become gentlemen and RNVRs were gentlemen endeavouring to become officers, but that snobbish doggerel had died a natural death some years back. The North Atlantic was a great leveller; it brought out the best and worst in people, and by 1941 only the best were good enough to hold a seagoing appointment.

Due to the refit, ninety percent of the ship's company were accommodated at the escort base on Staten Island and the captain was still ashore when Anderson arrived. The first lieutenant wanted to be helpful, but he thought it best if Anderson referred his request to the captain, whom he expected at any moment. As things turned out, he was wildly optimistic and it was past three o'clock before the captain eventually put in an appearance.

A somewhat taciturn officer in his early forties, the RNR lieutenant commander invited Anderson into his cabin and listened to what he had to say in complete silence. There were no interruptions, no raised eyebrows. He was a man who took everything in his stride and was not easily surprised by any story he heard, no matter now outlandish it might seem.

'You'd like me to monitor their frequencies?' he said presently.

'That's right. I think it's possible that this particular U-boat will send a tuning call to a German intelligence agent here in New York.'

'This is a dead ship, Commander Anderson. I'm dependent on the navy yard for power.'

'You're not likely to use much juice on listening watch.'

'And it'll be pretty much of a hit or miss affair. It's a pity you've no idea when he'll be transmitting. As it is, we could search the whole waveband and not pick up a damned thing.'

'There is that risk, but I still think it's worth trying. After all, we've got nothing to lose.'

'Of course, you realise that if we do intercept his signal, my yeoman won't be able to decode it.'

'I'm not worried about that,' said Anderson. 'The fact that a U-boat is transmitting a message to somebody ashore is all the proof I need.'

'All right, Commander,' he said. 'When do you want us to start?'

'Tonight – say from 1800 until first light tomorrow.'

'Two hours from now. You're not giving my first lieutenant much time to get things organised. We've only got one signalman on duty; the rest are over on Staten Island.' He broke off to take an incoming call, listened briefly and then handed the phone to Anderson. 'It's for you,' he grunted, 'A Lieutenant Canford.'

It seemed that running Uncle Walter to ground had not been the simple rask Ginny had imagined. She had tried his home in Georgetown, the Senate office, the Library of Congress and the White House before locating him at the Madison where he was entertaining his personal staff. 'You know how it is around Christmas,' Virginia said laconically, and he gathered Uncle Walter had not been pleased when she'd interrupted his lunch party. But somehow she had persuaded him to come to New York, and had convinced him that, despite the holiday rush, he would have no difficulty in getting a seat on the train.

'He'll be arriving at seven and will come straight to the Savoy-Plaza on Fifth Avenue.'

'The Savoy-Plaza,' Anderson repeated.

'That's right. I'll be waiting for you in the penthouse suite.'

He was impressed. She really must have pulled out all the stops to get the penthouse suite. It was one more eye-opener, one more reminder of the Canford wealth and influence. Anderson said he would be there before seven and then hung up with a wry smile.

'Problems?' asked the captain.

'None that I can't handle,' he said.

'Good. Now, about these signalmen of mine; I reckon we can get them back from Staten Island in time. But is this going to be a semipermanent arrangement or what?'

'With any luck, the coast guard will take it on tomorrow.'

'Is Lieutenant Canford trying to fix that?'

'More or less.'

'She strikes me as a very efficient and determined young woman.'

'She's all of that,' said Anderson.

People, Anderson reflected, rarely bore any resemblance to the mental picture you had of them, and Uncle Walter was no exception. He had thought the senator would be much like Virginia's father, but no two brothers could have been less alike. Walter Canford was much older, silver-haired and thinner in the face. An attack of polio in his youth had left him with a withered right arm and a noticeable limp. Although his physical disabilities were an obvious handicap, he made light of them and was not the kind of man who looked for sympathy. Apart from a ready smile that was wholly genuine, he had the knack of putting strangers at their ease and Anderson warmed to him the

263

moment they shook hands.

'It's a pleasure to meet you, Commander,' he said.

'And you, sir,' said Anderson. 'I hope you managed to get a seat on the train from Washington.'

'Old age has its compensations.' His eyes creased in a warm smile. 'That and being a senator.' He turned to Virginia. 'Well now, Ginny,' he said, 'suppose you fix us both a drink and then leave us in peace for half an hour?'

'What about something to eat?' she asked. 'Would you like a ham sandwich? I could ask room service to make you one.'

'A ham sandwich would suit me fine,' he said. 'But there's no hurry.'

Virginia nodded, went over to the cocktail cabinet and fixed a bourbon and branch water for her uncle and a scotch on the rocks for Anderson and then withdrew to the dining room.

'My niece never ceases to surprise me,' said Canford. 'I thought she would insist on staying.' He glanced sideways at Anderson. 'A very clever and astute young woman, Commander. She usually gets what she wants.'

'So I've noticed,' Anderson said drily.

'And that's why I'm here.' Canford placed his glass on the occasional table and leaned back in his chair. 'Ginny has told me most of the story, but I'd like to hear it from you.'

'Right from the beginning?'

'That's a good place to start.'

Choosing his words with care, Anderson told him about the report from the Norwegian Resistance that had led the RAF to fly a number of photo-reconnaissance missions over Bergen, about the mysterious security fence inside the naval barracks which had subsequently disappeared. He spoke of the duel between the RAF Liberator and the U-boat off Reykjavik and stressed the fact that all the sighting reports clearly stated that the U-boat had been specially modified. He explained why Vandervell was convinced the U-boat had been sunk by the USS *Pope* and why he held a contrary opinion. He allowed that the pilot and observer of the seaplane were inexperienced, but even so, he didn't see how they could afford to dismiss their report as a figment of the imagination.

'I agree that launching one or even two flying bombs against New York doesn't make an awful lot of sense from a purely military point of view, but it's the kind of spectacular act that would appeal to someone like Hitler.'

'I'd go along with that. The question is, what are we going to do about it?' Canford reached for the glass of bourbon. 'I take it you've given the problem some thought, Commander?'

Anderson wasn't sure that he had the necessary facts to make a firm recommendation and said so. He knew there was an antiaircraft site at Fort Hancock on the Sandy Hook Peninsula about fifteen miles from Red Bank, New Jersey, which was supposed to protect the New York metropolitan area, but that was the sum total of his knowledge.

'I don't think there's much point in strengthening the ground defences, sir,' he said. 'If you shoot the VI down over the city, it will still do an awful lot of damage. We should aim to intercept it out to sea.'

He thought the USS *Lovel* and her attendant destroyers could form an outer picket line, but the Tenth Fleet would need to reinforce the task force if they were to do any good.

'The USAAF has two antisubmarine squadrons in the area, one at Ford Dix, the other at Mitchell Field on Long Island, and they will obviously have to step up their existing patrol programme.'

'I think you'll find that steps have already been taken to put that in hand.' Canford smiled. 'I had a few words with a friend of mine in the War Department after Ginny spoke to me on the telephone.'

Anderson had no idea what she had said to him, but evidently it had been sufficiently forceful to spur Canford into action.

'The VI has a top speed of four hundred miles an hour, sir. Thirty minutes is therefore the maximum warning time we'll get from the radar.'

'I take your point, Commander.' Canford finished his

bourbon and set the glass down on the table. 'By morning, I guarantee the USAAF will have a squadron of P51 Mustangs at Mitchell Field.'

'What about night fighters?'

'It just so happens that there are four Northrup P61s at Fort Dix. They don't have the speed to catch a VI but with their radar, they can provide an airborne early warning system.' Canford smiled again. 'At least, that's what I've been assured.'

Anderson said, 'Do you mind if I ask you a rather personal question, sir?'

'Not at all,' said Canford. 'I might even answer it.'

'Why did you start the ball rolling before you left for New York?'

'Because I have a very high regard for Ginny. She said you knew what you were talking about, and that was good enough for me.' He chuckled. 'Anyway, as it happened, it didn't come as a total surprise to the Navy Department. And now it's my turn to ask you a personal question.'

'That's only fair,' said Anderson. 'I might even answer it too.'

'I'll come straight to the point then. What do you intend doing about my niece, Commander? I presume you do realise that she's in love with you?'

'I had noticed.'

'So?'

'I've seen Glendales and now this place – I can't compete with that.' Anderson shook his head. 'We're not in the same league, Senator. My people are small farmers and I have no private income. I could never support Ginny in the style she's accustomed to and I'm not prepeared to live off her.'

'I'm not going to ask whether you love her, Commander, because that's none of my business. What I will say is that you shouldn't presume to know what's best for her. She's old enough to decide that for herself. I also think she's entitled to know where she stands before you take off for the Pacific.' Canford stood up, obviously not in the least embarrassed by what he'd said. 'The lecture's over, now let's see about that ham sandwich.'

266

The senator stayed on only long enough to eat the sandwich. There was a train leaving for Washington at twenty past nine and he wanted to be on it. Nothing Virginia could say would persuade him to change his mind and stay for dinner, and in the end she rang the bell captain and asked him to hail a cab so that it would be waiting at the curb when they came down to the foyer.

Walter Canford was not a demonstrative man by nature, but he hugged his niece good-bye and there was a slight catch in his voice when he wished them both a Merry Christmas.

'I'm very fond of Uncle Walter, but there are times when he thinks he has a God-given right to sort out other people's lives.' Virginia watched the taillights of the cab fade into the distance. 'I hope he behaved himself with you.'

'We got along like a house on fire.' Anderson took her by the arm. 'I think we'd better go back inside,' he said, 'it's damned cold out here. Anyway, I've got to collect my overcoat before I leave.'

'Where are you going now?' she asked.

'Back to the escort base. I've arranged for HMS *Medina* to monitor the U-boat wavelength and that's where the officer of the watch will expect to contact me.'

'Tell me something,' she said, as they walked toward the elevator. 'What can you possibly do about it if they do launch a flying bomb against New York tonight?'

'Damn all, when you come right down to it.'

'Well then, why don't you call the ship and give them the telephone number of the penthouse suite?'

'Why don't I?' said Anderson. From what Senator Canford had said, the Navy Department in Washington appeared to have the situation under control and no great purpose would be served if he returned to the escort base on Staten Island.

Webber turned up the volume on the portable radio and then sat down at the kitchen table. The transmitter had been plugged into the mains, the copper wire aerial strung out of the window, and there was nothing he could do now except wait, wait for the minute hand to creep forward to 2240 hours. Sixty seconds to go: He stubbed out his cigarette and put on the headphones, adjusting them so that they fitted snugly over his ears.

Exactly on time and clear as a bell, U 195 rapped out his call sign and he answered it with a hand that trembled on the Morse key. There was a short pause and then the U-boat flashed the code word XYLOPHONE and he heaved a sigh of relief.

The attack on Grand Central had been cancelled and he could take it easy for the next seven days. Webber thought XYLOPHONE was the best Christmas present he was likely to receive from anyone.

CHAPTER 27

Christmas Eve

Sunday, 24 December 1944

An insistent purring noise woke Anderson and he reluctantly opened one eye. Virginia was lying on her stomach, fast asleep and breathing quietly, her head on one side and facing toward him. Trying not to disturb her, he raised himself up on his right elbow and, reaching over Virginia, lifted the telephone off the hook.

The first lieutenant of HMS *Medina* sounded weary, as if he hadn't had a wink of sleep all night. He said, 'I'm afraid we drew a blank, Commander. We did hear a station signing off, but it was just outside the normal range of frequencies used by the opposition.'

'When was this?' Anderson asked softly.

'2243 hours, according to the signal log. The call sign was QVH, but we weren't able to get a fix on the source with our High Frequency Direction Finder. However, the transmission was sent in clear, so it had to be a friendly station. I'll tell you one thing, sir – the operator was a rank

268

amateur. I doubt if his Morse speed was more than eight words a minute.'

'Really? Well, thanks for trying anyway.'

'What about tonight, sir? Do you want us to do the same thing again?'

'No, that won't be nececessary; our American friends are taking it on,' Anderson said, and hung up.

QVH: He made a mental note to check the call sign against the list shown in the annex to the Eastern Sea Frontier signals instruction. A rank amateur? Perhaps HMS *Medina* had picked up a radio ham? Anderson thought that couldn't be right; radio hams had been banned in England for the duration and it was likely the United States government had taken a similar line. He could verify that with the NYPD – there was that detective he'd met at the 18th Precinct. What was his name now? Delgado. Yes, that was it. Benjamin Delgado.

Virginia stirred and then turned over onto her left side.

'What time is it?' she mumbled sleepily.

Anderson peered at his wristwatch. 'I make it seven-fifteen,' he said.

'God, it's still the middle of the night.' She frowned. 'Did I hear you talking on the telephone just now?'

'Yes. I had a call from the *Medina*. It wasn't important.'

'Good; that means you haven't got an excuse to leave.' She reached up and slipping an arm round his neck, pulled him down into the bed. 'Have you?' she said and kissed him on the mouth.

'No.' He smiled. 'Not unless your uncle suddenly turned up again.'

'What would you do if he did?'

'I'd tell him I had a special license.'

A typically English pun, Virginia thought, one that was full of double entendre. But if only it were true, if only he did have a special license in his billfold. That would be some Christmas present, but of course he had this damned stupid hangup about her being a poor little rich girl.

'I suppose I should call my parents to let them know when to expect us,' she said, yawning.

'Us?'

'They're expecting you as well.'

He could guess how that had come about. Ginny had probably sprung it on them when she'd called her parents to explain why she would be staying the night in New York. The exigencies of the service, the difficulties of travelling in wartime, a seething mass of people at the railroad station – no doubt she'd had a dozen good reasons why it made sense to stay over, and no doubt the formidable Mrs. Canford had seen through them all. He could just hear her mother saying, 'It's that British naval officer, isn't it? I can't think why you're so interested in him – he's not for you, darling.'

'You're not on duty, are you, John?' Virginia asked.

'No. Vandervell took me off the roster. He said that as it would be my last Christmas in New York, he proposed to give me the opportunity to make the most of it.'

'That was nice of him.'

'Yes, wasn't it,' Anderson said drily.

It hadn't been an entirely friendly gesture. Vandervell was counting the days to when he left for the West Coast on the fourth of January and had simply wanted him out of his hair.

'Perhaps you've already made other plans?' she said.

Other plans? She knew he didn't have any. Left to his own devices, Anderson supposed he would probably spend most of the time on Staten Island gravitating between his cabin and the wardroom. The Elks were throwing a party for servicemen at their fraternity centre on Madison Avenue and 39th Street and there was some kind of shindig at the Music Box canteen, but they were strictly for enlisted men. There was an open invitation to breakfast from the National Catholic Community Service after the midnight mass at St. Patrick's, but as he wasn't a Catholic, that was out too.

'Have you?' she insisted.

'I'd love to spend Christmas at Glendales, if you're sure it's all right with ...'

Virginia placed a finger over his lips before he could finish the sentence. 'That's all settled then,' she said. 'Now,

270

what time do we leave?'

He would need to pack a change of clothing and collect the secondhand pearl brooch, a small gift for Ginny which he'd intended giving her before he left for San Francisco. Apart from that, he wanted to stop off at the office before he saw Delgado.

'There are one or two things I have to attend to first,' he said, 'but they shouldn't take too long. I reckon I'll be ready by twelve.'

'I'm ready now,' she said in a husky voice, wantonly pressing her naked body against his.

There was an air of festivity in the squad room. A small artificial Christmas tree decorated with tinsel and glass baubles stood on the windowsill among a collection of Yuletide cards from various well-wishers, including one from the owner of the nearby delicatessen who realised he had a nice thing going with the 18th Precinct. Crime didn't stop just because it was the season of goodwill but, as Captain Burns had observed, with Christmas Eve falling on a Sunday this year, business was bound to be slacker and they could therefore enjoy the party without much fear of interruption. It was all the encouragement the detectives had needed and the punch bowl had done the rest, so that by eleven-thirty everybody was in a very friendly mood. By then, the atmosphere was also thick with blue-grey smoke from a dozen Havanas, thanks to the owner of a local cigar store who had reason to be grateful to Delgado.

'You've had a good year, Ben.' Lieutenant Caskey clapped Delgado on the shoulder, a gesture that was largely prompted by the spirit of the occasion. 'A very good year. You cracked the Ziggermann case, and grabbing those cigarette thieves last Thursday night was a fine piece of detective work.'

Delgado figured it was the liquor talking, but accepted the compliment nonetheless. 'I got lucky.' Delgado inspected his cigar, tapped it over the ashtray on Ganley's desk and missed the target. 'There was a recognisable pattern,' he said modestly, 'and I happened to guess where the thieves would strike next.'

'Well, it still makes our record look pretty good.' Caskey helped himself to another glass of punch. 'Maybe we should loan you out to the 24th Squad, Ben. Then perhaps they'd find the wise guy who spread all that alarm about a fresh outbreak of rabies.' He turned to Ganley. 'What do you think, Jack?'

'It's certainly an idea,' said Ganley. 'I hear he was passing himself off as a police officer.'

'That's right; he had a shield too.'

Delgado began to edge away. The subject was too close to home for comfort and he could feel the blood rushing to his face.

'Are you okay, Ben?' Caskey asked abruptly.

'Sure I am. Why d'you ask?'

'Oh, I don't know, you look a bit flushed to me.'

'Well, it is kind of stuffy in here.'

'I hadn't noticed,' said Caskey.

A telephone started to ring behind Delgado and he whirled round to answer it. There was little love lost between him and Frank Toomis, but this was one occasion when he was glad the desk sergeant had called.

Toomis said, 'What d'you know? I've hit the jackpot. You're the very man I wanted.'

'What can I do for you, Frank?' Delgado said cheerfully.

'You've got a visitor, Ben.' Toomis lowered his voice. 'Remember the British naval officer who called here a while back to collect that Limey deserter?'

'Lieutenant Commander Anderson?'

'That's him; he's here now, asking for you. I hate to drag you away from the party, Ben, but I can't get anything out of him.'

Toomis didn't sound the least bit sorry, but neither was Delgado. 'I'll be right down,' he said, and hung up.

'Trouble, Ben?' Caskey asked.

'No – just some guy who wants to see me.'

'Tough, but there's no peace for the wicked, is there?' Caskey closed one eye in a broad wink and then moved away to hobnob with Captain Burns and the rest of the

272

squad, the genial host doing his best to make the party go with a swing.

Delgado went downstairs to the muster room and advanced toward Anderson, hand extended in greeting, a warm smile on his face. 'It's a pleasure to see you again, Commander,' he said.

'And you,' said Anderson. 'But I'm so sorry to have interrupted your party.'

'Think nothing of it. As a matter of fact, I was glad of an excuse to get away.' Delgado took Anderson by the arm and led him over to the bulletin board inside the entrance, so that Frank Toomis couldn't eavesdrop on their conversation. 'Now, what's your problem, Commander?' He grinned. 'Gunner Yates hasn't been misbehaving himself again, has he?'

'No, he's safely under lock and key. This has to do with a radio ham.'

'They're banned for the duration,' said Delgado.

'That's what I thought.'

'Something tells me you intercepted an unknown station. Am I right?'

Anderson nodded. 'HMS *Medina* did – last night at approximately 2243 hours. The station signed itself off with the letters QVH. There's no such call sign listed in our signals instruction.'

'QVH.' Delgado bent down and buried his cigar butt in the bucket of sand that was intended to be used in an emergency, like the fire extinguishers on the wall above it. 'I can't say it strikes a chord with me. Could be a military aircraft.'

'It wasn't on the frequency allocated to the USAAF.'

'A civil plane then? There were a lot of extra flights in and out of La Guardia last night.'

Anderson frowned. It seemed a likely explanation and he could have kicked himself for not having thought of it before. It was also possible that the plane had been out of voice range, which would explain why the radio operator had reverted to a Morse. Of course, his speed would have been slow, but perhaps he'd found it difficult to get through

273

to the control tower. Whatever the reason, it was a fact that no VI had been launched against New York last night. He was undoubtedly making a mountain out of a molehill. 'You're probably right,' he said. 'I'm sorry to have wasted your time.'

'You haven't. Like I said, I was grateful for the excuse.'

'Well, I'd better get going.' Anderson smiled. 'I've got a train to catch and I'm late as it is.'

'Sure.' Delgado stuck out his hand again. 'All the very best, Commander, and have yourself a merry Christmas.'

'The same to you,' said Anderson, 'and a prosperous New Year.'

Delgado saw him out into the street and then headed back upstairs to the squad room, his brow creased in thought. QVH: Somehow that call sign didn't sound as if it belonged to an airline operating out of New York. Although it was almost noon and he had promised Gina faithfully that he would be home in time for lunch, he figured it would only take a few minutes to call the local FBI office downtown.

The spirit of Christmas? After six years of war, Hartmann was no longer sure what it meant, but he supposed the fact that they were still alive was reason enough to celebrate the occasion. Six years: That first Christmas of the war seemed a lifetime ago now, but he could still remember it clearly, as if it were only yesterday, possibly because it was the only one he'd spent at home in Lübeck. The next two had found him somewhere in the North Atlantic, first with Prien on U 47 and then as commander of his own boat. The Christmas of '42 had seen them in the Bay of Biscay homeward bound for Brest, while '43 had been the year of the refit and Jeanne Verlhac.

Hartmann raised his eyes to stare at her photograph on the shelf above his bunk. It was looking a little worse for wear now, but that was hardly surprising. Two days ago, he had found the frame lying face down on the deck, the glass shattered into a thousand tiny fragments as a result of the hammering they'd received from the escort vessel. A bad omen, Peiper had muttered, as if the facts weren't grim enough already. With only fourteen tons of diesel oil left in the tanks, it was essential they set off on the return leg sometime during the next forty-eight hours; otherwise U 195 would probably run out of fuel before they met up with the 'milk cow.' To his dismay, the Führer had decided the attack should now be launched on the thirty-first of December. Galen had said it was undoubtedly a shrewd move, one that had been prompted by the knowledge that in seven days' time the Ardennes offensive would reach its final and decisive stage. A shrewd move? Bullshit. It was far more likely that the Führer had consulted his astrologer and been assured that the stars would be in their most favourable position on New Year's Eve.

Hartmann glanced at his wristwatch. 1500 hours: Best would arrive outside his cabin at any moment to report that the crew were waiting for him to say a few words. Of course, it was the wrong time of day, but Weihnachtsabend was invariably a movable feast in the U-boat arm, celebrated as and when the situation permitted. Right now, their situation was about as bad as it could be but the occasion demanded that he do his utmost to appear in a carefree mood. Wearing a determined smile, he drew the curtain aside and, stepping out into the passageway, came face to face with the first watch officer.

Best said, 'We're ready when you are, sir.'

'Thank you, Werner.' Hartmann moved past him and went forward. 'Let's hope this is the last Christmas we have to spend at sea,' he muttered to himself.

'Sir?'

'Nothing, Werner. I was just thinking out loud.'

Apart from those who were on watch in the control and engine rooms, the entire crew along with Galen's detachment had mustered in the bow accommodation room. Hartmann thought 'mustered' was not a wholly inappropriate description for the way the men were seated, jammed together like so many sardines in a tin. Still, at least there was tinned Danish ham to eat, and the cook had certainly produced a cake worthy of the occasion. The

275

imitation fir tree and the flag draped over the torpedo tubes at the far end of the compartment did little to improve the drab surroundings, but what did that matter when there were bottles of Niersteiner on the table? Looking around at the sea of expectant faces, Hartmann wondered what the hell he was going to say to them.

'I can't remember when I've seen so many anxious expressions,' he began. 'Anyone would think this was a dentist's waiting room.'

It wasn't a very good joke, but there was a faint ripple of laughter.

'I don't have any presents to give you this year, which may be a welcome relief.'

There were more smiles. In 1943, the flotilla commander had presented each enlisted man with a copy of *Schepke Fights On*, a badly written and thoroughly boring novel dedicated to the memory of the former U-boat ace who had been killed in 1941.

'I do, however, promise you one thing. God willing, this time next year you will be sitting down to dinner with your families.' Hartmann raised the mug of wine which Dietrich had placed in front of him. 'Let's drink to that,' he said.

No heroics, no rabble-rousing words to stir the blood and prepare them for battle, just a simple heartfelt wish. He could tell from the expression on Galen's face that the speech had not met with his approval, but he didn't give a damn about that. It was how he felt, how the crew felt.

'Prost,' he said.

'Prost,' they answered back, and then, much to Hartmann's surprise, the crew cheered him.

There was no air of festivity in the Delgado household. By the time he arrived home, the lunch Gina had left in the oven for him had shrivelled to an unappetising mess. Instead of blowing her top, she had greeted him with an icy politeness that was ten times worse. 'Don't you want to know why I'm late?' he'd asked. And Gina had answered with a cold stare that said she couldn't be bothered to listen to any explanations from him.

276

Of course, he had only himself to blame for making a production job out of a simple call sign. He should have let well alone, but no, he'd had to open his big mouth to Caskey who'd needed an awful lot of prodding before he'd eventually agreed to call the FBI office. Delgado had reckoned Hoover's people would pay more attention to a lieutenant than they would a second-grade detective, which only went to prove how naive he was. 'An unauthorised transmitter here in New York? You've got to be kidding, Lieutenant.' Jocular words that Caskey hadn't taken kindly to. If looks could have killed, Gina would now be making the necessary arrangements for his funeral.

Delgado ate another mouthful of the burnt offering and then, pushing his plate aside in disgust, lit a cigarette. It was amazing how quickly he'd lost his halo. One lousy phone call; that's all it had taken. Throw in a snotty FBI agent who probably wouldn't say hello to his grandmother unless he had written permission from J. Edgar Hoover himself, and you could understand Caskey's sudden change of attitude. Naturally, he'd tried to put things right, sucking up to Caskey in the hope it would smooth his ruffled feathers. And where had it gotten him? Nowhere. The Ziggermann case and the cigar store thieves? Forget them: Two successful cases didn't add up to a commendation. He'd spent three useless hours drinking with the brass, only to be greeted by the big freeze-up of 1944 when he finally arrived home.

Delgado stubbed out his cigarette, scraped the remains of his lunch into the waste can and then washed and dried the plate and silverware. Gina and he had better make up before the kids came home and the grandparents arrived for supper, otherwise this was going to be some lousy Christmas Eve. Easier said than done when there was no olive branch readily available. Not that Gina was in a receptive mood for an apology. He could hear her clumping around in the living room, and that was a bad sign because Gina always took it out on the furniture when she was good and mad. The radio was playing in the background, but Crosby dreaming of a white Christmas was not having a soothing effect on her. A white Christmas? There was not much chance of that, and right now he was prepared to settle for a peaceful one. Bracing himself like some battle-weary infantryman about to clear an enemy strongpoint, Delgado left the kitchen and walked into the living room.

Gina was balanced precariously on a rickety stepladder and was showing a lot of leg as she reached up to fix an angel on top of the Christmas tree. The dark, pleated skirt and the long-sleeved, red silk blouse emphasised every rounded contour, and she had never seemed more desirable than at that moment.

'Here, let me do that,' he said in a hoarse voice.

Gina ignored him and climbed one step higher, the ladder wobbling dangerously from side to side.

Moving swiftly, he grabbed the legs to steady it. 'What are you trying to do?' he demanded. 'Break your neck?'

'I-am-trying,' she said with heavy emphasis, 'to-fix-this-damn-angel-to-the-tree.'

'I can see that, but why do it now? You know Matthew and Francesca like to help decorate the tree.' He frowned. 'By the way, where are they?'

'At your mother's,' she said tartly. 'Where else would they be?'

Her tone suggested that he ought to have known, but for the life of him, Delgado couldn't remember whether or not Gina had mentioned it to him before. 'You have every right to be angry,' he said, 'but we can't go on like this, Gina. If we don't call a truce, we'll spoil the whole evening for everybody.'

'And whose fault will that be?'

'Mine.'

In sheer exasperation, Gina pulled the topmost branch toward her, dislodging three glass ornaments which shattered on the floor. The ladder swayed, and losing her balance, she fell into his outstretched arms, the pleated skirt riding high above her thighs as he grabbed her about the waist and hips and then gently lowered her to the floor.

'Are you okay?' he asked.

'Yes, I'm fine, Ben.' She smiled faintly. 'Just a little shook up, that's all.'

His arms still encircled Gina's waist, and pulling her close, he kissed her. At first, he thought she was going to push him away, but then her lips parted and a moist tongue sought out his. Slowly and tentatively, he moved his hands up under the skirt, stroking her thighs above the stocking tops until she began to quiver against him.

'Benjamin Delgado,' she breathed, 'now you just stop that.' But he knew she didn't mean it.

Christmas Eve was going to be the end of the line for Osprey, or so the FBI agents who'd arrested him in Newark that afternoon kept on saying. Osprey still couldn't figure out how they had gotten on to him, and that was one hell of a disadvantage when you were trying to guess how many jokers the interrogators had up their sleeves. He supposed the FBI must have been watching the house on William Street. But if that were the case, why had they waited until today to arrest him, when he'd been living there since the seventh of December? It simply didn't make sense unless they had been playing the waiting game, hoping he would lead them to his control.

Osprey turned his head away from the light on the table, which was shining into his eyes. Two men were questioning him. One was short and stocky with blond hair and gold-rimmed spectacles, the other lean but very muscular, a real hard-nosed son of a bitch who was sitting outside the pool of light, somewhere in the back of the room where Osprey couldn't see him.

'Look at me,' said the blond man. 'Look at me.'

Osprey turned his head toward the light again.

'Let's take it from the beginning again, shall we? What's your name?'

'My name is Osprey,' he said, 'Henry Osprey, and I'm an American citizen.'

'You're a fucking Kraut,' said the man in the shadow.

'That's right,' said the blond man. 'You came ashore with two other Nazis at Hancock Point on Wednesday, the twenty-ninth of November, shortly after 2300 hours

Eastern standard time. You buried your inflatable boat in a wood and the following morning you travelled to Boston by Greyhound bus. You spent four nights in Boston before moving on to Newark where you contacted Emil Pretzner.'

'Is that a fact?' Osprey drawled.

'Indeed it is. We know all about Emil Pretzner, the sixty-five-year-old ex-Salvation Army captain and Nazi sympathiser who gave you a room in his house. We've had him on a short leash since June 1942.'

Osprey stared at the blond interrogator, his face expressionless, his mind working overtime. Pretzner must have been involved in that abortive mission of '42 when the Abwehr had put eight saboteurs ashore, four of them on Long Island. Berlin should have dropped Pretzner right there and then, instead of which the stupid bastards had continued to use him.

The man in the shadow said, 'You know what we do to Nazi spies, Osprey? We burn them.'

'I am not a Nazi spy,' said Osprey.

'Bullshit. We've got your number.'

Damn right they had, but there were some gaps in their knowledge. They didn't know that he had stayed in New York, that he'd delivered a homing beacon to Webber.

The blond man said, 'Who's Amy Butcher, Henry?'

'Amy Butcher?' Osprey pursed his lips. 'I don't think I know the lady.'

'Why don't you make it easy for yourself?'

Was that a hint that they might be prepared to do a deal with him? No, it was too early for that.

'What's she like, Henry?'

'Who?'

'Amy Butcher.'

Amy Butcher was a recognition phrase, but they were looking for a woman, and he'd give them one if and when it proved necessary. He would give them Christel Zolf instead of Double Griffin, because they would fry him for sure if they discovered his connection with the projected V1 attack on New York. He didn't doubt that for one moment. Only this morning he'd read how three of Otto Skorzeny's men had been tried and executed for wearing American Army uniforms during the Battle of the Bulge. It would have to be Christel Zolf, but not yet. There was a long way to go before that.

'Why are you smiling, Henry?' the blond man asked.

'Because you two guys are a laugh a minute, that's why.'

Osprey saw the fist coming, but it was moving too fast for him to get out of the way. The short arm jab across the table split both lips and the blood began to trickle down his chin.

CHAPTER 28

New Year's Eve

Sunday, 31 December 1944. Morning.

The strident jangle woke him instantly, and reaching out, Webber shut off the alarm. Seven forty-five, the thirty-first of December, a day destined to be quite unlike any other that had gone before. This he had known from 2243 hours last night when U 195 had flashed the code word ACCORDION to signify that Double Griffin was on. He wondered if Christel Zolf had also been informed. On reflection, it seemed unlikely; she didn't have any part to play in the operation tonight and could fade into the background to be what she'd always been, an assistant cipher officer in the chancery of the Swiss Embassy.

Christel Zolf: Now there was a real enigma. Odd to think that after all the years they had worked together, he was no closer to her now than the day they'd first met. Of one thing he was reasonably certain; there had never been a man in her life other than the Führer. She was his handmaiden, chaste, celibate and totally antiseptic. Still, that was only as it should be. It helped to make her the perfect control, discreet, efficient and totally unobtrusive, qualities which they shared, or so he liked to think.

Kicking the sheet and blankets aside, Webber rolled out of bed, walked over to the window and, drawing back the curtains, gazed up at the sky. The visibility was poor, but the fog patches weren't thick enough to close La Guardia Airport and the moisture in the atmosphere suggested they could have some rain before the day was out. A dense, persistent fog would have made things a whole lot easier for him, but as it was he would just have to sound convincing when he called Hal Redmond, the operations manager at National Easter, to explain why he would need to line up a replacement.

Webber turned about, his eyes drawn to the extension on the bedside table. Better get it over with, he thought, there was no point in waiting. Whatever time he called, Hal Redmond would go off the deep end. Squatting on the edge of the bed, he lifted the receiver and dialed National Eastern.

Redmond said, 'Operations manager – what can I do for you?'

'Hullo, Hal,' Webber croaked. 'It's me, Paul Webber.'

'You don't sound too good,' said Redmond.

'I'm not exactly feeling on top of the world. I've got a hell of a sore throat and a temperature of a hundred and one. I reckon I've got a dose of flu. I felt pretty groggy on Friday coming back from Chicago. As a matter of fact, I let Dave Stamford, my copilot, do most of the flying.'

'What you're really saying is that you want me to find somebody to stand in for you today. Right?'

'Well, I spent the whole of yesterday in bed, but it didn't do any good.' Webber cleared his throat, making a rasping noise he hoped would sound convincing. 'Maybe you won't have to find a replacement, Hal. I mean, the weather looks pretty bad to me.'

'The weathermen say the fog will gradually clear,' Redmond told him. 'We'll have a grey, drizzly afternoon with some downpours toward evening. Above four thousand feet, visibility is moderate to good. A ten-knot southwesterly wind should help it to stay that way, so we don't expect to cancel any flights.'

'I guess I've landed you with a problem.'

'Don't worry, I'll solve it.' Redmond clucked his tongue.

'Will you be okay for tomorrow, Paul?'

'I sure hope so.'

Webber hung up, satisfied that Redmond had swallowed his story. In a very subtle way, he'd also gotten a weather forecast out of Hal, which would form the basis of the Met report he was required to transmit at 2000 hours. Previously, he'd only had to send the letters QVH, meaning message received and understood, but tonight he would be on the air for several minutes, which would increase the risk of detection. Opening the drawer in the bedside table, he took out a box of cartridges and the sub-nosed Colt .38 revolver that Spruce Airways had insisted he carry when they'd won the franchise to deliver U.S. mail to Seattle back in 1930. Drawing the revolver from the leather hip holster, he unlatched the swing-out cylinder, loaded it with six rounds and snapped it home. Pushing it under the pillow, he then went into the bathroom.

At ten-thirty, having read the *New York Times* over a leisurely breakfast, Webber called Cynthia Langdon and invited her to have dinner with him. 'I know a small, intimate restaurant not far from the Astor,' he told her. 'It's got lots of atmosphere and I know you'll like it.'

He liked it too. The restaurant was diagonally across the way from the Statue of Liberty reproduction in Times Square, and was exactly the right place to leave the homing beacon.

The staff of Eastern Sea Frontier were already assembled in the conference room by the time Anderson arrived at 17 Battery Place. Although some five minutes late, he wouldn't have been there at all had not Virginia Canford telephoned the escort base to warn him that Vandervell was about to hold a briefing. 'I expect it must have been an oversight,' she'd said in her usual diplomatic fashion, but he'd thought it much more likely Vandervell had wanted him out of the way. Vandervell had made that very clear when he'd reported for duty after Christmas. 'No sense you hanging around here, Commander,' he'd said bluntly. 'The Royal Navy isn't replacing you with another officer so you

283

might just as well take some time off to pack your gear.'

Ignoring the warning sign above the entrance which said, 'No admittance – Conference in Session,' Anderson opened the door and strode into the room, interrupting Vandervell in midsentence. 'Sorry I'm late,' he said cheerfully. 'I only heard about the meeting a few minutes ago.'

Vandervell glared, waited for him to sit down and then said, 'As I was saying, last night at approximately 2240 hours, Tenth Fleet intercepted an exchange of signals between a U-boat and an unidentified station here in New York. According to our people, the U-boat's position was then latitude 39 degrees 17 minutes north, longitude 71 degrees 22 minutes west.'

Vandervell indicated the position on the chart behind him and then turned about to face the audience again, looking anywhere but in Anderson's direction.

'Intelligence has reason to believe that this particular U-boat is carrying a flying bomb. Given the present situation in the Ardennes, we can be sure they intend to use it on us. The question is, where and when?'

It appeared the U.S. Navy's Intelligence Department was divided on that question. Since the U-boat was in a position to strike at either New York or Washington, there was one school of thought which favoured the White House or the Capitol, while the other reckoned the missile would be directed against Hyde Park in the belief that President Roosevelt was in residence there.

'If the President were to be killed, I don't have to tell you what a shock that would be to the nation.' Vandervell gazed around the room. 'However, the navy thinks it's possible they're just out to kill a lot of innocent citizens and tonight, if last New Year's Eve is anything to go by, there will be upward of two hundred and fifty thousand people in Times Square. We know that in 1943 the Luftwaffe used radio-controlled glider bombs to sink the *Roma* and severely damaged a second Italian battleship, so it's conceivable the enemy has developed a homing beacon for the V1. Anyway, early this morning the Police Department had a squad go over Times Square with a fine tooth comb. They didn't find

anything first time around, but they intend to keep on
looking throughout the day and into the night, just like the
navy and the air force.'

As Vandervell continued, it became evident that the
wireless intercept during the night had made the navy and
air force sit up and take notice once more. Partly as a result
of Senator Canford's influence behind the scenes, the
air/sea antisubmarine patrols had been stepped up from
Christmas Eve, but after seven uneventful days the majority
feeling was that it had been a false alarm. Prompted by a
newfound sense of urgency, the number of sorties had been
more than doubled, so that there would always be six B24
Liberators from Fort Dix and Mitchell Field constantly on
patrol, each aircraft searching a box embracing ten
thousand square miles. Two hunter-escort groups were at
sea, an airborne early warning system would become
operative at dusk to back up the existing radar and
antiaircraft picket line that had been formed around the
USS *Lovel* and her attendant destroyers, and four P51
Mustangs were at instant readiness.

'With that kind of blanket cover, the U-boat commander
may find it impossible to launch a V1, but should he
succeed in doing so, we are aiming to knock the flying bomb
out of the sky long before it reaches the coastline.'
Vandervell paused to take a sip of water from the glass on
the lectern. 'Nobody can be certain when or where the
enemy will strike. It could be tonight, tomorrow or a week
hence. If it's tonight, the target could be Times Square or
some other crowded place, like St. Patrick's Cathedral
where Archbishop Spellman will be conducting two holy
hour services. Since the exact time of the threat is still
vague, the civilian authorities are naturally reluctant to
order the population of New York to keep off the streets and
stay home; they think that would be tantamount to
conceding a moral victory. Nevertheless, they do realise
they can't afford to take any chances. The NYPD is
therefore setting up a field headquarters at the West 54th
Street station to control the Times Square-St. Patrick's
sector. They're relying on the armed services to keep them

fully informed about the military situation, and that's where we at Eastern Sea Frontier enter the picture. We have to provide a liaison officer.'

'I'd like to volunteer for the job,' Anderson said quickly.

'You, Commander?' Vandervell's stare was blank.

'Well, I've been involved right from the start and I'd like to be in at the end. I also happen to know one of the detectives, a man called Delgado.'

'Yeah, well, I guess you've earned the right,' Vandervell said slowly. 'The NYPD want you to report at 1800 hours, so if you come around to my office this afternoon, I'll give you an up-to-date briefing before you go on duty.'

'Right,' said Anderson. 'I'll stand by from 1600 hours if that's okay with you.'

Vandervell nodded and then looked round the assembled officers. 'Are there any questions?' he asked.

Virginia Canford raised her hand. In a firm yet tactful way, she suggested that it might be a good idea if they sent two liaison officers to the West 54th Street station. If the situation got hot and the lines became busy, she thought Commander Anderson might well need all the help he could get.

The Canfords had a lot of influence and Vandervell got the message in double quick time. 'Okay, Lieutenant,' he rumbled, 'you just talked yourself into a job.'

Hartmann couldn't stop yawning. It was purely a nervous reaction, which had started a few minutes ago when he'd walked into the bow accommodation room and found the army detachment busy cleaning their personal weapons. There was nothing unusual about that, it was part of the daily routine organised by Galen, but all the same, he couldn't help feeling that on this occasion there was a more sinister purpose behind it. Galen was a dangerous fanatic, the kind of man who would proceed with the operation whatever the circumstances and no matter how suicidal it might be. If necessary, he wouldn't hesitate to crush anyone who stood in his way, a fact Hartmann had been aware of from the moment Obersteuermann Frick had warned him about the armoury.

The keys to the armoury were and always had been the crux of the problem. Dietrich was responsible for the armoury, but since Galen and the second watch officer were the closest of allies, he couldn't ask the artillery officer to return the keys to himself or Werner Best without provoking the showdown he wanted to avoid. No, there was only one way to ensure the weapons were returned to the armoury and stayed there. He would have to convince Galen that he was equally determined to carry out the operation. It was too late now for a sudden show of enthusiasm and that wasn't his style anyway. First, last and always, he was a professional and that was a part he could play with conviction.

Hartmann glanced toward the passageway. 'Ah, Reinhard,' he said briskly, 'do come in and sit down. There are a number of points we need to discuss concerning Double Griffin.'

'So you said a few minutes ago.' Galen was more wary than hostile.

'Yes. Well, among other things, I want to discuss the question of air defence.' Hartmann smiled. 'Naturally, I have to know how long we'll be on the surface before we can decide what measures are necessary.'

'It will take a minimum of two hours to reassemble and prepare each missile for launching.'

Although they had two V1s on board, Hartmann had always understood that only one missile would be launched against the target. The other flying bomb was simply a backup in case the first went out of control on takeoff. However, it now appeared that Galen intended to use both missiles, come what may. That notion would have to be killed stone dead, but this was not the moment to do it.

'In that case, we'd better man all three gun positions,' he said slowly.

'You sound reluctant to do that, Erich.' Galen stared at him, his eyes narrowing. 'Why so?'

'I don't want our men getting in each other's way,' Hartmann said curtly. 'Confusion is the handmaiden of inefficiency.'

Numbers were all important. The more men there were up top, the more difficult it would be to execute an emergency crash dive, although it wasn't politic to mention that.

'I imagine you and Oberfeldwebel Meyer will need to be on the bridge with me?'

'There's nowhere else we can install the ignition and fire control panel.'

'That's what I thought. We'll dispense with two of the lookouts; that should give us more room.'

'Good.'

'Now, as regards the missiles,' Hartmann continued, 'I propose we bring the V1s up from the stowage compartment and position them in the bow accommodation room directly below the forward hatch. It will mean a lot of work under difficult conditions, but it will save us valuable time later on.'

'I think that's a very sensible idea,' Galen said affably. 'When do you suggest we make a start?'

'Now's as good a time as any,' said Hartmann.

The artillerymen would have to return their weapons to the armoury before they tackled the job. Once the small arms had been stashed away, it was Hartmann's intention to make sure that one of the missiles blocked the door. If he succeeded in doing that, he thought it wouldn't matter a damn who had the keys to the armoury.

CHAPTER 29

New Year's Eve

Sunday, 31 December 1944.
Night—6p.m. to 10p.m.

By six o'clock a demolition squad from the Department of
Public Works had joined the three police emergency
vehicles in Times Square. Also present in the area were two
ambulances and three engine companies of the Fire
Department with hose trucks and other equipment. By the
time Anderson and Virginia Canford reported to the West
54th Street station, four hundred patrolmen were already
out on the streets, the advanced guard of a small army that
one hour later would number some two thousand five
hundred men.

The muster room of the 18th Precinct resembled Grand
Central in the rush hour, with an irate Sergeant Toomis
trying to impose some semblance of order among the
reinforcements drafted from uptown. Easing a path
through the milling throng for Virginia, Anderson made for
the staircase and went on up to the squad room.

The squad room was equally crowded and just as noisy.
Although nobody stood still long enough for him to make
an accurate head count, Anderson couldn't recall ever
seeing so many people jammed into such a tiny space
before. It took him some time to spot Delgado among the
crush and even longer to catch his eye. When eventually he
did, Delgado pushed his way toward the rail, a broad smile
on his face.

'Well now, Commander,' he said warmly, 'what brings
you here?'

'We're your liaison officers.' Anderson stepped aside,
making room for Virginia. 'I don't think you know
Lieutenant Canford,' he said.

'Not by sight.' Delgado shook hands and then pointed to

a shorter, fair-haired man standing beside him. 'This is my partner, Jack Ganley,' he said. 'Jack – meet Lieutenant Commander Anderson and Lieutenant Canford.'

'You don't know me,' said Ganley, 'but I've heard of you.'

'Oh, really?' said Virginia. 'How come?'

'You were one of the witnesses to that traffic accident on Eighth Avenue and West 44th Street back in November.' Making no attempt to disguise his admiration, Ganley held on to Virginia's hand longer than was strictly necessary.

'I didn't know we were expecting a couple of liaison officers from the navy,' said Delgado.

'We're supposed to report to Captain Burns,' said Anderson.

'He's getting to be a popular man. First the Police Commissioner and now you two.' Delgado held the swing gate open to allow them to pass through the barrier. 'If you'd like to come this way, I'll show you where he is.'

Burn's office was right next door to the water cooler. A thin, balding man with a long, sad-looking face that reminded Anderson of a St. Bernard dog, he seemed unsure whether he was coming or going, and freely admitted it.

'I wasn't expecting two liaison officers.' Burns smiled at Virginia. 'Still, I daresay we can find room for you in Lieutenant Caskey's office, Miss Canford.' He turned to Delgado. 'Perhaps you'd like to see to that, Ben, while I have a word with Commander Anderson?'

Delgado took the hint and turned expectantly to Virginia. With some reluctance and smiling wryly, she followed the detective out of the room.

'Seems we're going to have a busy night, Commander,' Burns said when they were alone.

Anderson nodded. 'I hear there'll be upward of two hundred and fifty thousand in Times Square.'

'Three-quarters of a million is a more likely figure.'

'How will you cope with that number of people?'

'We've done it before. Among other measures, all vehicular traffic will be ordered out of the Square from 42nd to 47th Streets.' Burns shrugged his shoulders. 'Who knows? Maybe this rain will persuade a lot of people to stay home.'

'Let's hope so.'

'I know what you're thinking, Commander, but a word of warning. Only the Police Commissioner, the Chief of Detectives, Lieutenant Caskey and myself know why you're here and we'd like to keep it that way. We're not hiding our heads in the sand, but if word got out that we were expecting an air raid on New York, it wouldn't stop at one flying bomb. In no time at all, people would be spreading the news that a whole avalanche was on the way, and then we really could have a panic on our hands.'

'Commander Vandervell made the same point when he briefed us this afternoon.'

'Oh, I didn't know that.' Burns found a chair that had been pushed against the filing cabinet and placed it by the desk. 'Perhaps you'd like to sit there, Commander,' he said, 'and then you can tell me all about the navy's Intercept Service and the kind of information we can expect from you.'

Anderson told him about the setup as briefly as he could and in terms a layman would understand. There were grounds, he said, for assuming the agent in New York was using a transmitter that had ground crystals and was pretuned to a fixed frequency. This type of transmitter was easy to operate and thoroughly reliable, which was why it had been issued to British and American agents working behind the lines. However, the equipment did have one major disadvantage. Once a listening post picked up a signal from a clandestine station, they knew which frequency to monitor in future.

'So the navy will monitor the frequency this guy was using last night?' said Burns.

Anderson nodded. 'So will the FBI. They hope to run him to ground with their detector vans.'

'Hope?'

'Well, if they're to get an accurate fix on his position, he'd have to be on the air for at least three continuous minutes. Somehow, I don't see him doing that. Anyway, it's the U-

291

boat we have to worry about. Even if the message is decoded in double quick time, there's no guarantee it will disclose their intentions.'

Burns said, 'We don't intend to take any action until the flying bomb appears on your radar screens.'

'That should give you at least thirty minutes,' said Anderson.

'I could wish for more time, but we'll get by. Incidentally we had the telephone company put in some extra lines.' Burns pointed to a red telephone on the desk. 'That's yours, Commander – mine's the black one. I kid you not, the damn thing hasn't stopped ringing all day.'

As if to confirm his statement, it started to ring once more. Snatching the receiver off the hook, Burns answered the call with a grunt, something he continued to do at intervals while making notes on a scratch pad. From first to last, it was a very one-sided conversation.

'That was the FBI,' he said, replacing the receiver. 'Seems they've just busted a spy ring in Washington.' Burns glanced at his notes. 'Does the name Christel Zolf mean anything to you, Commander?' he asked.

'No,' said Anderson.

'Me neither,' said Burns. 'I can't think why they bothered to tell us.'

'All our people are interested in is the direction and speed of the prevailing winds from ground level up to six thousand feet.' Those had been Osprey's words, and looking at the message which he'd just encoded, Webber was glad they hadn't asked him to provide a more detailed Met report. Even though the plain text had been disguised by a very simple type of cipher alphabet, he reckoned the transmission would still take all of two minutes and that was quite long enough to be on the air.

Webber clamped the headphones over his ears and settled back to wait for the tuning and netting call. Right on the dot of 2000 hours, U 195 came through loud and clear. Answering with his call sign, Webber proceeded to tap out the encoded message. It took him two minutes to send it, but even when he had finished transmitting, the ordeal was still far from over. The message had to be decoded and if there had been an error or the operator had misread the signal, he knew they would come back at him, requesting a repeat of the corrupted group.

The seconds ticked away, multiplying into the largest silence he'd ever known. And then suddenly, U 195 flashed the magical letters QVH, and he breathed again. Curbing an impulse to rush things, he switched off the power supply, removed the plug from the mains and reeled in the copper wire aerial. Carrying the transmitter into the bedroom, he hid it in the closet, vowing that tomorrow night he would dump the damn thing into the East River.

Webber glanced at the alarm clock on the bedside table. Ten past eight: There was plenty of time yet, plenty of time to make sure he hadn't forgotten anything. The homing beacon? That was nestling in his overcoat pocket. The Colt .38 revolver? Did he really need it? You bet he did, it was the only form of insurance he'd have if anything went wrong. Did it show then? Webber opened the closet again and checked his appearance in the full-length mirror. The holster sat neatly on his right hip and there was no telltale bulge under the jacket. Those questions finally settled, he went into the living room and fixed himself a large scotch on the rocks before calling for Cynthia Langdon.

She was a Southern girl from Memphis, a tall redhead whose Tennessee accent was still as strong now as it had been the day she'd left her home state for New York some nine years back. Her real name was Margaret Rawlins, but to the johns and the other hookers on the street she was Paulette de la Salle, which helped to create a mysterious and enticing image, or so she liked to believe. Apart from the Gallic alias, Margaret Rawlins had several physical attributions going for her, not the least of which was a pair of shapely legs that were particularly eye-catching in high heels and a sensuous if somewhat sallow face.

Times Square was not her usual haunt, but on New Year's Eve there was no better place to turn a few tricks. In

293

less than two hours she had picked up three johns, a funny little cosmetics salesman who'd claimed he was from out of town, a soldier from Miller Field over on Staten Island and a baby-faced marine. Even by her standards, that had to be something of a record and for a while she'd had visions of making upward of a hundred and fifty bucks before the night was over. But now she wasn't so sure. The fine drizzle which had started earlier in the evening had suddenly become a heavy shower and the crowd in the Square had rapidly melted away to find what shelter they could. Worse still, from a business point of view, was the fact that the neighbourhood was crawling with New York's finest.

Offhand, Margaret Rawlins couldn't remember having seen so many bulls in one place before. It had been enough last New Year's Eve, but this time round they had really come to town. Wherever she looked, there was no avoiding the cops. There were literally hundreds of them, walking up and down the sidewalks, hanging about on street corners and prowling the dark alleyways, making life difficult for her and the other hookers. From where she was standing, sheltering from the rain under the awning of Loews State on Broadway and 45th, Margaret could see a whole gang of them examining the base of the Statue of Liberty reproduction and the underside of the platform that had been erected in front of it. She wouldn't be surprised if they were looking for a bomb; after all, there were all kinds of nuts in New York, a fact that she could personally vouch for, having met a fair number of them in her time.

One such little creep was eyeing her furtively right now. But even though he looked harmless enough, she wasn't about to make a pitch, not when one of the two attendants on duty in the foyer was watching her like a hawk. That guy was really bad for business, and she might just as well move on because there was no chance of making a pickup while he was around.

Braving the rain, Margaret ran toward the curb, determined to cross over to the centre island before the light changed. As she did so, a closed delivery van went through the stoplight and turned into West 54th, heading toward

Eighth Avenue. Jumping back out of the way, she whirled around to give the driver a piece of her mind and noticed a curious loop of wire on the roof behind the cab. A lightning conductor? On a delivery van? Some kind of aerial then, one that rotated like a weather vane. Maybe the vehicle belonged to one of the local radio stations? Yeah, that must be it. Nodding to herself, Margaret hurried over to the centre island and waited for the lights to change on Seventh Avenue.

The john was sheltering in a doorway in an alley off West 45th and she could tell at a glance that he was bored and lonely.

'Mind if I join you?' Margaret said huskily.

'What?'

'Until the rain stops.'

'Oh sure, be my guest.' He moved to one side, making room for her in the doorway.

'Thank you,' she said. 'My name's Paulette de la Salle. What's yours?'

'Ganley, he said. 'Jack Ganley.'

'Are you waiting for somebody?'

'Not especially,' said Ganley.

'I'm at a loose end too.' Margaret smiled. 'Why don't we get together and celebrate New Year's Eve? I've got a nice apartment uptown where we could have a fun time.'

'What do you call a fun time?' he asked quietly.

'Whatever gives you a kick – French style – Greek style – you name it. I'll do it for twenty.'

'I think we'd better go my place on West 54th.' Ganley reached inside his raincoat and produced his shield. 'You see, I'm a police officer, Miss de la Salle.'

'Aw, for Chrissakes,' said Margaret, wouldn't you just know it?'

Hartmann raised the sky-navigation periscope and slowly rotated it through three hundred and sixty degrees. Almost ninety minutes had elapsed since they'd received the Met report, and while the hydrophones hadn't picked up any propeller noises during that time, he wasn't about to take any chances.

'Visibility's poor,' he muttered.

'All the better for us,' Galen observed.

'You think so? Personally, I would be a whole lot happier if the men could see what they were doing.' Hartmann completed a full traverse and lowered the periscope. 'All right,' he said, 'stand by to surface.'

Peiper repeated the order to the engine room, waited for the chief engine room artificer to confirm that the E motors had been switched to full speed and the reserve fuel pumps had been turned on, and then released the compressed air into the diving tanks. As he did so, Hartmann climbed up into the pressurized cabin above the control room.

'Ten, nine, eight, seven ...' Peiper called off their depth. 'Conning tower clear.'

Opening the upper hatch, Hartmann scrambled onto the bridge. Galen and the two lookouts close on his heels. Two seamen emerged from the enlarged hatch, made their way forward to the bows and started to unshackle the jumping wire. In that same instant, the hatch above the galley opened, and with Dietrich leading the way, the gun crews spilled out onto the deck. Within a matter of seconds, the transit plugs had been removed from the barrels of the 20mm cannons, the waterproof ammunition containers had been broken open, and the guns, cocked and loaded, were trained port and starboard. By then, Oberfeldwebel Meyer and the artillery detachment were also on deck, struggling to erect a portable crane aft to the enlarged hatch. With rain driving into their faces, the foredeck casing partly awash and the boat rolling in the swell. Hartmann could appreciate just what a difficult task they had to contend with.

Galen's artillerymen were not the only ones faced with an uphill job. Down in the bow accommodation room, eight torpedo mechanics grappled with a V1, straining every muscle to drag the flying bomb up to the inclined chute that had been positioned under the forward hatch. They were obliged to work in pitch darkness, Peiper having removed the fuses in the forward section of U 195, a precaution

296

necessitated by the fact that over the next two hours the forward hatch would be opened and closed with irksome regularity. This too was a necessary precaution, one that was occasioned by the heavy swell and a desire to prevent a repetition of the Meyer incident when the boat had been contaminated with chlorine gas.

There was no frantic activity in the control room. For the two hydroplane operators, Obersteuermann Frick, August Peiper and Werner Best, it was practically a case of business as usual. There was, however, nothing usual about this particular operation and they were only too aware of the hazards that lay before them.

It was Best who gave voice to their inner thoughts. Turning to Peiper with a sickly smile on his face, he said, 'Even if you're not a religious man, August, this is the time to start praying. Our captain is going to need all the help he can get.'

Visibility at Mitchell Field on Long Island was poor and with rain falling steadily from the leaden sky, the flight commander could hardly see the end of the runway. Unlike the other pilots in the squadron, most of whom were fresh out of training school, the adverse conditions didn't bother him. He had completed a tour of operations with the 4th Fighter Group in England and could remember a time when, returning from Kassel, he'd found the whole of East Anglia so blanketed in mist that he'd had to rely on the control tower at Debden to talk him down. When you'd survived that kind of experience, a murky overcast was nothing to get excited about.

An Aldis lamp winked at him from the tower and then a green flare soared into the night sky. Glancing to his right, the flight commander gave his wingman a thumbs-up sign and opened the throttle. There was a deep-throated snarl from the Packard engine and he could feel the P51 Mustang trembling like a greyhound straining at the leash before he released the brakes. Freed of all restraint, the plane began to move forward, the runway lights seeming to merge into one unbroken line as it rapidly gathered momentum. In response to his light touch on the stick, the Mustang lifted off as gracefully as a bird taking wing.

Climbing swiftly, the flight commander levelled out above the overcast and throttled back. His wingman was alongside, close enough to make out the blurred outline of his flying helmet, and presently he heard the other two pilots report that they were tucked in behind him. Seconds later, Fighter Control at Air Defense Command Headquarters came through loud and clear to direct their every move. This was the seventh combat air patrol they had flown in as many nights and, as usual, they were instructed to orbit Sector One at ten thousand feet.

Although the top brass had gone out of their way to make a big production of their mission tonight, the flight commander reckoned the next five hours would be wholly uneventful. If precedence was anything to go by, this particular patrol was destined to be every bit as boring as all the other sorties that had been mounted since Christmas Eve. Of course, past experience had taught him never to underestimate the Germans, but even if they did succeed in launching a V1 from the deck of a U-boat, he thought it highly unlikely the missile would reach the outer limit of the Metropolitan Air Defense Zone. The flying bomb would have to evade the P61 Black Widow night fighters from Fort Dix and the Navy's antiaircraft picket line before it entered their air space.

By eight-thirty, according to one police estimate, there were some two hundred and fifty thousand people in and around Times Square. Despite a persistent drizzle, their numbers had continued to swell. At nine-twenty a sudden downpour had emptied the Square, but not quite in the way the police had hoped. Instead of going home, the crowd had simply taken shelter wherever they could find it: under theatre marquees, in bars, restaurants, hallways and subway kiosks. However, as Burns pointed out, at least the crowd was now partially dispersed and would be that much easier to control if they had to evacuate the area. The rain had given them a valuable breathing space and Anderson

298

just hoped it wouldn't ease up before the navy succeeded in decoding the transmission they had intercepted at 2000 hours. 'A cipher alphabet,' Burns had told him, 'they'll crack it in no time,' a confident assertion that had been thoroughly discredited by the time Virginia Canford relieved him at nine forty-five.

'How are they making out?' she asked.

'They aren't,' said Anderson. 'All they've got is a string of letters interspersed with numbers.'

'When did you hear this?'

'About five minutes ago.' Anderson stood up, making room for Virginia at the desk. 'Sit down and make yourself comfortable, Ginny,' he said. 'I'm going to stretch my legs for a bit and get us something to eat.'

'You're surely not going out in this, are you?' Virginia waved a hand at the streaming window.

'A little rain never hurt anyone,' he said. 'What do you fancy – a hot dog?'

'Nothing,' she said. 'I'm not hungry.'

'How about you, Captain?'

'Me neither.' Burns patted his stomach. 'I have to watch my ulcer.'

The squad room was a vastly different place than when Anderson had seen it last. At six o'clock there had scarcely been room to breathe; now, almost four hours later, Delgado and Ganley were the sole occupants. Delgado was leaning against the water cooler watching a pot of coffee on the electric ring. Across the way, Ganley was talking to a bored-looking redhead.

'A hooker, calls herself Paulette de la Salle,' explained Delgado. 'You could say this hasn't been her lucky night.'

'Why so?' Anderson said without interest.

'She tried to proposition Jack.' Delgado rubbed his jaw. 'Still, all kinds of screwy things are happening tonight, aren't they, Commander? I mean, we've always been able to handle New Year's Eve without the navy's help before.'

Anderson waited, sensing there was more to come.

'And then we've got this special squad in Times Square. As soon as the crowd dispersed, they began to search the

299

area, something they've been doing all day, on and off. What d'you suppose they're looking for? A bomb planted by a saboteur? Or some nut?'

'I wouldn't know,' said Anderson.

'I recognised one of the guys,' Delgado said slowly. 'He's with the FBI – works in their office downtown. And that set me thinking.'

'Really?' Anderson tried to move on, but Delgado barred his way.

'I remembered the unidentified radio station you came to see me about on Christmas Eve.'

'Oh, that,' Anderson said airily. 'It didn't amount to anything.'

'It didn't?' Delgado smiled and shook his head. He was curious about what was going on, and he thought he had a right to know. After all, hadn't Anderson come to him for information in the past? He tried to think of a convincing argument that would make Anderson open up. 'I think you're snowing me, Commander. Look, I realise secrecy is necessary in wartime, but sometimes it can be a double-edged weapon. I mean, you could be sitting on a vital piece of information and so could I.'

Anderson thought Delgado had a point. Any number of disasters had occurred during the war because the left hand hadn't known what the right was doing.

'Are you working with the FBI, Commander?'

'They're involved,' said Anderson.

'Have you heard from them tonight?'

'They called Captain Burns about four hours ago. It seems they've uncovered a spy ring in Washington led by a woman called Christel Zolf.'

The name sounded vaguely familiar and Delgado wondered where he'd heard it before. Obstinately, his mind remained a blank, and then suddenly the tumbler began to click. Walking over to his desk, he stared at the signature on the crumpled piece of paper under the sheet of glass. The letters 'Ch' followed by a straight line with a dot above it and ending with an 'l'; the surname shorter, beginning with a 'Z' and finishing with an 'f' or a 'b.' Making a stab at it,

Gina had suggested the girl's name was Christine Zulb.

'Jesus Christ,' he said hoarsely. 'Paul Webber – the pilot with the National Eastern Airlines – he was with Christel Zolf the night of the traffic accident.' He swung round to face Ganley. 'Forget the broad, Jack,' he snapped. 'Get a squad car out front.'

'Are we going somewhere, Ben?'

'Damned right we are – just as soon as I've seen Caskey.'

'I'll come with you,' said Anderson.

'I don't think so, Commander,' said Delgado. 'This is a job for the police. And don't you worry, I know where he lives.'

'Suppose he's not at home, supposing you have to go looking for him?' Anderson persisted. 'Would you recognise him?'

'No.' Delgado turned to his partner. 'How about you, Jack?'

'Never laid eyes on the guy,' said Ganley.

'I have,' said Anderson. 'I was standing right beside him when the patrolman took his name and address.'

'On second thought,' said Delgado. 'I guess we do need you after all.'

The rain gradually eased off and then, quite suddenly, it stopped altogether. A few minutes later, a steady trickle of revellers began to move back into Times Square, their numbers swelling rapidly as word got around that it had stopped raining. Within an incredibly short space of time, the crowd had grown to more than a quarter of a million, and observing the milling throng from the tenth floor of the *New York Times* building, the Assistant Commissioner of Police decided they would have to close the area to vehicular traffic.

CHAPTER 30

New Year's Eve

Sunday, 31 December 1944.
Night – 10 p.m. to midnight.

Ganley pulled to the curb outside the apartment house on East 93rd Street and killed the motor.

'You'd think the licensing bureau would have turned up the registration number of Webber's automobile by now,' he grumbled.

'I have a feeling we're going to need it,' said Delgado. 'Seems to me he's already flown the coop.'

'How do you make that out?'

'You found a vacant slot outside the house, didn't you? That could mean he's not at home.'

'You reckon?' Ganley said doubtfully.

'Well, we won't know for sure if we just sit here on our asses. Let's go check the apartment.'

'I don't know, Ben.' Ganley sucked on his teeth. 'Maybe we should wait for the other guys Caskey said he would send.'

'Screw the other guys.' Delgado twisted round to face Anderson. 'You stay here, Commander,' he said, 'no matter what happens.'

'Are you expecting trouble, Ben?' Ganley asked in a subdued voice.

'I think Webber's already killed one man – a cab driver by the name of Janowski.' Delgado opened the door and got out. 'If I'm right about that, he's got nothing to lose.'

The list of tenants was just inside the porchway. Anxious not to waste any time, Delgado pressed every button with the exception of Webber's. Seconds later, there was a faint whirring noise followed by a sharp click as the lock was tripped. Pushing the door open, Delgado slipped inside the hallway and then went up the staircase, Ganley close behind him. Halting outside Webber's apartment, he drew the .38 Police Positive from his shoulder holster and, backing against the wall, motioned Ganley to stand on the other side of the door where he would be out of the line of fire.

'If Webber should answer the bell,' he told him, 'we go in fast – me first, then you. Got it?'

Ganley nodded. Reaching sideways, Delgado pressed the bell. Getting no answer, he pressed it again. 'Looks as if you were right, Ben,' Ganley whispered. 'He's not at home.'

'I think we'd better talk to the nieghbours, Jack. They may know something.' Delgado holstered his revolver, moved across the landing and pressed the buzzer to the Langdons' apartment.

A grey-haired, spritely woman with quick, darting eyes opened the door as far as the security chain would allow.

'Mrs. Langdon?' he asked, flashing a smile.

'Yes. What do you want?'

'We're police officers, Mrs. Langdon.' Delgado produced his shield in case she didn't believe him. 'We want to see Mr. Webber.'

'Captain Webber,' she corrected him. 'He's not in.'

'So we've discovered.' Delgado stretched his mouth into a broader smile. 'I don't suppose you know where he's gone, do you?'

'Why do you want to see Captain Webber?'

God give me strength, Delgado thought. 'National Eastern wants him,' he said. 'Some kind of emergency.'

'Oh, I see.' She nodded her head several times like a pigeon pecking at corn. 'Well, as it happens, he's taken my daughter out to dinner.'

'Where?' asked Ganley.

'Where?' She frowned. 'I seem to recall Cynthia saying they were going to Mario's.'

'Mario's?' Ganley repeated.

'It's a small restaurant near the Astor.'

'Thank you, Mrs. Langdon.' Delgado started to move away. 'You've been very helpful.'

'If you'd like to leave a message with me ...'

'Thanks all the same.' Delgado called back, 'but we'll catch up with him.'

'Something tells me we're going to Mario's.' Ganley panted as they took the steps two at a time.'

'You can bet on it,' said Delgado.

'What about Lieutenant Caskey? Shouldn't we wait for him?'

'We've got a car radio – what's wrong with using that?' Delgado opened the front door and plunged out into the street.

Webber finished his coffee and moved the cup and saucer to one side. 'I guess it must have stopped raining,' he said. 'The bar's not nearly so crowded now.'

Cynthia Langdon leaned across him to get a better view. They were sitting in a corner booth at the back of the restaurant, near the kitchen, and the bar was just inside the front entrance.

'Why are they leaving this early, Paul?' she asked. 'It's only ten-fifteen.'

'Search me.' Webber shrugged his shoulders. 'Maybe it's the herd instinct at work. A few people start to leave and the rest follow suit, thinking that if they leave too late, there won't be room for them in Times Square.'

'Perhaps we should go too, Paul?'

'Is that where you want to see in the New Year?' he asked.

'Don't you?' she countered.

No, he did not. Times Square was the last place he wanted to be when the midnight hour struck. 'Not particularly,' said Webber.

Her face registered disappointment, but he didn't care about that. He had dropped the homing beacon into a litter bin less than sixty feet from the entrance to Mario's. He had intended to plant it in the restaurant until the litter bin had caught his eye and he'd thought it the perfect hiding place. Taking advantage of the crowded sidewalk, he'd shortened his stride until Cynthia was several paces ahead of him.

Then he had withdrawn the homing beacon from the pocket of his overcoat and pushed it under the rubbish in the bin.

'I had a more intimate celebration in mind, Cynthia.' Webber stroked her knee under the table. 'Somewhere quiet.'

'Your place I presume?' she said.

'That's right. Where else can we talk in private?'

'Talk?' She smiled knowingly. 'Somehow I don't see us doing much of that.'

'Maybe it's time I turned over a new leaf; made a few resolutions for the future.'

Like breaking with Cynthia, Webber thought. He had never intended to take up with her. It had happened because, in an unguarded moment, he'd called her Christel. And yet, for all that he hadn't planned it that way, she had served a useful purpose, providing him with a cloak of respectability when he'd needed it most.

'What kind of resolutions, Paul?'

'Can't you guess?' he said in a voice full of innuendo.

Of course she could. He could see from the expression in her eyes that she had visions of confetti and rice.

'What are we waiting for?' she breathed.

It was exactly what he wanted to hear. Signalling the waiter to bring him the check, Webber examined it briefly, left twenty dollars on the plate and, sliding out of the booth, backed up a pace to make room for Cynthia. As they moved down the aisle, three men entered the restaurant, one of them dressed in navy uniform.

The naval officer looked familiar, and at the same moment that a flash of recognition appeared on his face, Webber knew where he had seen him before. There were no prizes for guessing that the other two men were police officers, and reacting swiftly, he gave Cynthia a violent shove in the back to send her stumbling into them. Turning round, he ran back toward the kitchen.

Ganley saw the woman coming and for a split second was undecided whether to get out of the way or try to break her fall. By the time he had made up his mind, it was too late and the woman crashed into him, instinctively wrapping both arms round his hips. Ganley lost his balance, fell sideways and, caroming into Delgado, knocked the detective off his feet. Somehow Anderson managed to avoid the ruckus, and, jumping over the heap of bodies on the floor, he went after Webber.

The Colt .38 in his right hand, Webber hit the swing door with his left shoulder just as a waiter was about to enter the restaurant, bearing a tureen of soup and half a dozen plates on a large tray. The resultant collision had all the ingredients of a Mack Sennett comedy, except that neither man was in the mood for laughter. Cursing at the top of his voice, the waiter went over backward, upending the tray and spilling the contents of the tureen on the tiled floor. His feet swept from under him, Webber ended up on all fours and was still struggling to get up when he was grabbed from behind. Wriggling like an eel, he managed to break the grip on his right arm.

Anderson could feel Webber slipping from his grasp. He had tried for a bear hug, hoping to pinion both arms to his sides, but it hadn't quite come off. The floor was like a skating rink, and with both feet slipping all over the place on the greasy tiles, it was difficult to get any kind of leverage.

Webber twisted again, and suddenly they were face to face and Anderson could feel the revolver pressing into his side. There were no flashbacks, no images of his past life, only an ironic thought that, for a British naval officer, he'd chosen a strange place to die. The gun went off, making a funny kind of popping noise as if somebody had burst a balloon. Anderson felt a searing pain across his chest, and then all the lights exploded before his eyes.

Delgado had been quick to recover, but even so, by the time he arrived on the scene, Webber had reached the tradesmen's entrance and was about to open the door.

'Freeze,' Delgado roared. 'Freeze you bastard.'

A sixth sense warned him that he was dealing with a man who knew he was dead and his finger had already taken up

306

the slack on the trigger when Webber turned and fired. The rest was pure reflex and he squeezed off two shots, aiming for the trunk, the way he'd been trained. Both rounds struck Webber in the chest, the impacy slamming him against the door. His face a picture of bewilderment, he slid down onto the floor and then, still in slow motion, rolled over onto his left side and lay still.

Delgado holstered the revolver and, ignoring the chefs, the waiters and kitchen hands who were staring at him open mouthed, dropped on one knee beside Anderson. He thought the Englishman was in bad shape; his face waxen and there was a bluish tinge to his lips.

'How is he, Ben?'

Delgado looked up at Ganley. 'Not too good,' he grunted.

'I don't understand what made him go after Webber. I mean, he knew we had the rear exit covered.' Ganley chewed his bottom lip. 'I guess he's the stuff heroes are made of, huh, Ben?'

'I'll tell you one thing,' Delgado said angrily, 'he'll be a dead hero if somebody doesn't get a fucking ambulance.'

Hartmann looked up at the murky, overcast sky. They had been fortunate, exceptionally fortunate, and he just hoped their luck would continue to hold. All they needed was another five minutes grace and then their uphill task would be completed. Racing against time, the artillerymen had winched the V1 up the inclined chute to position it on the ramp, aft of the enlarged hatch. Despite the fact that U 195 was making heavy weather of the swell, the crane operator had managed to lower the pulse jet engine onto the mounting pylon at the first attempt. That done, Oberfeldwebel Meyer and the rest of the attachment had then bolted on the short stubby wings and filled the tank with low-grade aviation spirit.

At that stage, Hartmann had thought their problems were over, only to discover that this was far from the case. They still had the Dampferzeuger to prepare, a propulsion device that utilized the powerful reaction between

307

hydrogen peroxide and sodium permanganate. Apart from that, Oberfeldwebel Meyer was obliged to wait until they were exactly on station before he was able to set the magnetic compass to the required course.

'We're almost ready, Erich.' Galen clapped him on the shoulder. 'Another minute or so and we'll give the Americans a New Year's Eve to remember.'

The artillerymen filed past the conning tower, Oberfeldwebel Meyer bringing up the rear as they made their way aft to shelter behind the lower gun platform. Leaving them to carry on, the warrant officer climbed the rungs set into the port side of the conning tower to join Galen on the bridge and report that everything was in order.

'Excellent.' Galen moved to the fire control panel and then glanced over his shoulder at Hartmann. 'Better keep your head down, Erich,' he advised. 'We don't want to set fire to your beard, do we?'

Slowly, as if savouring every moment, Galen pressed the ignition button. The pulse jet whined and fired into life, making a deep-throated snarl like a a heavy diesel truck with a loose baffle plate in the silencer. A tongue of flame from the engine licked the conning tower and soared above the bridge. Exactly thirty seconds later, Meyer tripped the firing switch and there was a deafening whoosh from the Dampferzeuger as the hydrogen peroxide reacted with the sodium permanganate. Propelled up the ramp, the V1 lifted off and, climbing rapidly turned onto the preset course.

Hartmann straightened up and moved to the voice pipe. Removing the cover, he whistled up the control room and said, 'All right, Werner, stand by to submerge when I give the word.'

'What the hell do you think you're doing, Erich?'

Galen was standing right behind him and Hartmann could feel a hard round object pressing against the nape of his neck. A Walther PPK: Dietrich was probably armed too. He might have known that Galen would outsmart him. The artillery officer had obviously guessed what had been at the back of his mind when he'd suggested they transfer the missiles from the stowage compartment to the bow accommodation room, and had removed the automatic from the armoury before it was blocked off.

'We've fulfilled our mission,' he said calmly. 'It's time to go home.'

'We still have another missile on board and I intend to use it.'

'With such fanaticism you should be in the SS,' Hartmann said contemptuously.

'I am.' Galen jabbed the automatic into his neck. 'Now, cancel your last order.'

Hartmann weighed the risks. To remain on the surface for another two hours was to invite certain death. On the other hand, if he gave the order to dive, everybody on deck would be drowned. Twenty-three men up top, twenty-eight below. After a moment's hesitation, Hartmann decided in favour of the majority.

Bending over the voice pipe, he shouted, 'Now hear this: Dive, dive, dive.'

Galen clubbed Hartmann over the head with the automatic and then swung round to cover the open hatch.

Best heard a loud grunt over the voice pipe and exchanged glances with Peiper. 'Something is terribly wrong up top,' he said in a voice hoarse with alarm.

'That's obvious,' Peiper muttered.

'I think I'd better take a look.'

'Do you think that's wise?'

Best had a feeling that it wasn't, but he put the thought aside and went on up the ladder. One thing at a time, he told himself. First thing you've got to do is close the upper hatch. When that's done, you can then decide what to do next. He looked up, saw Galen standing above him and realized he was staring death in the face. The bullet hit Best above the right eye, and losing his grip on the steel rungs, he fell back into the control room.

In a loud, hectoring voice, Galen said, 'Is there anybody else who wants to question my authority?'

Nobody answered.

Inspired by a wry sense of humour, the crew had christened their B24 'The Holy terror' in recognition that while the Liberator hadn't succeeded in frightening the enemy yet, its alarming behaviour in the air certainly put the fear of God into them every time they went up in her. Like the other B24s from Mitchell Field, the crew of 'The Holy Terror' had been given a specific area to patrol, a box embracing some ten thousand square miles. Equipped with a sideways-looking radar, capable of searching out to a range of twenty miles, it was theoretically possible for them to cover their allotted area in five sweeps. In practice, however, a five mile overlap was allowed so that in effect the area was subdivided into seven lanes.

At 2331 hours 'The Holy Terror' was flying due west on the fourth leg when the radar picked up a U-boat on the surface. At precisely the same moment, the pilot observed a fiery comet receding into the distance. Instructing the radio operator to send a sighting report to Tenth Fleet and Air Defense Command, the pilot altered course to port and, descending to one hundred and fifty feet, came in on an attacking run. The nearest surface vessels at that point in time were the Buckley Class destroyer escorts *Kirkwood* and *Robert E. Hales*.

The Metox receiver failed to warn them, and it was Dietrich who spotted the glowing exhausts in the night sky. As he screamed a warning, the Liberator switched on its L17 eighty thousand candlepower searchlight. Blinded by the glare of white light, the gunners found it well nigh impossible to align their sights on the attacking aircraft and so they merely blazed away, hoping that by putting up a curtain of fire in its path, the plane would be forced to take evasive action.

It was a forlorn hope. The return fire from the nose turret of the B24 was both accurate and devastating, the .50 caliber bullets turning the bridge into a collander and scything the gun crews down like corn before the reaper. At exactly the right moment, the Liberator released eight depth bombs to obtain a perfect straddle.

The depth bombs were set to detonate hydrostatically at twenty-five feet, with the result that U 195 was practically lifted bodily out of the water. In addition to crushing the outer shell, the destructive force exerted by two thousand pounds of Torpex severely damaged the rudder, the propeller shaft and the keel. The seams of the inner pressure hull were also badly strained, and within seconds Peiper learned that there were five major leaks in the engine room. With U 195 settling by the stern, he gave the order for all hands to abandon ship.

'You two.' Peiper tapped both hydroplane operators on the shoulder. 'It's time to go. And you,' he said to Frick.

There was no need to say 'look lively.' Nobody wanted to be trapped inside a steel coffin and they moved fast, trampling over the dead body of Werner Best in their anxiety to reach the ladder.

The bridge was a bloody shambles. Galen lay on his back on top of a pile of bodies, his arms outstretched as if in supplication. At least, Peiper assumed it was Herr Major, but with the head missing, it was difficult to be absolutely sure. What about Hartmann? After all they'd been through together, he couldn't leave without knowing what had happened to him. The same thought occurred to Frick, and they set to, heaving the bodies aside, burrowing through a mass of human offal to find him laying face down under Oberfeldwebel Meyer. Although there was a nasty looking gash in his head and his right arm was obviously broken, they saw that Hartmann was still alive, breathing shallowly.

There was no time for niceties, no time to handle him gently. Bending down, Frick lifted Hartmann across his shoulders and, with Peiper leading the way, carried him to the upper gun platform. Waiting until the chief engineer had descended to the lower platform, he then lowered their captain to Peiper's outstretched arms. Repeating the process in reverse order, they finally reached the deck and, positioning themselves on either side of Hartmann, jumped overboard.

Moments later, as if suddenly tired of the unequal

311

struggle, U 195 went down fast, her bows pointing up at the sky in a last defiant gesture.

The *Robert E. Hales* was the first destroyer escort to arrive on the scene. Of the U-boat's fifty-one officers and enlisted men, she found only six survivors: one able seaman, one diesel mechanic, one hydroplane operator, Obersteuermann Wilhelm Frick, Kapitänleutnant August Peiper and Korvettenkapitän Erich Hartmann.

Delgado removed the cigarette that was burning down between Virginia Canford's fingers and stubbed it out. 'Everything's going to be all right,' he said. 'This is the best hospital in town and I know he'll pull through.'

'You think so?'

'Sure I do.'

'How long has he been in the operating room now?'

It was the second time she'd asked him that question in almost as many minutes. 'About an hour and a half,' said Delgado.

'It seems longer.'

'It always does when there is nothing you can do except sit and wait it out. But like I said, there's nothing to worry about. He has the will to live and that's half the battle.' Delgado smiled reassuringly. 'And of course, he has you. He knows you're worth fighting for.'

'I wish I could believe that,' she said with a catch in her voice.

'Well, it's true,' Delgado said firmly. 'I should know; I was there in the ambulance with him and he never stopped asking for you.'

'You're a nice man, Ben.'

He could tell that she wanted to believe him, but for some reason there was still an element of doubt. 'Now you listen to me,' he said quietly. 'I wouldn't lie to you about a thing like that.'

Virginia nodded. No, he wouldn't. Delgado was an honourable man, the kind you instinctively trusted. She knew now that John hadn't meant it when he suggested they wait until the war was over in order to be sure how they really felt about each other.

'I think maybe this is the surgeon,' Delgado murmured.

Virginia looked up, saw a figure in hospital garb striding down the corridor toward them and went to meet him on legs that felt decidedly shaky. There was a reassuring smile on the surgeon's face and she knew even before he spoke to her that Delgado was right, that John was going to pull through, and the tears began to run down her face.

Patrolman George T. Pappas wasn't too sure what he was supposed to be looking for. The sergeant in charge of their four man detail had said they were after some kind of transmitter that was probably smaller than a walkie-talkie radio and acted like a beacon. It was also very likely that this device had been disguised to resemble something else, an afterthought which had caused a certain amount of confusion in Pappas's mind, because if left the field wide open. Given those guidelines, almost anything you could name, from an empty beer can to a bag of popcorn, could be classified as a suspicious object.

Pappas also had the feeling that the whole thing could be a wild-goose chase. There was not a shred of evidence that the guy who'd been killed in the shoot-out at Mario's restaurant had planted a transmitter in the neighbourhood. Naturally, detectives from the 18th Precinct on West 54th Street were still questioning his woman companion, but from what the sergeant had said, it seemed she was still in a state of shock. All the same, he could see that they couldn't afford to take any chances, especially when there were upward of half a million people jammed into Times Square. More were arriving every minute and that was the whole trouble. There was hardly room to breathe, and with the crowd standing shoulder to shoulder, it was virtually impossible to make a thorough search of the area.

Inch by inch, Pappas elbowed a path through the crowd on the sidewalk. Progress was agonizingly slow and it took

313

him a good twenty minutes to cover the block between 43rd and 44th Streets. Although he did his best, checking every entrance and recess along the way, it was easy to overlook a potential hiding place in the crush.

As it turned out, the search was destined to become even more haphazard. As he approached Broadway and 45th with the sergeant and the rest of the detail some distance behind, Pappas observed a man behaving suspiciously. At first sight, it looked as if he was about to molest the young woman who was standing in front of him, but drawing nearer, Pappas saw that he was fiddling with the catch of her handbag. Before he could reach him, the thief snatched her purse and made off toward Eighth Avenue. Yelling for the other officers to follow, Pappas went after him.

A good sprinter in his day, it was more like an obstacle race, but, weaving and dodging, Pappas managed to catch up with the thief inside fifty yards. Much to his surprise, the man put up one hell of a fight and it took the combined efforts of three police officers to subdue him. By the time they located the nearest patrol wagon and bundled him into it, the crowd in Times Square had become so vast that from thereon the whole search ground to a halt.

The V1 flew on, bearing a charmed life. A P61 Black Widow from Fort Dix had tried to intercept the missile some twenty miles from the navy's radar and antiaircraft picket line, but with its superior speed, the flying bomb had outdistanced the night fighter. Flying straight and level at an altitude of six thousand feet, it had then swept through a hail of fire from the USS *Lovel* and her attendant destroyers. At 2347 hours, exactly sixteen minutes after it had been launched from U 195, the V1 entered the Metropolitan Air Defense Zone, one hundred miles from the selected taget.

The four P51 Mustangs patrolling at ten thousand feet were not equipped with radar, but complying with the directions they received from Fighter Control, the pilots had little difficulty in vectoring onto the target. The missile was flying above the overcast and the sheet of flame from its

Argus duct engine was clearly visible to the naked eye. Unlike the Black Widow night fighter, the P51 could match the speed of the flying bomb in level flight. Splitting his force in two, the flight commander executed a half roll and went into a steep dive, his wingman close behind him.

There were two ways of dealing with a flying bomb. From various combat reports he'd seen, the flight commander was aware that some RAF pilots liked to fly alongside the missile, creating such a turbulence under the wing of the V1 that the flying bomb eventually overturned. Others preferred to come in from behind, opening fire at a range of two to three hundred yards. Of the two courses of action, the flight commander chose the latter. Levelling out, he closed on the target and opened fire. He kept his thumb on the firing button for a good four seconds, sending a stream of tracer rounds into the missile. Bits and pieces flew off the engine but the bomb flew on, seemingly indestructable.

Then, suddenly, there was a violent explosion and the air was full of debris.

The babble of noise from the seven hundred and fifty thousand people assembled in Times Square gradually died away and was replaced by an expectant hush. A few minutes later, loudspeakers relayed the carillons of St. Thomas's Church, and then, on the stroke of midnight, the glowing globe atop the flagpole of the *Times* Tower made a slow descent to signify that 1944 was over.

After a momentary blackout, the electric moving bulletin sign on the tower proclaimed: 'It is now twelve o'clock. The New Year is here. Let us make it a year of Victory. Let us pledge ourselves to get on with the job so that those we love may soon be home with us again.' On the platform in front of the Statue of Liberty reproduction, Lucy Monroe began to sing 'The Star Spangled Banner,' but although the microphones amplified her voice a hundredfold, the roars and cheers from the crowd were such that only those at the front could hear her.

In the litter bin near Mario's reastaurant, the homing beacon continued to send out a lonely mating call.

EPILOGUE

The potential high-fliers of this world often have a habit of falling by the wayside, and in this context, Delgado was wrong about Jack Ganley. His partner never did make it to the top. In January 1947, Ganley received a knife wound in the stomach while attempting to arrest a dope pusher, and although he subsequently made a complete recovery, he resigned from the force less than a month after returning to duty. Ganley never admitted to it, but Delgado was pretty sure that his sudden decision owed much to the persuasive influence of his fiancée, a very bright and ambitious young lady who worked for an advertising agency and whose future plans for Jack did not include slow promotion in the NYPD. Following their wedding in June of that year, the couple moved to the West Coast where Ganley founded a security company and apparently did rather well for himself. Although both men vowed to keep in touch, their letters gradually became more and more infrequent, until finally they stopped altogether shortly before Christmas 1950 when the Ganleys moved on to Florida and Delgado mislaid their new address.

For all that Delgado believed that his ethnic background was a distinct handicap in a force then largely dominated by the Irish, he was in fact promoted to lieutenant in 1952 and could have made captain had he so desired. However, as he pointed out to Gina, he was a detective first, last and always, and while running a precinct might appeal to some men, he didn't relish the thought of becoming an administrator. When Delgado finally retired in 1968, Gina was in favour of moving to warmer climates but somehow

317

they never got around to it and they still occupy the same apartment on East 92nd.

After his capture and interrogation, Hartmann was sent to a POW camp in Kansas where he was kept in solitary confinement until the eighth of May, 1945, when the war in Europe officially ended. U-boat men had a reputation for being the most persistent escapers and it seems the authorities feared that Hartmann would organize a mass breakout, which would explain why he was singled out for special treatment.

Repatriated to Germany in 1948, Hartmann spent the next two years searching for Jeanne Verlhac, but although the International Red Cross eventually traced her to Chartres, there was to be no happy reunion. Jeanne had married someone else. She had two children, a girl aged five and a boy of eighteen months, and she made it very clear to the Red Cross representative that she didn't ever want to see him again. Hartmann didn't blame her; he was a ghost from the past, and believing him dead, Jeanne had picked up the pieces and built a new life for herself.

Hartmann also put the past behind him and made a fresh start, first in Cologne and then in Munich where, after qualifying as a lawyer, he became a public prosecutor. Along the way, he married a very practical German girl, as different from Jeanne as chalk from cheese.

Although Cynthia Langdon and Christel Zolf never met one another, the pattern of their lives was remarkably similar. Apart from the fact that each had been close to Webber, both women remained single and, perhaps even more curiously, both died of cancer in exactly the same month in 1957, Cynthia in New York, Christel in Zurich.

The penalty for spying in wartime is death, but three factors saved Christel from the electric chair. First, she was extremely cooperative; second, the war was drawing to a close; and last, but not least, she was a Swiss citizen. Her trial in April 1945 virtually went unnoticed which, in a way,

318

was only to be expected in view of the major events that were taking place elsewhere in the world. Sentenced to twenty years' imprisonment, she was released in 1956 and deported to Switzerland with maximum secrecy.

Anderson was discharged from the hospital in March 1945 and was immediately sent on twenty-eight days' convalescent leave. As he said later, with a slight lift of an eyebrow, there was nothing very restful about the honeymoon Virginia had organized, but the recuperative effect was miraculous.

Some other officer was appointed to HMS *Aden* in his place, but Anderson stayed on in the Royal Navy until 1953, when he retired voluntarily in the rank of Commander. During those eight postwar years, he served in the Home, Mediterranean and Far East Fleets, including a spell of combat duty in Korean waters aboard the aircraft carrier HMS *Glory*.

Virginia followed him around the world, with the result that their first child was born in Portsmouth, the second in Malta and the third in Hong Kong. It was this constant upheaval and disruption to family life that finally convinced him he should leave the service, a decision which surprised Virginia because she had never so much as dropped a hint in that direction.

Anderson still had a hang-up about the Canford wealth and influence, which he freely admits helped to get him established when he decided to open a management consultancy in New York. However, he came to realize that while nepotism can certainly give a man a head start in life, there comes a time when he either makes it on his own or goes under. Anderson didn't go under, because he showed an uncanny knack for finding the right people to fill the right job, and became so successful at it that he eventually opened another office in London.

Virginia never did get around to writing the novel of the year; raising a family took up too much of her time for that, but when the children were old enough, she rejoined the family law firm and made quite a name for herself at the bar.

If they have a mind to, most married couples can go back to a certain place and say this is where we first met. The Andersons can't, because 17 Battery Place no longer exists. The old shipping offices where so many sailing conferences were held were demolished to make room for the World Trade Centre. The architects probably never gave it a thought, but it is a fact that quite inadvertently they succeeded in building what is possibly the most ironic war memorial of all time.